FACES TELL ALL

PHILIP WOLFSON

Published by Blast Press
324 B Matawan Avenue
Cliffwood, NJ 07721
gregglory@aol.com

gregglory.com/blastpress

This is a work of fiction. Names, characters and events are either the products of the author's imagination or used in a fictitious manner.

ISBN 978-0-9984829-9-6

FACES TELL ALL

When avid face reader Harold Savitt comes on to fashionista Trish Donlon about her perfect nose, he gets the cold shoulder. But his drunken prattle about the science of beauty had intrigued Trish and would lead to their partnering on a face-reading phone app for the dating crowd—designed as they put it, "to help lonely hearts find the love of their lives."

Although Harold and Trish intend the face-reading app for matchmaking, its potential for espionage attracts the CIA, enemy Chinese Intelligence and Chinatown gangsters, while the app's brilliant Chinese programmer may be a double agent.

In the climax, staged in a gigantic movie studio, Harold's quest for glory and the girl hinges on a showdown demonstration of the app that reveals good guys and villains—as all battle for the coveted faces technology, including a game-changing weapon of propaganda warfare.

"No image is more compelling than the face and its features—animated by expression, and reflecting all of life's drama and human nature; so that even a child can read at a glance all that history has recorded in the mind and heart of our species: the primitive fear and rage of the cave dweller, despair and distrust turning to hope and faith as man struggles to civilize through the ages, exultation and bliss as he reaches for the heavens—all expressed in the face. Its power to arrest and control our attention cannot be overestimated."
—Dr. Philip Wolfson.

"The centrality of the face as symbolic of personality permeates the fabric of human experience." —Michael Eigen Ph.D., On the Significance of the Face, The Psychoanalytic Review, 1980-81.

As part of China's "...multibillion-dollar effort to burnish its image worldwide....the government has methodically worked to cast China as a progressive, welcoming model for the rest of the world to admire and emulate." —Jonathan Ansfield, New York Times. October 2010.

"We get the faces we deserve: inappropriate diet, persistent negative emotions, drugs, toxins, and stress all contribute to lines, congestion, and colours on the face." —Coco Chanel, quoted in Chinese Face Reading For Health.

ACKNOWLEDGEMENTS

This novel is dedicated to the over 7 billion faces of the human "race", diverse enough to comprise all of our distinct identities, yet homogeneous enough to mark us, unmistakably, as members of the same family.

My interest in the science of faces began in the 1960's when, working as a medical advertising writer in New York City, I discovered among the Argosy Book Store's vintage tomes, *The Encyclopedia of Face and Form Reading* by Stanton and *Redfield's Comparative Physiognomy*, both from the 1880's. Although clearly racist and pseudo-scientific by contemporary standards, I believe these books accurately reflect deeply ingrained biases that formed the basis for Western imposed criteria of beauty—including our biases about the looks of certain animals that carry over to humans thought to resemble those animals.

Elements of Chinese and Western Medicine, as well as Jungian and other observations on the psychology of faces help form the main premise of this book: the unique power of the human face not only to reflect our underlying physical and psychological natures but also to affect our conscious and subconscious beliefs and behaviors.

In documenting the long, uplifting history of our Chinese-American fellow citizens, New York Chinatown's Museum of Chinese in America (MOCA), a small jewel of a museum, proved an invaluable resource—as was The Metropolitan Museum of Art, whose world-famous collections testify to man's remarkable and universal preoccupation with his own image.

In *Faces Tell All*, fictional characters discuss notions of esthetic beauty relating to symmetry, proportionality and balance that stem not only from ancient Greek and Renaissance sources, such as the Golden Mean and the Fibonacci number, but also from equivalent Chinese concepts Yin and Yang and the 64 hexagrams of the I Ching. Thus, coincidentally, from numerologies of both East and West are derived lines, curves, forms and shapes that appeal to people across all cultural divides.

Many thanks to my publisher Gregg G. Brown of Blast Press for his support and guidance and to the Monmouth County Fiction Writers Guild, for theirs; for the extraordinary work of my website and marketing professionals Steven Kass and David Leta of ShoreSite Web Designs, photographer Patty Marchesi and model Nicole Lippert; with special appreciation for early reviewers, so generous with their time and praise: Dr. Michael Eigen, Thomas Bird, T.J. Lloyd, Richard Dery and Bruce Ferguson.

Finally, gratitude to professional colleagues, friends and family for their advice and encouragement: Dr. Paul Mailshanker, Dr. Xin Liu, Dan Walsh, Esq., Peter Lyden; my children Lisa Copeland, Stephen and Jacob Wolfson and my loving wife Inge, whose beautiful face and personality are an inspiration beyond words.

PROLOGUE

CHINATOWN, NEW YORK

Orphaned at age fourteen and still unmarried at fifty, Mary Shun none-theless considered herself a happily-assimilated Chinese-American; that was, until recent events threatened to shatter the life she had carefully crafted as if it were a delicate Ming figurine.

The original stench of racism in her adopted country had faded to only a faint odor, and Mary was proud that she had stuck it out. First employed as a shop girl, she had mastered English at night school, worked hard at clerical jobs and after many years had risen to Assistant Curator at the Chinese American Museum (CAM), an organization devoted to understanding and tolerance between the peoples; whites were now among her best friends.

But Mary's otherwise bright outlook was clouded by a sinister new reality: the cousin she had sponsored the year before when he had emigrated from Hong Kong was being corrupted by a few remnants of the once-notorious Triad gangs in Chinatown. Mary Shun had offered Shun-Fa-Ting, now called Billy Shun, a corner of her small apartment on Mulberry Street and had paid for his business computer course. A few months later, Billy started his own computer business and was soon doing well enough to want his own place.

Mary could hardly wait for that to happen. She did not like the looks of Billy's companions and she was sure their murmurings about street activities were gang-related. Hoping to expedite his move, when the museum needed its computer system repaired, Mary provided Billy with an introduction, and he successfully bid the job.

CAM spotlighted anti-Chinese racism that had occurred over the past two hundred years. Posters, books, magazines and videos of old movies depicted Chinese "villains" of the white American imagination, such as Dr. Fu Manchu, and the Dragon Lady, alongside stereotypes of "good" Chinese, like Charlie Chan, Anna May Wong, and the China Dolls. Nearby were photographs of actual Chinese-Americans who, like many others, were loyal and productive citizens. Mary Shun had helped research much of the background information for the exhibits.

One day, Billy Shun seemed to take a new interest in the displays, especially one reporting massacres of Chinese coolies in the 19th century. Billy's black eyes burned like coals. Charging into Mary's office, he shouted curses against the "White Devil" that were overheard in the museum. Fearing that Billy might turn violent and ruin her hard-won reputation and career, Mary begged him to "give America a chance" as she had done.

The next night—it was mid-December, 2016—she was shocked to find Billy at the museum, e-mailing display images to a trading company that was a suspected front for the Peoples Republic of China intelligence services—the Ministry of State Security, a.k.a. the MSS. Mary was furious but decided to hold her tongue for the moment. She was not unsophisticated about such matters. While in a restaurant, months before, she had overheard a reputed former Ghost Shadows gangster boast that he was getting orders from Beijing.

Mary had informed her friend, Lieutenant Henry Juen of the local Fifth Precinct, NYPD; he, in turn, introduced her to a U.S. government official named Van who gave her a list of suspected MSS-infiltrated organizations in Chinatown as well as their fronts in Hong Kong.

Mary had met Van downtown at the huge Gothic-style Federal Building. He was a very tall, older man with piercing blue eyes who seemed remarkably fit for his age. Van had offered his phone number and an encoded e-mail address, asking her to contact him if she had any tips about gang-related activities.

Before calling Van, Mary decided to confront Billy at their apartment. She practically spat out the words in their native Cantonese: "Billy, I cannot stand by if I see you doing something that would bring dishonor and loss of face to our family and our community."

Billy glared back, hands on hips, fists clenched. "What do you mean 'you cannot stand by'? You'd better not interfere."

Mary's answer was a grim tightening of her lips and jaw.

Billy Shun read her face well. He knew what he must do.

The next day, Mary called Van; he advised her to immediately take a cab to his Federal Plaza headquarters. Mary bundled up against the late fall chill with a thick coat and a wool hat that shaded her eyes and covered her ears; she did not see or hear the hooded figure following her as she emerged from her apartment building. Seeing no available cabs, she approached Canal Street and decided to take the subway.

After a short wait amidst a sizeable crowd on the downtown platform, Mary stepped toward the approaching Q train. She never saw who delivered the explosive kick that sent her tumbling and screaming to her death under the wheels. The high-pitched cries of horrified onlookers blended with the screech of brakes—applied too late.

Within the hour, Van learned of the horrific incident. But there was more disastrous news: a search of Mary's apartment by Fifth Precinct detectives revealed that her computer, despite the installation of firewalls and elaborate pass codes, had been hacked, and its confidential files compromised.

Van was summoned to headquarters in Langley, Virginia the next day to explain the security breach. Doubly hard to swallow was the dressing down from Tim Peters, his division chief, who Van grumbled was "half my age and half my size." Van thought the chief's patronizing tone complemented his tailored blue blazer and Hollywood haircut. A bow mouth and button nose completed the twerpy picture. Equally calculated to annoy Van was Peters' habit of fidgeting with a school ring while turning slowly in his swivel chair. To confidantes, Van dubbed Peters "the fidget midget".

"Bad idea, Van, to trust this Mary Shun with your codes just because Lieutenant Juen vouched for her. Problem is, over the years, you've become too high profile, and..." he smiled, "I'm not just talking about your six-foot-six. Too much publicity, too loose with your name and your codes. Now, more than ever you're a target of the MSS."

3

Van wasn't smiling; his sapphire eyes blazed in anger. An old-school Ivy Leaguer who scorned "dressing to impress", he sported a blousy Russian tunic under his one sop to convention: a greasy, well-worn Burberry trench coat.

The division chief continued. "The better news is, we've gotten a storm of Chinese chatter from satellite surveillance since the murder yesterday. We've pinpointed some receivers in the Los Angeles area, near South California University. We might be close to ID-ing them. Meantime, I'd lay low, if I were you."

Van's eyes still glowered beneath his massive brow. That prominent feature together with a hawk nose, receding hairline and his usual belligerence led colleagues to call him (behind his back) the "mad eagle". "Over the years, as you put it, I've carefully developed street contacts in Chinatown and elsewhere and never before lost an operative or a source. You don't read these people—and they don't read you—by electronics. It's *face to face*. As for publicity, shining a light is often the best way to see how the rats run. I'll take my chances."

Turning to leave, he heard the other man say, "Don't let me read about *you* in the papers, Van."

PART ONE

HUNTING AT THE
SERENGETI BAR AND GRILL

I.

Glancing at the massive Cape Buffalo horns above the entrance, Harold Savitt ducked inside the restaurant like a thief on the run, thinking, *I hope nobody from work sees me. Besides, only nerds go hunting at the Serengeti armed with a rolled-up New York Times.*

A dashiki-clad hostess escorted him to a booth upholstered with simulated leopard skin. Harold unrolled the newspaper carefully, intending to indulge a favorite pastime of skimming the headlines, but first, he looked expectantly toward the mirrored bar where bobbing heads were silhouetted against shining rows of bottles and glasses.

Above the bar, the vast, golden-hued Serengeti Plain spread across a forty-foot photorealistic mural. Zebra and wildebeest grazed amid clumps of flat-topped Acacia trees, as a pride of lions crouched in tall grasses—the snowy peak of Kilimanjaro looming in the distance. Bird cries, muffled roars and the thumping of distant drums arose from speakers embedded throughout the restaurant.

Harold was about to order a drink when he spied the news article: **NYPD, FEDS Suspect Chinese Gangs in Subway Murder.** A Chinese gang member is suspected of having thrust Mary Shun, 50, an employee of the Chinese American Museum (CAM) under the wheels of the Q train early Wednesday morning, according to a spokesperson for a join task force investigating Tong and Triad criminal activity. Onlookers reported seeing a martial-arts kick delivered from behind the victim, propelling her onto the tracks. The fleeing suspect was described as Asian and wearing a maroon-colored hood. The remainder of the one-column piece described the mission of the museum and gave a brief background on Mary Shun along with her photo.

Harold blanched as he envisioned the grisly event. That poor woman! He remembered briefly meeting Mary at the museum's previous location in Chinatown.

He had planned to visit the renovated CAM, but now that prospect was shadowed by horror and fear. Harold admired much in Chinese culture, such as face reading and Kung Fu. A responsible Black Belt, he flinched at the thought that martial arts were misappropriated for murder; his cinema heroes, Bruce Lee and Jackie Chan, had only fought in self-defense.

To quell his agitation, Harold ordered a double martini. He pulled off his soup-stained paisley tie and stuffed it into a side pocket of his rumpled tweed sports jacket. Sitting back, he tried to appear blasé while managing to sneak looks at passing women. Soon, the server, with a conspiratorial wink, delivered a cone-shaped glass brimming with the icy libation.

Five ounces of Grey Goose Vodka and thirty minutes later, a primitive part of Harold's brain began to perceive the bar patrons as animals milling around the water hole: pursuers and pursued, predators and prey. In his 80-proof hallucination, they became slow-motion caricatures playing out an existential drama: nervous pawing at hair, tentative smiles dissolving into grimaces, furtive glances searching for clues of intent, trembling mounds of flesh arousing blood lust in carnivorous eyes.

Then, Harold's attention locked onto a nose—a tapered, well-proportioned nose that seemed to fit its female face, which was oval, with roundish eyes and a flirtatious, upward-curving mouth. *A perfect nose,* Harold thought, among the thousands he had seen and amassed—along with mouths, eyes, foreheads and chins—as illustrations in antique texts of physiognomy collected during his Columbia College days.

Back then, he and his chums (usually when drunk) would play the timeworn game of rating women's looks on a scale of one to ten. Admittedly, this was sophomoric and a loser's game: winners *got* the girls; they didn't need to *rate* them.

But Harold declined to analyze his own face—believing that studying other faces was research, whereas studying his own was narcissism.

In fact, Harold's eyes were deep-set and elliptical; the irises, hazel. His nose was straight, with a slightly rounded tip; his chin square and slightly protruding. A broad brow and forehead were topped by thick, curly, chestnut-brown hair—features he considered quite ordinary.

An only child, Harold had gone to high school in the Long Island suburbs. He'd been a good student, engaged in many activities, but never felt popular. His father was an ophthalmologist who'd expected that Harold would also become a doctor. His mother had often fixed him up with friends' daughters. He'd liked a few of them, but saw himself swimming in a fishbowl of family scrutiny and always managed to wriggle off the hook.

Having reached his thirties, Harold was still frequenting places like the Serengeti Bar. And now, suddenly smitten by the perfect nose, he made eye contact and pushed through the crowd toward the object of his affection. She was sitting at the bar, dressed in an expensive looking velvet black jacket over a white silk blouse.

"This is not a line, but…" Harold froze.

"…No? What is it?"

"Well, believe it or not…it's your nose."

"What's wrong with my nose?"

"Nothing, it's perfect."

"It must be, the way you plowed through that crowd."

"Not just that, but, your eyes…"

"I've been told I have a good nose, but what *about* my eyes…or my mouth?"

"Th—There's nothing wrong with your eyes or mouth!"

"Now *there's* a compliment!"

His face fell.

"Relax," she said, "I'm just messing with you. By the way *your* eyes are really something. Have you seen them lately?"

"Pretty red, huh? I guess they give me away."

"Too trashed to lie convincingly and the evidence convicts you."

"Guilty as charged. What are you, a lawyer?"

"Yes, as a matter of fact. I don't practice law but I sometimes use it in business."

"What business would that be?"

"I'm a fashion consultant."

"That's interesting. *Seriously,* how bad are my eyes?"

"They glow in the dark. But you don't *seem* as drunk as you look."

"I'll take *that* as a compliment. Maybe I'm just drunk enough to be honest."

"Now, why do I expect the next line to be a lie—as in *You Lie,* the T.V. show?"

Harold laughed apologetically. "I've seen the show, and yes—faces and body language do tell the truth. But I make a specialty of noses. Eyes and mouths are the moving parts, and usually get all the attention. Noses are overlooked, unless they're very good or very bad. *Seriously,* books make a system of it. But I'm more into the pure aesthetics."

"Are you an artist or just a snoop with a college education?"

"I'm no artist but, yes, I like to think of myself as a connoisseur of female beauty."

"I'll take that as a compliment. But there's another French word to describe it: *voyeur.*"

Harold's brows knitted in earnest; his head was swimming from the martinis. "*Seriously,* people *are* attracted by certain faces. It's instinctive, like a sixth sense drawing you to the right partner. My grandmother used to say: "For everybody there's a somebody."

"You keep saying *seriously* and I won't believe a thing you say."

Harold eked out a nervous laugh. Avoiding eye contact with the woman, he was momentarily distracted by revelers occupying a nearby "zebra-skin" banquette.

She continued, "It's not men's features, *per se,* that interest women, it's what they *express.* Men usually tell women they like their looks or they're pretty. You're the first man I've met who analyzes the component parts."

"Being analytical comes naturally to me. "By the way, I'm Harold Savitt."

"I'm Trish."

"Not to go on about your nose, Trish, but you have what the Chinese sages would call a Mountain Root Nose—according to the *Mian Xiang*. You know, men may not mention it, but noses are actually more important than they let on. *Seriously...*"

Trish's faux frown seemed to mirror the fierce ebony masks glaring down at him from the walls.

"I—I mean, *honestly,*" blurted Harold. "I think guys would take bad eyes over a bad nose, every time."

"Now my nose is a *mountain?* On that note, the conversation with this mouth is over. Just kidding. I've really got to run. I will say, as a fashion person and as a woman, if you must *get into people's faces*, pun intended, the eyes *do* have it—windows on the soul, that sort of thing." Her face softened. "Women like to be admired but not ogled like a specimen. And," she said with a friendly smile, "don't take yourself so *seriously*."

Harold laughed weakly. Trish arose and left. The room was spinning. He hadn't asked her last name. Feeling squelched and spent, he decided to call it a night.

II.

Next morning, thoughts penetrated the thudding pain behind his eyes. She told him last night he was "too trashed to lie convincingly". *In other words…when you're drunk, the truth comes out, but not the way you intend. Shot down again!*

Plodding glum-faced down the brownstone steps of his West 23rd Street apartment, Harold fetched his copy of the *Times*. Back inside, trying to ignore a throbbing headache, he found the follow-up article: **Murdered Museum Worker and Cousin Quarreled About Anti-Chinese Racism.** The gist was that Mary Shun's cousin, Billy, was a suspect because of their overheard quarrel and his disappearance after the murder. Billy Shun was a recent Chinese émigré whose companions included Chinatown gang members possibly tied to Intelligence for the People's Republic of China. The kick that had sent Mary onto the subway tracks was thought to be typical of the deadly martial arts practiced by both warring "Ghost Shadows" and "Flying Dragons" gangs. They were known to train at a few small studios in Chinatown and the "House of Kung Fu" in Flushing, Queens. Some of the gang members were thought to be illegal immigrants.

Harold knew of Flushing's large Chinese-American population. *Hmm*, he mused, *that's only a few miles from where I used to train in Little Neck. This gang barbarism definitely gives the noble arts a bad name.*

Needing a bite of breakfast and more sleep to nurse his hangover, Harold called his publishing office, saying he'd work from home that day. When he awoke two hours later, thoughts of the subway murder and the aborted hunt at Serengeti no longer rankled as much. He thought of calling Carlos. They hadn't spoken in weeks.

Back when they were classmates, Harold, as copy editor for the *Columbia Spectator*, had approved two humorous pieces of Carlos's: "Girl Watching at the West End", an off-campus bar, and "Sightseeing in Morningside Park", a nearby mugger's haunt. Harold and Carlos had hit it off and become roommates during their writing collaborations; Carlos's literary flair—he had been an English Lit major—paired well with Harold's editing skills.

Harold had been pre-med but had blown his medical school chances and was nearly expelled for stupidly cheating on a biochemistry final that he could have passed legitimately.

After graduation, Harold used his sciences background (and an uncle who knew the boss) to get an ad-writing job at Harris, Pierson Pharmaceutical Advertising, Inc. However, Harold was long on big words and short on creativity. He was indecisive, seldom met deadlines, and ultimately lasted less than two years at the agency.

Carlos Manuel Ponce Morales y Bermudez was born in the United States after his family had emigrated from Cuba. His father, once well off, had lost almost everything to Castro's confiscations but parlayed a small loan from relatives into real estate empires in Dade County Florida and Hudson County New Jersey. Like Harold, Carlos had the head but not the heart to follow his parents' ambitions for him—in this case, property management; Carlos originally dreamt of becoming a fiction writer.

One year and a pile of rejection slips later, Carlos, at Harold's suggestion, took his unsold short stories about Cuban-American life in New Jersey to Vic Rothko, the hardboiled Creative Director at Harris, Pierson.

Vic liked Carlos's work, including a heart-rending story about a closeted gay man growing up in a super macho Hispanic environment. Vic rightly guessed that he could refine raw nuggets of Carlos's literary talent into advertising gold.

As Harold floundered at Harris, Pierson, Carlos prospered. He was well liked for his witty personality and dashing looks reminiscent of actor Eric Estrada. Within weeks, he created an ingenious advertising campaign for an established anti-depressant—promoting its off-label effect as a mood stabilizer. But Carlos's accomplishment had a chilling effect on his friendship with Harold, which, shortly after, plunged into deep freeze when Harold was fired. Carlos regretted that turn of events and still felt affection for his former roomie. Since then, they had talked little: about sports, women and family, but never shop.

Eventually, Harold had called Carlos to grouse about his demise at the agency. They'd met at Rosa Mexicana Restaurant and munched on taco chips and guacamole.

Carlos tried to console Harold. "Look, we both settled for second-fiddle careers. I'm a failed writer and a sell-out to crass commercialism. You have a solid science background and might still have a shot at medical school."

"I'm not sure I still want medicine or ever did. When I was a kid, I think my father misunderstood my fascination for that optical instrument with the sliding lenses. It looks like a mechanical face, with those round, staring eyes. Yes, I'm still interested in science, but I'm not one to hack up people's eyeballs like my dad or make a splash on Madison Avenue like you did."

Carlos thought, but didn't say, that Harold's bitterness was still coming through. Truth was, his former roommate's encyclopedic knowledge and love for research made him better suited to be an editor, as he had been in college, rather than a writer.

A few weeks later, Harold had caught on as a research editor for a small scientific publishing house and was feeling a little better about things. The publishers appreciated his thoroughness as a researcher and a concise editing style, honed by the discipline of ad writing. Assignments were more long-term, deadlines not as pressing. If advertising was a bit like show business, publishing was more like academia: plodding and predictable, if a bit dull. Diligent to a fault, Harold had chalked up a solid, if uninspired, seven years at Fortune-Estes Publications.

So now, the day after Harold missed his kill at the Serengeti, Carlos's phone rang. Seeing the familiar name on the digital screen, he smiled, expecting that Harold was feeling more chipper. "The one and only Harold Savitt! What's up, old chap?"

"I think my approach to women is getting tired and lame. And it's all your fault."

Carlos guessed Harold wasn't really serious. "*Getting* tired, he says, like that's something new. And why is it *my* fault?"

"Your *Spectator* piece on girl watching started me on this physiognomy kick and I've become a voyeur of female body parts. Jeffrey Dahmer the cannibal had nothing on me."

Carlos laughed. He took Harold's joking as a sign that the old tensions between them were indeed easing. "The problem is, you're focusing on the means instead of the ends. Ask yourself: what do I really want in a woman *or* what kind of relationship am I looking for?"

"I haven't thought that far ahead yet. I figure: unleash my instincts and hope for the best." Afraid that he was sounding pessimistic, Harold glanced hopefully at his reflection in the bedroom mirror, but the unmistakably sad face looking back couldn't be denied.

"I haven't heard your scripted line with women lately, but I bet you're coming off *mucho* hungry and needy. If your instinct is for meat and blood, you're scaring off the animals. You're like this intellectual, horny kid that's trying to seduce women with your braininess. It's nowhere. Just relax, be yourself, and have fun."

"But I don't know who I am, or what I want. Even in high school, getting good marks and all that extra-curricular stuff may have impressed other people, but not me. I was just going through the motions, trying to live up to my parents' expectations. Lying in bed, I'd hear snippets of their big plans for me, and then I'd fall asleep and dream about them. I didn't know my dreams from theirs. These days, I don't know my personality from the actors I admire. Who is the real Harold Savitt?"

"Just stop with the pseudo-scientific persona. The true you will come out. That faces thing is just a game. Don't take it so seriously, or expect other people to. And ease up on the hard stuff. It's messing up that loveable you that's in there somewhere."

"I think I see it now. That girl last night said I didn't seem as drunk as I looked. Maybe for a few moments I seemed authentic and honest. And, in spite of myself, the real me came through."

"Yeah, the authentic bullshit came through. Don't overthink it. You're trying to be on both sides of the booze barrier - drunk and sober - at the same time. You can't handle the stuff. Start from that premise."

"You know, I thought I could handle weed. Remember that great stuff I used to get from Albert and Chickie on 96th Street?"

"Wasn't really my thing. A real Cuban man smokes good cigars and drinks Bacardi 151, not that girlie Grey Goose stuff. Marijuana is for maricons and your Puerto Rican buddies."

Harold snorted. "Listen to the Cuban racist! What's up with the Cuban-Puerto Rican wars?"

"Not exactly a war—maybe like the friction you guys had between the German and Russian Jews. Everybody winds up getting along. And forget about the pot too. Try it straight, and get back to me."

"You know, the PR's had their nobility too. I remember Marife Hernandez on *The Puerto Rican New Yorker* when I was a little kid. She had a great Castilian nose: arched and aristocratic…!"

"Basta—enough! Let me know when the real you is ready for the real world."

***

Harold thought about his conversation with Carlos, who always seemed so self-assured. Whenever they compared notes, Carlos, unlike Harold, never seemed to have a romantic hard luck story, nor did he ever brag about female conquests. He was too cool to indulge in kiss and tell. Actually, Harold hadn't heard any specifics on Carlos's women in a while. Maybe he was spending more time with his men's book and writer's club, a group of young literary aspirants and published authors whom Harold envied because they had real talent. If only he could accept his own limitations and find happiness with perhaps an ordinary girl, who was only ordinary looking like him. Oh well…

***

Carlos thought about his conversation with Harold, who, despite his resentment of Carlos's success, still looked up to him as the "real Cuban man who drinks 151 rum". Actually, despite Harold's insecurities, worn candidly on his sleeve, there was innocence and integrity about him that Carlos admired. Yet, his own "image" as polished and suave made him feel like an actor or imposter, developing a reputation as a playboy he scarcely deserved. For example, last night's cavorting in a mid-town dance club: he could have had his pick of several ravishing women who practically threw themselves at him. But, as always, he fled, feeling a deep distaste. The sameness and futility of it all, year after year, left him exhausted, empty and wondering what he was trying to prove. Women, starting with his mother and sisters, had always gushed about how handsome he was. Funny…he had thought Harold was actually better looking but he probably didn't think so himself.

Yes, his outward success in advertising was substantial and satisfying, but he felt blocked in pursuing his fiction writing; ironically, his own life was a work of fiction. His mother mourned his bachelor status; his father told him it was *improprio*—unseemly—not to have married by now. However, he could not settle for a "proper" woman just to satisfy them. And he could never be honest enough with Harold to admit he was a hypocrite, a fraudulent Romeo, and an unhappy one at that. Harold was his best friend…or at least he used to be. Perhaps filling that gap now was a writers' group pal, Geoff Sutter, to whom he had recently been drawn. But guilt-ridden and dismayed by the eclipse of his friendship with Harold that he had, albeit unwittingly, betrayed, he vowed to somehow rebuild it. If only that social ease and finesse that came naturally to him didn't threaten Harold so much. Dammit, it wasn't all *his* fault.

III.

Billy Shun sat cross-legged in the center of an antique Ningxia rug, opposite his Chinese interrogator, Gao-Ting-Ren. Through the airfreight terminal window, Billy spied the distant, familiar skyline of Manhattan.

The interrogator spoke in Mandarin. "You are an embarrassment. Your *operation* was a piece of bad luck. The Americans are looking for you with photo ID's, so we can't pass you off as Air China crew. Your undeserved good luck: this rug you'll be rolled into is covered by original bill of lading as a return, and won't go through outgoing customs." The interrogator smiled. "We considered sending you back in bamboo coffin, which they never check. But symbolism of your death might be too tempting for some."

Billy was not amused. "I know the killing of my cousin made me immediate suspect, but I did achieve uncovering codes and identity of American agent Van."

"We have been onto Van for years and have plans for him. You achieved nothing except to warn him he may be imminent target. If your luck holds up, you will return to the motherland and not be seen in America again. Otherwise, you will promptly join your cousin among the ancestors."

IV.

Operative Ching-Li-Ho, code-named "Yellow Dog", had contempt for the handler who had locked him at gunpoint into an office in the Air China freight terminal at Kennedy Airport. He spoke in English, "You, a clerk, hold a gun on a real warrior of the motherland?"

Through the mail slot, the handler spoke, "I am following orders, which is something you might live to learn. You are lucky to have an opportunity to explain yourself." Just out of Ching's earshot, he spoke with someone on a cell phone, then handed him the phone through the slot.

The voice on the phone spoke in a Hong Kong dialect of Cantonese. "Yellow Dog, listen without speaking. Operative Shun, whom you claimed was reliable, was rash in bringing attention to himself. You were rash in following his orders without clearance from local agent. Your action of liquidating contact of American agent was risky and only alerted American counterintelligence that we may be tracking him. They are also tracking us."

"It was believed that…"

"Silence! Home headquarters has alerted our agents in L.A., Chicago, New York and Dallas to eliminate electronic communications that do not involve approved operations. You are not to call us. We will call you. You are fortunate that your skills are still needed, for the moment."

"May I speak?"

"Yes."

"Operative Shun told me he was acting on approved orders…"

"…And you failed to verify that with me."

"Yes, but…"

"There is no but. You are to remain under guard, until an available U.S. flight can be found for you. I will check to see if agents in L.A.,

Chicago, or Dallas might use you. Is your cover alias still valid on an up-to-date passport?"

"Yes."

"Good. You will hear from me by morning. Meanwhile, you are to stay overnight in that office, which has basic amenities."

"I am grateful for chance to redeem myself."

"Do not squander that chance."

V.

For the most part, Trish Donlon and her associate, Jennifer Santoramo, got along well—both on the job and socially. Trish was from the Bronx, New York; Jennifer from suburban Connecticut. Originally roommates at nearby Manhattanville College, they'd been drawn by its serious academics and former reputation as an enclave for the style-setting Kennedy women. They had much in common: love of fashion, dressing-up to visit the city, and a past affair of the heart gone awry—Trish's with a neighbourhood boy her parents disapproved of, and Jennifer with a young Tuscan aristocrat during a vacation in Italy. Having matured into confident, worldly-wise, beautiful young women, they resolved together not to become romantically involved prematurely again.

Trish had majored in business; Jennifer in psychology, with a minor in Italian. After graduation, they set firm career paths: dating was fun, but strictly recreational. Trish got an accelerated-program law degree, intending to use it only for business. Jennifer got an MBA, figuring it would pay off faster than a masters in psychology. The two women remained roommates during grad school and made the most of city living. They shared a zest for fashion, the arts and nightlife, but seldom double-dated.

Trish Donlon's auspicious start as a buyer for Macy's had led to an offer from Spence-Iturbi, Inc.—consultant to high-end fashion houses. Esteban Iturbi was enamored of his young associate. He used her to dazzle clients at fashion-insider events such as the America's Cup and the Cannes Film Festival. She managed to climb well up Spence-Iturbi's corporate ladder without sleeping with the boss and headed a staff of eighteen in Marketing.

Jennifer Santoramo had wowed the brass at Gucci and Giorgio Armani with her movie-star looks and knowledge of Italian; both firms wanted her. But she decided to teach marketing at the Fashion Institute of Technology for a year before joining Trish as her associate at Spence-Iturbi. She loved Trish, and it looked like a plum job. Even so, Jennifer hoped she wouldn't spend her life as Trish's assistant, and she preferred to get her own apartment.

Trish and Jennifer's stratagems improved the bottom lines of their luxury brand clients—Louis Vuitton, Gucci, Prada, Giorgio Armani, Hermes and Chanel—and earned them bonuses, flex hours and junkets to places like St. Tropez and Ibiza. They also turned bar hopping into a fine art. Working as a team, they attracted interesting people and evaluated them for social or business purposes—always ready to co-opt a new look or idea to help their clients. Not surprisingly, they drew plenty of handsome, eligible men, but Trish and Jennifer kept things light with the opposite sex, and never discussed their individual dating experiences.

This penchant for privacy extended to correspondence with their respective families. Jennifer's parents in Connecticut kept in close touch and still hoped that their gorgeous single daughter—now in her thirties—might find the right man. However, she kept them in the dark on that subject.

Strong-willed Trish had been estranged from her parents in the Bronx ever since she was a teen, having defied them and become involved with "that boy" of a different religion and ethnicity. Except for some contact with her younger brother—also a rebel—she hadn't spoken to her family in years.

Trish ribbed Jennifer about the weekly calls she made to her parents in Wethersfield, but she secretly envied Jennifer's close relationship, especially her ties to her father, a retired former banker. Jennifer's offhand "psychoanalysis" of Trish's fractured family grated a bit, even though she knew Jennifer meant well.

For her part, Jennifer admired Trish's independence while still chafing at being her number two. They had talked about starting their own agency together someday but Jennifer eventually wanted to run her own show and was carefully biding her time.

Trish's attitude toward Harold, given their first meeting, had not been as dismissive as it seemed. She told Jennifer about it the next day, at the office. "I see this guy with laser-beam eyes, rushing over like I'm his long-lost inamorata. He's cute, but a bit drunk; tells me I have a perfect nose, and comes on about his hobby of face reading."

"Not too smooth," replied Jennifer.

"Right. At first, I'm thinking: here's another brainiac—all dull, intellectual talk. But he seemed so sincere about beauty as a science. So it got me thinking; let's research faces, you know, like what makes certain faces great and why they go with certain styles."

"Let's do it," Jennifer enthused. "We already survey face shapes in cosmetology. Maybe faces suggest certain roles—like business faces go with business styles. Role-playing is big in psychology."

"Right up your alley," replied Trish, with a tinge of sarcasm not lost on Jennifer.

They agreed to research face reading, and learn more from this guy, Harold. They would hunt him at the Serengeti, if he were a regular, which Trish suspected he was.

***

Jennifer thought about her conversation with Trish. She had to admit her own mixed feelings about their relationship. True, Trish had been her entrée to a great life and an impetus to change, starting during their undergraduate years when she had prodded her to stop lazing around in the academic fluff of psychology. After that, Trish had urged her to leave the cozy cocoon of teaching at FIT—daring her to dive into the high-charged, glamorous world of women's fashion. She had to concede she loved it, but were the two of them locked in a paralyzing embrace? Now in their thirties, they were fiercely independent, highly respected in their field, but still unmarried—and faced with what: more of the same forever? She would always be Trish's number two if they stayed together. She thought, *maybe face reading for fashion is hairbrained and will come to nothing. But it's really all about psychology. Maybe a lifeline to pull me out my comfortable trap...*

***

Trish thought about her conversation with Jennifer. As for the obvious tension between them, Jen clearly needed to spread her wings in some way. Trish didn't want to lose her; they were a unique and unbeatable team. But was Trish the evil twin who was suffocating her sister? No, Jen was nobody's doormat; she had a mind of her own. But was Jen staying with her out of loyalty or obligation? What did Trish herself want? To be the Doyen of Seventh Avenue…? Not really. Coco Chanel had been one in a billion; *she* didn't need to hang out in bars; people of significance came to *her*. So, who was Trish? Just a perpetual playgirl with a fast Irish mouth who could make people laugh and command respect? Here she was, thirty-one and still looking for the guy who could stand up to her and yet be trusted. *Was there anything there with this Harold? Not likely. Just another nice Jewish boy—emphasis boy—who's bright but not smart. Still, instinct tells me to follow up, just in case…*

VI.

Two nights after his regrettably drunken introduction to Trish, Harold returned to the Serengeti, resolving to do better. An hour later, while dawdling over his third glass of ginger ale, he twiddled an elephant-head stirrer in rhythm to the African folk music undulating out of the sound system.

Emitting a sigh, Harold almost got up to leave the bar—before Trish walked in with an equally good-looking female companion. Noting details more carefully this time, he observed that Trish did have bright blue eyes and wavy, shoulder-length auburn hair to go with her perfect nose. She was wearing a burgundy-colored waistcoat and matching slacks that fit her perfectly.

Her companion had equally long, brunette hair, almond-shaped, dark-brown eyes and what Harold thought was a classically sculpted nose. An emerald-green dress and pearls offset her creamy complexion. They were seated into a nearby booth.

Harold ambled over with a practiced nonchalance he'd admired in actor George Clooney—wearing his new mohair sports jacket, purchased for the occasion. Seeing Trish up close, he detected faintly etched laugh lines bracketing her mouth—a good sign according to *Mian Xiang Face Reading*.

Trish spoke first. "The nose man! Pardon me while I go powder mine. Just kidding, Harold. The schnozz over here belongs to Jennifer."

"Hi Jennifer."

Jennifer nodded and smiled warmly. "Hi, Harold."

Harold smiled hesitantly, turning to Trish. "Listen, Trish, I'm sorry about how I came off the other night—too trashed for prime time."

"I *did* bust you a little," she said with a sympathetic smile. "But actually, you got me thinking. Women *do* care about their features: enhancing eyes and eyebrows, shaping hair and lips, fixing noses and sagging chins. Glamming-up is already big. But maybe there's a new fashion idea in face reading."

Jennifer cut in. "We work together in fashion, to find marketable ideas. We've done some research since Trish spoke with you, but we haven't found any original sources for face reading. That's where you come in."

"You were looking for *me?*" Harold's face lit up, his mood heightened by the driving tempos of *This Time For Africa* bursting from a large-screen video.

Trish raised her voice to be heard. "Yes, we were stalking you at the Serengeti."

Jennifer laughed. "We work together like lionesses on the hunt. When we were roomies at Manhattanville, we shared our kills."

Enjoying the repartee, Harold wanted to say he and *his* college roommate were still friends—but thought better of it. "You're talking marketable—how else could physiognomy be marketed for fashion or cosmetics? I assume you Googled all the listings on face reading?"

Both women nodded, smiling.

Harold continued, "And the websites that invite you to match your face with celebrities?"

"We saw them too," said Trish.

"Even nip and tuck surgeons have these programs that let you preview your new face, feature by feature," Harold added.

Trish spoke, "And photo booths show couples how their child's face would turn out. Even with all that, we should be able to find a new *wrinkle*—excuse the expression."

"Isn't Trish the punster," said Jennifer, barely hiding her acid tone. "By the way, have you seen these new face reading apps for camera phones? They supposedly help you find a mate."

Harold shrugged. "I've seen them, and some claim to be scientific, but I'm not impressed…too much like astrology."

"I've seen the reviews of those face reading apps," said Trish. "They wouldn't appeal to me if I was in the marriage market."

"*Aren't* you?" teased Jennifer.

"Only after you, my dear older step-sister by three months."

Both laughed at the inside dig.

"Basically," continued Trish, "I wouldn't want a machine telling me what to do or how to think. There's a very short list of humans I allow to do that."

"*Tell* me about it," said Jennifer.

Not up to trading zingers, Harold stayed serious. "But what if there was a scientific machine that reads faces? Wouldn't your clients want to know about it? You know, one that match faces with fashions?"

"Like they say," said Trish, "great minds run together. We were wondering the same thing about dressing people to suit their faces—and their bodies, of course."

"I know from cinema and my experience in advertising," said Harold, his mouth twisting cynically, "faces send powerful messages that are often more persuasive than words…"

A striking, dark-complexioned waitress, dressed in a low-cut dashiki, interrupted them, flashing a dazzling smile. "Have you tried the new Mombasa Cocktail? It's awesome and the next best thing to being there."

The women laughed and settled for Kir Royales. Harold was tempted, but decided to stick with ginger ale—livened up with a cherry—hoping no one would say it was a Shirley Temple.

"Speaking of persuasive, *there's* a face," said Trish, looking at the waitress, "that's hard to say no to."

Intimidated as he was by all these beautiful and powerful women, Harold's smile looked a bit pinched, his ears flushed around the edges. "I agree, but I think I'll take it easy tonight—big day in the office tomorrow."

"Aren't they all?" said Trish, her tone clearly facetious.

Harold tried to sound authoritative. "You mentioned original sources. Mine have real science behind them—like the Greek Golden Mean. Chinese face reading uses geometry also, with Yin and Yang corresponding to hard lines and soft curves in faces."

"Fashion and cosmetology are all about lines and curves too," said Jennifer, brightly, also anxious to sweeten the conversation. "How does it work in face reading?"

"Well," said Harold, "the experts say we're hard-wired to prefer symmetrical and proportional."

"Maybe so," said Trish, "but I'd call it instinct or intuition, which is how I size-up people. And not just features…expressions too—like I told you the other night—people with interesting, expressive faces. And you know what else is important? Whether they've got a healthy glow about them."

Harold hoped he looked healthy. "That healthy aspect is a good insight. It's right out of Chinese Medicine. I agree that features and expressions are both important. Maybe there's a connection between them. I bet if people like their own features, they'll make nicer facial expressions." Harold forced a smile.

Trish decided she liked Harold's features, but suspected he didn't like them much himself.

"I think so too," said Jennifer. "Say Suzy second-grader has a homely face everybody frowns at; she frowns back, and grows up a sour puss. It would take a strong personality to overcome that handicap. But, then again, people could be counseled to like their faces, smile more, and improve their overall appearance, which includes dressing properly." She winked at Trish.

"That's Jen, *always* the psychologist" said Trish.

"No really!" said Jennifer. "I see a role for a face reading therapist—with maybe a subspecialty in fashion therapy."

"Maybe so," said Trish, sounding conciliatory. "You'd be selling hope for all those unbeautiful faces. Got a potato nose like what was his name…Karl Malden? Maybe not a heart-throb like Brad Pitt, but a guy who can be trusted."

"I could have my *own* institute for face and fashion consulting," said Jennifer, emphatically. "My father's been looking for something to invest in."

"Easy, girl," said Trish.

Harold tried to ignore the tension between the women, pleased that his own ideas were gaining traction. "No, I think Jen's idea is sound; assure people who feel insecure about their looks that irregular features can convey character. For instance, the Chinese love chins. A big chin, like on Kirk Douglas, the old actor, should command respect for a guy who thinks he's a wimp." *Like I hope I'm not*, Harold thought, self-consciously stroking his own ample chin.

Jennifer leaned forward with a tolerant smile, thinking, *he's not a wimp exactly, but a basically nice guy with self-esteem issues. Maybe a project for me. I wonder if Trish likes him?*

Harold perked up, trying to remain assertive. "So are we talking about promoting a scientific face-reading program to the dating crowd? Simply comparing your own face to those of celebrities has been done already. But tying in fashion, and emphasizing healthy models, that's different. Convince people there's value in every face, and show sample faces they might be attracted to. Try to find a compatible match."

Jennifer raised an attentive eyebrow. "Compatible could be ones like your own or ones you're attracted to. Maybe strong faces would be attracted to sweet ones, or vice versa." She thought, *I'm not sure which one I'd prefer...*

"Looking strong and healthy is huge," said Trish, flexing a bicep. "I saw a documentary once about women who judged possible mates on how healthy and potent they look. Guys that were classically handsome but didn't look potent didn't make it." She aimed a foxy grin at Harold.

The flush around Harold's cheeks was visible, even inside the low-lit booth. "That's all right. Maybe more choices for us healthy types—men and women."

Trish thought, *I don't think he knows he's cute.* She struck a commanding pose. "Harold, what do you think? A new app for a camera phone? Maybe a book. An interactive web site that includes face-reading therapy." She aimed a condescending smile at Jennifer. "There are all kinds of possible spin-offs. Obviously, we'll need a computer maven to make it work. First, let's have a working meeting—put all our ideas together. And keep it to ourselves, for now."

Eyes narrowed, lips pursed, Harold pictured himself as movie mobster Edward G. Robinson, planning a caper. "Right. Keep a lid on it. But we have to check out all sources, Western and Chinese." He thought about visiting the CAM museum and shuddered, remembering the murder of Mary Shun.

"We're with you on that," replied Trish. "Jennifer and I do tons of research to see what's been done or needs to be done in terms of marketability. We can meet in my office on a Saturday. I'm Trish Donlon; Jen's a Santoramo. Got a card?" She handed him an expensive-looking, engraved business card:

Patricia M. Donlon
Marketing Director - Spence-Iturbi, Inc.
Fashion Consultants
810 Seventh Avenue, New York, New York 10019
212-646-7000 ext. 214 siturbi@comcast.net

Shuffling through his wallet, Harold produced a well-worn, dog-eared business card.

Harold B. Savitt, B.Sc., Associate Science Editor
Fortune-Estes Publications
313 W. 43 Street, New York, N.Y. 10029
212-439-6007 hbsavsw@comcast.net

"This is the only one I've got right now. Disregard the phone number penciled on the back. I think it belongs to a blind date I never called."

"Don't give it away...It could be 'Miss Perfect Eyes'," sniped Trish.

Harold laughed faintly and handed her the card. "It's Ok. You can have it."

Trish offered an understanding smile. "Don't worry. I'll call you.

VII.

Harold awoke feeling much better than after his first encounter with Trish Donlon. Could she be both a romantic *and* a business interest for him? Carlos's question echoed: What do you really want in a woman? What if I wound up liking Jennifer better? She was also smart and good-looking. Trish was friendly, although a bit bossy and sarcastic. Looks-wise, she was easily a 9 in the rating game and so was Jennifer, compared to his own, maybe 5 or 6. Best to concentrate on the business aspect.

Harold realized he'd always lacked self-confidence but he couldn't understand why. Back at Great Neck South High School, he was an all-around student—he played clarinet in the school band, was president of the Science Club, and a Merit Scholar. Physically fit and fast afoot, he lettered on the track team but passed on football because his parents disapproved—although they weren't against Kung Fu and other martial arts.

Excelling at everything became a pointless game—like amassing a full inch of extracurricular activities printed under his yearbook picture. But it did lead, along with high S.A.T. scores and straight A's, to an Ivy League college acceptance, that first step toward his parents' dream: medical school. It seemed like they were always pulling his strings. Then, in his senior year at Columbia, his parents couldn't understand why Harold cheated on that exam and failed to make medical school when he admitted that he knew the answers anyway. Dr. Farkis, the psychologist, told him it was self-destructive, rebellious behavior—subconsciously punishing his parents by failing. Harold wondered whether his later downfall in advertising was more of the same. He really wanted to succeed, but on his own terms, where he was the originator.

Nowadays, his job as a science editor was dry work and not high-paying, although he excelled at the research aspect of it. He could make his own hours as long as assignments were completed. Even so, it irked him to be a "re-write man" as he put it, and not a true creator. Both his love life and career seemed in a slump.

Before meeting Trish and Jennifer, Harold had worried that his proclivity for research might become a paralyzing obsession—a cover-up for procrastination and fear.

But now, if he could use his research ability to partner with these attractive, smart women, he might make a giant leap forward—like jumping a piranha-infested stream in a T.V. reality show. He thought he had the guts; he just needed a friend to confide in before deciding to jump—one that he could totally trust.

VIII.

There *was* somebody: his uncle, Dr. Paul Wallach, his mother's brother. Uncle Paul had helped Harold get the advertising job with Harris, Pierson Pharmaceutical Advertising. Wallach had eventually become a dentist, like others in his family, after flirting with the possibility of becoming a Foreign Service officer, specializing in China. He'd passed the difficult examination, but getting a State Department job hadn't been easy. While waiting months for an FBI security clearance, he took a "temporary" job at Harris, Pierson that turned into a successful five-year stint. But somehow, it never felt like a career. He applied for and gained acceptance to dental school; Foreign Service was put on hold, perhaps forever.

Harold thought, a *guy with a storied resume like that would understand my career missteps—and he was a blood relative to boot!* Uncle Paul might give him a key to Chinese face reading he hadn't heard of yet, maybe about the persuasive power of faces. No doubt about it: faces and the roles they represented were what drove T.V., Hollywood, advertising and the tabloids.

Before phoning, Harold remembered something. Going to his computer, he quickly scrolled down the search engine topics and found the listing—one of his favorite old movies. He scanned the summary. *It's fiction, a bit far-fetched*, he thought. *But who knows? The hypnotic power of facial imagery...mind control.*

He punched the New Jersey number:

"Harold! How's life in the wicked city?"

"Hi, Uncle Paul. It's a mad chase and I can't keep up."

"The Columbia Lion not getting his share? Time to change your luck."

"My luck hasn't been great. But lately there's reason for optimism."

"Well, the Chinese say bad luck can become good and then change again."

Harold laughed appreciatively. "That's actually why I called you. I remember you studied Classical Chinese at Columbia. I've used *Mian Xiang Face Reading* to help me find the perfect woman. But now my motive is profit, and I need to find something new and marketable."

"How can I help?"

"I'm planning a new app for smart phones based on face reading and also Western ideas like Greek geometry, the premise being that your face reveals your character traits, your fitness, and, in effect, your fortune. The main market would be matchmaking: trying to find the user a compatible face and personality."

"Sounds pretty ambitious."

"It is. It would also use celebrities' faces especially character actors, as benchmarks to show that all kinds of faces have value. Two possible business partners of mine have even suggested using facial analysis in psychotherapy, or for fashion consulting. But the design would have to be based on some real evidence or science."

"What could I possibly add to that? Unless it's maybe a periodontist's perspective on the importance of a healthy smile."

"That's good. But aside from aesthetics, some of the newer face-reading apps I've seen online claim to be based on methods used by law enforcement and national security. I thought you might have some insights in that area based on your knowledge of Chinese politics and their military."

"I'm not really up on Chinese intelligence methods."

"Well, maybe the Chinese read faces to judge the fitness of the enemy—like if we're healthy, or stressed out. Using strategies like that, we might help Miss Lonely Hearts tell Mr. Right from Mr. Wrong. But, like I said, it's got to be based on solid science."

"I'm not familiar with *Mian Xiang* but I do know something about another great source for fortune telling: *I Ching, The Book of Changes*. It shows how different personality traits play out in different life experiences. It's also based on Yin Yang, hard vs. soft personality traits, and how they balance."

"Really? *Mian Xiang* is also based on Yin Yang balances—the way faces and features are shaped, lines versus curves and hard structures compared to soft. Maybe there's a connection between face reading and *I Ching.*"

"Maybe. You'd definitely need a computer nerd, probably Chinese, to figure it all out. But don't overlook *I Ching.* I bet the Chinese wouldn't, when dealing with the enemy. Research the field before you work on strategy or tactics; that's right out of the Chinese Art of War."

"Speaking of war, remember that great old movie, *The Manchurian Candidate?*"

"I do. It's about brainwashing."

"Right. I was just looking it up before I called you. The Chinese brainwash an American P.O.W. into becoming an assassin. Seeing the Queen of Diamonds—a face on a playing card—triggers his killer instinct. It's like post-hypnotic suggestion, mind control."

"What's the tie-in to face reading?"

"Maybe the Chinese are not just reading faces…maybe they're using them as a subliminal weapon, getting through to the subconscious in a way that words can't. I'm not saying they could get masses of people to commit murder, but influence their behavior in more subtle ways."

"You're not saying *you'd* want to influence behavior with facial images, are you?'

"Not in a harmful way. But think about it: even if our program was only about reading faces to interpret the personalities behind them, you're still projecting images of influential faces out there to impressionable minds, and you have to be aware of the impact they might have on the psyche. As it is, some social scientists think society's gone to hell in a hand basket because we worship celebrity faces on tabloid covers and T.V. screens."

"That's true. Some people think that projecting evil faces, like the ones in the Batman movies, could trigger psychopathic impulses in some loonies out there. It's worth researching. As far as espionage, I'm sure the Chinese are spying on us. And police and security people, all over, are reading faces, trying to read the intentions of criminals and terrorists. Casinos want to find cheats and corporations want to ferret out industrial espionage. They're probably all using scanning cameras to spot known and maybe potential bad guys,"

Wallach continued, "I have no idea about the subliminal use of faces by the Chinese to influence people. Facial recognition software and surveillance, especially in China, is getting big. I know someone who might know about these things: Van Lear, a buddy from Chinese class at Columbia. When he dropped out of sight, back in the mid-sixties, we all thought he might have gone CIA, China Division."

"What made you think so?"

"Well, we had been playing I *Ching* fortune telling, just for a lark, the week before he disappeared from campus and it predicted the CIA for him. He wouldn't admit he got the appointment but he got really red in the face. Just a few years ago, I found a website which quoted him as an expert on China. Of course, they didn't mention CIA, but even if he didn't go into the Agency, he might know whether the Chinese are making a major push in face reading, for espionage or propaganda."

"Uncle Paul, on the subject of national security and the Chinese, do you remember two news items about the murder of a Chinese woman by a martial artist in the subway."

"Yes. What's the connection?"

"The Feds and local police suspected Chinese gangs, some of whom were Kung Fu masters and some who were illegals from China. The murder victim worked at CAM, a Chinese museum—actually, I met her once. The article said her cousin was a suspect because they were over-heard arguing about anti-Chinese racism and he disappeared after her death. He was a recent émigré from Hong Kong and a suspected gang member. Maybe your probable CIA man might know if China was involved. I was just curious."

"We could ask him that, along with your questions about face reading. It would really be a kick to hook up with Van again."

"On second thought," said Harold, "my partners—one of them's a lawyer—might be leery about involving the CIA. I better check with them first."

"Ok, I won't try contacting Van until you say so. He's hard to find anyway. Back in the day, he let us skulk around with him in dingy bars around Morningside Heights with these Iron Curtain characters he'd found somewhere. I remember this six-foot-ten Latvian that Van let on was a hit man. The Latvian bragged that he'd cut a Russian Commissar in half with a burp gun. He was scary *without* the gun."

Harold laughed. "Spy stories from a real Cold Warrior. Did you wear trench coats? I'm talking *The Third Man* with Orson Wells, Joseph Cotton…"

"Yeah, most of us, like me, played the role; a few, like Van, were for real. Why don't you e-mail me the details of your online face reading programs? I still feel the key is finding a Chinese software techie. Let me think about what other contacts I might have to help you find one."

"Ok, Uncle Paul. Thanks for helping. I'm anxious to tell Trish and Jennifer about our discussion."

"So, are you in love? Is that what this is really all about?

"She'd be easy to love. Trish is a beauty, with a perfect nose."

"Let's hope for your sake she has a nose for business. We'll talk."

IX.

The Wallachs were childless and Dr. Paul Wallach had always thought of his nephew as a son. He empathized with Harold's career confusion, given his own vacillations between dentistry and what he had considered more adventurous fields like advertising or the Foreign Service. Originally pre-med/pre-dent at Georgetown University in the late fifty's, he was friendly with students in its Foreign Service School, and dated Mary Jo Frazier, the blonde, winsome daughter of a former diplomat. The Fraziers liked Paul, and introduced him around at garden parties in the posh Georgetown section of Washington, D.C.

Paul was attracted to the WASP-y, elitist lifestyle, as was Mary Jo to his darkly sensitive, Russian-Jewish looks and quirky sense of humor. But after she embarked on a study year abroad, Paul felt marooned and homesick for the New York metropolitan area. He transferred to Columbia University's School of General Studies and continued to hedge his bets on a career, taking courses in biology, international politics and one Chinese language class—where he met a brilliant, irascible graduate of Princeton University named Vandersloot "Van" Lear.

X.

In 1962, Vandersloot W. Lear had graduated from Princeton, majoring in Russian and political science. Van's senior thesis took the form of a spy novel entitled *Helsinki Summer*. It featured the emerging technology of miniaturized electronics surveillance and the use of well-camouflaged dead drops for concealing messages and photographic images. Drawing on his own experience as a high school "junior-spy" at the 1956 Helsinki Youth Festival, his novel became a best seller and drew attention from important people in Washington. After graduation, Van took a government job for one year that involved foreign travel but the nature of it was hush-hush to family and friends.

An autocratic bearing came naturally to the tall, powerfully built Princetonian descended from English and Dutch colonial gentry. (Elizabeth Schuyler, the wife of Alexander Hamilton, had been an ancestor.) Van Lear's haughty intelligence and brusque charm quickly attracted Columbia students and faculty when he began graduate classes at the Morningside Heights campus in New York City in the fall of 1962.

Van's social circle at Columbia included Paul Wallach and Charles Wu, a Taiwanese Ph.D. candidate. In 1964, when Van suddenly disappeared after graduating from the School of International Affairs, their assumption that he had gone into the CIA's China Division was correct, but remained unconfirmed. After his first posting to Taiwan, the Agency stationed him first in Latin America, and then in Africa, where he specialized in drug interdiction.

Now, all these years later, and unbeknownst to Wallach, Lear had returned to Chinese operations, from a Counterterrorism Center in downtown Manhattan. Working with NYPD's Lieutenant Juen, and an FBI colleague, Lear monitored foreign-based crime and anti-terrorist intelligence. His special targets were New York's Tong and Triad gangs, some of whom were now suspected of conspiring with agents of the Chinese People's Republic, Ministry of State Security (MSS).

The recent murder of his source, Mary Shun, gave Lear new reason to anticipate moves against him by the MSS. An old reason would stem from his 1999 turning of their prize Chinatown operative, a man named Fong, into a double agent who then helped him—aided by the FBI colleague—to break a Chinese-instigated counterfeiting ring. However, during the operation, Van's identity and role had become known to MSS's Bureau of Counterintelligence who then added him to their target list of enemies for capture or elimination. The FBI had arranged for Fong to disappear into a witness-protection program in a remote US location in order to protect him from the vengeful MSS.

From his earliest days in the Agency, Van's hard-to-hide stature and remarkable brain power better qualified him to be an analyst in The Directorate of Intelligence—an inside job. Nevertheless, he had always demanded, and been given, outside operations work. In fact, on China-town streets, Lear had used his towering presence and bounding strides to great advantage in both surveillance and capture of alien suspects. Fleeing his pursuit, bad guys would run into the grip of waiting FBI and police plainclothesmen—a tactic his superiors tried to discourage, but Van usually got his way.

Combing for leads in Chinatown, he could rely on Lieutenant Henry Juen's investigative prowess. From Juen he knew that Billy Shun, a prime suspect, seemed to have made a clean getaway, leaving behind nothing directly incriminating, and apparently taking his own laptop computer. Perhaps more information on Shun would be forthcoming.

The FBI colleague he had worked with on the counterfeiting bust—despite strained relations between the CIA and FBI—was Agent Jacob Ritter. Agent Ritter had at his disposal a vast surveillance apparatus, including electronic, which dwarfed the domestic capabilities of the CIA. He could trace suspects—in this case probably Chinese—who had traveled from Chinatown and New York in recent days, particularly on planes or trains. It would be a matter of casting a wide net while looking for patterns of activity, travel, and communication generated by "people of interest".

Lear also had a good friend in Charles Wu, his former classmate at Columbia. Wu had become a highly regarded professor of Chinese studies and library curator at that university whom he could rely on for advice and information. Although not directly employed by the CIA, Professor Wu was retained by the agency as an advisor and consultant. Van thought Wu was one of the smartest men he'd ever met, and one of the few that Van trusted with details of his, often clandestine, counter-terrorist activities. For his part, Wu needed Van as a preeminent China expert and operative within government to lend weight to, and act on his own recommendations.

Assigned nowadays as a Case Officer, Van was pro-active in his work habits, and impatient by nature. His Division Chief's warning to lay low stuck in his craw, but all he could do was wait for developments.

XI.

Trish Donlon's Seventh Avenue office occupied an elegant, designer-renovated art deco bank building trimmed in the original sculpted stone, gold leaf and mosaics. The door of her glass-walled corner suite bore a bronze nameplate inscribed: *Patricia M. Donlon, Director of Marketing* and consisted of thick, bevelled glass, a bronze handle, and chrome pneumatic hinges.

Harold approached, carrying two heavy, leather satchels. With a free finger, he jabbed at the handle of the door and pivoted nimbly through as it sprang open—imitating a young, acrobatic Cary Grant.

Trish laughed. "Nice move. The gag is, you don't need pull to get into this office."

"Just some heavy lifting. Wait 'til you see all this stuff."

"Bring it on. I'll buzz Jen." She pressed a button.

Jennifer Santoramo's office was adjacent; she entered through a connecting glass door a few seconds later. "Hi Harold. What have you got for us?"

"Hi Jennifer." Harold deposited the satchels on Trish's stainless steel and glass desk, took a deep breath and sighed. "…Before we begin, I've got a confession to make."

"Uh oh," said Trish, "he's dumped us for some better-looking bimbos."

"Impossible," said Jennifer, her jaw dropping in mock surprise.

"Hardly," said Harold, with an ironic smile. "I know you said be discreet, Trish, but I *have* involved another person—my uncle. He's got a varied background, which might be useful to us: advertising, science, and even Chinese studies. He might have some contacts to help us find technical help. And I can trust him."

"It's nice to have family you can trust," said Trish, with her own ironic smile. "What's your uncle's take on our little project?"

Trish sat at her desk, head held high as if presiding. Harold perched upright, eager and attentive at one end of the adjacent red leather couch; Jennifer slouched languidly at the other end.

"Speaking as a former advertising guy," Harold said, wincing as if reliving the experience, "and Uncle Paul agrees—there's a good, and…well, a dark side of communicating facial images. A lot of it is subconscious. Some people may have a secret agenda."

"You mean like in subliminal advertising," asked Jennifer, "where you influence people without their realizing it? I saw this *changing-minds.org* website, where they say peoples' attitudes and behavior can be changed by body language—including faces." She sat straight up, dark eyes sparkling in anticipation.

"Definitely," said Harold. "I realize it's only fiction, but in the movie *The Manchurian Candidate*, a captured G.I. is brainwashed by the Chinese to become a killer, and the subliminal trigger is seeing a face on a playing card. I'm not saying we'd be brainwashing anybody, but we should be aware of the potential power of facial imagery—some of it subconscious."

"Aware of what, exactly?" asked Trish, raising a skeptical eyebrow while biting the edge of her lower lip.

"Well, for one thing," said Harold, "if you use celebrity matching, and you suggest your client looks like some fearsome Hollywood heavy, or even a cartoon character—you might be insulting some people and scaring others. Or God forbid, you could trigger some lunatic impulses when people watch monster movies."

"Maybe so…" answered Trish. "Instead, why couldn't we substitute faces that are *similar* to these Hollywood heavies but ones with nicer reputations?"

"I think that's a way around it," said Jennifer. "You'd want to keep a positive spin for clients with sensitive feelings. What else from the dark side?"

Harold pulled out two ancient-looking hardcover books from one satchel. "These physiognomy textbooks from the 1880's are dripping with racism, but don't be put off by that. They typecast people as to what animals they might resemble. That doesn't sound scientific, but it might have some validity because humans seem to have universal biases toward some of those animals."

"Such as?" asked Trish.

"For example," said Harold, "some people have predatory faces like lions…or hawks. Other strong faces might look like bulls or horses. On the other hand, some people look like…well, sheep or other animals of prey. Stature or build can enhance an image. Of course, personality doesn't necessarily follow, but the faces and bodies could be suggestive of those traits."

"Ok," said Jennifer. "But say our program could spot predator versus prey types. Just like with the Hollywood heavies, you want to spin it positively—tell the lions they look…uh, assertive or powerful, and the sheep…How about even-tempered or easy-going? Something like that?"

"Good way to handle it," said Harold. "But here's another point on the subconscious power of faces; based on what my uncle knows about the Chinese, they're probably experts on face reading and might be doing it themselves, not only to read the enemy, but also to influence through propaganda images."

"What's that got to do with us?" asked Trish.

"Because", answered Harold, "We should find out what they know in case they are the best source. And that goes for what national security people know too. If their methods are based on really good data, like from controlled studies of thousands of faces, some other outfit in the dating market might beat us to it! Even for the dating crowd, you'd want to distinguish between predator faces, and, let's say…friendlier faces."

"I guess so," said Trish. "Have you seen any such data?"

"Well, listen to this," said Harold, reading aloud: "According to *Health News*, West Point cadets whose faces projected dominance were more likely to become generals…The same was also true for C.E.O.'s of Fortune 500 companies and law firms; those with power faces made more profits."

"Probably true of our bosses too," said Jennifer. "Estaban and Jim both have strong, masculine faces."

"Makes the point," said Harold. "Face reading principles like that would be interesting to people involved in military or industrial espionage. If we rule out that stuff, we may be losing the guts of a really good program. I don't think we should rule out any raw data until we see what it all adds up to."

"If you say so," said Trish. "Anything more, before we show you what we've got?"

"This," he said, holding out two sheets. "These are printouts from *You Lie*, the T.V. series you mentioned at the Serengeti. They explain the science behind how facial expressions and body language give you away."

"I'll take your word for it," said Trish. "But I fly mainly by my own homing instincts…women's intuition."

"Ok," said Harold. "So, what does your intuition tell you about what women might want from face reading?"

"What women *really* want is to look beautiful," said Trish. "…to find the right look for themselves, and attract the right partner. We could package our app as a beauty aid or a fashion accessory. It analyzes the shape of your face and your features, your complexion, and maybe also your height and your figure type. That would go beyond anything that's out there now."

"The program, as we see it," added Jennifer, "could give women tips on which hairstyle, eyebrow shape, makeup and lipstick to use plus the most flattering styles and colors of clothes. Best of all, it helps you find a compatible face or body in a crowd because it reads a woman's frame as well as her face. What do you think, Harold?"

"The fashion angle sounds great, especially adding a body scan. But to make it really scientific you'd need to include Chinese Medicine in your face reader. It diagnoses chronic stress in the face: deep lines in your skin, a pale or blotchy complexion, rings under your eyes, blood shot eyes, that sort of thing."

Jennifer spoke, "Ok. So, why not first use the camera phone to check yourself out? You can see that you're well-groomed, but also that you're looking healthy and not stressed out."

"I can see it all now," said Harold. "When you read another person's face in your camera phone, you're not only receiving information in your conscious brain, but also your subconscious. We could have a voice-over or a text say something like: "This is a healthy, confident face that you have zeroed in on—one that is destined to play a powerful role in your life.""

"…*Or*," said Jennifer, overdramatizing like a magic show barker, "these deep-set eyes and massive brow indicate great intelligence that will provide handsomely for you in the future."

They all laughed.

"But *seriously*, as Harold would say," replied Trish, "what if people did say they were hypnotized—I'm speaking as a lawyer now—and claimed they were intimidated or…even *seduced* by these facial images?"

"C'mon now, Trish!" said Jennifer. "You're afraid of matching up the wrong people, and having it backfire on you legally? I say we should first lay out all the research, and then choose our next move."

"Maybe so, Miss *Associate* Marketing Director," said Trish, patting Jennifer on the shoulder. "I'm only saying we should be cautious."

"Cautious…fine," said Jennifer, rolling her eyes in exasperation. "But Trish, let's not miss out on a new way to empathize with women who aren't conventionally beautiful. And open up whole new markets in the process…"

Just then, a loud rap on the glass door announced the presence of a hulking, uniformed security guard. His brutish face reminded Harold of the classic Hollywood heavy, Broderick Crawford. Pulling the door ajar, the guard squeezed out a perfunctory smile. "Everything Ok, Mizz Donlon?"

"Oh yes, Mike. Jen and I couldn't feel safer."

The guard nodded gravely, closed the door, and moved on.

The women tittered.

Hmm, thought Harold. *If I were paranoid, I might take what Trish just said the wrong way—like I'm so harmless, of course they feel safe. Now why do I think like that?*

"Mike the guard," said Jennifer. "Now *there's* a face that fits the outfit."

"—And the job," said Trish. "Except, the guy happens to be a total mush."

"*Except*," said Harold, "that I bet the people who hired him expect his face to have the desired effect. The average bad guy wouldn't be hanging around long enough to get to know the warm and fuzzy Mike."

46

"Good point, Harold," said Jennifer, laughing. "So, if you're at the Serengeti, with our new and improved face reader, how can you tell the cops from the robbers—if both are tough looking guys?"

"You can't, but that's precisely my point about the need to look deeper: you know, greasy complexion, lines on the face—none of that healthy glow that Trish was talking about. You might even detect corrupt cops...ones on the take that look worried or stressed out. It all comes down to finding that software technician, probably Chinese, because most of this deep face reading is Chinese in origin. You hope he knows digital cameras too, and we run it all by him. Maybe Uncle Paul, with his background in Chinese studies, can help find someone."

"Ok. Sounds like we've got more searching to do. Jen and I can also do a market study to see if women might be interested in a face-reading app—to find the right outfit, or the right guy."

"It's a start," said Harold.

XII.

Two days later, Harold's phone rang. "Harold, it's Uncle Paul. I got the stuff you e-mailed. Too much to discuss over the phone; let's meet somewhere in the city."

Harold thought of his favorite research venue. "How about the 42nd Street Library?"

"Great. I'll drive in. See you in about an hour."

Harold Savitt and Paul Wallach met just inside the gigantic metal entrance doors of the New York Public Library. Harold had arrived fifteen minutes earlier and had time to browse the stacks. Stepping forward to embrace his uncle, he held a large book in his other hand. Harold and Paul strode through the high-ceilinged Rose Reading Room and sat together at one of its long oak tables.

In the perfectly balanced light streaming from an overhead bronze lamp, Paul's smile seemed restrained. "Don't be discouraged, Harold, but a lot's been done already. A program called MALINTENT, developed by The Department of Homeland Security, uses scanning cameras that read facial expressions to determine the intentions of terrorists. They might even read pupillary dilatation, which shows excitement. Or close-up, they might read irises, which are unique—like fingerprints. Nothing about facial structure—your area—but they might be developing it. You've got to beat them to it."

Harold shifted nervously in his seat. "We'd have to come up with something they don't have. Something truly original."

"Don't forget expression…only, a lot's been done, probably protected by patent."

"Ok. Maybe we could include the facial lines and contours that come with *habitual* expression; those *become* structure, over time. That comes right out of the Chinese Medicine part of face reading. It would show chronic stress and a debilitated state, not just the immediate nervousness that a suicide bomber's face might show."

"Maybe, but just for *matchmaking*— boy-girl stuff. Anything that encroaches on national security or law enforcement—like we talked about—you might first want to vet through somebody like Van, my buddy who went CIA."

Harold saw that a nearby patron was observing them. He leaned closer to his uncle and spoke in a stage whisper. "The women and I were discussing just that, and they seem reluctant to involve the Feds unnecessarily."

"Did you explain to them that the underlying principles might be the same for spotting both an ordinary rat and a terrorist?" said Paul, softly.

"I did," said Harold, raising his voice a bit. "And I told them that, in any case, our competition is liable to use it, whether we do or not."

"Right. Which brings us back to the need to find a Chinese software engineer. And unless that guy was a double agent from China, we'd need someone like Van to find out what the Chinese might know about it. I'd love to get Van involved—talk old times, and maybe get to work with him."

Harold sneaked a peek at the nearby patron, noticed he was reading a book, and raised his voice a bit more. "I notice you used the word we," said Harold, with an indulgent smile. "Are you planning on joining us?"

"Would you have me? I'd donate my services on behalf of the family."

"That's very generous of you Uncle Paul. But probably not necessary. It's premature to say that this project is really coming to something. I'd love to have you as a partner, but it's only fair to get Trish and Jennifer's approval first. When it comes to involving the CIA, I think they're going to need a little more convincing. And to tell the truth, so will I."

A stern-faced female librarian whom Harold thought looked the part seemed to descend from nowhere and, in a severe, loud whisper, reproached them for talking. Moments later, they were led to a private conference room, and sat themselves on either side of a metal table equipped for Internet service.

"Now we can talk," said Paul. "Like I said before, I can hold off on the CIA thing. Maybe I can help find you another Chinese source. And I agree we should research as widely as possible. The program should blend the best from East and West.

The Greeks *did* have some good ideas about form and beauty. Look at the statues of their gods for example: they were models of handsome Greek people and they became the standard. Nowadays, cosmetologists and cosmetic dentists use Greek principles of symmetry and proportion too."

"Precisely, Unc'. Look at this book I just picked up...John Cleese on *'The Human Face'*. Remember him from *Monty Python*? They discuss those classical models—faces representing beauty, fame, heroes, villains, and mating types. My female partners and I agree that humans may admire the faces of handsome people, like with celebrities, but we think when it comes to finding a mate, most people are probably more comfortable seeking someone their own level. I've seen studies that confirm that."

"Probably true. Let me see that book...this was based on a BBC documentary from years ago, all about diversity and prejudices about faces."

"Speaking of prejudice," said Harold, "my *Redfield's Physiognomy*, from 1884, is laughable, if you can stomach the racial stereotyping. They despised the faces of non-European type people."

"Makes sense," replied Paul. "Seems when people don't like other peoples' faces, their features or skin color, they tend to treat them badly."

"Trish and Jennifer and I came to the same conclusion. Humans tend to favor their own kind and mirror each other. That's another way that facial expression plays into it. You'll smile at a pleasing face, but maybe scowl at a homely face. And people's reactions to your face can reinforce what you think about yourself."

"Probably happens often enough. Now here's something else: look at this chapter on animals and how our features resemble or differ from other animals, such as apes."

"Yeah, the women and I also think animal faces are important. But, some racists despise human faces that remind them of apes—the animals that resemble us *most* and are closest to us *genetically*. It's a contradiction! You'd hesitate to tell somebody they resemble a gorilla, even though they're considered noble beasts—intelligent, brave and defenders of their families. Go figure."

"That's so true. We probably killed Neanderthals off because they resembled us enough to be competition, but were different enough to look like animals. Again, you can't prove it, but it seems intuitively true. Racism nowadays against other humans must be just a variation of that."

"Concerning racism, I can't stop thinking about that subway murder of the Chinese museum worker. I looked up the museum website and the place is really devoted to celebrating Chinese-American history. Why would her cousin blame her for anti-Chinese racism? They were both Chinese. Maybe there was some other issue between them. I wish I knew someone in the Chinatown community. Maybe your friend Van *could* help, if he knew someone down there."

Paul's face brightened. "I just thought of someone who might know how to find Van. He's a Chinese professor who might also know how to relate Chinese face reading to Western theories."

"Let's ask him," replied Harold. "But, I'm betting he'd agree that the Chinese didn't start from theory. Just by simple observation they would have concluded that certain faces coincide with certain personality types—maybe because people could be conditioned to *act* like their faces. Doesn't that explain it?"

"Not entirely. I think you'll still need *I Ching* because it describes so many aspects of human nature and situations that can occur. Individual examples of face type and personality may not jibe, but add enough samples and you could get a tendency or a trend. This is all very Taoist. That's why this guy I just thought of up at Columbia could be key. He's an expert on Tao. Meanwhile, why don't you work on your own to find a software guru and see who you come up with."

"I will." A dollop of guilt settled in Harold's stomach. There was another important source of help he'd overlooked—deliberately.

"You know, Uncle Paul, there's someone else who might help."

"Who's that?

"My former roomie at Columbia, Carlos Morales. Maybe Carlos can help find a technician or make a real contribution to our project. This book on faces makes me realize that media and advertising could be front and center on face reading."

The two men soon parted, agreeing to stay in touch on the technician search, and Harold promising to broach the subject of his uncle becoming a partner to Trish and Jennifer. He admitted to himself some qualms; obviously, he needed help with the project, and he hoped he could trust Carlos. Also, Uncle Paul seemed a little too anxious to play spy. That might not sit well with his women partners.

XIII.

That night, Harold steeled himself to make the call. "Carlos, it's Harold…Here's an update on the face reading, and maybe you can help." He related the gist of the Serengeti meeting with Trish Donlon and Jennifer Santoramo, the follow-up at their office, and his conversations with Uncle Paul.

"Good! These women think you might have a marketable idea with face reading. It sounds like Uncle Paul wants to re-live *Foreign Intrigue*. But how are you going to find a Chinese software nerd?"

"I thought you might help. Maybe there's one working in Hollywood re-creations—the kind you guys must have used in that commercial starring Harold Lloyd, the silent film comic—remember? He's this maniac who's all thumbs, and becomes a confident hero— thanks to one tablet of long-acting…"

"…Facultin. It's for anxiety and memory loss in early Alzheimer's. I didn't work on the account, so I don't know exactly how they made it. But what's the connection between face reading and digital re-creation?"

"To re-create faces, I would think you would scan every contour of the original face—just like military satellite systems that visualize every pebble on the ground. Scientific face reading has to scan the face also."

"Not my field. You're asking if our guys know somebody…a digital re-creation who knows Chinese face reading because he's Chinese. Who knows? I'll talk to our T.V. production manager and try to find out something."

"That would be great."

"Assuming we find this guy, what do we offer him, or tell him to set up a meeting? I don't want my people to think I'm freelancing. Saying it's for you might be a non-starter."

"Probably true," said Harold. "I'm not sure what to tell them. Let me ask Trish and Jen. Maybe they could say their fashion clients are interested in Hollywood star re-creations: using legends like Bette Davis or Joan Crawford to sell cosmetics, or women's fashions. That might work…I'll get back to you. Thanks for helping." Ending the call, Harold thought, *Could this really lead to something? As long as I don't screw up.*

XIV.

Hearing Trish's melodic *Hel-lo!* on the phone, Harold tried to match her exuberant tone. "Is this Spence-Iturbi's answer to Coco Chanel?"

"I wish. Aren't we in a good mood today. Have you already found *The Manchurian Candidate?*"

"Not yet, Trish, but the plot thickens. My uncle has offered to help, as sort of an unpaid partner. And, I've involved my ex-college roomy who works in advertising at my old agency, Harris Pierson. Carlos is a good guy and smart. He has contacts in cinema that might help us."

"Ok. But the more people we tell about this, the greater the chance of somebody stealing our ideas—which is why we can't advertise openly for a tech that knows face reading. Meanwhile, our little market research project also takes time."

"The market survey *is* important, Trish. But you can help in another way. Carlos doesn't want anyone at his agency to think he's free-lancing or that I'm involved, since I used to work there. But you could call Harris, Pierson and ask for a meeting on how re-creations of Hollywood glamour queens could sell anything fashion-related: clothes, jewelry, perfume… cosmetics. You know your field."

"Why, sir," said Trish, in a 'presenting' voice, "our clients also promote home décor, art work, automobiles, even sports equipment—all as fashion accessories! *Confidentially,* we're recommending a Far Eastern motif next season. Could you find an imaging consultant with experience in that area?"

Harold imagined an impish smirk on Trish's face. "Trish, you'd make a great undercover agent. The fashion world's Mata Hari!"

"Thanks, but my little presentation is only a twist on your clever subterfuge to get me into your former agency. Give me the contact names to ask for and I'll take it from there."

"Fine!" Harold was enjoying this praise from Trish. "You'll speak to Carlos first; he'll pave the way. And please, don't mention me to the other agency people." He gave Trish Carlos's last name and the agency incidentals.

"Great. I'll get Jen on board with all this. She'll need to prepare some specifics back at our place, in case, your...I mean, Carlos's agency calls back with more questions."

Trish's slip of the tongue about "your" agency was innocent enough, but it stung anyway. "Yes, *Carlos's* agency," Harold said, exhaling audibly. A bubble of worry was surfacing about the meeting at Harris Pierson. Would Carlos upstage him again, perhaps unintentionally, as before?

XV.

Billy Shun's Chinese interrogator, Gao-Ting-Ren, learned of Billy's return to China. The "cargo" had arrived in good condition. The interrogator's team of MSS agents, in New York and other American cities, could now plan against the feared agent Van.

Assassinating Van was considered, years ago, by Triad gangs, when they were first infiltrated by the MSS. Now, because of all the intelligence data in Van's conscious and subconscious brain—accessible by certain extraction methods—Liang, the MSS Deputy Minister of Operations in Beijing had decided that he was much more valuable alive than dead.

A kidnapping and transport operation to China would be ideal, if Van could be lured back to Chinatown, near the Oriental Rug Emporium on Mott Street—useful for human trafficking. There, the perfect vehicle could be found for his delivery to the motherland—a rug much larger than Billy Shun's 7' by 9' Ningxia. Gao-Ting-Ren hated to admit it, but the clever idea had come from Minister Li-Jian-Shui and his weak-kneed lot at the Ministry of Science and Technology; they claimed the source was an American Charlie Chan movie—of all things!

The aforementioned Deputy Minister Li, a fifty-five-year-old bachelor, sat in his cramped office in the dilapidated concrete building of the MSS's Tenth Bureau: Science and Technology. *Modern Beijing is springing up with new construction all around us*, he knew, *but our Bureau has been neglected—not just the buildings, but our work as well.*

Li's work involved a new plan called "Operation Spotlight" that would focus a spymaster's lens on the American enemy. It had a unique two-fold purpose: espionage *and* propaganda. But it had been a tough sell to superiors in the Standing Committee of the Chinese Communist Party, the CPC. His propaganda films produced in the 1980's on behalf of the People's Liberation Army had won praise from Party bigwigs for their use of dramatic cinematic techniques—especially the close-up, angled shots of the modern Chinese warrior with his "bold and resolute visage".

Li was a student of propaganda documentaries, including those of legendary Nazi filmmaker Leni Riefenstahl. But it was Li's reliance on such "foreign influences", as charged by envious bureaucrats in the Operations Ministry that had led to the Standing Committee's foot dragging on the approval of Operation Spotlight. In his last-year's report to the Standing Committee, Li assured them that, at last, plans had been completed to infiltrate American media and entertainment centers with Chinese "visitors" and Chinese-American software technicians and engineers—all of who were operatives. They would spy and report on Western cinematic technology. At the same time, fellow operatives would plan to use spy lenses embedded in critical locations to scan the enemy. Such lenses would also be placed in computers, T.V. sets and automobiles. The net result in espionage would be information about the readiness and number of the enemy, both ordinary citizens and officials; one could even eavesdrop on important conversations. And face-recognition would allow identification of individuals and increased hacking into vital data.

The propaganda spearhead, on the other hand, would counter Western-imposed standards of physical beauty and strength, in face and body, which had erroneously persisted for centuries, and replace them with the naturally superior images of Chinese and Asian people. This cultural offensive had its counterpart in the spectacular showing of Chinese athletes and performers in the 2008 Beijing Olympics along with its musicians, film actors, acrobats and dancers the world over. Agents were now stationed in major American cities to relay instructions, run operations and report on new developments.

It was imperative that communications be restricted to approved operations so as to minimize opportunities for the enemy's counterintelligence efforts to intercept them.

According to CPC supervisors, the recent unauthorized assassination of a Chinese-American woman by one of their own free-lance operatives was a mistake that brought increased attention from the enemy, and was not to be repeated.

XVI.

The next morning, over coffee, Trish briefed Jennifer about the proposed role-playing at Carlos's agency. She arose from the couch they were sharing, a sly smile playing on her lips. "You know what else I'm thinking, Jen?"

"I can guess. Aside from the face reading, we'll be making a good contact for Spence-Iturbi Fashion Consultants."

"Bull's eye," said Trish. "Even if Carlos's agency doesn't find us a Chinese software tech, we can still look into re-creations of former stars for our fashion clients."

Jennifer turned to face her. "But let's be honest, Trish. How solid is this business proposition really?"

"I must admit, I'm going mainly on pure instinct with Harold. He's a little unsure of himself, but he seems like a straight shooter and has good ideas. Only one thing troubles me…"

"What now?" asked Jennifer.

"Harold and his uncle seem to welcome getting the CIA involved in our little project. Outside of researching patent protections, I'd just as soon avoid government agencies, even supposedly friendly ones." Taking her seat at the desk, Trish stuck out a recalcitrant lower lip.

"But Trish, what about the argument that the People's Republic of China might have the best info on face reading, and that the CIA would be in the best position to confirm that?"

"Frankly, I'd like to see if we have any contacts ourselves that could look into the technology behind facial imagery. I have an idea I'll tell you about in a minute. We can't involve Spence-Iturbi, yet, for obvious reasons. They'd co-opt our idea just like the CIA might."

"And so would FIT, much as I'd like to play the big shot over there. But frankly Trish, there *is* one thing I've got to tell you that is troubling me."

Crossing her arms, Jennifer leaned toward Trish.

Trish stood up, as if refusing to be cornered. "Let *me* guess. You think I might be holding you back from flying off on your own with the therapy or the fashion angle."

"You read my mind, if not my face," said Jennifer, scowling.

"Look Jen, we've got to trust each other, and that means presenting a united front. I wouldn't want Harold to think we're squabbling, or to distrust us either. We should be totally above board with him about what might happen."

Jennifer sat back luxuriantly onto the couch. "And...we should all agree to be equal partners in any spin-off from the face reading app for the dating public."

Trish laughed. "The way we finish sentences for each other, it's no wonder we're a double-barreled threat in the fashion industry."

"Except your barrel is over mine and it's bigger caliber."

"The way it's got to be in this corporate set-up," said Trish in an apologetic tone. "But in any spin-off, whoever has the natural advantage, as you do with psychology, would be the natural leader. I would be your partner, but definitely under you in any face reading therapy institute. We'll never know what Harold knows about Chinese face reading, or his uncle about the political aspects of facial imagery, so they'll be the natural leaders of that—I hope." Trish chuckled softly. "You may think I'm being overly cautious, but I wouldn't want Harold to be corrupted by anybody."

"You mean anybody but us."

Hooting laughter, Trish and Jennifer slapped hands in a high ten.

"I trust Harold to be honest," said Trish, "but not necessarily to have the best judgment. So, I'd like to keep some controls on him..."

"...Like you do on me, Madam Control Freak."

"I'll wear that title as a badge of honor," said Trish, with a proud smile.

"That's how you got to be boss lady, which I'm not challenging. But be real: wouldn't you want to break away from Spence-Iturbi if this thing got big?"

"Maybe eventually, but meanwhile, there might be an opportunity for them to cash in too, with Hollywood re-creations selling fashions and cosmetics. Estaban and Jim have been very good to us. Of course, I would insist on retaining rights to the face reading property. Let me play it my way, at the right time."

"Alright—as long as we're really equal partners," said Jennifer.

"Of course. But now, to make things more interesting we're on the verge of dealing another wild card named Carlos into the game—an advertising type like Harold, but I'll bet a whole lot slicker. That's where you come in, my little pretty, said the Wicked Witch."

"Wait a minute, Witchy," aren't you running this little play at the agency?"

"Only at first. Actually, I was planning on turning Carlos over to you. Not that I have exclusive designs on Harold, but pairing off seems the right way to go. I know you can handle it."

"Anything for good ol' Spence-Iturbi. So, what's this other idea you were hiding up your sleeve?"

"Hoda. I was thinking about using her as a consultant, in case Harold comes up short in finding a guru." The reference was to their former college classmate, Hoda Ramsis, a native of Cairo, Egypt, and now an associate curator of Egyptology at the Metropolitan Museum of Art.

Jennifer had to admit that her boss was always thinking. "Good idea, Trish. She might know somebody at the Met who does facial analysis of art works."

"She's helped us before," said Trish, "researching statues and paintings for fashion styles. Let's see if fine art has gone scientific—at least enough for our purposes."

"I'll call her in a second." Jennifer pressed keys on her calendar app. "Let's see if we can get a private tour or something, maybe with one of the Met techies, ideally somebody Chinese to satisfy Harold's specifications."

"I'll bet Hoda's face is one he wouldn't mind studying," said Trish.

"Too late for him—she's married," answered Jennifer.

"It's Ok. Harold said he's only interested in the pure aesthetics of faces. You could trust him anywhere, I guess."

Jennifer laughed. "Call him and see if he wants to go."

XVII.

Harold jumped at Trish's plan. He had previously wanted to see the current Chinese Mongol exhibition. Now, of course, it might be relevant to their work. Anyway, he could hardly object to a new person being injected into the project, since he was pushing for his own uncle's participation—with some privately held reservations.

He babbled on for a few minutes to Trish, excited that the face reading project was gaining ground. But going to the Met had to be scheduled around a Medical Monograph assignment due for Fortune-Estes. Luckily, he needed to be at the Mount Sinai Medical Library for two days, and could dovetail that with the museum visit—only a short jaunt down 5th Avenue. Trish sounded very encouraging. But juggling all these new balls—Uncle Paul, Carlos, another person at the Met—he might drop one and sabotage himself again.

XVIII.

A forecast of light snow—it was now mid-December—prompted Trish and Jennifer to have one cab pick them up, at their respective apartments, for the ride to the Metropolitan Museum.

Next morning, Trish scooted in beside Jennifer in the rear seat of the cab, which instantly began to maneuver through midtown traffic. "Harold wasn't just excited Jen—he sounded like he was going to climb right through the phone. I'm not saying he's coming on to me, but I'd like to keep things…"

"…Under control," said Jennifer.

"Of course. Just like I wouldn't want to see you going off half cocked and waste all that energy, in case this whole thing goes kaphlooey."

"And how are you going to keep Harold under control?"

"Actually, I'd like to give him his head and let him run with the project. I think it would be good for his self-esteem."

"Now who's playing Dr. Freud?" said Jennifer.

"*Touche.* But, honestly, I would like to see him stand up to his uncle or the Feds, and even us, if it came to that. A good test for his taking charge would be coming up with that Chinese techie. And let's see how he handles himself today with Hoda."

IXX.

Twenty minutes later—it was 10 a.m.—Harold greeted Trish and Jennifer in front of the Metropolitan Museum of Art as tiny snowflakes swirled around them. Slung over his shoulder was a leather strap and case holding his new Nikon Digital SLR, a gift from his parents. Walking up the granite steps, the three passed under a huge banner announcing Kublai Khan and the Chinese Art Exhibit.

Harold said, "Glad you called me on this. I thought we could see what kinds of faces get immortalized in museums…Maybe discover a tie-in to Chinese face reading in the China exhibit and take some pictures."

"I'm always inspired here," said Trish, "like for reviving historic clothing styles. And our friend may have some ideas."

Once inside the grandiose Beaux Arts lobby they waited in a coat check line. Harold anxiously rubbed his hands together. "Are you sure she can be trusted, Trish?"

"Relax, Harold," said Jennifer, putting a hand on his shoulder. "We know her to be a good friend. She was a classmate, and an anthropology major, which explains why she wound up here. She might know about scientific analysis of faces in the art world. As for her own face, well, you'll see." Jennifer phoned Hoda as they checked their coats. "She'll be down in five minutes. Meanwhile, we can browse."

A few steps into the Egyptian section, the group encountered a stone lion that seemed ready to pounce. On a nearby wall were paintings of men in Roman tunics staring out with bold, black eyes. The legend explained that these had been Egyptians under Roman rule. Harold examined their faces studiously, and took pictures. "Look at their large eyes, very Egyptian. Large eyes are considered amorous or innocent, like in children who have relatively large eyes for their faces. And the Chinese agree."

Jennifer's large, dark eyes shone like polished onyx. "Amorous," he says. "If you are drawn to Egyptian eyes, beware, they may cast a spell!"

Jennifer and Trish parodied a haunted house laugh.

Enjoying the fun, Harold waved them over to mummy cases seven feet tall. The faces painted on the cases had enormous eyes, shaped like those of the men in Roman tunics.

Trish said, "Those eyes are really hypnotic."

Harold snapped photos of the mummy faces.

Jennifer answered her cell phone. "Ok, See you there." She turned to Harold and Trish. "We're meeting her in her office right around the corner."

Following Trish, Harold walked several steps and turned quickly into a small corridor when his head almost collided with a female chin.

"Hi, Hoda. This is Harold," said Trish.

Harold, who was five-foot-ten, lifted his head to make eye contact with a statuesque, dark-haired woman whose face resembled one he'd just seen on a mummy case. She wore an Egyptian headdress that reached her shoulders, a tailored skirt-suit and high heels.

"Hi Harold. Welcome to my inner sanctum." Hoda spoke in a deep, velvet purr, her accent Middle Eastern with a British upper-class inflection.

Harold managed a soft, "Hi".

Hoda led them inside her office dominated by a large Sandalwood desk and seated them around it.

"She has this effect on people," said Jennifer. "Sitting down, she's not so scary."

"I'm really only six feet," said Hoda, modestly lowering her eyes. "In America, even tall women wear heels. Back in Egypt, not so much."

"Here at the Met," said Trish, "she plays Cleopatra, or is it Nefertiti? We knew her when she was just another Manhattanville dorm rat."

Hoda laughed. "This would be normal dress for a professional woman in Egypt—minus the heels. I'm Associate Curator in Egyptology here; it doesn't hurt to look the part."

Harold surveyed Hoda's desk. On it were pictures of her, a man—apparently her husband—who was Caucasian-looking, and two pre-teen children, along with a bronze, pyramid paperweight, inscribed *Hoda Bahur Ramsis.*

He noted Hoda's distinctly Egyptian eyes; they were large, black and exotically shaped, reminding him of actor Omar Sharif's. The contours of her face were different, more roundly female, but mask-like in their perfection. "Sorry to stare," he said, "but I see you as a model of Egyptian beauty, or any beauty for that matter. Do you mind if I take your picture—for scientific purposes only." Harold's coy smile showed he was half-joking.

"Not at all, I'm used to it," said Hoda, without a hint of false modesty. She posed, smiling, as Harold raised the camera and snapped the picture.

"Harold's hobby is collecting female features," said Trish.

"*In books,*" said Harold with a wry smile, remembering his grotesque joke about Jeffrey Dahmer.

"Well," said Trish, "Queen Nefertiti here has made the books. Show him, Hoda."

Hoda closed the door to the small office. "I don't mind fitting a stereotype, as long as it's attractive." From a desk drawer, she removed two 8"x10" glossy photographs. "Trish means these famous busts of Nefertiti."

Harold recognized the one painted bust of Nefertiti; it had the same, bronzed coloration and facial type as Hoda's. The other, in grey granite, resembled her even more, with triangular planes that ran from the nose across the cheekbones up to the ears, suggesting cat-like features. "You didn't have to interview for this job," said Harold, "your face did it for you."

"Maybe partially," Hoda laughed. "Not to blow my horn, as the Americans say, but my resume includes a Doctorate in Egyptology and Hieroglyphics. I speak Arabic, as well as Coptic, the ancient Egyptian language."

"Not just another pretty face, as the Americans say," added Trish.

"Not what I'd expect to find in museum staff," replied Harold. He suddenly thought of CAM, the murder in the subway, and the postponed trip to Chinatown. "The one place I haven't seen is the new CAM, the Chinese museum. Know anything about it, Hoda?"

"Actually, yes. I've been there. I know some of their staff through the American Association of Museum Curators. One was murdered recently in the subway—Mary Shun. I knew of her. Horrible! It is a great little museum, though. Surely a good place to study Chinese faces."

"But about the murder," said Harold, "the papers said the police suspected Mary Shun's cousin. The police said he may have been a gang member and that he seemed angry about anti-Chinese racism. But why would he take it out on his cousin?"

"I can't imagine," replied Hoda. "A personal issue? To silence her up about something?"

"Terrible," said Jennifer, looking pained and sympathetic.

"Who wants coffee?" asked Hoda, smiling briskly, happy to change the subject. "I've got American and Egyptian, which is like Turkish coffee."

All chose Egyptian with sugar.

Hoda quickly made and served four cups of the characteristically thick coffee; its sweet, earthy aroma filled the room. "Makes a cup in thirty seconds. Pretty pricey, but Asher says I'm worth it."

Harold looked expectantly at a photo on the desk. "Who's Asher?"

"My husband."

"I was wondering. Asher is a Jewish name."

"Yes, Asher is Jewish."

Harold looked surprised.

"I'm Coptic Christian and he's Messianic Jewish. They both believe in Jesus. So, we're not as different as you think."

"I'm traditional Jewish, and not particularly religious," replied Harold, "but I can appreciate diversity, in faces and otherwise."

"On the subject of diversity," said Jennifer, "whatever people *say*, most are ambivalent about it, which is not necessarily a bad thing, if they own it."

"How do you mean?" said Harold.

"Opposites can attract, legitimately, if it's a clear choice, and not, say, a rebellion," said Jennifer. "For example, Hoda and Asher, if you don't mind my saying so." She looked expectantly at Hoda.

Hoda smiled graciously. "Not at all."

Jennifer continued, "Theirs' is an example of a good marriage between two different cultures, and both families are cool about everything. On the other hand, it's a natural tendency to favor your own similar-looking and like-minded people. As long as it's your own choice, and you're not just aping your social group or your parents' choices."

Harold wondered if he "aped" his parents' choices and then subconsciously rebelled. "Speaking of apes," he said, "my uncle and I were discussing how humans prefer cat-like looks to ape-like looks—in *humans*."

Hoda seemed to purr her answer: "As you probably know, the ancient Egyptians worshipped cats. Other peoples did too."

"The cat's eye has magnetic power," said Trish. "When we promoted winged eye-shadow and mascara for Max Factor a few years ago, it was the cat-eye look."

"My physiognomy books say that lion-faced people intimidate and command people," said Harold. "We're trying to find a scientific basis for why faces have the power to attract. We've been talking about it, and just sitting here now, I've been experiencing it."

"If you mean me," said Hoda, "I don't think of myself as particularly powerful."

"Oh yes, people must be drawn to you," replied Harold.

"Your face is cat-like and your eyes are really powerful. Maybe your face can be expressed by a mathematical formula and into a program. Everybody's got some kind of appeal. Even ordinary faces could be analyzed to get people matched up to their type, or to what appeals to them."

"Your idea is to match people by their faces?" asked Hoda.

"Yes," answered Harold. "We may worship beautiful faces or fear powerful faces, but in choosing a mate, we're more practical, probably based on survival instincts. Most people seek their own comfort level, in faces, so to speak."

Harold was speaking in a matter-of-fact, almost professorial tone, but another track of his mind was shouting: *Is she ever beautiful! I knew that Asian looks had to be included along with classical European, but I'd totally overlooked the ancient Egyptians, who were both African and Middle-Eastern, which is Asian. I'm a blend of Middle-Eastern and European; Trish*

and Jen are European; we're all linked together. That's me, the missing link.
He couldn't suppress a self-deprecating smirk. *I could never land a classy chick like this one.*

"But, Harold," said Jennifer, with her own coy look, "if you don't have a cat face, you might be a teddy bear or puppy dog—the cute, fluffy look."

"Like Harold?" said Trish.

He blushed. "Very funny. I look like a dog?"

"No," said Trish, "but you are cute and fluffy".

The three women laughed in delight.

"I think you should take it as a compliment," said Hoda.

"I'll think about it," said Harold, forcing a smile.

"This is all very interesting," said Hoda, "but how can I help?"

Trish spoke up. "We were hoping you could help us find a software technician who studies facial images in museums. You could also be a live model of a non-Western beautiful face, or consult on the Egyptian look in fashion, like we've discussed before."

"I'd be willing," said Hoda. "Off hand, I don't know any software people that study museum images, but I will ask around for you."

"Thanks, Hoda", said Jennifer. "Faces are also about archetypes…how facial types match roles or personalities."

"How does that work?" asked Hoda.

"Archetypes come into it when people assume roles that seem to fit their faces. Powerful people may act that way, partly because of how they relate to their own faces, or how other people react to them. A lot of powerful faces seem to have angular features with more massive brows, cheekbones or jaws. Kind or compassionate-looking faces are often rounder or curvier, like in children or babies. People with such faces might act friendlier or compassionate if people see them that way. The power of suggestion. It doesn't necessarily follow, of course, because personality can override everything."

"I couldn't sum it up better," said Harold. "For example, I don't think it's a coincidence that the police and the military have a lot of tough-looking people, or that Hollywood draws pretty faces. Naturally, there are mixtures and exceptions. Archetypes are only generalities, but we think they're influential."

"So," said Hoda, "as archetypes, we may act out our faces, and play defined roles in life?"

"We think some people do. Can you think of any archetype examples shown here at the Met?" asked Trish.

"Perhaps. Our new Chinese exhibit shows little clay actors playing roles in theatre companies. I don't know what their faces show exactly, but you could look."

Harold spoke, "We were hoping to find something Chinese, because Chinese face reading seems to dominate the field. Please lead the way."

"I really have to go. But let me take you upstairs and get you started."

A few minutes later, they approached the Mongol-Chinese exhibit. A museum guard handed them a pamphlet and explained that they couldn't take photographs.

Hoda assured them she'd send pictures of whatever they wished. Following thanks and hugs all around, including Harold, she departed.

Hardly believing all this female favor, Harold felt almost giddy. Mesmerized by Hoda's beauty, he would enjoy the opportunity to study her further— strictly as a naturalist would examine a specimen, of course. He laughed to himself, remembering Trish's admonition against ogling *her* at their first meeting.

They split up for a short time. The women gravitated to medieval female dress, Harold to swords, shields and armor. He tensed up at the sight of a stern-looking Mongol statue, labeled Military Officer. An adjacent Civil Officer statue seemed kindly looking. Harold remembered the brutal general in *The Manchurian Candidate* vs. the kindly Charlie Chan: classic archetypes.

Trish touched Harold's arm. "I do want to get another possible issue straight between us, Harold."

Her smile seemed especially warm, but Harold felt an icicle in his stomach. "Wh...what do you mean?

"We are, of course, partners with you in this venture, but that is separate from our work as Spence-Iturbi fashion consultants. Since I am representing my firm in dealings with your old agency, I couldn't pass up

an opportunity that would benefit our fashion clients. You do understand that, don't you?"

"Of course I do…" But Harold's words caught in his throat. He
understood from a business point of view. However, anticipating the
upcoming meeting of Carlos and Trish, he feared the worst: no Chinese
face-reading technician would emerge from it. Instead, the upshot would
be a fashion victory for Trish and Jennifer, *through Carlos,* that would
leave him out—again.

Harold took a deep breath and steadied himself. He extended his
arms around both women, feeling like a gallant Jimmy Stewart, and
escorted them over to an exhibit entitled "Chinese Theatre, 1276-1368".

"This must be the guided tour," said Trish, trilling a laugh as she
felt Harold's arm circling her waist. Jennifer giggled. Harold blushed and
dropped his arms to his sides.

In front of them were glass cases containing clay figurines. They
were labeled: Official, Leading Man, Secondary Male, and Comic.
Adjacent was a Newlywed Couple: the Bashful Bride, and the Awkward
Husband. The three visitors became absorbed in the figurines for a few
moments.

"Notice," said Harold, "that the faces are simple drawings in clay,
but they are perfect caricatures of the actors' roles. The faces and personalities match."

"These remind me of the opera masks I saw at a Chinese New Year
celebration," said Trish, "But only the Newlyweds shows a real female.
I'd be initiating a sexual discrimination suit."

"You'd be filing it posthumously," said Jennifer. "In those days,
women were seldom seen or heard in public."

"Even in Shakespeare's day," said Harold, "men actors played wom-
en's parts."

"Definitely a man's world, then and now," said Trish, playacting a
hopeless tone.

"No question," said Harold. "But maybe they weren't enjoying it
much. Why does the Leading Man need a Second Banana?" He thought
of playing second to Carlos.

"I'll psychoanalyze this one," said Jen. "The Secondary Male is jealous and threatens the Top Banana. The Official warns them to behave. And the Comic relief cracks jokes and keeps everybody loose."

Harold and Trish laughed out loud; drawing dirty looks from nearby people.

Jennifer said, "We better leave before we're asked to. Actually, it's almost noon, and I have a working lunch with Jim Spence. He's one of our bosses, Harold."

Trish explained, "We like our bosses. They appreciate our hard work and trust us to find new business on our own."

Harold answered, "My bosses aren't so social, but they leave me alone as along as I get my work done. Obviously, I don't have the kind of freedom you have away from the office. If I could somehow tie the study of faces into my other work without my supervisor knowing, I could more easily justify the kind of time we're taking for our research. I need to think about that. I sure hope we accomplished something here today."

Jennifer answered, "We certainly saw today how roles and faces can match. In our business, we see how clothes can help you look the part. Maybe the right face helps you look the part, too? It's like what you said about soldiers that look tough, and it's certainly true of fashion models."

Trish added, "I guess we saw how ancient faces are still in vogue, like Hoda's, for instance. And she did reinforce your point about the importance of certain animal faces, like cats and cute puppy dogs."

The women's laughter sounded soft and encouraging, but Harold felt himself blushing again "It was...I think, a worthwhile day." With effort, he summoned a breezy smile, imagining himself the dapper, confident William Holden in *Sabrina*.

He and Trish walked Jennifer to the museum entrance, saw her into a cab, and then decided to have lunch together over on nearby Madison Avenue.

XX.

An enclosed sidewalk café provided ample warmth from the cold and a close-up view of the passing crowd. A waiter seated them and took their order.

Harold stretched out, affecting a carefree air. "People watching is obviously more fun in the summer. More people, less clothing."

"I'm always looking at clothes and people," said Trish. "As we say on Seventh Avenue, there are shoppers and there are buyers." Smiling, she leaned pointedly toward Harold.

"I'm a typical man, meaning I hate shopping. Except that I do shop for women, I guess." Surprised at his own openness, Harold wondered if he could break through a fear barrier with Trish.

"Unlike clothes," replied Trish, "you can't very well try women on for size. Only marriage really proves if you've got a good fit; you don't want to make a mistake."

"You sound like the voice of experience."

"I was married. I was just a kid." Trish shyly lowered her eyes. She reminded Harold of Hollywood legend Maureen O'Hara—the auburn hair, the sapphire eyes, the sudden lilt in her voice and the dreamy expression that came over her. He was moved by Trish's unexpected show of vulnerability and her trusting him with personal information.

Trish's steady gaze projected a warmth Harold had not felt before. "I'm Bronx Irish and fell in love with a nice Jewish boy from Riverdale— maybe it was rebellion, or attraction of opposites, as Jennifer was talking about. Our parents fought it but we went ahead and married anyway in a civil ceremony. Only our friends and his sister came. My side of the family was really terrible."

She continued, as Harold inched his chair closer. "My mother is from a big Irish family in the Bronx—athletes, cops, priests, military, mostly Mt. St. Michael's alums, and all devout Catholics…You can't imagine what we went through." She murmured, "We broke up less than a year later. It was not meant to be."

"At least you had the guts to try," said Harold. "I feel like I've been sneaking around in the shadows my whole life. Trying to please my parents; afraid to think about what I really want—in a career or in a mate." Harold realized he was baring his soul to a woman he was attracted to and hardly knew. Was he going too far?

Trish smile seemed reassuring. "In finding my path in life, humor has helped a lot. Growing up, a fast mouth got me smacked. It works better in business."

"You know those Chinese figurines in the museum. You'd never be the Bashful Bride."

"Maybe she was pretending, Harold," said Trish with a shrewd smile.

"How do you mean?"

"Maybe she didn't want to show up her Awkward Husband."

"Oh, you foxy Irish lass! You belong in that Chinese troop after all."

"Why?"

"You'd be the Comic, keeping everybody loose."

They both laughed.

"My role in life…" she said. "And it pays the bills."

"I used to be funnier sometimes, with Carlos; ethnic stuff, silly conversations, but something happened…"

Deli sandwiches and coffee came. Harold was grateful for the interruption; they switched to small talk. Later, sharing a cab to Trish's East 44th Street apartment, Trish reviewed what she was to say at Harris, Pierson, with Carlos's help. Harold took the cab to his office, thinking that, perhaps, despite his past doubts and fears, he was connecting with women on a deeper level than ever before. Trish was no longer on a pedestal; she seemed more approachable.

XXI.

As planned, the following day, Trish spoke briefly with Carlos at Harris Pierson. Because he did not work on the Hollywood re-creations account, they decided to concoct a story that Carlos reputedly had some fashion knowledge. (He was a snappy dresser and thought he could pull it off.) This would allow him to sit in and perhaps help guide things along. He then transferred her over to Burt Johnson, the T.V. Production Manager, and, in a five-minute conversation, Trish was persuasive enough to set up a next-day meeting at the agency.

Burt promised to include a representative from the New York office of the affiliate that shot the Harold Lloyd commercial. Although Harris Pierson was primarily a pharmaceutical agency, Burt made clear to Trish that they were prepared to compete for the fashion consumer accounts that were her clients.

The next morning, Trish was escorted into the staid boardroom of Harris, Pearson. She made a mental note: Early Harvard Club; needs a makeover.

"Hi, I'm Trish Donlon, Spence-Iturbi Fashion Consultants."

"Pleasure to meet you, Trish; I'm Burt Johnson. *Carlos*, you already know."

Trish didn't, except by phone, but smiled appreciatively at the man who nodded and smiled at the sound of his name. She seated herself in the tufted-leather chair next to Johnson.

"And this is Mark Fallon, from ImageGraphics."

They exchanged greetings.

Mark had a bearded, cherubic face and a booming bass voice. "Trish—Burt briefed me...No problem doing commercials with re-creations of certain stars. Bette Davis and Joan Crawford may be difficult because their estates own the rights and will probably play hardball." Mark's round face twisted into a scowl.

Trish smiled broadly, wanting to stay positive. "I agree. We've found that it's usually easier to deal with living, past stars or their agents."

Mark sneered. "Exactly. Many *older* beauties, faded but hanging on, are anxious to see themselves re-born as their former gorgeous selves. Trouble is, image rights are now big business and lawyers run those. God save us from lawyers."

Trish kept her smile but thought, *what a blowhard!* "Yes, obviously, we'd need a rights release that's bullet-proof. Sometimes it's easier if the star had an arrangement with a cosmetics company; we represent many of those. By the way, did Burt mention that we're recommending an East Asian accent to fashion next season?"

"Yes, Trish," said Burt. "Since you called, I was thinking of some glamorous Asian types, or Caucasians playing Asians, like Jennifer Jones, where she played a doctor in Hong Kong."

Trish replied, "*Love is a Many Splendored Thing* was the movie. She was smashing in that Chinese sheath skirt with the high collar—a look that could be revived."

Carlos joined in. "Yes, that was a chic Asian look. Remember *Suzie Wong*—played by Nancy Kwan? She was a sensation, the innocent femme fatale. Very appealing; might still be."

Hmm, Carlos does know his fashion, thought Trish. *He's ruggedly handsome with a roguish glint in his eye, but not really my type—maybe Jen's.* "Yes, a very appealing look," she said. "But our star doesn't need to look or be Asian to make the fashion statement; even an Asian atmosphere or style can create the brand. I'm thinking Rita Hayworth in *Lady from Shanghai*. And how about Fay Dunaway in *Chinatown*? She played a straight-arrow American. But what a great body and face to model Asian clothes and accessories! I wonder if *she's* available to approve a re-creation?"

Mark's deep voice rumbled on. "We can have our media and production departments make a composite list to search for who's available, and for how much."

He looked at his notes. "Trish—Burt also mentioned you were looking for a Chinese digital production guy within our group, someone who knows something about Chinese fashion…We do have a liaison, a Chinese guy, at South California's film school in L.A. He helped develop the original re-creation technology. I might be able to get him to talk with you on the phone or email. He's a great guy, but hardly a fashion plate…more like baggy jeans and bad ties from K-Mart." Mark's deep laugh boomed across the table.

"Actually, said Trish, in a serious, measured tone, "speaking Chinese and knowing Chinese culture are more important. Maybe he could introduce us to some Chinese people who do know fashion. I suppose we could go to L.A., if need be."

"Well, Trish," said Mark, "when you're ready to make a proposal— you know, with product lines, estimated billings and all the rest—let's all get together. Between us, we'll have available stars, media and costs all lined up and ready."

"Sounds like the way to go," said Trish.

"Meanwhile, I will call Ma. Ma-Chang-Kou is his name. He's *Chinese* Chinese, but speaks perfect English. He worked with Dr. Barry Daveneck on the pioneer digital work at South California. Give me your card. Maybe he'll be your guide to Chinese culture and you can be his fashion consultant." Mark roared over his own joke.

XXII.

Gao-Ting-Ren, the MSS operative who had interrogated Billy Shun called a local New York Chinatown number; he spoke in the Shantung dialect—difficult to understand for Mandarin speakers who might be eavesdropping. "This is agent Blue Lotus. We are planning operation against American agent Van, using your rug Emporium. Best time would be Chinese New Year, because of crowd cover, but we must be ready anytime."

"Very well. We will prepare in usual way."

"At proper time, you will spread word that smuggled MSS agents are hiding in Emporium. Make sure Fifth Precinct knows; they work with Van and will tell him, which we want. Police may be watching, but do nothing unless Van is spotted. Then one of your people approach him with Emporium tip and run in that direction."

"What if my man is apprehended?"

"No problem. We will create diversion and distract police. Van will be disabled quickly and brought to you. Speed is essential."

"Don't worry. As soon as rug is rolled up for shipment, truck is waiting at back door, motor running, as before."

"One more thing. Agent White Tiger in Los Angeles will be alerted for possibility. He will be notified, as soon as cargo is loaded here in airplane. White Tiger will inspect it at his end. Tell your driver to call you, after takeoff, and you will call me."

"Understood."

XXIII.

Right after seeing Trish, Jennifer and Harold at the Met, Hoda had made two calls. The first was to a colleague in the museum's Department of Scientific Research; she left a voice mail requesting anything on computer analysis of artwork. The second was to her beloved Uncle Makram in Cairo. He served on Cairo Museum's Supreme Council of Antiquities and been the primary inspiration for her becoming an Egyptologist. Makram Salama Ramsis was a trusted family confidant as well as one of the world's leading authorities on Pharonic Egypt.

Despite comprising a large segment of Egypt's intellectual and professional elite, Coptic families like theirs had suffered discrimination at the hands of the Muslim majority for centuries. Ironically, they were Christians who claimed to be the true ethnic descendants of the ancient Egyptians and as such, had assumed patrimony over that "pagan" culture.

Since it was evening in Cairo, Hoda reached Uncle Makram at home. They spoke first in Arabic for a few minutes—solicitous inquiries about family—after which Hoda slipped into Coptic. "Uncle, maybe you can help me. Friends of mine are researching the subject of faces— the power of faces. What might Egyptian scholars of the ancients have to say on that subject?" A few quiet seconds passed. Hoda inquired, "…Uncle Makram?"

His answer was hearty laughter.

"Have I misspoken, Uncle?"

"No, my sweet. I will explain why I am amused in a moment. But first I must ask, does this concern Met business?"

"Oh no. This is a totally private venture involving my girlfriends from college and another man. I would not presume on you otherwise."

(It had been long understood—despite their bonds of blood—that uncle and niece would respect the rival interests of their two great museums.)

"Good. I will explain why the power of faces is amusing…it is because of a pet nickname you had as a child—one which we never told you about."

"What name is that?"

"The name is Udjat—short for Wadjet."

"Wadjet? The goddess who personifies the Eye of Horus?"

"The very one. Even as a baby you had that bewitching Eye of Horus."

"Why keep it a secret? Everyone knows Horus is a good omen who wards off evil."

"You were always a good person, powerful yet modest, even as a child. But we didn't want to give you an extra sense of privilege or importance—by, in effect, worshiping your beauty. That would have been idolatry and un-Christian."

"Thank you, Uncle, but would not our Coptic faith consider using the Eye of Horus—even for good—a form of witchcraft?"

Makram laughed gently. "Ah, precisely the point. The Coptic Fathers would judge that as permissible magic in the service of healing and protection. So, I trust you would always use your powers wisely."

"I *am* liable to get a swelled head—as the Americans say—from all this talk of my power. A male friend of my girlfriend said the same to me today about the power of my face. He is looking into the mathematics of beauty and wants to learn more in order to develop a software program."

"I advise you to research further the Eye as hieroglyph and symbol of action, protection and wrath. I will send you something by special messenger that is seldom seen outside of Egypt. It contains the arithmetic values represented by parts of the Eye of Horus. I will say no more for now, except to say that it is an example of the power of numbers known by the ancients."

"Thank you, Uncle. I will treat this information carefully."

"I trust that you will. It will enhance your already considerable powers exponentially, and must be tempered with wisdom and prudence."

PART TWO

THE EAST ASIAN LIBRARY

I.

It had been decades since Paul Wallach passed through the lattice-metal gates of Columbia University's Department of East Asian Languages and Cultures and its C.V. Starr Library. It had always struck him as a marvellous blend of West and East: Romanesque arched ceilings and stained glass windows contrasting with a Shinto Shrine, East Asian relics and rice-paper manuscripts. Those writings bore the ancient Chinese pictographs that fathered modern Chinese, as well as the Japanese, Korean, and Vietnamese languages. The enclosed space seemed monastic, yet inviting, as much a sanctuary as a place of study.

Charles Wu was Trustee of the library and Curator of the Rare Books Reading Room. Wallach had first met him when they were students in the 1960s. Wu was Chinese-born, but American-educated, having arrived as the son of an émigré former diplomat from Nationalist China. Soon granted advanced standing at the then East Asian Institute Charles Wu received his well-deserved doctorate in only one year; he had also been memorable for wearing three-piece suits from Dunhill and expensive Italian shoes.

Wallach had not been the star pupil in Wang Shen Shang's (Mr. Wang's) Mandarin Chinese class, nor in the Classical Chinese courses that Wang taught—unlike classmate Vandersloot Lear who was a superb student, took advanced courses at the Institute, and could order with aplomb at Chinese restaurants.

Wallach still regarded Wu with the same veneration as he did most of Chinese civilization. Flustered as they shook hands, Wallach saw in Wu's dark eyes both affection and a timeless serenity that belied his razor-sharp intellect.

"Paul, so good to see you, but you seem troubled." Wu's plumpish face and impeccable attire were just as Wallach remembered them from student days.

"Charles, the last time I set foot in this library, I was sweating the upcoming final in Classical Chinese. No final this time, but I'm still sweating Classical Chinese."

Wu's empathetic smile relieved Wallach's anxiety only slightly. "You're here as a visitor, but more importantly, as a friend. How can I help?"

"Charles, they say a little bit of knowledge is dangerous. I might know just enough Taoist philosophy to get into trouble."

Wu arched a curious eyebrow. "What kind of trouble would that be?"

"Well, what would you get if you put *Mian Xiang Face Reading* and *I Ching Book of Changes* into a blender?"

"What kind of dish are we cooking?"

"Could be a mix of high-stakes espionage and boy meets girl at a matchmaker's party. Chinese divination seems to be the common ingredient in the two books, but does it really make sense to combine the two?"

"Here's a Chinese riddle for you: the answer is yes and no, and both easy and complex."

"I knew you were going to say that."

Their shared laughter made Paul feel more like a colleague and less like a pupil.

"This may be a generalization, Paul, but as you know, there's a tendency in the West to see things as yes or no, black or white, polar opposites, and so forth. The Chinese, on the other hand, believe that everything fits together, if you understand the context…Follow?"

"Yes and no."

They laughed.

Wu continued, *"Mian Xiang* and *I Ching* both divine the future, in the larger context of Taoism. As you know, *Tao* means 'the Way'. So, if *Tao* is a way of cooking, think of it as an Haute Cuisine cookbook, and *Mian Xiang* and *I Ching* are recipes with common ingredients. On the phone, you mentioned these Tao classics and face reading. I've prepared a brief visual aid presentation. Let's step into the Rare Books Reading Room."

"Do you mind if I videotape this session for my nephew and his business partners?"

"Feel free." Charles Wu led Wallach into a smaller inner office containing two chairs, a small desk and a multi-media projector. The room was semi-dark. As they sat, Wallach pressed the record button on his Sony Camcorder.

Wu flipped a switch, flashing the image of an enormous face on the wall.

Wallach was visibly stunned. Glaring at him with fiery red eyes was an ancient Chinese warrior—thick, black eyebrows slanted upward in anger; huge mouth curved downward in defiance.

Charles Wu smiled sympathetically. "Sorry to startle you, Paul, but, it illustrates how even a picture of the face can rouse our emotions."

"It certainly makes the point. Do you think the ancients deliberately used facial imagery as a tool of power?"

"Let me answer with these power portraits from China, 221 B.C." Wu clicked the remote. "This first one is the official portrait of Emperor Qin Shi Huang, first ruler of Unified China."

"Whew! Wins no beauty contest either."

"Exactly. This emperor so believed in the power of *Mian Xiang Face Reading* that, when his portrait showed unfavorable features, he ordered it destroyed, along with the secrets of *Mian Xiang*. And to improve his public image, he commissioned a fabricated portrait of himself using ideal features from *Mian Xiang.*" Wu clicked the next image. "And here it is: Emperor Qin then presented himself as this benevolent-looking ruler—not the despot that he really was."

"Portrait of Dorian Grey, in reverse," said Wallach, laughing.

"Yes, a fraudulent but effective public relations campaign. Practically nobody in the kingdom knew what he really looked like: no photos, no T.V. Now, let me show you some other ingredients in this Chinese dish you're cooking."

Wu projected images of charts entitled *Harmony, Entirety, Ying Yang, Qi (Spirit)* and *Wu Xing* (Five Elements). "The Five Elements are found in both *Mian Xiang* and *I Ching*. They represent wood, water, fire, earth, and metal. Since we're talking about face reading, each element corresponds to a facial shape, such as round, square, rectangular, oval, and so forth—and to a type of personality."

"So, I was right…a lucky guess about the linkage between these two Chinese classics."

"Yes, you're a better Chinese scholar than you thought. But there's more. Another key ingredient they share is Yin Yang. Yin generally refers to softer, rounder feminine features, and Yang to sharper, angular, more masculine features. Yin and Yang have their soft and hard personality types too."

"This is unbelievable!"

"It gets better. The Jungian archetypes known in the West correspond quite well with five Chinese archetypes: there's the King and the Queen—who are Leader-types—the Magician-Joker, the Sage, the Warrior, and the Lover. These are five classic, universal roles in all human societies, usually represented by dramatic facial images. Notice also that the number five in numerology is still working for us."

"Yes, numbers seem to have symbolic values revealed when a code is broken, like in *The Da Vinci Code*."

"Indeed. In the Dan Brown novel, there are anagrams and number puzzles to be solved; it is a work of fiction and very controversial. But can you guess where *The Da Vinci Code* was outright banned—in addition to the Vatican, of course?"

"No. Where?"

"…In the People's Republic of China. I doubt that it was in deference to the Pope, with all due respect. Remember that in the story, Mona Lisa, Da Vinci's masterpiece, is supposed to represent, with her male-female features, a mystical union of the two—in other words…"

"…Jesus!"

Wu chuckled. "Be careful; the Opus Dei Police may be listening."

"…In other words, Yin Yang! The mystical union of male and female."

"Yes, Mona Lisa is an iconic portrait, demonstrating the power of the face to beguile, and a perfect balance of Yin and Yang. Perhaps the Chinese considered it a subliminal threat, if only a cultural one. Now, this next part really fits in also."

Wu projected photographs of Chinese masks. "These are masks from the Chinese Opera. They have exaggerated or caricatured faces like those on Tarot fortune telling cards because they are true archetypes of behavior." Wu flashed a red laser pointer at the screen.

"First, there's the benevolent, happy mask. Next is a fearsome warrior mask. Below are the ruler types, then, the wise man or sage. Finally, we have the child or woman masks, representing innocence or the lover. So, you see, East and West agree on categories of human nature, and matching faces. Personalities and faces often match. I think we're really onto something."

"It's wonderful…beyond what I suspected. But Charles, two questions: could the Chinese intelligence services use this kind of information? And, can it be translated into a software program?"

"I would imagine that any intelligence service might want to survey pictures of the enemy to see if there's a quota of healthy, strong-looking faces, and a proper blend of various archetypes—thinking it takes all kinds to make up a fully-functioning society. Also, faces can be used as propaganda—for effect and to influence people like we've demonstrated here. My software knowledge is limited, but for expert advice on the People's Republic of China, I suggest someone we both know: Vandersloot Lear."

Wallach laughed softly. "Charles, I was hoping you'd say that."

"Why?"

"It so happens I've been looking for Van. I'm on a team working on a camera program for the dating public that evaluates people based on Chinese face reading. The Chinese government might be planning to survey the faces of the enemy using these principles…perhaps even influence people through mind control—you know, *The Manchurian Candidate* kind of thing. Maybe Van would be able to say if we've got a potentially hot property."

"Why not contact him directly?"

"Easier said than done. If Van went into the CIA and isn't listed anywhere, how would I reach him? We haven't spoken in many years."

Wu replied, "I might be able to contact him through school connections that you probably don't have. Meanwhile, you'll have to find software help on your own. I'll write notes of our discussions and an outline to help your software person. For now, let's exchange cell phone numbers, and I'll set up a secure email using security walls and passwords."

Ten minutes later, Paul Wallach was saying thank you and good-bye: "*Syeh Syeh*, Charles. *Tzai Jian*."

Charles Wu grasped Wallach's hand. "Well pronounced, Paul. *Tzai Jian!*"

Wu walked his visitor to the door, then returned to his desk and jotted a few words in his diary, thinking that face reading could be important to intelligence work. He knew Van had scoffed at *I Ching* as a party game—considering Paul Wallach to be a bit of a kook. He'd also probably dismiss the idea of face imagery as a propaganda weapon and face reading as an espionage tool. But because Van was Wu's main contact to CIA and his only one to the FBI, he preferred to persuade rather than go around him if we need to alert higher-ups somewhere along the line.

Paul Wallach walked a couple of dozen paces into the open space between Columbia's quadrangle of buildings and halted, remembering another question he had about the Chinese Intelligence Services. Charles Wu may not know the answer, but it might be found in a brief stop at the cross-campus Lowe Library. He headed in that direction.

II.

Thirty minutes later, at a newsstand, Wallach bought the Celebrity Edition of *People Magazine*. Flipping through it, he waited for the 8th Avenue subway train to the Port Authority Bus Terminal. Entering a crowded car, he began to study the faces of passengers. Not wanting to stare, he pretended to read, while stealing looks at surrounding people. He reviewed in his mind the archetypes Charles Wu had mentioned. That bull of a man with heavy brows suggests a warrior. The matronly-looking woman next to him has round, soft features and could represent motherly compassion. There's a professor or sage type. The woman over there has deep-set eyes, a strong nose and a broad forehead—definitely a leader type. Of course, actual personality would rule, but if enough observers act on their perceptions, face types could be strongly influential.

A split-second of eye contact drew a flicker of annoyance from the leader-type woman. Obviously, some people don't like to be stared at. Wallach thought to check his reflection in the subway car window; he realized he'd been grimacing and glaring at her. She was only frowning *back* at him.

Embarrassed, Wallach poured his attention into the magazine faces. He realized that he was looking at the practiced smiles of trained actors—facades put out to entertain and fool the public. He glanced again at the woman. Their eyes met again; this time she smiled back. Now he saw in the window's reflection that his own face looked friendly.

He looked around. Several people looked weary and had bags and lines under their eyes. A few others looked pasty or sallow, as if they were also stressed or worn-down. *My God, if the Chinese or anyone else spied on our faces, how would we measure up?*

Scanning the crowd, Wallach felt his face and lips ease into a mellow smile. As he made eye contact, his fellow passengers' expressions became brighter; even their complexions appeared to gain color.

He couldn't wait to tell Harold about Charles Wu's revelations about face reading as well as his own experience of people watching in the subway. Realizing how faces can act powerfully on the psyche, Paul Wallach wondered if facial imagery, produced on a mass basis, could be used as a weapon by nations against each other? Van's opinion would prove invaluable...

III.

Instead of boarding the NJ Transit bus, Paul Wallach called his nephew and arranged to meet at Harold's West 23rd Street apartment. Wallach also called his wife Lorraine to let her know.

They had married while he was still working in pharmaceutical advertising. Afterwards, working full-time as a history teacher she helped support them through six grueling years of dental school and postgraduate periodontics. Lorraine encouraged Paul's ongoing interest in international politics as well as this new project with Harold.

Harold's brownstone apartment encompassed two large rooms with French doors, bay windows and brick walls. It reminded Paul of his own two-room, West 83rd Street brownstone whose carved bronze fireplace had lent a romantic setting to his courtship of Lorraine Saperstein back in the early 1970's.

Familiar with the ways of bachelors, Paul brought Chinese take-out food to Harold's. And, on the spur of the moment Harold invited Trish and Jennifer to come over. The women had said to go ahead and eat, that they'd join them soon. Harold uploaded Paul's Wu video as they dug into the still-steaming food.

Harold enthused, "Sun Luck combination dinner…Maybe the best egg roll north of Chinatown". It crossed his mind that he still felt uncomfortable about visiting that part of town because of the subway murder.

Paul chewed on the crispy eggroll. "You know, I can't picture Charles Wu—he's such a classy guy—eating Chinese take-out at the East-Asian Library. It would blow the image completely."

Harold laughed. "I see what you mean from the video: the sage professor in jacket, vest and tie—I can't imagine him eating with his fingers."

"He used chopsticks, of course, like any Chinese person would," said Paul, as he demonstrated a surgeon's skill by grasping a single grain of rice between his own wooden pair.

Harold looked impressed. "You've got the right touch for Chinatown *restaurants*, Uncle Paul…even seminars in Chinese politics, but Tong gangs—forget it. And when it comes to the Chinese intelligence services…"

"…You mean the Ministry of State Security? I'd be over my head, assuming we had something that made the big boys nervous. That's why involving Vandersloot Lear is critical. Let me show you something I downloaded from the Lowe Library, right after I saw Charles Wu." He handed Harold a printout.

Harold read silently: GlobalSecurity.org. Intelligence: The People's Republic of China, MSS, Ministry of State Security: Aside from professional agents, the MSS co-opted low-profile Chinese nationals or Chinese-American civilians…businessmen, students, and researchers formed a large pool of potential agents. The FBI estimated that over 3,000 companies were fronts set up for Chinese spies.

Harold frowned. "No mention of Tong gangs, which doesn't mean they haven't infiltrated them. The police suspected Tongs in the murder of that Chinese museum worker. Maybe she was onto some illegal activity…"

The intercom beeped. Harold heard Jennifer's voice and buzzed them through. Seconds later, Harold opened his door—to Carlos who shouted, "Surprise, roomy!" Trish and Jennifer were behind him. The visitors barged in, carrying bags of food, and flashing wide grins.

"Hey, you guys have gotten acquainted in a hurry," said Harold, hoping his half-smile didn't reveal displeasure over Carlos's newest intrusion.

Paul greeted Carlos warmly—they'd met before—and introduced himself to Trish and Jennifer. "If the subject is faces, Harold started with two winners here."

Trish fluttered her eyes like an infatuated teenybopper. "Oh, you Ivy guys can really lay it on. Flattery will get you everywhere."

"Like the high-rent district of West 23rd Street," kidded Carlos.

Everyone laughed except Harold, resenting what he thought was Carlos's jibe about his rent-controlled apartment. Feeling like George C.

Scott playing *Patton,* he barked, "Are we ready for the video? Uncle Paul engaged in some important deliberations up at Columbia today. Let's get started!"

"Yes, sir!" said Paul, snapping off a theatrical salute.

Trish and Jennifer exchanged glances and playacted timid expressions.

Carlos's reaction was a weary smile.

Realizing he'd been rude and feeling foolish, Harold composed himself, graciously seated his guests and served soft drinks; tensions seemed to ease.

Paul set the large laptop on a table, positioned the monitor, and prepared to speak.

Carlos spoke, "While you bring us up to speed, we'll catch up with lunch, too."

Jennifer chimed in. "Carlos has introduced us to—would you believe—Cuban take-out?

"Nothing against Chinese food," said Carlos, "but let's expand our cultural horizons."

"Looks like you're fully up to speed with Jennifer", said Harold, feeling a pang of jealousy.

"I can't show you a video of *our* deliberations, old man..."

Everyone, except Harold, laughed again.

"But," Carlos continued, "as the point man at Harris, Pierson, I got us acquainted over a culturally neutral pizza. Actually, no, it's Italian, Jen's heritage."

Jennifer retorted, "Yeah, except American pizza is to Italian pizza like the *Sopranos* is to the Sicilian Mafia. A knock-off, but not the real thing, as we say on the Avenue."

"All kidding aside," said Carlos, "to clear up any misunderstanding between us, just remember, pal o'mine, that you and Trish called *me* into this. I'll admit, I was a little skeptical, but now, I'm a believer—especially with the Chinese contact Trish made after the agency meeting."

Harold looked aghast. "What contact?"

"Not to steal Trish's thunder," said Carlos, in a conciliatory tone, "but she was just about to tell you..."

Trish interjected, "No secret, Harold. We had to finesse our little skit with Harris, Pierson. Burt Johnson, bless his adman soul, is hot to trot for our clients to do fashion commercials with his agency. Jen and I decided—I told you this this might happen—while we pursue this strategy with Carlos's help, there's no reason why we can't show our clients digital re-creation work, especially if it's Ok with Ma."

"Who is Ma?" demanded Harold.

"Ma-Chang-Kuo," answered Trish. "He's the Chinese digital imaging guy we were looking for. Thanks to Carlos's agency and the affiliate the Chinese guy works for, we had a great conversation. I'll explain more but first, I'm going to tear into this…What is it?"

"Camerones Empanizados," Carlos enunciated, trilling the "r". "Breaded shrimp. Try some. How do you like this Ropa Vieja? It's like shredded beef stew."

"Yummy," said Jennifer, stopping to chew. "I know you're anxious to brief us Harold, but if you're concerned about extra-curricular activities, yes, we did sort of bond."

"As in James Bond and his women?" Harold was only half-kidding.

"No, as in the Cuban and Italian thing," she said. "Both recovering Roman Catholics, families that own you. More importantly, Carlos has a good eye for fashion. We'll need him to keep up this cover story until we rope our man—hopefully, this guy named Ma."

Harold again felt embarrassed. "Carlos, I'm sorry. I guess I'm a bit jumpy over not being up to speed myself on all these developments. We do need your help, and if you're willing to work on this project with the rest of us, I want you in, as a full partner—if everyone else agrees. I mean that…" Harold clasped Carlos's hand firmly, but realized his own smile felt tight.

"I accept," said Carlos, smiling whole-heartedly and grasping Harold's shoulders. "And not just because I've bonded with Jen over pizza… and now, Cuban food."

Everybody laughed—Harold reluctantly.

Trish spoke. "Let me explain about Ma. We exchanged emails. He's actually from Shanghai, not Manchuria—speaks almost perfect English. He was educated over here at South California University and works in the digital re-creation lab at their film school. Then we hooked up via a Skype phone call, which I video recorded."

"Great," said Paul. "What did you tell him?"

"I told him that once, during Chinese New Year, I was fascinated not only by the masks and costumes, but also by the fortune tellers and face readers. I said I'm curious as to whether we can work Chinese fortune telling or face reading into fashion ideas. Then, unfortunately, we lost the Skype connection. I texted him and I practically held my breath until he texted back. He said he wasn't an expert on Chinese face reading—he knew more about Chinese Medicine—but he could get me started. I wrote back: 'I would be happy to get a foot in the door, please excuse the American expression.' He answered back, 'Confucius say, when putting foot in door, make sure it isn't closing.' Can you beat that? Your Chinese techie has a sense of humor!"

Harold beamed. "Trish, you are one slick operative. Uncle Paul, you should use her to get in touch with your reclusive CIA buddy."

"A Yin Yang combination of beauty and brains," said Paul. "And Trish got Ma to mention Chinese Medicine. We've known that Chinese doctors read facial complexions to predict a person's medical future. Charles Wu touches on that in the video. Wu's also keen on the power of facial imagery. Let's watch…"

The video lasted fifteen minutes. Afterwards, Paul summarized the implications: how facial analysis could predict someone's personality and future—to the extent that people act out the traits that features suggest—and if sickness or good health can be spotted in the face as Chinese doctors are trained to do. And, as Charles Wu demonstrated, facial images, from Mona Lisa to a Chinese warrior, could also be used as weapons of propaganda to captivate or intimidate.

Paul paused. "Then, on my subway ride, I realized that both facial structure and expression are important. They both make impressions on us, and, we use facial expressions to show our reactions to them. Expressions can be weapons too."

"Faces are some of the games people play," said Trish.

Carlos lit up. "Exactamente! Whatever we come up with— *real* games could be part of it. I'm talking about video games, card games, board games, game shows—all based on faces. Merchandizing offshoots like that could be bigger than the original concept."

All agreed that Carlos had a good idea. Again, Harold eked out a smile.

Trish said that Ma agreed to meet her and a colleague in L.A. This was all to be on spec; compensation wasn't yet necessary. It was ostensibly a meeting about fashion. But if Ma had the know-how, we might induce him to build a practical face-reading app for the dating public. Creative spin-offs like games could follow later.

As they were about to leave, Paul Wallach spread his arms like a father gathering his family. "I think we should mention something that maybe we shouldn't need to mention."

"Uncle Paul," said Harold, "You sound like a Chinese riddle, like in the Charles Wu video."

Wallach chuckled. "Right. And to help solve it, I propose we ask Charles, one piece of the puzzle we trust, to help check out Ma, another piece we don't yet trust. What I was going to say before is that this partnership seems to be built on trust—no contracts—just sharing information completely and being totally honest with everyone."

All agreed to ask Charles Wu to vet Ma, and to keep Charles in the loop. The five people placed arms around each other's shoulders. The shared goodwill felt visceral.

Harold could hardly believe that this unlikely mix of people had come together on an important project, and *he* was in the middle of it. Still, a tiny worm of doubt wiggled at the edge of his consciousness.

IV.

Agent White Lotus patched into the diplomatic cable from the Los Angeles Legation of the People's Republic of China. He spoke with Deputy Minister Li of the MSS in Beijing. "Here is update on Operation Spotlight. I intercept and monitor all work coming from our operatives in American cinema and T.V. Your initiative to bombard American media with attractive images of China progresses well. Propaganda war includes Chinese movies, documentaries and images of Chinese leaders, film stars, broadcasters, athletes, military and scientists. Our agents and operatives are well placed among American producers of entertainment, news, popular magazines and communications technology. Perhaps most important, we are buying distribution rights for all American movies so that we can modify them for our own purposes."

"You say update. Is there anything new on our plans to monitor the American enemy through scanning lenses embedded in T.V.'s, computers and automobile dashboards?"

"We are in process of planting factory technicians who install the lenses in China, Taiwan, the U.S., South Korea, and Japan. The attached wireless transmitters will allow monitoring of conversations and identification of targeted individuals. Also, I can report on conversation between Chinese technician, Ma, in Los Angeles and American media group wanting information about Chinese face reading for use in fashion and communications."

"What is the importance of that?"

"It is not yet clear. Chinese face reading may have significance, particularly if the enemy thinks so. Ma is expert in digital re-creation of faces. We are privy to many of his conversations and as a Chinese national, he is vulnerable to our pressure on his family in Shanghai. If he helps Americans create images to sell fashions, we expect his technology to also be available to us to help spearhead our cultural propaganda against the West."

V.

During the nearly two weeks since Mary Shun's murder, Agent Vandersloot Lear waited for Lieutenant Henry Juen to conduct his investigation in Chinatown. Juen had multiple contacts in the Chinese Benevolent Association, among others. But, as Lear knew from the intelligence trade, information flowed both ways. Informers were often double agents, and misinformation, also known as playback, was a tactic both sides used to mislead the adversary.

If Chinese gangs—likely involved in the murder—were being run by the Chinese MSS, they might be particularly expert in playing the double game since they were nominally American and could easily infiltrate local institutions.

Mary had not given her cousin Billy's name to Agent Lear—only that she suspected someone she knew of possible anti-U.S. activities. But Billy became a murder suspect because of his overheard argument with Mary, and his disappearance within a day of the murder. Incriminating also was that Mary's computer files were hacked by someone with access to her apartment. And, although Billy was not known to practice martial arts, he could have had an accomplice.

Lieutenant Juen informed Van Lear that the reported killer wore a maroon, hooded, sweatshirt-type garment (not unusual), that he was East Asian and of average height (as was Billy). He had probably escaped to the street, as staying in the station would have been risky. Nearby business workers didn't remember seeing someone of that description within a few minutes of the murder, although the killer may have discarded or lowered the hood, thereby altering his appearance.

Informants, walk-ins, Youth Association members and others all reported nothing. Surveillance was put on Billy's known acquaintances, haunts, and businesses he had serviced. Even Chinatown's infamous

Doyers Street tunnels, used in "evade and escape" tactics by Tong and Triad gangs were searched—to no avail.

After years of jointly combating the smuggling and counterfeiting of goods, Agent Lear and Lieutenant Juen had developed a good working relationship. They now spoke on an Incidental-Capacitance telephone line that couldn't be traced or tapped.

"It's Van, Henry. I got your report…not much to go on so far."

"Hello, Van. We are squeezing some of Billy Shun's associates, especially parolees and other bad guys like Flying Dragons and Ghost Shadows we suspect are dirty. They might know something. We've stepped up plainclothes patrols, follows and electronic surveillance."

"Good. He may have flown the area, and maybe even the country. We do have photo IDs circulating through INTELLENET. He's probably the one who hacked Mary's computer, and he might be hanging around to target me or others."

"We could start a rumor that you're on the streets, like in the old days, and use a decoy, instead."

"I thought of that, but I'm not sure. Mary Shun was vague on the phone about what she suspected. I'm concerned about Billy's possible ties to the Chinese MSS, or their Cheng Pao K'o Intelligence Agency. We've got electronic monitoring of cable transmissions and satellite stuff. There's been a lot of telecom buzz from China, recently, both to this area and L.A. As they say, the wires are humming."

"I get it. Let me know if you want us to use a Van double as bait. Back in '08, those fake Rolex and Gucci peddlers, and a lot of other people, got a good look at you, your six-foot-six and your patented trench coat."

"And don't forget my loping walk. This decoy would have to be like a movie double to really resemble me; let me think about it." Lear remembered his Section Chief's caustic warning to lay low.

Also disconcerting to Van was Charles Wu's secure e-mail reporting that former classmate Paul Wallach wanted to ask Van something about face reading and the Chinese—some silly business about mind control and *The Manchurian Candidate*. Wallach had been a likeable-enough guy, but as a wannabe agent, he could be a loose cannon. Wu, however, had thought enough of Wallach's ideas to forward a brief description: the

Five Element and Yin Yang principles of face reading might provide a basis for character analysis and health status: both potentially useful for intelligence.

Van did remember playing *I Ching* for laughs while drinking with Paul Wallach and other elbow-benders at a pub near Columbia back in the sixties. Wallach had a knack for it. Van was always skeptical. But when Wallach threw the coins and asked the *I Ching* "Where is Van going?" the hexagram in the book answered: "The hidden Dragon is exposed in the field". Paul guessed that meant Van was the "field" agent who was going to spy on the Dragon (code for China). When Van scoffed, Paul asked *I Ching* the same question again, and the answer was, "It furthers one to cross the great water."

Van had turned crimson, smiling grimly and said nothing. He remembered the incident—just a coincidence. Yes, he had flown the Pacific ("the great water") to Taiwan on his first CIA assignment, back in '67. But it had hardly been cloak and dagger: analyzing Red Chinese farm journals, from Taipei, in a drafty garret the size of a walk-in closet.

About this face reading business, Van needed to hear much more; so far, he wasn't buying it. Meanwhile, better to keep Paul Wallach at arm's length, and Charles Wu as the intermediary.

VI.

The following week, Harold and Trish shared a taxi to Newark Airport for their Los Angeles flight. Paul Wallach drove up from Monmouth County, New Jersey and joined them in a coffee shop for a strategy session. Harold was taking two vacation days and had accepted his uncle's help with costs. Trish was on expense account for this speculative venture with Carlos's agency. She and Harold were excited as they gulped milkshakes and watched Wallach sip a decaf. Through a window, they could see runway lights flash on as dusk was falling.

Paul needed to sound a cautious note. "It was almost too easy that, right off, he seems to be exactly what we are looking for—a Chinese digital techie who's familiar with *Mian Xiang Face Reading*, although, you'd expect many Chinese would be. By the way, I emailed Charles Wu about Ma. He's agreed to check him out through his own sources."

"Good. But, with Ma, we shouldn't lead off with the matchmaking," said Trish, "because I don't know what Burt Johnson or Mark Fallon, at Carlos's agency, told him about me or my Spence-Iturbi fashion clients. He might be still thinking this is primarily about fashion. I don't think we should play all our cards just yet."

Harold added, "That's why we suggested to Ma an itinerary of L.A.'s Chinatown, Uncle Paul. Here is a printout of the shops and events from the Chinatown Los Angeles Website. Trish told Ma that we'd like to take the walking tour and get the full flavor of traditional Chinese culture, and especially the clothing styles."

"And so Harold won't be too bored with fashion talk," said Trish, "we're hoping to see the Moon Festival with Shaolin Warriors performing martial arts."

"If Charles thinks Ma is legit," said Uncle Paul, "I suggest we go full speed ahead and not beat around the bush. If he's able to do the face reading program and if he's media and marketing savvy, I'm sure he'd be impressed by the possible uses for propaganda and even espionage, even in what's offered as a matchmaker's program. And somebody like Van could help protect our interests. To clinch the deal, you may have to reveal my connection to him."

Harold replied, "To be fair, Uncle Paul, it's only a possible connection. Although I do admit having Van as a consultant could mark us in Ma's eyes us as serious players and thinkers."

"Serious enough to scare him away," said Trish.

"I wouldn't worry about that," said Harold. "Like our research on Chinese spying shows, he's probably already been contacted by the Chinese to spy because he's an émigré and works in an influential field. He shouldn't be thrown by such talk."

Trish insisted. "I still think we should draw him out carefully."

"Well," said Paul, "you've proved yourself to be a pretty slick operative in the advertising wars so far. I'm sure it will all go well go well in L.A. Here's a *People Magazine* to read on the plane: the new Celebrity Edition—lots of great faces to ponder."

VII.

The Continental 767 took off at 6 p.m. for the five-hour flight. Harold figured that arriving at 8:30 p.m., Pacific Time, they would probably stay up late talking with Ma at the hotel, so he would try to sleep now on the flight.

Trish read the *People Magazine* that Uncle Paul had given them. As Harold slept, she thought about the famous faces of yesteryear and today. Each star is unique, but types of faces and personalities seemed to re-occur and always be popular. There's that nerdy look of Dustin Hoffman, starting in the 60's, followed by Robin Williams; then, in their day, Mike Myers, Ben Stiller…Adam Sandler…nerds all. These days, there was Seth Rogan, Jessie Eisenberg and Jason Schwartzman—all young-ish—playing awkward, but mischievous munchkins that females can't resist. It was subliminal soft power, used to seduce American woman-hood! *Can you stand it?* she thought, as she laughed aloud.

Harold roused slightly. "Huh?" Still sleeping, he turned toward the window clutching a pillow.

"Nothing, Harold." Trish looked fondly over at Harold. In some ways, he seemed like an overgrown adolescent, but sweet. *He just needs to believe in himself more. I'm going to let him take the lead and deal with Ma. We'll see how that goes.*

Reading the "Hollywood Through the Ages" section, Trish noticed how the Warrior-Action-Hero types seemed to be in demand, along with the Innocent-Ditzy-Babe types, and the Femme-Fatales. It was interest-ing how men got addicted to these different kinds of women. But then, some women go for the bad boys, and some want to mother the more stable but nerdy types. *I wonder where I fall on that spectrum and what type of man I'll wind up with?* She looked over at Harold, sleeping peacefully beside her. *Who does Harold remind me of? Actually, he's a lot like the actor Seth Green, but with a little rounder end to his nose. Cute…and fluffy…*Still contemplating, Trish fell asleep.

Harold was awakened hours later by the flight attendant picking up snack containers; reaching over, he picked up the *People Magazine* that had fallen from Trish's unconscious grasp, and saw the article on a print out stuffed into the magazine:

The Attractiveness Halo: Mere physical attractiveness exerts a generally positive influence on the attitudes and behaviors of observers. An opposite, negative halo for especially unattractive faces also exists. It also operates in dating and mate selection.

Harold couldn't contain himself. "Trish, sorry to wake you…"

"Nnnnnnnn…Are we landing?"

"Not yet." He had reset his watch, which now read 7:30. "We've got about an hour to go. Trish, I'm embarrassed to ask you this, but we've developed some trust between us…"

"Well?"

"Do you think I'm physically attractive?"

Trish looked at Harold with deadpan seriousness. "Now you're putting me on the spot."

Harold looked crestfallen. "You can tell me the truth."

Trish played it to the hilt. "If you think you can handle it…"

Harold squirmed in his seat while holding his breath.

"…Harold, you idiot—you're very cute!"

"You mean it? You're toying with me again."

"Now I'm really going to be honest," Trish said sternly.

"Here comes the real truth," said Harold, tensing in anticipation of the worst.

"The truth is that you *are* cute. But it means nothing unless you think so, and also act as if you are."

"You mean…?"

"Yes, not to act stuck up about it, but naturally confident—like we were talking about with Jen before."

"I don't know how to act confident like you do."

"I don't try to *act* confident; I'm just being myself, having fun." Trish made a funny face.

Harold laughed. "I take myself and my face too seriously. I don't even like to look in the mirror; I'm afraid I won't like what I see. I'm afraid to laugh at myself and afraid to laugh with others, for fear of offending them."

"Why not laugh? Every relationship should be light-hearted—not too serious."

"Are we having a relationship?" Harold looked hopeful.

"We certainly have a business relationship, which is built on trust...And it's a good place to start."

"Start on what?"

"Who knows? I just follow my instincts—like I should have done when a little voice in my head said that boy in the Bronx wasn't right for me."

"Follow your instincts? That's *my* line. I just hurl myself ahead and see what happens."

"I got the hurling part that first night. I like you better sober...Still a bit analytical, but having more fun."

"What's wrong with analytical? That's what's got us this far, on a three-thousand mile goose chase for all we know."

Trish laughed. She had to admit, that was a good one. "Let's be realistic. The science about faces and personalities may show general tendencies, but individual people are more unpredictable. For example, we throw market research at clients about what women want, because that's what clients expect, but..."

"...Let me guess," interrupted Harold. "What really sells the client are those moments when you tell the truth and come across as authentic."

"...And they buy in! It's hard to fake. If you try to sell something you don't really believe in, you may get away with it, short term. But they'll cancel or short the project, eventually."

"That's just like advertising. But sometimes you have to sell something you wouldn't buy yourself."

"That's a compromised success." Trish mustered a compressed-lips smile.

"What kind of success should we look for in L.A.?"

"The kind that comes from selling something solid. I can certainly believe in East Asian fashions, so I haven't really misled Ma."

Harold thought that Trish may be a practical, hard headed-businesswoman, but she did appear to have ethics and standards. "So, Trish, you really *do* believe in face reading?"

"I think face reading looks promising, but this won't be easy. The variables are endless. Many kinds of faces, mixtures of faces, all complicated by facial expression. You ought to know, you're the scientist."

"It's complicated all right. Look at these other items Uncle Paul gave us." Harold read aloud: "Subliminal Manipulation: sub-lim blogspot.com. Anything programmed subliminally to your subconscious, from every stranger's face or spider's web you have glanced at, is stored in your brain and is capable of influencing your judgment, behavior and attitudes." He turned toward Trish, "So maybe *The Manchurian Candidate* isn't just fiction. I believe in it, but I bet half the world thinks covert hypnosis is total b.s."

"Yeah, and that half might be the Chinese. All I know is that every day, megabucks are spent to influence people with facial imagery of one kind or another."

"Without a doubt. But I wonder if Ma will really buy into all this. Maybe he just wants to create a thin Fatty Arbuckle to sell diet pills."

Trish laughed, thinking that Harold was funnier than he realized.

They leaned back and drowsed until the plane began to land.

As they were taxiing in, Harold grasped something small and rectangular in his pants pocket. "Trish, I have another confession to make."

"Oh repent, my son."

"Uncle Paul slipped this little baby into my hand as we were leaving." Harold held up a steel-cased digital voice recorder. "I don't know how it works. We need to ask Ma's permission to use it, if only to help us turn it on."

"You're funny; the spy has to ask the spied-on for help. Ma didn't mind being recorded on Skype, but still, we should ask. Meanwhile, why don't you two get acquainted? Call him on my cell and let him know we're arrived…Here's the number."

PART THREE

CHINATOWN, L.A.

I.

Ma-Chang-Kuo was waiting at baggage pick-up, holding a sign reading: "Harold and Patrician"—not that Trish would have missed him: the jovial-looking Asian man with a bad tie whom she recognized from the Skype conversation. To complete the incongruous picture, he was wearing blue jeans and cowboy boots.

Ma spotted them riding the escalator. He guessed that the phone voice he had just heard belonged to the anxious-looking man speaking to a woman Ma recognized; but her Skype face hadn't done her justice.

After introductions and pleasantries about the flight, Trish felt she had to correct something. "On your sign, Ma, putting an 'n' at the end of Patricia makes me some kind of an aristocrat. Your prices are liable to be higher," she said with a sly grin.

Ma laughed apologetically. "Oh, sorry. No extra charge. But I thought maybe you spelled like Patrician McCarthy, with an 'n'."

"No, I'm Patrici-a Donlon—same Irish tribe, different clan. But I don't know her."

Ma spoke with only a slight Asian intonation. "You probably will in future, if you're interested in Chinese face reading. She's president of *Mian Xiang Institute* out here."

Harold felt anxious. "We've heard of *Mian Xiang*, but I'm surprised someone named McCarthy would be an expert." He cast a worried glance at Trish, which Ma also caught. Harold thought, *I'm glad Ma's up on Mian Xiang. But is he doing a commercial deal with someone else—an American?*

Ma gestured with open arms—his smile equally expansive. "Welcome to the Pacific Basin. California is the Gateway. Ideas from East and West exchange very freely out here. Movie people, surfer dudes, hippies …everybody is into Tai Chi, martial arts, Fung Shui, Eastern religions, and yes, face reading. Out here in Movieland, faces are the *thing*. Obviously, Chinese décor, fashion, and food are popular too. But with me, not so much. I like Western barbeque, R&B, and country music." Ma laughed good-naturedly at his guests' astonished faces.

As they walked across the street to the parking area, Trish said, "You're full of surprises. The boots should have been a clue. The tie— forgive me, I'm a fashion person—is not." Trish smiled indulgently as she inspected Ma's chartreuse polka dot tie.

"Oh yes," said Ma. "Everybody knows I'm *not* - a fashion person, that is. Trust me, there's no dress code at the South California film school, but I started one of my own. Once I borrowed a funny tie for staff meeting, and it became my signature prop. Lots of funnies in the movie business."

Harold and Trish chuckled.

As soon as they got into Ma's Chevy SUV and started driving away, Harold said, "I'm still not over the fact that Patrician McCarthy is the president of *Mian Xiang* Society."

Ma corrected, "*Institute...*She's a celebrity in Chinese community. Patrician instituted Medical Diagnostic Face Reading out here. She studied with Chinese sages, and now teaches Chinese Medicine to Chinese people."

Harold asked anxiously, "Do you know her?

"Oh yes, but only as acquaintance. We haven't worked together."

Harold felt a bit mollified, but worried that someone else might be beating them to the punch on face reading.

Most of the thirty-minute trip to the hotel was spent discussing New York, which Ma seemed to love. "Coming to L.A. for Chinese atmosphere is Ok," he continued, "But on that score, you may be disappointed."

"Why is that?" asked Trish.

"I've been around since the nineties and Chinatown has faded. Truth is—it never was that great, compared to ones in San Francisco or New York."

"So, you'd sooner visit our Chinatown?" asked Trish.

"Oh no. I prefer uptown Manhattan; eat barbeque, listen to country music, shop Bloomingdales."

Harold said, "So you're laying in the weeds like they say in the country. You *do* know fashion!"

"Not really. My mother in Shanghai goes on-line to Bloomingdales. Whenever in New York, I have shopping list for sales. Makes up for being bad son who went to America." Ma laughed.

Trish thought Ma was charming, but the cowboy routine was a bit overdone.

Harold said, "If, you don't mind my saying so, Ma, you'd make a heck of a spy."

"Oh no. Much too obvious attempt to blend in."

"You'd fool us. So, what are the best rockin' rib joints in New York?" asked Harold, still not sure this wasn't all a put on.

"No state secret. My favorite is Hill Country on East 26th Street—great ribs and hoedown…your kind of thing?"

"No Memphis pig-out at my house. I'm already the bad son."

"Tomorrow, in Chinatown, I'll show you place where bad sons make up to mothers. Why you bad son?"

"Because I didn't become a doctor like my father."

"Oh, my father is doctor too, back in Shanghai. But only Chinese Medicine."

Only, he says, thought Harold. *I'd like to know even the face reading part of Chinese Medicine.* "Tell us, Ma," said Harold, anxious to move things along. "How does *Mian Xiang* play into your work with digital re-creations of famous faces?"

"Two different subjects, Harold. Classical Chinese Face Reading principles haven't really been incorporated into our scanning technology."

Harold looked deflated.

Ma continued, "On the other hand, idea of mapping the face, dividing it into sections, facial topography—they both have those in common. Anyway, I'll show you Chinatown and the film school. Lots of facial images to see."

The need to persist plagued Harold like an annoying itch. "So, I suppose no one has developed a software program that performs *Mian Xiang Face Reading*?"

"Not that I know of," replied Ma, in a patient tone.

Trish thought things were moving too fast and away from fashion. *Let's play it straight for a while yet,* she thought. "On the subject of re-creations of stars' faces, I wonder if Nancy Kwan is available to meet with us. She'd be a great consultant on Chinese styles here in L.A."

"Oh yes. I doubt if a Kwan meeting can be arranged. But definitely, you'll get flavor of Chinatown. Your reservation is at Best Western Dragon Gate Inn, comfortable and right in Chinatown. After that, special tour of SCU Institute for Cinematic Technology—sorry, only available in afternoon. You're only staying two days, right?"

Harold nodded. "Right. We're leaving tomorrow night on a red-eye."

"So, you'll miss Chinese New Year, which starts in February. But maybe see costumes, masks, floats being built. See lots of Chinese faces." Ma chortled softly as before in what was sounding to Trish like a predictable laugh track.

Minutes later they drove through the Dragon Gate Inn's pagoda-style archway. Ma said, "It's late, New York time. Sleep in. See you eleven tomorrow morning."

Looking forward to a good night's rest himself, Ma, was easing the SUV back onto the freeway when his second smart phone signaled an incoming text. He pulled over. It was from his parents in Shanghai who used a special encryption based on Hokkien, an ancient dialect, to thwart eavesdroppers: "Dear Son, the MSS has threatened us again if you fail to complete the mission they have given you. But, please do not concern yourself with our safety. They will not harm us as long as you are useful to them. Be vigilant. They can make you disappear even in America. We know these despotic bandits will always oppose free expression in the motherland and inhibit Chinese enterprise.

Do what you must do to save yourself even if it means cooperating with them. We may not be able to join you in the U.S. but beware of tricks. The Americans may also be testing you. Signal back that you have understood this message without replying. Your devoted parents."

II.

After inspecting their adjoining rooms, Harold and Trish sat in her room. It was furnished with Chinese-motif chairs, tables and beds, all framed in dark-lacquered wood. Trish snapped photos from her phone. "Not bad," she said to Harold. "Maybe a bit institutional. Tomorrow, hopefully, we'll see some real designs for fashion possibilities."

"Hopefully…" Harold said, intent on working the mobile control of the cable T.V. He clicked onto a video of dragon-suited performers dancing to tinny music, and then, a clip of sleek Chinese women in form fitting dresses, boogying to a facsimile of Western rock music.

It was an infectious beat. Harold found himself moving to the pulsating rhythms and beckoned Trish to join in. Soon they were dancing close, and in sync.

"Hey, lookin' good," said Trish.

As their cheeks touched, Harold inhaled the enticing fragrance and warmth of her breath. "Looking good, yourself," he said. Up close, Trish's eyes seemed especially beguiling now, with inner corners that curved upward; her pupils dilated, encouraging him. Their bodies swayed back and forth for a time; Harold's hands were now around Trish's waist; his lips gently brushed hers. "How's that for research into faces?" He couldn't believe his own boldness.

Trish stepped around Harold and kissed him on the cheek. "That kind of research should stay theoretical for now."

Aroused by the contact, Harold hoped for more, but Trish, as usual, had the last word.

III.

When Ma-Chang-Kuo arrived, promptly at 11 a.m. the next morning, Trish and Harold had already browsed the mini-mall within the hotel, finding a Chinese apothecary and magazines. Trish noted *Glamour*, *Vogue* and *Elle* in Chinese/English editions—all with close-up photos of Chinese glamor girls.

"This sort of thing," said Harold, "would have been banned during the so-called Cultural Revolution in Red China."

"Looks like a new one is underway—this time with prettier faces."

Ma greeted them at the hotel entrance with his unfailing wide smile. "Good morning. I already checked you out. The SCU campus we're visiting is back near the airport. I asked the Dragon Gate to hold your bags until we get back this afternoon."

"Hospitality with a smile," said Trish.

The trio started walking up Hill Street past East Asian-style buildings. They passed through a large pagoda-styled gateway into an open square and pedestrian mall.

Ma pointed to the gateway. "This is Gate of Filial Piety, Harold. Here, bad sons do penance for mothers." He chortled.

"Please, Ma, take our picture," said Harold. "My mother has a sense of humor."

"She'll love this," said Ma, snapping a photo of Harold and Trish under the gate.

Harold noticed something flashing between the tiers of a pagoda-like building. It had a glass front and was moving. "Ma. What is that?" Harold pointed. Looking at the object, he missed what Trish saw: Ma's mask of joviality had slipped, revealing one of anger—eyes narrowed, lips tight.

Trish thought, *what's his problem?*

Ma's smile returned as though it hadn't left. "Oh nothing. Scanning camera is security system against shoplifters and undesirables. Chinese Business Association is finally going hi-tech."

Harold asked, "What kind of undesirables?"

"Some Chinese gangs used to be around. Maybe the police are looking for somebody."

Harold looked around, wondering if Tong gangs were a problem in L.A. "I see a lot of tourists like us. I'm no expert, but I don't see any suspicious types."

"That's just it. Many suspicious types learn to blend in. That camera may use face-recognition technology to find people they have on file. At South California, I'll show you more interesting technology."

Trish wondered how Ma knew about the habits of suspicious types, like how to "blend in".

After twenty-minutes of browsing souvenir shops, Ma, Trish and Harold stood at the railing of the Seven Star Wishing Well.

Harold dug in his pocket for loose change, and found the Olympus recorder. Following an honest impulse, he held it out; a red light flashed. "Oh, Ma. I meant to ask you. Is it alright to record?"

"Has it been on?

"I…I think it may be. To be honest, I'm not sure how to work it. Trish and I decided to ask you. And then I forgot."

"Forgot to ask how to work it? Or forgot to ask is it all right to record?"

"Well—both."

Ma's laugh gave way to a knowing smile.

Flushed with embarrassment, Harold thought Ma had his number.

Ma said, "No problem, Harold. I didn't say anything bad on the recorder. Did you?"

Everyone laughed, Harold and Trish a bit too loudly. They exchanged relieved glances.

Ma examined the recorder. "Press here to record, this button to stop. Here turn off to save battery. File management…Figure it out later."

Harold placed the recorder into his shirt pocket with the red indicator light showing "on". He pulled out a nickel from his pants' pocket.

Leaning over the railing of the wishing well, he hesitated. "Ma, don't people usually throw regular coins into the wishing well?"

"I suppose."

"What about *I Ching* coins?" Harold said, hoping the subject would lead to face reading.

"Ah, you know about *I Ching*. *Those* coins would work just as well. Maybe better. Let's find out."

Ma stepped into a shop and emerged moments later carrying a clear baggy of brass Chinese coins, each about the size of a quarter, with a square hole in the center. "These are lucky *I Ching* coins, called auspicious coins. They magnify your wealth or good fortune."

"So, can we do *I Ching* also with them?" asked Harold.

"Only if you were doing *I Ching* coin tosses and using the book, which you are not. Also, with *I Ching*, you ask questions. With wishing well, you ask for good luck. So, if lucky *I Ching* coins are thrown in wishing well, it's like loading dice, as the Americans say," said Ma with his patented laugh.

Trish was thinking he used it as a punctuation mark.

"Why can't you load the dice in *I Ching*?" asked Harold.

"Simple answer," said Ma. "You are not asking *I Ching* to change your luck but how to act in changing circumstances. Make sense?"

"Yeah. Like a solid house built on shifting sand."

"Now, you're getting it!" said Ma, laughing at Harold's perplexity. "Whole idea of *I Ching* is to advise you what to do in different situations, depending on which personality trait you're using. Everybody has Yin traits and Yang traits, soft traits and hard traits—that come into play when the challenges change."

Harold remembered his Uncle Paul said the same thing. "I've heard of that but can you give me an example?" asked Harold.

"Let's see… Oh yes. A minute ago, you were confronted with, if you don't mind me saying, a little dilemma."

"How so?"

"When I asked you a double question about the digital recorder, you gave me a double answer but you didn't try to lie."

"I'm a bad liar."

"Which was clear then." He laughed softly. "But you were honest about it and in your reaction. Please forgive my bluntness."

Harold felt himself blush again. "Go ahead. It's all right."

"You showed a classic trait much prized in Chinese culture."

"What is that?"

"*Humility.* I explain. There are sixty-four basic behavior themes in the *I Ching.*"

Harold nodded. "Ok."

"One of my favorite is number thirty-three: the theme Withdrawal. It is represented by typical mix of Yin and Yang traits. I paraphrase: It is prudent to withdraw when you are at a disadvantage, and at same time to be steadfast and true." Ma's smile was forgiving. "You withdrew by humbly admitting truth about the recorder. If you had tried to lie or bluster, the conversation and our business relationship might have taken a negative turn."

Harold and Trish were struck speechless. Finally, Trish said, "Our colleague Jennifer studied psychology. She'd be taking notes."

"No big deal. Everybody in China knows *I Ching.* Want to try your luck at the wishing well?" He handed several coins to Trish and Harold.

Impressed as she was by *I Ching* wisdom, Trish thought the Seven Star Wishing Well was a monument to high kitsch. It looked like a lava field—bilious green in color—flanked by a pair of dime store Buddha statues. Little caves containing metal pots perforated the "lava". These were labeled: Love, Luck, Home, Wisdom, Health, Wealth, and Joy.

Ma spoke. "If you look at the coins, one side shows Yin Yang and the Chinese characters for Wealth, Luck, Contentment, and Magnificence. The other side shows symbols for Dragon and Phoenix, to match male and female for harmonious relationship."

"I'd like the male-female to win," said Harold, shooting Trish a mischievous grin; she returned a demure smile.

Ma replied, "Here, it doesn't matter. Either side wins, if you get it in the pot."

"My father's advice at Belmont Racetrack," said Harold, "was if you spread your bets too wide, like shooting for too many pots, you reduce your chances of profiting on a winner. So, I'll double or triple down on my favorites…Concentrate on just a couple."

"Makes sense," said Trish. "Which horses are you betting on?"

"I'm putting my money on Love and Luck." Harold leaned far over the railing and tossed a coin toward the Love cave. It missed the metal pot and landed with a dull *clink*.

Over the next minute or so, he and Trish tossed about a dozen coins. A few bounced in and out, but none stayed in the pots.

Trish looked frustrated. "Did Confucius say anything about man or woman who tries too hard?"

Ma laughed. "Let me think… Something comes to mind. This, maybe, is close, and again I paraphrase: The superior man does not set his mind for or against something; instead, he follows what is right."

Harold asked, "How does he know what is right?"

"Instead of trying too hard, like Trish said, sometimes just relax and trust the universe." Ma backed against the railing, grasped the remaining coins and tossed them over his shoulder. All missed—except two that stuck together and landed with an unmistakable *clunk* in the Joy pot.

"Amazing!" yelled Harold. Trish whooped; passersby spun around to look.

Trish thought Ma's ecstatic face resembled the nearby Buddhas. "You've been practicing," she kidded.

"I throw coins here before, but never practicing; never try too hard."

"OK," said Harold. "I've seen it all. You're the Magician-Joker and the Sage in one package."

"Thank you, Harold," said Ma. "But some would say, just a lucky throw. The Chinese believe don't push your luck like you Americans say, But anticipate and prepare yourself for good fortune."

"Are you always so happy?" fired Trish, remembering Ma's momentary loss of composure with the scanning camera.

"Oh no. Big act. Just like everybody in Movieland," Ma said.

"I think you're a big kidder," answered Trish, with a cagey smile. "It takes one to know one, like we say in New York."

Trish's sharp tongue sounded provocative to Harold. But Ma appeared unflappable as ever, answering only with a cagey smile.

"What *would* it take to really bother you?" Trish insisted.

"Let me think…" Ma's eyes narrowed. "What would bother me, right now, is that I bore my guests. Keeping them from what they really came here for." Ma's smile was the same full curve, flowing into smile lines from his mouth to his eyes.

Trish, however, detected tightening brow lines.

"I'm not bored," said Harold, "but I am hungry—for Chinese food. I can smell it from here. That's part of what we came here for. What do you say?"

"I say, Harold, you smell good place, around the corner, probably Yang Chow Restaurant."

IV.

Back through the Gate of Filial Piety, they walked around the block and entered the Yang Chow. Ma took charge, and got a table in a private corner. "Let me be your guide in the restaurant also. I order wonton to start, spicy but not too hot." Ma's face turned severe as he ordered in Chinese to a waitress bearing menus. "I'll also order rice and tea. *Fan, cha!*" Ma commanded the waitress.

Harold asked, "Isn't wonton a kind of dim sum?"

"Not exactly—coverings and fillings are different."

Harold thought Ma seemed to control every scene and had an answer for everything. Needing to gain the initiative, he found himself welling up with candor. "You know, Ma, my uncle is a partner with us on this project. He was trained for Foreign Service, specialty China. But he says his only claim to fame is handling chopsticks."

Trish wondered where Harold was going with this particular ploy, but her face stayed placid—eyebrows elevating only slightly.

"Oh, handling chopsticks is very important," replied Ma, smiling.

Harold wondered whether Ma was serious.

Trish guessed he wasn't.

"Where did your uncle get his diplomatic and chopsticks training for China?" Ma asked, with a playful smile.

"At Columbia University, and the Chinese restaurants around Morningside Heights. I studied there also—without taking the course in chopsticks."

Ma smiled faintly.

Harold realized his wisecrack missed the mark. "Uh…where did you go to college, Ma?"

"National Shanghai University College of Digital Arts. Also have Masters from SCU in Animation and Digital Arts."

"How did you happen to get into computer-generated advertising?" asked Harold.

That's better, thought Trish, *leave the verbal fencing to me.*

"Advertising agencies want computer graphics like ours for all kinds of products. We talk to many agencies." Ma smiled apologetically. "But some of us freelance."

He winked at Trish.

She smiled coyly in return.

The soup arrived; the hungry trio dived into it, along with the house specialty, Slippery Shrimp"

Trish was also getting impatient to ask about the face reading program, but thought she'd play her last "fashion" card. "Ma, I know you worked with Mark Fallon at ImageGraphics."

Ma nodded, with a trace of a pleasant smile.

"Mark and I discussed doing digitally-created former stars for fashion products."

"Oh yes," replied Ma.

"When it comes to photo rights for stars," Trish went on, "we could be waiting for months. Working freelance might be faster."

"I suppose," said Ma. "What do you have in mind?"

"Well…"

"If I may, Trish…" said Harold, suddenly trusting the universe. "Ma, to be *honest,* we want to confide in you about another idea. We hope you'll want to work with us on it, exclusively."

Ma's smile slipped only a little. "I'm listening."

"Well, it's really all about face reading. As you say, the movie business is all about faces."

Trish thought, *good intro, keep going!*

Harold continued, "Trish and I, my uncle, and two other colleagues wonder whether *Mian Xiang Face Reading* and maybe *I Ching* principles could be combined into a digital-imaging software program that scans faces and analyzes personalities."

"Hopefully not mine!" laughed Ma, his brow and cheek lines contracting slightly.

"We agree not to do each other," Trish joked.

Harold's face stayed serious, his eyes narrowing slightly. "A Chinese consultant up at Columbia told my uncle that he thinks it's theoretically possible, although he is not a software person."

"What is the theory?"

"Basically, *Mian Xiang* and *I Ching* share principles of Yin Yang, and The Five Elements, and also revolve around Chinese and Western personality archetypes, expressed in faces. We think this is all ground breaking."

"Very interesting." Ma's smile was compressed, but his eyes widened.

"As I understand it," continued Harold, "or better, *don't understand it*, mathematical algorithms could convert facial shapes into numbers, which can then line up. Perhaps, you know about that."

Ma retrieved a small computer from his bag. Within a few seconds, he found a website. Scrolling down to *I Ching*, he stopped under the subtitle Binary Sequence. "Nothing more secret than Wikipedia. It says the *I Ching's* sixty-four hexagrams are basis for binary sequences we use in computers."

"Took the words right out of my mouth," cracked Trish.

"Go on," said Harold, trying to comprehend.

"Subtle curves in face can be mathematically plotted in algorithm or mathematical formula. At SCU, we made algorithms for computer-generated images, in Spiderman movies—faces and bodies. Did you see movies?"

"Yes," said Harold, but I wasn't relating it to face reading then."

"Chinese consultant up at Columbia: did your uncle mention his name?"

The change of subject took Harold by surprise. "Well, uh…" He thought, why hold back? Charles Wu's identity would be easy to find out. "Charles Wu is his name. He's prominent in the Department of East Asian Languages and Culture there."

"Oh yes, very interesting." Ma's face seemed expressionless.

"Ma," said Harold, "if we came to an understanding, we would give you Charles Wu's notes and ours in order to develop a face-analyzing program built into a cell phone camera for the dating public. It could be important enough to interest governments."

"Why so important?" Ma leaned forward.

"We need to be sure we can trust you, with well…sensitive information."

"Speaking of sensitive, you and Trish are getting insider look at SCU Institute of Creative Technology—not your children's tour of Universal Studios." Ma laughed.

Harold replied, "Fair enough. If you are willing to reveal the heart of your technology, we'll tell you our concerns about the ultimate implications of Chinese face reading. After your tour, we can both decide if there's enough substance here to make an agreement."

"Fair enough," said Ma.

"Well, here goes. My Uncle Paul, Charles Wu and a *third man…*" Harold smiled at his own double-entendre about the Orson Wells' spy movie. "…Anyway, the three of them were students at Columbia. This other man went into Foreign Service, specializing in China. We think if we can develop a software program that evaluates faces for personality traits and health, based on Chinese models…" Harold paused for emphasis. "…Governments might be interested in spying on whole populations, or using facial imagery on them as a tool of social control—subliminal stuff like in *The Manchurian Candidate*. I'm not sure I buy that part, myself." Harold tried to smile.

Ma wasn't smiling.

Harold continued, "Anyway, maybe this man could tell us if governments—U.S. or Chinese—might already be working on this. In other words…"

"…In other words, you are shooting for *espionage* work?" Ma interrupted, with a surprising edge to his voice.

"Oh no!" said Harold. "We think we can only succeed with face reading for the girl-meets-boy market, or for fashion. We wouldn't try to do surveillance…like that scanner back at the Gate of Filial Piety. My Uncle Paul tells me that Homeland Security or CIA or whatever wouldn't let us do it. They already have sophisticated programs for scanning possible terrorists, wouldn't you think?"

"I wouldn't know." Ma's smile seemed painted on.

"How about MSS, the Chinese Security Services?" asked Harold. "Wouldn't you think they might be interested?"

Trish watched as Ma's smile extended beyond his eye wrinkles and joined the brow lines above his eyes.

He replied, "Only if Americans did something the Chinese hadn't thought of themselves…something Americans might use against them. I have no special knowledge. That is just logic." Ma's tone of voice had been rising.

"I see what you mean," said Harold. "Why pirate something, if you've got it already?" Both he and Ma laughed loudly.

Trish got the impression that both men had been verbal tightrope walking, and were happy to jump off. "Ma," she said, wanting to change the subject, "Can we simplify this faces concept for simple people like me, and the average Joe and Jane? Faces seem to boil down to a few basic types —power or predator, pretty, smart, kind or friendly and well, average faces, like most people have."

"That's a pretty good list," said Ma. "Casting directors think that way. But don't forget, there are blends of those faces too, like Yin Yang."

Harold joined in. "What makes it even more complex are factors like facial expression and the unique body language of the person. The strength of the voice could come into play too, which is partly a function of personality."

"I agree," said Ma. "But how could you measure personality through facial expression?"

"Good question," answered Harold. "Maybe our program could establish a base-line of each person's facial expressions…say, relaxed and unemotional, and then compare that to…how happy—or at the other extreme, how aggravated they might look when subjected to a stimulus. The *You Lie* T.V. series shows how faces react to questions or situations when people are lying or stressed out. A similar algorithm could be also added to our program."

Ma's expression seemed to change within a few seconds, from that of self-satisfied—almost smug—to wonderstruck at Harold's apparent ingenuity. "Maybe so!" exclaimed Ma. "When we map out movie face re-creations, we take facial expression into consideration. The stars were also known for their smiles and scowls. Body language and voice would be comparatively easy to factor in. You'll see later how we handle scale with film school technology."

"We are really looking forward to that," said Harold.

"I'll demonstrate how all faces and their movements can be traced with grid lines that expand and contract. We do this in computer-generated images all the time. You see grids in movie techno-thrillers. It's a way of expressing curves with lines."

"And those can relate to algorithms, right?" asked Harold.

"Right," answered Ma. "The tricky part, for those in re-creation who connect the dots, is to read and reproduce subtle differences in texture of skin. Things that Chinese doctors notice when they read sunken cheeks, puffiness, colorations in the eyes…"

"I'm amazed," said Harold, "with your detailed knowledge of Chinese Medicine. Did your father teach you this?"

"Many Chinese know these things. *My* turn to be amazed, Harold and Trish, with your ideas to make algorithm and software out of face reading in Chinese Medicine. Also new is your thinking about expression, and using posture and voice as factors. And bringing in *I Ching* is really new. Good ideas, but not easy to do."

"What would it take to find out," asked Trish, angling for the sale.

"Let's go over to SCU," replied Ma. "I'll show you interesting technology. But first you need to see ladies' dresses and masks?"

"You know what, Ma?" said Trish, "From what you've told me, New York's Chinatown would do just as well. And I think we'd rather spend the time on face reading technology." She shot Harold a knowing glance.

He nodded. "I *was* hoping to see the Shaolin Warriors martial arts, if possible. Martial arts are an interest of mine."

"Martial arts demonstration is here day after tomorrow," Ma replied, "so you'll miss it. But maybe you can see in New York Chinese New Year, in February. They have it too."

Twenty-minutes later they were in Ma's car on the 110 Freeway, approaching South California University Institute of Cinematic Technology.

V.

A briny aroma and the cawing of gulls confirmed the group's close proximity to the ocean as they parked near a cluster of contemporary, glass-wall buildings. Ma led them inside the largest one, where his cheery hello satisfied security at the main desk. He rushed his guests through the reception area and straight to an elevator.

One floor down, and after a short walk down a corridor, Ma opened a locked door with a key. Stepping from the semi-dark hallway, Harold and Trish were shocked by the blazing light emanating from a twelve-foot illuminated globe. Harold recognized the structure as a geodesic dome; inside it was an ergonomic chair and electronic paraphernalia.

"This is Agora Dome," said Ma, puffing out his chest. "Makes its own public relations statement, yes?"

"Incredible," said Harold. "Looks like a giant Times Square New Year's Eve globe."

"Oh yes," replied Ma. "Many LED lights and also little mirrors and cameras embedded in structure. It shoots faces from all angles and gets photo-realistic detail in re-creation."

"The spherical dome gives you a complete three-hundred-and sixty-degree image," guessed Harold.

"…And without shadows or distortion from change of perspective," added Ma.

"Which movies used this technology?" asked Trish.

"*Spiderman 2* and *3*, and *Superman Returns*; also *Benjamin Button*. More recently, *Captain American…Doctor Strange*. Current projects—I'm not at liberty to discuss."

"Understandable," she said.

"The big payoff for us movie people is going beyond conventional photography. We create 3-D models with life-like appearance. Who wants to be model?"

"You can't mean me," said Harold. "How about Maureen O'Hara here?"

"My big chance for Hollywood…What do I do?" asked Trish.

Ma stepped over to a console and punched a keyboard several times. More lights blinked on within the globe. He escorted Trish through its opening and into the adjustable chair. "Just look straight ahead and sit still." Ma pressed buttons. An image of Trish's face appeared on a large monitor screen.

"Now watch this," said Ma, twisting dials. "Changing proportions, light and shadow makes features different. Now I add grid lines that overlay whole face."

Trish's face and features began to change. Faint grid lines flexed and shrank with the changing features like volleyball netting deformed from a ball's impact.

"There goes your nose!" said Harold.

"Not my mountain of power?"

They all laughed.

"Notice," said Ma, "Very slight changes make for completely different face."

He dialed Trish back to her own features. "Notice how grid lines show exact change. You can copy and re-create any star's face, synthesize totally new faces never seen before…types of faces people like."

"Can you measure standards of beauty with an algorithm?" asked Harold.

"Oh yes," answered Ma. "Thanks to technology from cross-town rival L.A. University. Dr. Quadrano developed Esthetic Mask based on Golden Mean. Mask is template, with grid lines you measure your face against. Beautiful faces all seem to fit template."

"Can we use that, or build on it to make our own face reading program?" Harold asked.

"*Esthetic Mask* is patented by Dr. Quadrano, but original geometry was used by Leonardo da Vinci to paint Mona Lisa—remember? We found on Wikipedia, and also *I Ching* Hexagrams. Bringing it all together with *Mian Xiang* face reading and Chinese Medicine is difficult job. But then you really have something!"

"You hear that, Trish?" said Harold, "the Mona Lisa mystique is measurable and probably reproducible...You could make new and maybe better Mona Lisa's."

"She wasn't a conventional beauty by today's standards", said Trish. "But women with plainer faces could think of themselves as classically beautiful, if they fit the Mona Lisa template." She thought, *Jennifer had said something like that.*

Ma turned off controls to the dome, and led Trish back out of the structure. They sat around a steel and glass table, lit by a pin spot ceiling light.

Harold felt that he had to get past Ma's sensitivity on the espionage issue. "Ma, ...oh, what the hell..."

"Something wrong?" Ma sounded solicitous.

Harold shrugged in resignation. "Ma—whatever commercial product we come up with, my Uncle Paul seems determined to vet it through his old CIA buddy, Van." Harold did not see that Trish was glaring at him.

Ma was carefully reading his guests' eyes. "This *Van* was in CIA with your uncle?"

"Oh no, Uncle Paul was never in CIA. Van was, and maybe still is."

Trish recognized Ma's new double question. This time, Harold didn't answer properly; he fell into the trap of revealing unnecessary information. Her objecting, though, might upset this Ma unduly.

"Why does this Van have to vet your face reading idea?" asked Ma.

"Because he is an expert on China," said Harold, "and would want to keep this technology out of Chinese hands—if it's valuable...Or, I guess, he might tell us if they already have it...Or maybe even that the U.S. has it."

Ma's voice took on a stony edge as his smile faded. "You realize that any government agent could put an end to anything they consider harmful to national security and put an end to whoever is producing it?"

Harold replied, "I think Uncle Paul trusts Van, but also Charles Wu, up at Columbia. They were students together and drinking buddies."

"*Drinking buddies,*" muttered Trish. She tried to read Ma.

Ma was smiling again, but with hardened eyes. "So just how much does this Van know?"

"Little or nothing, I believe," said Harold. "Uncle Paul hasn't been able to reach him, although Charles Wu might have given him a hint. The idea is to tempt him with some information. Just enough to indicate we might have something valuable."

"I think we should give him something," said Ma.

Trish wasn't sure she heard right. "W…We should what?"

"I am willing to produce this software package, for a fee equivalent to equal partner's share; expenses to be shared and come off the top. We can work out details in e-mails and further meetings. If you want to tempt this Van with something really good, there is something in Dallas—I doubt you've seen it yet—that is just as impressive, or even more so than this technology. A Chinese contact of mine would help you down there."

Harold was dumbfounded. Ma was not only unbothered by a CIA vetting, he was offering more bait to lure the vetter. If that was all it took to make Ma their man, it seemed almost too easy. Harold glanced hopefully at Trish. She looked both leery and perplexed. "So, why not Trish?"

"I'm not saying no. With all due respect and thanks to Ma for this wonderful presentation, I just think we should run everything past our partners, with a mutual promise to respect the confidentiality of all these ideas."

Ma was careful not to intrude.

"Would that be acceptable to you, Ma?" asked Harold.

"Absolutely. I have property and ideas to protect also. And this other technology I mentioned—I will hold back until I hear from you."

"Totally fair and understandable," replied Harold.

VI.

Ma offered to show Trish and Harold around the adjoining Marina Del Rey before driving them to the nearby LAX airport. Viewing the profusion of sea craft, Harold asked, "Are you a boat guy, Ma?"

"Not *me*," said Ma.

Harold thought Ma's smile was benign, but the voice still sounded superior. "Back in Long Island, they say better to have friends with boats than have a boat. Did Confucius say anything like that?"

"Confucius *did* say, 'Ambition is like water with boat. Can float boat, but can also sink it.' You agree?"

"I wouldn't contradict Confucius," said Harold. "My problem has always been too little ambition, not too much."

Trish cringed inwardly. *Don't reveal a weakness! I'm starting to think like the Chinese.*

Ma spoke, "Like friends with boats, you have friends to help ambition. Good ideas you presented make for good start and good fortune in the future."

"Thank you, Ma," said Harold. "I have a good feeling about all this."

Trish thought, *Well, I don't....*

Soon they were at LAX. Harold and Trish thanked Ma, said the necessary good-byes and promised to call soon. They checked-in their bags, picked up boarding passes for the 9 p.m. flight and began a long wait in the Club Lounge.

The mediocre airport food did nothing to relieve Trish's gut-level distress. "Harold, I suppose you hoped to win Ma over by being so candid, but I wish you hadn't spilled the beans on Van—you know—his name, and the CIA business."

132

"It had to come out sooner or later. Ma was totally forthcoming with his technology—almost all of it. And we haven't given him everything, like Charles Wu's notes and the video."

"I don't know," said Trish. "Something doesn't ring right. First, you lead him to believe that the CIA has a veto over this project, which one would think might bother him. Then, he jumps in and wants to help make sure the CIA is involved. Also, he seemed to be rattled by that Chinatown scanning camera, which bothered me. It doesn't all add up. He's already got a basic outline from us. His potential for knowing the details of Chinese classics beats ours, hands down, exceeded only by somebody like Charles Wu, who can't do software. With all of Ma's technical know-how, it makes you wonder what he needs *us* for to come up with a super software package on face reading. Maybe he does want Van, although I can't imagine why."

"Wait," countered Harold. "His ace in the hole seems to be this *other* technology, which he is willing to share if we say yes to his essentially becoming a partner. Maybe he does need Van and us. And maybe we couldn't do this project without the other technology. So, I guess we need each other. Maybe Van becomes our ace in the hole."

"Yeah, a card that wasn't ours to play, not yet anyway. Let's see your uncle's reaction to this. Maybe it *would* take Ma's know-how, plus the extra technology to make this project happen. But what will your uncle say if we don't land Van—his *drinking buddy*? Do we really need the CIA to pass muster on our business? I would say no, and I rest my case."

"You're the lawyer. And why are we arguing? You may be right about my playing the Van card. Maybe it was premature. But we *do* call Ma's bluff by saying yes to his joining the project—regardless of whether Van is reeled in or not. Once we say yes to Ma, even if Van stays away, I agree, we still go ahead."

"All in favor?" said Trish. Seeing Harold's raised hand, she raised hers, then covered a yawn. "Unanimous. But I must say, the guy is a Confucian mind-bender. And he isn't always Mr. Happy Face; I wouldn't want him for an enemy. Now, I move we nap 'til boarding time, which is still ninety minutes away."

VII.

It was early next morning when Agent White Tiger in Los Angeles phoned Agent Blue Lotus in New York. "Listen carefully. Based on conversations of Ma, Chinese cinema technician in L.A. and American face reading group, we believe American agent Van Lear could be lured out here. That is because he has a connection to the group and they are trying to interest him in their project. Ma has also hinted to group that Lear's participation would not be unwelcome. Perhaps Lear will accompany them or appear as an uninvited guest. This is only a plan B that we need to further organize, in case New York abduction fails."

"We will not fail."

"I hope so for your sake. In any event, the bait and trap out here won't be ready for some time yet. If you don't flush him out before that, then plan B becomes plan A. Maybe best to wait until Chinese New Year in New York. Big crowd will give you better chance to take him without police interference."

"As time approaches, let me know what you intend."

"He may be wary since his contact was killed, and may assume his identity is confirmed. I am not so confident in you or your operation, after Billy Shun disaster."

VIII.

Like all Chinese nationals who were to travel to the U.S. on a student visa, Ma-Chang-Kuo was originally screened by the MSS for possible employment as an agent. The Intelligence Ministry had been quick to take advantage of the economic and trade policy of *Zou Chuqu* "Going Out" first promulgated by President Jiang Zemin in the 1990's.

For those with advanced technical training like Ma (and with family back home essentially held hostage) the pressure to spy and work against the Americans—rather than completely join them—could be especially intense. Ma kept his options open by feeding the MSS tidbits of digital re-creation technology developed at SCU, some of which the Chinese already worked on. They did consider it a good sign that he had never filed for U.S. citizenship, and was probably headed home, like many others, for his most productive years after gleaning the most from his overseas experience.

Some of the digital technology displayed in popular Chinese action films had, in fact, been developed in Mainland China and Hong Kong studios. The MSS had actually encouraged this open sharing of Chinese technology by Ma and others in order to gain access to American technology "by any means necessary"—a PRC mantra. In some of these films, Ma had collaborated with two technicians in particular, a Ms. Ren and a Mr. Ho, as their British and American cinema colleagues in Hong Kong knew them. Coincidentally, they bore some resemblance in age and appearance to Ma's parents whom he had hoped to someday bring out of China.

Ma knew that he couldn't sit on the fence forever. Going by the experiences of others, chances are he would eventually succumb to the pressure of the PRC. Certainly, his fear of their threats presently outweighed his desire to totally cast his lot with the Americans. That his parents were feeling the heat more intensely only underscored his predicament.

And now, developing a face-reading program for Trish and Harold that had national security implications might open up new possibilities for placating his MSS handlers, if he could tantalize them with a few crumbs. This CIA friend of theirs could be a useful new connection for him—or an adversary. And the name Charles Wu he recognized from an MSS list of probable enemies of the motherland. Wu could even be a plant of the MSS floated to test his loyalty. Ma had to be careful.

He knew that the well-heeled Chinese Ministry of Commerce (MOFCOM) had been funding scholarships for "deserving" Chinese students to enroll in SCU telecom courses. He assumed that such students could "repay" the motherland by tapping Ma's cell and office phones. To be on the safe side, Ma often spoke ambiguously and in riddles to keep any listeners guessing. His messages to his parents continued in coded Hokkien.

IX.

Agent Vandersloot Lear was not sleeping well. Dreams and fragments of memory nagged at him. There was no word from Henry or Jake Ritter. Mainland Chinese chatter, he knew from his own sources, had greatly lessened. In fact, it had practically stopped. That in itself might be suspicious.

He glanced at his own Super Watch, basically a three-inch wide minicomputer that was almost always on his wrist. It was 3 a.m. What *was* on his mind? Charles Wu's comments about Paul Wallach—that *would-be* agent—flitted about like gnats in his half-conscious brain. He hated to admit it, but there had always been something about Wallach that got under his skin, despite some things he admired. Wallach had not been an outstanding student, had not gotten a good handle on Chinese, much less mastered it as he himself had. But Wallach was always coming up with these crackpot theories that nobody could really demolish: like how the Chinese, despite their supposed ideological rigidity— remembering the "Great Leap Forward" and its agricultural disasters— would ultimately turn pragmatic and take advantage of Western technology.

Van remembered Wallach defending this "minority of one" position against a scathing attack from their seminar leader. The support for this, Wallach explained, was in the *I Ching*, which teaches one to adapt to changing circumstances. That got a laugh at the time. But he certainly was right about Chinese pragmatism: how they've turned Marx *and* Capitalism "on their heads" and taught everyone a lesson or two about production and international markets—not to mention showing the Ruskies and Americans how to run a spy network. *Not that we've learned much back from them*, thought Lear. *Now what's this seminar I'm having with myself? Oh well, as long as I'm up, where is that I Ching app I found on my Super Watch?*

Part Four

"Big D"

I.

The day after their overnight flight back to Newark, Trish summarized the trip in a text to Paul, Jennifer and Carlos: Ma was willing to work with them—but also with the CIA, which was surprising, as was his bringing up "other technology" in Dallas. They proposed having a face-to-face meeting of the entire group.

Jennifer surprised Trish, in turn, with news of a call from Vera Tang, the fashion mogul, looking to discuss promotion ideas with Spence-Iturbi Inc. Trish was pleased, but her mind was still on L.A. and that other Chinese VIP. Jennifer also reported that she and Carlos had made progress in the face reading market research study. Ninety percent of three hundred respondents would buy a camera phone app that could read faces and match the user with a prospective romantic partner. Carlos reported to his agency, Harris, Pierson, about a "fashion research study" in the works with Spence-Iturbi—referring to Trish's L.A. meeting with the Chinese digital technician.

Harold had thought of a way to justify time away from the office; he suggested to his senior editor the idea of a new periodical topic: the disease of *Prosopagnosia,* the inability to recognize faces. The subject would pair well with that of autism, whose sufferers had trouble understanding facial expressions. The editor thought it promising. Since these were fields related to face reading, Harold could move forward on both tracks and cover his own.

Despite progress on all fronts, however, fears and doubts still bedeviled him. Even if Carlos and the women were trustworthy, what about Ma, who seemed to toy with him, showing him up in front of Trish? Could Harold trust himself to outwit or face down adversaries? As for romantic possibilities, one way to bag a top-drawer woman like Trish would be to triumph in this complicated business venture, and become a hero in the eyes of those who might underestimate him.

To be dead honest, the only thing he ever felt truly confident about—man-to-man—was his martial arts ability, and *that* he had neglected lately. While still in college, under the tutelage of his Master-Instructor in Little Neck, he was awarded a 5th degree Black Belt, performing a blend of Chinese Wu Shu and Korean Taekwondo techniques.

Master Choi Hong taught him that Wu Shu's upper limb grabs and swings married well with the leg lunges and kicks of Taekwondo. Although Harold had never hurt anyone himself, he knew that some kicks were powerful enough to break ribs, vertebrae, or windpipes. In fact, it was probably a killer kick that had sent poor Mary Shun to her death. He didn't anticipate having to fight Chinese gang martial artists trained for mortal combat, but, let's face it: he was hesitant to set foot in Chinatown. Was he really afraid? Was he ducking a challenge? He could understand Uncle Paul's wanting to play the hero a bit and prove himself, once and for all. *Hmm, I was thinking of calling Master Choi just to say hello, anyway. And maybe I can see Mom and Dad as long as I'm visiting the North Shore…*

***

Paul Wallach was glad the L.A. trip had gone well. He reported that Charles Wu had emailed him a flow chart showing how *Mian Xiang* and *I Ching* could be combined for face reading. Wu had reached Van Lear on their behalf, but Lear was non-committal about Wallach's ideas on face reading and questions about the Chinese. Wu cautioned Wallach not to be discouraged—that Lear's disinterest probably had less to do with the merits of the face reading idea than his reluctance to involve Wallach in national security matters. Wu was also happy to hear that they had found Ma apparently capable and willing to take on the project. Wu also related that he had made his own inquiries about Ma through trusted and confidential Chinese channels operating between Columbia and SCU; nothing untoward had showed up regarding Ma's credentials or anything else, but he had promised to look further into the matter. What Wu did not tell his periodontist friend was that he intended to make personal contact with Ma.

With Christmas intervening, Paul invited his partners for a discussion and dinner the Friday night before New Year's at the Wallach family's Victorian mini-mansion in Marlboro, New Jersey. Carlos, who lived across the river from Manhattan in Weehawken, would pick them up at the ferry docks in his father's car.

Meanwhile, the holiday meant time off for Harold, and opportunities for Connecticut-native Jennifer to visit her folks up in Wethersfield together with Trish (a recent tradition). Christmas also allowed Carlos to resume his role as a favorite *tio* to nephews and nieces at his parents' home in nearby Union City, New Jersey.

II.

Harold arranged to first visit his parents in Great Neck, and then Master Choi in Little Neck, on the Saturday before Christmas. The Martial Arts Studio was normally closed that day but Choi had agreed to see him for a private lesson—one that Harold said was urgent. He rented a car for the occasion and met his parents for brunch at the North Shore Country Club, which afforded matchless views of Long Island Sound. The Savitts had largely recovered from their dashed hopes of Harold becoming a doctor. They were pleased to hear that he had interested his Uncle Paul and others in a promising business venture. Harold left them in good spirits.

Within twenty minutes, he had parked the Ford Focus in a small lot adjacent to a yellow-brick building in Little Neck. Moments later, he sat opposite Choi-Hong at a small metal desk surrounded by framed photos of martial artists on the walls. Harold had always felt completely at ease with Master Choi, a pleasant-faced Korean-American; he came right to the point: this was to be more of a consultation than a lesson…Had Choi heard about the killer kick subway murder that the cops thought was gang related?

By the way, the victim had been a friend of a friend (a slight stretch of the truth since Hoda had known Mary Shun only slightly). Had any martial artists discussed the killing? Wasn't this a black mark against the sport in the public eye? Although ashamed to admit it, Harold confided in Choi that he had been hesitant to go to Chinatown since hearing of the murder.

"Harold, I remember telling you that some former Tongs used their martial arts skills to muscle people in the city. Yes, I did hear of the murder and I do know that former Tongs congregate regularly at a Kung Fu studio in Flushing. But I'm not aware of any tie-in. To answer your question, certainly this kind of violence discredits us all. However, before I tell you the name of the studio, I need to ask why you would want to know."

Harold hesitated before speaking. He knew that the Flushing section of Queens, New York City contained a huge Chinese population rivaling Manhattan's Chinatown. It was fair to ask: what was his plan? To find the killer of Mary Chen himself? And if he did, then what? *No, I don't see myself as a warrior or a detective—more like a humble practitioner of martial arts defending against their criminal misuse. But look at me—scared away from Chinatown by a subway murder. Am I man or mouse?*

"Master Choi, I am not a vigilante. But I would like to be able to walk the streets of Chinatown, face possible gangsters and not show fear, especially in front of women," *one in particular*, he thought.

"Harold, I will show you an ultimate killer kick which is also a supreme confidence builder. But only if you promise to use it strictly in times of extreme danger."

"I promise, Master." Harold meant it.

They donned uniforms and warmed up until both were freely perspiring. "You are still in decent shape," said Choi, "but probably a little rusty. What I will show you is a lethal martial arts kick from Brazil, called the *capoeira*. You can deliver up to eighteen hundred foot-pounds of force at the point of contact. The move is actually derived from a dance step; how well do you dance?" Choi laughed.

"I had some practice a few days ago in L.A., but I was always a better runner than a dancer." Harold assumed a sprinter's crouch, and alternately flexed his well-muscled thighs.

"Ha!" laughed Choi, hands on hips.

"What's so funny?"

"Harold, I'm not making fun of you. I laugh in appreciation. No one would be better prepared for the *capoeira* than a powerful runner like you."

"Really?

"Yes. It requires spinning lunges from a deeply bent leg. We'll see how good you are. Anyway, I'm going to put you through the workout of your life—hopefully not *for* your life."

They both laughed, Harold feeling a bit uneasy.

An hour and a half later, as Harold toweled himself off in the shower room, he thought the workout *had* been taxing beyond his expectations; despite the hot shower, stiffness and soreness was already setting in. Master Choi was satisfied with his progress, and his promise not to play Steven Seagal, the avenging martial artist of the movies. In return, he entrusted Harold with the address of that Kung Fu studio in Flushing.

III.

Trish had stayed over at the Santoramo's after Christmas; they were also hosting Jennifer's brother, Bart and his family who lived locally. At one point, Jennifer steered the conversation to their new face reading project, which did not bother Trish—at first. But then Jennifer brought up possible financing, especially for her idea of facial counseling. That interested both her father and Bart, who were investment bankers. Trish thought such talk was premature, but said nothing, until they were driving back to the city.

"I guess you're lining up your backers, Jen."

"*Our* backers, boss lady...you're included. And if my end of it, the psych institute, takes off and the face-reading app doesn't, you can sit back and trust your older buddy—by three months—to take care of you."

"A Golden Parachute...Sorry, Jen, I misspoke. Your brother and dad are darlings. I'm sounding like Harold now: afraid somebody's going to get the jump on me. Come to think of it, maybe he and I are not so different—he's underachieved to spite his parents, and I've overachieved to spite mine."

"I know we never discuss our dates, Trish, but since we might get involved with these guys, business and otherwise, just how are things progressing between you and Harold—if you don't mind my asking?"

"Maybe I sounded like a scheming woman," said Trish, "when I told you I was sort-of testing Harold to show me his leadership qualities. But I'm not going to mother him, because I don't want a little boy, either as a romantic or a business partner. I'd say he's got potential, but I'm not allowing possible romance to get ahead of business. How about you and Carlos?"

"We've had two dates, mostly discussing business, and, as you'd probably guess, Carlos has no problems with self-confidence, but frankly he hasn't made any serious moves. Sounds like you and I have both got things well under control." Jennifer expertly zoomed the company Lexus onto the southbound lane of Interstate 91, headed back to New York.

For the next hour, she and Trish talked about ways to coordinate facial as well as body types with couture styles in Vera Tang's new collection—one they'd recommend have Chinese styling and flavor.

IV.

That next Friday at 4 p.m., Carlos picked up the group at the Weehawken Ferry slip in his father's new Cadillac Escalade. Forty minutes later, Lorraine and Paul Wallach greeted them all at their front door, in Marlboro, New Jersey.

Lorraine was the consummate hostess in the Wallach's spacious Victorian home, which featured high ceilings and antique furnishings. She sat in on their discussions during dinner, which were video-recorded. "As a teacher," she said, "I can see discussing all kinds of faces in art classes. I would show how every face has value and a role to play."

"Yes," agreed Jennifer, "and bringing animals into it which children love. It might help them develop empathy and understanding of how we react to faces."

Lorraine replied, "As long as your Chinese software guru can deliver the goods. Paul told me about wanting to involve his old buddy who went into the CIA; this Chinese guru seems almost too willing to encourage that. I'm worried about your safety."

"Who knows if there is anything to worry about", said Paul. "As long as Van Lear keeps mum, it's a guessing game. Lear probably doesn't think face reading has much to it."

"And you're determined to prove him wrong!" replied Lorraine.

"I guess I am."

She continued, "That's what bothers me. Maybe you wanted to be, Paul, but you're no professional spook, to use your spy lingo. Perhaps Lear's reticence is his way of discouraging you from involving the CIA."

Harold spoke, "We have two Chinese experts who *are* willing to help; one at Columbia—the other at SCU. We could pool their findings and even get them together. Maybe Van and the CIA don't matter…"

Paul answered, "Charles Wu is a friend and, so far, just a consultant. By the way, I think we should offer him a paid honorarium, or make an outright donation to the Starr Library, in his name, if anything comes of this. As for Ma-Chang-Kuo, he wants to be paid like a partner but didn't ask to be one. That avoids extra complications."

"The best news," said Carlos, "is that you've got a software engineer who is willing to make this happen. What's hard to understand though, is why he wants to involve the CIA himself by offering this *other technology* as bait?"

"I think," replied Jennifer, "that regardless of his motives, we should agree to use him, and the other technology. If he can make it work, let the bait issue play out by itself."

All agreed, and decided to send a text message to Ma—the basis of a written agreement—that they would use his services to build a software package under the payment conditions he suggested. All parties would share all information, including "other technology".

Trish quickly composed an email message, in appropriate legalese, inviting Ma to provide feedback and revise as he saw fit. She added that the CIA man's participation could not be compelled, promised, or guaranteed; they would attempt to solicit his reaction to their work. But, in any case, release of the product would not depend on it. If this draft was satisfactory, they would send signed final copies, which Ma was to counter-sign, and return. She pushed *send.*

Dessert was served; the mood became lighter.

Carlos spoke, "Don't forget—we were going to think of video or party games using faces…"

"Any ideas?" asked Trish.

"Let's brainstorm a little, like in advertising," answered Carlos, "that's how we come up with winning ideas."

Harold flinched but shot up straight as if suddenly electrified. "Aunt Lorraine— "do you have a black board or large pad to write on?"

She returned moments later, carrying a two-foot square pad, an easel, and a box of Magic-Markers.

Harold began to write. "I suggest we dumb this down to cartoon archetypes. Carlos was talking about a society…How about a small city where everybody works, intermarries and interacts with each other and the outside world? Every type of person is needed sooner or later and their face represents a particular role."

"What if," said Jennifer, "a mate seeker has to select a favorite from several categories, say: a lover-type, a power-type, a kind or compassionate-type or a joyful-funny-type—all from a pool of actual faces known to have those qualities. He or she can see how well they've selected. A lover-type shouldn't be so much about beauty, but more about health and strength. Users would be guessing which faces turned out to have the most kids, stayed healthy and had the longest-lasting marriages."

Harold furiously sketched arrows connecting the cartoon heads.

"That's good. Here's another variation", said Paul. "Say you need to select a representative team to the outside world, either to colonize another territory or…to defend against attack. In either case, you want a full range of human archetypes: planners and managers—also warrior and worker types. You'd also want to include artists, writers and other creative types. Charles Wu at Columbia actually thought intelligence services could survey the enemy in this way to see if they were a fully functioning adversary."

Jennifer added, "Or how about a twist on that; a game, like a T.V. reality show, where you need the right mix of characters to survive a life-threatening experience. Points would be awarded and the better-selected team survives. The other doesn't; all in good fun, of course."

Carlos spoke, "From what Trish and Harold told us about Ma's presentation at South California, this is not just about analyzing known faces. There is also a tremendous potential for creating new faces. Once you've scanned a million power faces, beautiful faces and all the rest, you've got the models for synthesizing new ones in movies and commercials. Ideal faces could be created, and then a contest held to find the closet real-life look-a-like."

Harold leapt in. "Yes, Carlos, think about it. You could fabricate thousands or millions of fictitious faces known only through their images on T.V. and movies, and then mount a huge public relations campaign to changing public perception of whole nations. Other cultures tend to worship ideal models as idols, just as we do with our celebrities."

"Flood the world with perfect noses, and all the rest," said Paul, winking at Trish, "And create new standards of beauty…Great propaganda for the nation or culture looking to extend its influence." Paul thought of the Chinese.

Trish's iPhone beeped. Ma had texted back his agreement to the proposal. He wanted to see all of their notes from Charles Wu and anything else they had on the subject. Upon receipt of that, he was prepared to deliver information about the "other technology" and to await signed final copies of the official contract.

Trish, Jennifer, and Carlos briefly huddled on how to transmit their response.

Trish used a server connection called "You Send It" and sent Ma the uploaded emails from Wu as well as the video of their current dinner meeting.

One hour later, as the visitors were preparing to leave the Wallach's, Trish received another text from Ma: 'Please send final copies of agreement. For *other technology* please visit, ASAP, Branson Robots Laboratory in Dallas, TX. They are expecting your call.' The contact person listed was Feng-Tzu-Wo. Postal and e-mail addresses, and phone number were supplied.

Paul Wallach suggested they thank Charles Wu again for his help, inform him about the agreement with Ma and send him a transcript of the audio recording of the L.A. meeting. All agreed. Paul showed Trish the special pass code for Wu at Columbia. She promised to e-mail Wu everything that next day.

As to who would go to Dallas, little discussion was needed. Riding home, Carlos and Jennifer exchanged knowing smiles. "Our turn," she announced.

V.

The next day, Jennifer called Branson Robotics in the Dallas suburb of Richardson, Texas and spoke to David Branson. Branson asked if Jennifer had seen the edition of *Discovery Magazine* featuring his robotics group. She said no. He suggested that Jennifer visit his website.

"Oh, this is incredible," gushed Jennifer, an hour later, to her partners on a conference call. "Apparently, they have a life-like polymer skin that moves like real skin during facial expressions. The complexion can darken or lighten according to different emotions. The robots react to human facial expressions by mirroring them back and can talk and even sing. So, machines can read human faces...Watch out!"

"I see where Ma was heading with his synthetic faces," said Harold. "You can create new ideal faces, digitally, or build actual robot faces. The robots will eventually have artificial intelligence and think for themselves. It's Ok, I guess, as long as humans have ultimate control."

Jennifer replied, "I spoke with both David Branson and Feng, who is apparently Ma's friend. They invited us to come out and video, take notes—whatever. They'll be working with Ma doing entertainment robot models. I imagine that could include fashion."

"This could be dynamite for Seventh Avenue," said Trish. "Instead of temperamental anorexics sashaying down runways, you could have perfectly-designed models, always looking and acting right."

Jennifer replied, "For matchmaking, you could design your own robot, or get fixed up with the mechanical man or woman of your dreams. I did notice on their website that there was a link to a Japanese robotics company that makes The Perfect Woman. I ran the video. Hard to believe it's a robot; every feature is perfect. Sorry Trish, only your nose is perfect. You can't compete."

"Forget plastic surgery," answered Trish, "I'll get robotized—the bionic woman."

More laughter erupted.

Carlos chimed in, "The American Airlines flight to Dallas-Fort Worth leaves tomorrow morning, 8 a.m., out of LaGuardia—gets us in well before noon. We'll spend the afternoon and evening; come back next morning. It should be enough time."

VI.

That night, in his walk-up studio apartment on Greenwich Village's Bank Street, a restless Agent Vandersloot Lear was killing time playing *I Ching* on his Super Watch. He "threw" the coins and asked it where Mary Chen's assassin was headed. Under Hexagram 39, it read, "the Southwest furthers". Now what the hell did that mean? The Super Watch signaled an incoming confidential email from Charles Wu. It said that Wu had received a digitized audio of Paul Wallach's nephew speaking with a Chinese technician in L.A. named Ma, who was connected to SCU. The nephew had mentioned Van's name, which really interested this Ma—who then suggested the nephew confer with another Chinese in Dallas, working for Branson Robotics. Wu was passing the complete audio along, as an attachment, "for what it was worth".

Van's initial anger at Wallach gave way to a budding curiosity. He was about to respond to Wu, when he saw that he had received another encoded message—this one from FBI agent Jacob Ritter, which read: "Sammy Chu, a former Flying Dragon, might be *flying* to prison again. He admits driving two guys who were in a hurry to Kennedy Airport the day of Mary Chen's murder. He didn't deny it was them, meaning Billy and an accomplice. We'd like to put him into protective custody but can't really hold him. He's scared shitless and will probably try to lam."

The message continued: "Unfortunately, TSA doesn't routinely scan photo IDs of passengers unless there's an alert. There were ninety-five passengers with Chinese names who flew out of Kennedy that day. Most have been checked out. Their destinations were L.A., Hong Kong, Shanghai, Chicago, and Dallas-Fort Worth. We've re-sent the photo ID of Billy Chen to TSA and Homeland Security and alerted them to look for him and a possible companion. Will keep you posted. Jake."

Van thought, *Now isn't that something? Two different sources mention Dallas. And the I Ching did say, "The Southwest furthers". This is plain silly...Just coincidence again. Come on, even if I really believed in Taoist fortune telling as an intelligence tool, I'd never admit it to Charles Wu, much less headquarters. But, just in case, I'm asking for an NSA spy in the sky probe of that Chinese technician in Dallas—and let's include his buddy in L.A.*

VII.

Back in his apartment, Harold was savoring a year-end vacation day and a modicum of satisfaction that people were approving his ideas. Respect from others was important, but he had to make that final leap from self-doubt to self-confidence.

Sitting at his desk, he pored over a subway map: the Broadway local from 23rd Street to 42nd, and then the number 7 train to Flushing. The House of Kung Fu, on Northern Blvd., he estimated to be only a few blocks walk from the elevated Main St. station. Dressed in street togs, he packed his knapsack with his workout gear, Nikon camera, Scotch Tape, a Magic Marker and the two Times newspaper articles dealing with the subway murder. Exactly how he would confront a possible Tong warrior, Harold wasn't sure. But when the moment arrived, he knew he wouldn't shirk his self-appointed mission to defend the noble arts. If not do battle directly, then at least deliver the strongest possible message.

It was early afternoon when Harold descended the stairs of the Main Street Flushing station. His stride was deliberate and unhurried, his eyes serene and trained on a distant point as if in a trance. Rounding a corner, he was startled by a flaming red neon sign wrapped around a four-story, ultra-modern commercial building. On it, gold metallic letters spelled, House of Kung Fu with accompanying Chinese characters.

Drawing closer, Harold was stirred by the splendor of the building: panels of jade-like ceramic alternated with those of chrome and stainless steel; floor-to-ceiling glass walls revealed brilliantly-lit interior spaces, populated by men and women in various martial arts uniforms and poses. He realized that the building's appearance—and its purpose—formed an organic unit: Yin and Yang.

Inside, a few people, mainly East Asian, waited to register at a polished granite counter. A semi-circular lobby, resplendent in green marble, opened left and right to corridors lined with overhead banks of blinding white-fluorescent lights. Walking down the right-side corridor, he could see training rooms and people he had viewed from the street. Harold found the intense light bewildering; he stopped and was confused about what to do next. Was he going to ask for a challenge match with someone, and also ask if they had gang connections? *Don't be absurd*, he cautioned himself.

Although none of the several passersby seemed to notice him, Harold felt self-conscious. He removed his Columbia Lions wool cap, took off his backpack and began to shuffle through its contents. Facing the wall, he was relieved to see a glass-encased bulletin board on which to focus his attention. Prominently displayed were a dozen or so headshots of uniformed martial arts champions wearing medals. He imagined them all to be the faces of powerful warriors. In bold type above each were their club names: Dragons, Eagles, Shadows, and so forth. Harold's eyes flitted over to an adjacent magazine spread pinned to the corkboard. The article featured photos of some of the same champions and was headlined: **Tong Thugs or Martial Arts Heroes?** Many "reformed" Chinese gangs have changed their names— from Ghost Shadows to Shadows, for example—but have they changed their games? Some of New York Chinatown's martial artists are national champions, but time will tell whether they become real heroes to neighborhood Chinese-Americans, their former prey. Certain elders of the Chinatown Benevolent Associations—who wish to remain anonymous—are skeptical....

Feeling a rush of excitement, Harold tried to appear calm. He composed himself by reading the entire four-column article over the next minute or so.

Finally, he looked around and noticed two groups of people in the corridor who were absorbed in their own conversations. He pulled out the two newspaper clippings about the subway murder and quickly taped them to the glass next to the magazine articles. Magic Marker in hand, trembling slightly, he strained to write legibly on the paper: ***Kung Fu heroes don't murder!*** Another glance around confirmed that he was unobserved. He raised the camera to the glass over the magazine article and depressed the shutter. The flash briefly blinded him as it reflected harshly off the glass. Turning around, he saw others looking in his direction. Harold felt a stab of fear in his abdomen and a prickly burning around his scalp and neck. Turning, he saw out of the corner of his eye another bright glint—all too familiar—the lens of a scanning camera. Harold couldn't resist looking directly at it. A flutter of panic in his chest rose to his throat; he gasped and coughed.

Oh my god, what have I got myself into, trying to play the big man? Harold thought, controlling an impulse to run that might draw further attention. But he *was* distraught, and looked it; people began to stare.

He tried to smile and walk casually toward the lobby but his face felt frozen and his legs stiff as if constrained by giant elastics. He found the presence of mind to slip on his backpack with its belongings inside, and placed his Columbia cap back on his head.

Harold became acutely aware of his rising heartbeat, took a deep breath, backed against the corridor wall and closed his eyes almost shut—remembering a Shaolin training meditation: upright relaxed stance, eyes and mouth eighty-percent closed, inhale through nose, exhale through mouth, left palm over right across the abdomen. Almost immediately, he felt tensions lessen and his breathing normalize.

Blinking his eyes open, he was jolted by the sight of two grim-looking men—wearing black martial arts tunics imprinted with "Shadows" in white lettering—blocking his path. Both moved toward him.

Harold would remember the next sequence as a blur, although several seconds passed. Dropping into a one-legged crouch, he extended the other leg and an arm for balance and whipped that leg around in a high arc, his shoe just missing the heads of the Shadows men. They backed way. Harold took advantage of the opening between them to bolt toward the front door. From ten yards away, he saw a man exiting, accelerated into full sprinter's mode just as the door swung open and zipped past him to the outside. A backwards glance told him he was being pursued by one of the black-clad men. He also saw he had dropped his Columbia cap.

Harold thought he'd never run so fast in his life—at least while in civvies. Not hearing footsteps behind him over the next couple of blocks, he was apparently outdistancing his pursuer, but realized that reaching the station, he might still have to wait for the train and be caught.

Luckily, a vacant New York City cab, roof light alit, was cruising slowly just ahead of him on Northern Blvd. With a burst of speed,

Harold reached it and rapped on the back window. Panting and perspiring heavily, he had to catch his breath and, entering the cab, haltingly gave the cabbie his home address. Sitting back, he felt the frenzy and fear dissipate, only to be replaced by wrenching bitterness and despair. He had failed to really confront anybody—verbally or physically. He had run. Maybe he had discovered a hangout of gangsters, maybe not. But in trying to beard the lion in its den he had proved to be a coward. And worst of all, he had gone back on his word to Master Choi about not being a vigilante.

So much for self-respect and self-confidence. These self-inflicted blows of defeat hurt deeply. How could he find the intestinal fortitude to go on from here? How indeed? Exhausted, he dozed off but awoke suddenly and clear-headed just as the cab was emerging from the Manhattan side of the Queens Midtown Tunnel. As if guided by an unseen hand, Harold reached for his cell phone and found the number. *Surely, he'll see me in an emergency.* He punched the number displayed for Alvin Farkis, PhD., psychotherapist.

VIII.

Van had gotten back to Charles Wu via secure e-mail. It was important to keep Paul Wallach's group on a tight leash and not let them insinuate themselves further in agency matters, including bandying Van's name about to impress people or to involve him. He conceded to Wu that the "coincidence" of Dallas had prompted him to order surveillance of certain Chinese persons in L.A. and Dallas. With Jake Ritter's help, he had obtained their full names and addresses and identified their vehicles. The satellite's zoom lens produced close-ups within six feet. This would permit accurate identification of target subjects as well as lip reading of conversations. He didn't bring up what he considered to be that *I Ching* "nonsense".

An academic with national security connections, Professor Charles Wu was uniquely positioned, both as official advisor to the CIA and personal confident of Vandersloot Lear. As such, he had to walk a fine line between his responsibilities to his adopted country and his friendship and loyalty to his friend. Van did not yet seem to appreciate the possible espionage and propaganda value of Chinese-based face reading and facial imagery. And Wu thought that, even if unproven, this was something the Chinese should not get their hands on. Even so and although he had other CIA connections, Wu preferred to work *with* Van and not around him, if possible.

Professor Wu was Library Curator at Columbia's East Asian Languages and Cultures Department, but he had to share his secretary, Eileen Cheung, with the Lowe Library; and, he was not aware of the exact hours that she was available to him. So, he was frequently surprised when she popped up—as she had now—unsmiling and eyeing him intently through the glass wall of the Rare Books Reading Room.

Earlier, he had asked her to process notes of his own library business and she had begged off, citing another assignment. She had, in fact, been in the Lowe Library, looking through Columbia College yearbooks of the past ten to fifteen years. This was for a "cousin" in Flushing who worked at the House of Kung Fu. He had forwarded a digitalized photo from a security camera, hoping to match it with a graduation picture and a name.

IX.

Earlier that same day—at 5:30 a.m.—Carlos and his father's driver, picked up Jennifer at her apartment in the Escalade.

"Now that you've seen my morning face, you've seen it all," Jennifer said to Carlos as she was helped into the rear seat.

"Sorry for the early pick up," said Carlos, "but even domestic flights can be a hassle with security delays."

"I'm curious," said Jennifer, "if you don't mind my asking, just what have you told your folks about our little escapade?"

"Not much…Just that I've got to go to Dallas on business. I don't think they'd be particularly interested in Chinese face reading or even robots. Why? What have you told yours?"

"I do keep them abreast of business. If this thing looks like it's taking off, they could offer some financial support. So, I did give them a brief summary."

"Does that extend to personalities too?"

"A bit. I told them you were Cuban. Mom wanted to know if you looked like Desi Arnaz, from *I Love Lucy*. I told her you were much cuter."

Carlos laughed. "Desi Arnaz! Everybody's stereotype of the Cuban. Our folks are so yesterday. That's why I keep mine on a need to know basis. They're in their late sixties and don't even own a computer. Over four-hundred properties here and in Florida, and he jots everything on one big notebook." Carlos put his arm around Jennifer and apparently changing his mind, withdrew the arm.

She thought, *That's a liberty I'd allow, considering the brief goodnight kiss he ventured two nights before. But, whatever.*

They both dozed for the twenty-minute drive to LaGuardia's Departures Terminal.

Once aboard the two-and-a-half-hour flight, Carlos tried to sleep, while Jennifer pulled out a hardcover book: *Man and His Symbols*, by Carl G. Jung, that had been assigned reading for Psych II at Manhattanville College. Inserted in the book was a printout from *World Psychology Journal* entitled: "*What Faces Mean—a psychological and philosophical study based on Jung's Symbolism.*"

Feeling roused, Carlos looked over at her. "Hey, Dr. Freud, what's this?"

"Jung's my man; he should appeal to you too, Mr. Hemingway."

"Why so?

"Literary types like you," she said, "should appreciate Jung's work on dreams, role-playing, and our new buzzword—*archetypes*."

"I like the role playing…Like in our faces games. What's this chapter about?"

Jennifer pointed to a heading entitled: *Beauty and the Beast*. "That's a key chapter."

"Let's play the roles," said Carlos. "You're Beauty and I'm the Beast."

"You're more like the handsome Prince. But if you kissed me, you'd turn into the Beast." Jennifer realized that she was challenging Carlos, almost daring him to kiss her.

"Well in that case, I'll stay the prince—no offense."

"None taken." Jennifer laughed. She was relieved, in a way, that he hadn't taken the bait, but also surprised. She looked over at the passenger seated next to her: a well-dressed, middle-aged, brown-complexioned man wearing dark sunglasses. He seemed indifferent to their conversation.

Carlos read in a low voice: "Young girls share the hero myths that come with firm bonds to their fathers; they break away and become fully women when they break from their fathers.'" His eyebrows and lips formed a devilish smile.

Jennifer wondered if Carlos was really coming on to her or just role-playing. She again glanced at their neighbor whose features were finely chiseled, his hair dark and curly. He apparently continued to stare straight ahead, but his eyes were still covered in tinted glass mystery.

Carlos continued, "Well, *aren't* you ready to break away from your father?"

"What makes you ask that?"

"I'm not saying you're tied to their apron strings, but you do check in with them pretty regularly."

"Look who's talking? Don't you run home for Cuban cooking at least once a week and use Daddy's car practically whenever you want it?"

"Yeah, but they don't intrude or question me too closely. And they don't meet the shaggy bookworms I hang out with."

"What you're saying is that they don't have hooks into you as much as you have into them."

Carlos laughed. "Aha! You've got me psyched-out, Dr. Freud. What else does Jung have to say?"

"Speaking of the beast," Jennifer said, as she read aloud from the book: "All primitive instincts and archetypes of man have their place, because they are fully in the nature of man. These are sometimes represented by masks which represent faces of man."

"Well, Lorraine Wallach seemed to agree," replied Carlos. "She said every archetype, and its face, should be acknowledged in her classroom."

"Quite so," said Jennifer. "Jung says here that 'civilized man must heal the animal in himself and make it his friend.' Speaking of healing, therapeutic face counseling could be the wave of the future, like treating people like Suzy Sour Puss that I talked about a few weeks ago. Faces aren't just flesh to gawk at on movie screens; they represent our sensitive inner selves. Let's see what this article says…"

Carlos held up the magazine reprint and read aloud: "*The Meaning of Faces.* Faces reflect the total psyche as described by Jung—our noblest intentions and our basest instincts." Carlos whistled. "You could carve that into the cornice of your Face Counseling Institute."

Another whistle, long and piercing, came from somewhere in their midst. Carlos and Jennifer whirled to face the man behind the shades.

"Excuse me?" said Carlos.

"No, excuse *me!*" the man said, suddenly animated, with arched eyebrows and a broad smile. "I've never overheard such a conversation in my life!"

Jennifer and Carlos gaped at the man, then at each other.

"Please excuse my eavesdropping; I couldn't contain myself," continued the man. His accent sounded West Indian and cultivated. "I am Dr. Alphonse Maupassant from the Université Notre Dame d'Haiti. I teach cultural anthropology and my special interest is voodoo." Dr. Maupassant's eyes remained obscured behind his sunglasses; he was exquisitely dressed (so thought Jennifer) in a tailored, blue serge suit and red tie silk tie, adorned with a diamond stickpin.

Carlos reached a finger into his shirt pocket and switched on Paul Wallach's audio recorder, while pretending to adjust his tie.

"You mentioned voodoo," said Jennifer, as the tension eased. "I can see the connection to masks that Jung wrote about, in...uh, primitive societies."

"No apology needed; voodoo *is* a primitive belief, which makes it all the more valuable to study. But I must apologize for reading over your shoulder; if I may, could I read you another paragraph from Jung?"

Jennifer handed the book to Dr. Maupassant, who quoted: "The mask transforms its wearer into an archetypal image of his *totem animal*, thus creating a bonding between the animal soul and his own."

"So, psychologically speaking," said Jennifer, "you could say that accepting your own face means you are reconciled with your animal soul and nature."

"Undoubtedly," said Dr. Maupassant.

"To be sure," said Carlos, flashing a saturnine smile. "I am fully reconciled with Jennifer's face and her animal nature. I'm just too much of a gentleman to be the Beast." *Actually*, he thought. *I don't know what I am, but I'm tired of playing the rake, for sure.*

"Silly boy," said Jennifer, giving Carlos a mock perturbed look. "Carlos thinks we're getting too serious."

Dr. Maupassant looked briefly startled and then laughed as he got the joke. "Why not break up a serious discussion with a little humor? But I must say I am impressed with your conclusions about masks, and finding your own roles in fairy tales such as Beauty and the Beast. You see, in the Islands, we also have fairy tales, like in voodoo, and masks and faces are so important.

I remember an Oscar-winning Brazilian movie called *Black Orpheus*, which featured the Black community in Rio. It takes place during

Carnival. Faces and masks are central to the action. There are tragic deaths. Did you ever see it?"

"Yes," answered Carlos. "It was a classic, and I understand quite a bit of Portuguese. The bossa nova music was hypnotic."

The Caribbean man's voice was deep and resonant. "Yes, the facial images, the masks and the music wove a mysterious spell."

"Speaking of mysterious, I would love to see your eyes, if possible", said Jennifer, in a deferential tone.

Smiling, Dr. Maupassant removed his sunglasses with a flick of the wrist—revealing eyes of lustrous, light blue; he seemed to relish the couple's astonishment. "So, you see, I am a living example of Jung's 'bridging of the opposites'. I am also an expert on this book. It is a classic in psychology and in anthropology. Let me quote another paragraph: "The Negro is for some people the archetypal image of the *dark primal creature* they do not want to admit, exists in themselves, of which they are unconscious, and that they therefore project in others.""

Jennifer looked pleased. "Some of our group also believes that such an attitude is behind racism, and a reason why certain faces suffer discrimination. Would you agree?"

"I would," replied Dr. Maupassant.

"With all due respect," said Carlos, with a polite smile, "This is all very interesting and probably true. But as a guy who's trained in simple selling strategies, I'm concerned that discussions of race may be controversial and over the heads of our main consumer market. Trying to psychoanalyze racism may not be good for business."

"Oh, I'm sorry to intrude on your business discussions," said Dr. Maupassant.

"Not at all," replied Jennifer, smiling at the stranger and then frowning back at Carlos. "We've been conducting research on the power of faces to influence our psyche, and even our dreams. We are drawn to them in cinema, theatre, the arts, fashion and certainly popular culture. Even governments may deliberately use facial imagery for its propaganda power."

"I couldn't agree more. So, the psychic power of faces is what you and your partners are working on?" asked Dr. Maupassant.

"Yes," said Carlos, looking stern-faced at Jennifer. "Without going into details, our partners are all sworn to keep this confidential for the time being…you understand."

"I do, entirely. I don't wish to pry. But if facial imagery is your project, maybe I can help you. I am going to Dallas to lecture on voodoo masks and imagery at Western Methodist University. Please come by if you are going to Dallas and you have time. By the way, my eyes are otherwise normal—just sensitive to bright light—a legacy of my Norwegian mother." He handed Jen a brochure announcing his lecture, scheduled for the following day, together with his his business card:

Alphonse Lars Maupassant, Ph.D.
Professor of Anthropology and Cultural History
Université Notre Dame d'Haiti
Port-Au-Prince, Haiti 2003004
Tel: 3-855-700-7002 almaupassant@edu.org

Jennifer took the card. "We don't have a card yet. We are all freelancing this project apart from our own regular jobs. I'm Jennifer Santoramo, fashion consultant. This is Carlos Morales, advertising copy writer."

"Pleased to meet you," answered Dr. Maupassant. "If you can't make my lecture, please check in at my website. I hope we can stay in touch. I believe your inclinations are humanitarian as well as commercial."

Carlos thought the conversation finished well, but couldn't stifle a yawn. "Perhaps we can catch up in Dallas. Sorry, but we've been up since 4 a.m. Sleep is a top priority at the moment."

Two hours later, after bidding goodbye to their new acquaintance, Jen and Carlos deplaned and approached the arrivals gate. Facing them, among the greeters, were two East Asian-looking men. One held a sign that read Jennifer and Carlos; the other wore a maroon, hooded sweatshirt.

X.

Speaking with Dr. Farkis in the mahogany-panelled library that was his office, Harold allowed that he had seen progress in overcoming feelings of inadequacy about career, women and his looks. But he voiced doubts about his physical courage and his ability to complete this new face reading project—what had become his "life's work".

Dr. Farkis turned to something in the bookcase behind him and resumed facing forward.

Continuing, Harold stated that even his confidence in martial arts, "the core of my fragile ego", was shaken by the fiasco in Flushing. It seemed irrational to want to face down the presumed killers of a Chinese woman he hardly knew, but he needed to break through some psychological barrier that was holding him back from becoming a "complete man."

"Doctor, I feel like I was climbing a mountain, trusting my know-how, my strength and my courage. The top was in sight, but I slipped and fell most of the way down. Now I've lost my nerve."

"Interesting metaphor, Harold." Dr. Farkis's face was roundish, like his eyes, which together with a long nose gave him a bird-like appearance. His eyes were bright brown and crinkled merrily at the corners when he smiled, which was often. "Mountains can represent your intentions, which are high-minded and altruistic."

"Thank you," said Harold.

"Problem with mountains, though…"

"…I know—what goes up must come down. So, the mountain is not my destination?"

"Here's a more pertinent question: Do you think it is possible for you to climb that mountain—if you really want to? In other words, do you have the smarts and the talent, aside from confidence or motivation, which we could call true desire?

"Yes, I suppose I do."

"Suppose? You believe you have it or you don't—yes or no."

"Yes, I do; of course I do. Nobody on this project has a broader base of knowledge or a greater intrinsic feel for it than I do. That's not bragging; that's fact." Deep within him, Harold felt something shift or click.

"I believe it because you believe it, Harold. Does something feel different about that?"

"It does. But do I dare trust my feelings…or instincts—something my female business partner flies by? I wish I could."

"You could. But seeing is believing, wouldn't you agree?"

"How do you mean?"

"I took the liberty of video recording our session without telling you, because I didn't want you to be self-conscious, particularly about how you look."

"So?"

"Let's play back the video and see if you see what I saw—right when you said, "Yes, I do". Dr. Farkis rose to replay the video on the large monitor screen behind him, and then moved his chair so he could view it with Harold. "I'm going to turn down the audio and zoom in so you can concentrate on the changes in your face."

In the video, Harold saw the tightness around his eyes and mouth suddenly lessen, his gaze soften and his pupils dilate. His jaw relaxed and shifted slightly forward as he mouthed the words, "…of course I do." There was a muscularity and fullness in his jowls and cheeks that he hadn't noticed before—a look of strength and power. His lips formed an easy, confident smile. "Well I'll be…"

"And so Harold…" Dr. Farkis broke in, "Now you know what this feels like and what it looks like. Do I dare use the 'B' word?

"*Believe?*" asked Harold.

"That's a good one too; the word I was thinking of was *breakthrough!*"

XI.

Meanwhile back at the Dallas airport, the two greeters who had met Jennifer and Carlos introduced themselves as Feng and Danny. Soon, all were loaded inside a white Dodge Van bearing the name Branson Robotics. Feng drove with Danny upfront.

Once on the interstate highway, Feng spoke English with a slight Chinese accent that reminded Jennifer of Ma's voice. "So, you folks are from New York, one of my favorite cities. Ma tells me you might work with him."

"We're exploring many possibilities," said Carlos, "including yours."

"We are eager to show the world what we are doing," said Feng. "Humanoid robotics has wide applicability: cinema, advertising, education, even fashion." He turned and smiled at Jennifer.

"Yes," replied Jennifer. "We were imagining robot supermodels strutting down runways in Milan, New York, and Paris. Your website videos looked very promising."

Feng laughed heartily. "I think you will be really impressed with how life-like our robots are. We have the faces virtually perfect, although it may be years before we refine body movement. We'll show you things the videos didn't show—externals of course, not software."

Carlos said, "We understand the need to protect your work."

Danny turned and looked back for a long moment at Jennifer and at Carlos; their eyes met. Danny's face was calm but unsmiling.

Jennifer ventured a smile but Danny had resumed facing forward, showing just the trace of a smile in the rear-view mirror.

Feeling a chill, she said, "I'm sure Ma assured you that we are trustworthy; we trust him. We gave him our detailed notes, and he shared a lot of his technology with us."

Feng said, "By the way, Danny here is our security; sometimes a driver. He's relatively new, so he's riding shotgun today to learn the route. We've got about twenty minutes to go, mainly highway."

Feng then spoke to Danny in Chinese mixed with English words—the route numbers—for the next few minutes. Danny replied in English as well as Chinese.

Carlos and Jennifer were absorbed in looking out the windows at the high-quality masonry and concrete buildings reflective of Texas's vaunted prosperity.

Danny suddenly came to life. Turning, with a bland smile, he addressed Carlos and Jennifer in accent-free English: "We have booked you into a nearby Hyatt Regency for tonight. I will be your driver today and to the airport tomorrow."

"Well, thank you…uh, Danny," said Carlos.

Several minutes later, they arrived at a mission-style building whose sign read: Branson Robotic Laboratories.

Feng ushered them into an adobe-accented lobby and turned to speak, "Mr. Branson is out of town today. But in regards to projects with Ma, I am your man. By all means, ask questions, record and take notes as you wish."

"Thank you," said Carlos. "We appreciate your making all this available." With the Sony Camcorder slung over his shoulder, he began to compose and shoot, while switching on the audio recorder in his shirt pocket.

Feng and Danny escorted them into a room containing a large projection screen and an oval table with accompanying chairs, most of which were occupied. A dozen or so familiar-looking figures were sitting at the table. Jennifer recognized one from the online Branson video.

"Meet Dr. Einstein," said Feng. "We call him Albert."

As the robot's head swung toward the visitors, its eyes, brows, cheeks and mouth assumed a friendly, life-like expression. The resemblance to iconic photographs of Albert Einstein was uncanny, down to deep wrinkles, leathery skin, and mournful brown eyes.

"Hello, welcome to Branson Laboratories," said the robot in a German-accented baritone.

Feng spoke, "He realized you were visitors and made eye contact with you two only. His eyes are cameras that connect with face recognition software. We have integrated everything with memory, cognitive function and voice responses. Thank you, Albert." The robot resumed facing forward and relaxed its expression.

Feng gestured toward two adjacent empty seats at the table; the visitors seated themselves. Carlos and Jennifer looked around the table and recognized a veritable *who's who* of historical figures and celebrities.

"I'm sure you know, if only by reputation," continued Feng, "F.D.R., J.F.K., Churchill, Mao Zedong, Gandhi…"

"I see Clark Gable too," said Carlos, "and there's Marlene Dietrich and Greta Garbo sitting together. I didn't think they got along."

Feng laughed. "Oh, we could get some pretty spirited discussions here, especially with the likes of Kathryn Hepburn, Sarah Bernhardt, Rudolph Valentino, Elvis Presley, and Princess Diana, but robot Artificial Intelligence isn't advanced enough for that yet."

"So why this particular choice of characters?" asked Jennifer.

"Because each represents a certain type or quality. They were all the rage in their day, and still command attention today."

"Yes," said Jennifer, "In our work, we have considered various facial types, like power faces, pretty faces, friendly faces, and blends of those."

"Good examples. Speaking of blends, look at Princess Diana," said Feng. "She was a special blend of what you might call a power face combined with child-like innocence. Noble brow, eyes deep-set but roundish—like a child's."

Hearing its name, the Diana robot looked at them, smiled and spoke in the upper-class British voice that had enthralled millions: "Pleased to make your acquaintance."

"Unbelievable. What will these models be used for?" asked Carlos.

"To show clients the kinds of faces that telegraph leadership or power, beauty or innocence, intelligence, humor or compassion. Iconic faces like these are always in demand, whether they act on the world stage, the concert stage, or the silver screen,"

Feng lowered his voice ominously, "But there's another even more exciting potential; someday, the only evidence of today's history, outside of books, will be movies, video, and digitized recordings. But, recorded images can be doctored or synthesized—in other words, faked. Someone could make life-like robots of Hitler and his Nazi henchmen, and re-create documentaries with top-flight Hollywood production values—visual proof that Hitler was really misunderstood, and that reports of all the crimes he was accused of were lies. Fifty or more years later, the few eyewitnesses to what really happened might just be called old cranks with an axe to grind. How would the average person know the truth?"

"I agree!" said Jennifer, taking a breath. "I realize how images can be manipulated, for good or for ill purposes."

Danny edged toward them. He had lowered the hood of his sweat-shirt, revealing his full face. It reminded Jennifer of a Mongol warrior face from the Met Museum Chinese exhibit: massive cheekbones, protruding jaw, and deeply slit eyes—all exuding malice.

Feng continued, a hardness coming over his face. "Ma said one of your associates mentioned a CIA connection named Van, I believe. Was he interested in getting involved in our work?"

Looking disturbed, Carlos arose from the table. "That's something our group really hasn't decided to encourage." He brought his camera around to focus on Feng, and then Danny, who seemed camera-shy—dodging out of camera range and forcing a smile.

Hoping to diffuse the tension, Jennifer pointed towards the robots. "Uh…The movie queens here would be interesting to us… we may want to re-create them for modeling clothes, jewelry and such."

"Yes," said Feng, "let's change the subject. Here's Kathryn Hepburn. She's really very approachable, once you get past her hauteur and the steely-blue eyes. Hepburn really did have that ruddy, vibrant look for most of her life. According to our experts, her face is a mix of fierce determination, intelligence, and female vulnerability."

The Hepburn robot projected her well-known glacial stare, which quickly morphed into her equally familiar, incandescent smile. The New England twang seemed equally authentic: "Sometimes I wonder if men and women are really suited for one another. Perhaps they should just live next door and visit now and then."

Feng laughed. "That's one of her better-known quotes. Even today, Kate Hepburn could write her own script and draw a world-wide audience."

"This is all very entertaining and educational," said Carlos. "But, frankly, I don't quite get what images of robots can do that Ma's digital re-creations can't?"

"Good point," said Feng. "Two things: first, our robots' skin and underlying structure simulate real tissue and look more authentic than even the best digital video. And second, when fully functional with complete bodies through animatronics, as we've imagined, robots can actually go out and create live history, not just portray past history. You see?"

"Truly amazing, Feng," said Carlos, realizing that Harold had posited a similar idea about creating history during their games session in his uncle's house. "But I have to ask you outright…we may have our own reasons for contacting a CIA agent because of a personal connection, but why would you want such people to see your technology?"

Feng's smile faded. He glanced at Danny, who was looking at Carlos. "I was just trying to be accommodating since Ma said you folks brought it up in L.A., and you do again here. I got the feeling you felt safer with government protection. Believe me, that's not necessarily the case with us." He glanced again at Danny.

They burst out laughing at the apparent private joke.

"Oh, but…," said Jennifer insistently, "Our agreement with Ma does not require the participation of this CIA person. Honestly, I think, our partner, Dr. Wallach, was more interested in renewing his old acquaintance with this CIA man. They hadn't seen each other since foreign service school…"

"This Van," said Feng, thrusting his jaw forward. "I understand the CIA sometimes uses code names. Was that his real name or a code name? I'm just curious."

"I have no idea!" said Carlos, turning his back on Feng. He remembered something, grasped his cell phone from his pants' pocket hidden below the table, and probed for a button. The musical ring tone was clearly audible throughout the room. Excusing himself, Carlos stepped into an adjoining hallway.

A minute later, he returned to the room, and motioned Jennifer to follow him outside. "Excuse us, for a minute," he explained to his hosts. "We have a bit of an emergency back home."

Jennifer sprang up and followed him into a small, empty office. "What's up?"

"It's no emergency. It's me calling me—an old trick from West End Bar days. This place is, frankly, giving me the creeps. I'll tell them that something urgent has come up and we have to get the next flight home. We'll keep them posted. Ok?"

"I'm with you entirely," said Jennifer. "I've been getting bad vibes since the van ride over here. Great stuff they showed us, but they weren't doing any more than the usual tour anyway. Ma can help us tie up any loose ends. Or will he?"

"I don't know. I think this outfit must be legitimate. They've been too widely written up not to be. But something isn't right."

"I'll smooth things over," said Jennifer. "I suggest we keep everything non-confrontational with these guys. They may be playing mind games, but we don't have to over-react. I'm sorry I brought up the CIA, but maybe I felt the need to sort of warn these guys that we had powerful friends."

"That's Ok. They seemed to know all about it. As far as mind games, remember that dialogue at the wishing well in L.A. that Harold recorded with Ma? I got the same feeling of double talk from Feng. These guys must be masters at it. Give them no extra information, and keep smiling."

Back in the presentation room, their hosts were understanding and solicitous. Even Danny summoned up a warm smile. "Hope it's nothing too serious," he said. "I'll zip you back over to DFW. There are plenty of flights to New York. I'll cancel Hyatt Regency for you."

"Thank you," said Jennifer. "It's not a medical emergency or anything like that, but pressing business." Jennifer wondered if it sounded legitimate.

"It happens," said Feng. "Don't worry. You're working with Ma. That's almost like working directly with us. We will make all information available to you or to him that you need going forward. Stay in touch. Do you have a card?"

"Not yet. We'll call you. Ma is already working with Carlos's boss, that is, Harris, Pierson." *Oops,* thought Jennifer. *Unnecessary information. I'll have to watch that.*

For the next few minutes, Danny couldn't have been nicer to Carlos and Jennifer. He suggested they refresh themselves and take a bite to eat from the lunchroom; he brought back their bags from a locker while he went to check on plane schedules.

A smiling Feng shook hands good-bye, twenty minutes later. "Thanks for coming. Short trip but hopefully worthwhile."

"Absolutely," said Carlos. "And thank you, Feng. We'll be in touch."

They followed Danny who carried both their bags to the van.

XII.

Jennifer was dreading the ride back to the airport. Was Danny going to be the blank-faced mute they first met? Was he merely moody before? Would he challenge them about Van?

Once underway, Danny glanced back at both passengers and flashed a seemingly genuine smile. He drove smoothly and was taking what appeared to be the same roads back to the airport.

Carlos and Jennifer visibly relaxed. He held her hand. It felt cold and clammy. Within a minute or two, her grip loosened and felt warmer. Carlos made sure his audio recorder was on.

"No sweat," said Danny in a reassuring tone. "It's now twelve-thirty. You've got a shot at a two o'clock flight, but should certainly make the three. You folks from New York?"

Carlos answered, "Yes, or close to it. We work there. How about you?"

"My folks brought me here as a baby from Hong Kong. Spent some time in New York's Chinatown. Been there much?"

"No," said Carlos.

"Not much," said Jennifer, almost in unison.

"I guess the consensus is no." Danny laughed. "I get back there every so often. After school, I spent three years in the Marines, got special training and got to see some of the world."

"How did you happen to hookup with Branson robotics?" asked Jennifer.

"Answered an ad, sort of, through Chinese channels. Friends of mine knew Feng. They needed a driver and security man. I freelance around. I have the training."

"What sort of training might that be?" asked Carlos.

"Mainly martial arts, that sort of thing. Being bi-lingual is a plus. We are seeing many Chinese clients and Japanese. I also picked up some Japanese in the Marines."

"Really?" asked Carlos. "So, the Chinese are interested in robotics too. Doesn't surprise me. Would they be buying the technology? Or…"

"…or *borrowing* it?" Danny laughed. "You really mean stealing it."

"No…I mean,…" said Carlos.

"That's Ok. We're all Americans here. The Chinese steal or pirate as much stuff as they can. The rest they buy, as cheap as they can." He laughed.

"So how does Branson Robotics prevent people from stealing its technology, Danny?" asked Jennifer.

"That's where I come in. Certain visitors might think of stealing. But not if they read me well. They can tell that I read them well too. Others know me by reputation. Stealing doesn't happen when I'm around."

Several seconds passed, as Danny's words sank in. Jennifer felt her blood run cold again. Carlos couldn't think of anything to say. He looked at Danny's rear view mirror in order to see his face. Danny was smiling, but that fierce glint in his eyes had faded.

Carlos and Jennifer felt too unsettled to continue any conversation. Carlos worried about upcoming meetings with partners and whether arguments might ensue. Jennifer wondered if Danny was a freelancing x-factor beyond anyone's control, or if this was a deliberate sales technique of Branson, calculated to scare off potential bad guys.

Parting conversation with Danny was perfunctory, involving minimal eye contact. Once in the terminal, Carlos seemed to be stewing; Jennifer tried to appear calm, hoping to stifle her inner turmoil. They did make the two-o'clock plane back to LaGuardia. Short on sleep since the middle of last night, the couple felt fatigue pulling heavily on them.

Carlos exhaled a breath through pursed lips. "I needed to get us out of that freak show, and I don't mean the robots. It has been a freaky day in general, including our interview with the witch doctor from Haiti."

Jennifer nodded soberly. "Dr. Maupassant was a bit strange, although he might be a help in researching the psychology of faces. I don't get the Chinese being Ok with CIA participation, or is it just Van they want? And Feng says he is just "curious" about Van's code name?"

"I know," said Carlos. "What's that about? But then, Danny totally blows my mind. With him, they seem to be saying: beware, you better be careful dealing with us. It doesn't add up. I've got most of it on audio, some on video. We all need to talk."

Jennifer's smile seemed hopeful. "As bad as this sounds, let's not panic yet. Maybe we're overly suspicious. Maybe it's gamesmanship—the way certain Chinese negotiate. They like to get an edge, throw you off balance, and see how you react. All's fair in love, war and business. But let's see what positive things we *did* get out of this trip."

"Well, Ok," Carlos sounded wary. "I admit we did learn something about the power of faces. Voodoo faces, robot faces or 'hit man' faces... they all have power. Glamorous faces like Diana and Kate may move the heart in nicer ways, but the power of faces to seduce or scare people is even stronger."

Jennifer replied, "They say Helen of Troy's face launched a thousand ships. She must have been quite a looker."

Sleep came easily. They awoke two hours later as the airliner taxied into LaGuardia with winter darkness falling.

XIII.

Agent Green Dragon, in Dallas, spoke the Fukien dialect reserved for calls to Agent White Tiger in Los Angeles. "The New York visitors to Dallas were given a brief tour of the robots. They took videos and abruptly departed as if they were frightened by something." He snorted a laugh.

"Very good. The desired effect. What was discussed?"

"I will send you video. But, in summary, the bait to attract American agent Van was made very enticing. The robots showed potential for mass propaganda. And the entire presentation showed potential to fear the Chinese."

Both men cackled as if vanquishing a hated enemy.

"Anything else?" asked Agent White Tiger.

"The New York face readers have sent interesting data on face reading to the L.A. technician, which is in his possession. Soon he will have final product that Van will hopefully find irresistible, in event we don't get him in New York."

PART FIVE

NEW YORK CHINESE NEW YEAR

I.

Jennifer's same day text to partners was brief: "Things are too complicated for a conference call. Let's get together."

In the two days before they could meet, New York was blanketed by a ten-inch snowstorm and freezing cold. The trains were running and not much else. The group agreed to rendezvous at the New York 42nd Street Library. Harold had pre-booked a small group meeting room. They sat around a conference table large enough for six people.

Carlos had brought his Mac laptop—onto which had been loaded the Branson video and the audio recording from the Dallas trip. "Let us give you this chronologically, so you get the whole picture. We should title it Carlos and Jennifer meet witch-doctor and the hit-man—with apologies to Abbott and Costello."

"Sounds like you had a bang-up time," said Paul, with a soft chuckle.

"There was no banging," said Jennifer, "but plenty of mental violence. Bottom line though, it seems everybody in L.A., Dallas and Haiti wants to work with us. We'll give you the blow by blow."

Jennifer had brought the Jung textbook and enclosed article for reference. She related the plane incident, and read pertinent passages from the written materials. "Too bad we couldn't have videoed the Haitian witch-doctor, as Carlos calls him. Actually, he was very nice."

"Nicer than I was, in the beginning," said Carlos. "The guy is eavesdropping and suddenly breaks into our conversation. Imagine Harry Belafonte in a Saville Row suit and dark sunglasses. Then he blows us away with Carl Jung and voodoo…whips off the shades, and underneath are baby blue eyes…"

"…With a voice as sweet and mellow as sugarcane honey," added Jennifer.

"He says he is living proof of the *bridging of opposites*," continued Carlos. "Basically, he explodes all your notions about faces and races." Carlos played the five-minute airplane conversation he had audio-recorded surreptitiously.

"So," commented Harold, as the audio ended, "he invites you to attend his lecture, visit his website—and maybe work with him in the future? Voodoo might be another example of the power of faces to work for evil, as well as for good, but why does everybody want to get in on our act?"

"Maybe we're getting too popular for our own good," said Trish.

"Exactly my point, Trish," said Carlos. "I picked up on your remark about Ma being so willing to show our work to the CIA, and, as it turns out, Feng sings the same tune. But, he insists that *we* brought it up." Carlos then played the Branson video and the audio recording.

Everyone agreed: the most arresting moments, including meeting the robots, belonged to Danny, the hit man.

"Ok," said Paul. "I think I get it. The deeper message coming out of Dallas and Los Angeles was not about the robots, or the Agora Dome. I think these Chinese gentlemen are trying to tell you they are serious players—not to be trifled with, and not intimidated by the CIA. Remember, they are business associates, not friends."

Harold looked hopeful. "Maybe they think, like you, Uncle Paul, that interest by the Feds means we're ahead of the curve in face reading and also in re-creation. Maybe that's why they want to entice CIA with this *other technology*—something really advanced and sexy, like humanoid robots."

Maybe that's wishful thinking, thought Trish.

"I'm not sure," replied Paul. "Right now, our most-trusted consultant is Charles Wu, a friend—and our best bet to contact Van Lear. I think we should show Charles Wu the Branson video and audio."

"Why not bring him up-to-date?" said Carlos. "I believe we've sent everything we have to Ma; aren't we just waiting for him to come up with the master software package? Should anything else be included?"

"Oh yes. I did hear back from Hoda," said Trish. "She said her uncle in Cairo sent her some ancient Egyptian info about the Eye of Horus, which could be useful, but she's not at liberty to discuss yet. She says she'll divulge it when the time is ripe."

"Ah, mysteries from the tombs of the Pharaohs," said Paul.

"She also asked," said Trish, "to be included in any field trips we take in the vicinity, and I don't see why not; she can be trusted not to blab or interfere unduly."

"She'd be a welcome addition. That reminds me," said Harold. "In two weeks, Chinese New Year celebrations start in Chinatown. There's the parade, martial arts exhibitions—we missed them in L.A.—and I've wanted to visit CAM, the Chinese American Museum. How can we overlook CAM if this is about Chinese face reading? I've been hesitant about going down there since that subway murder, last month, but I think it's safe for us now."

"I'm not scared," said Trish. "It could be a fun outing. We could ask Hoda if she wants to join us. She could be our guide and our in at the museum. She knows people there."

"I wonder," said Harold, "if they're skittish about discussing the murder of a fellow worker. We should let them know we're in solidarity with them."

"OK, said Jennifer. "But let's update Ma immediately...and not convey any of our misgivings to him. Tell him we are keeping our consultant, Mr. Wu, fully informed on all developments and tell him we are going to Chinatown, New York for further research. Don't mention the CIA to Ma. He can draw his own conclusions. Don't bring it up unless he does."

"Good thinking, Jen," said Paul. "Agreement or no agreement, I'm not sure we can trust him one-hundred-percent—yet. Let him worry a little bit about powerful friends we might have on our side."

"Right," said Trish. "We can play mind games too, and our cards close to the chest. Wait for his next move. Mirror that smile right back at him, and keep him guessing."

"I agree," said Harold. "After we visit Chinatown in two weeks, if we haven't heard from Ma, we'll ask him for a progress report. We might get his take on the Dallas visit."

"I'll call Hoda," said Trish, "and set up the day—see if it works for her."

Carlos was surfing the Internet for information on Chinatown New Year's events. "Here it is. February fifth...that's a Sunday. The parade starts at 11:30 a.m., with floats, dragon dances, bands...and martial arts.

I wonder what time the CAM museum opens?" He clicked on the CAM website. "It opens at 10:00 a.m. We can go there first, and then to the parade, without killing the whole day."

***

Trish called Hoda at the Met the day after the team decided on their Chinatown visit. She invited her to participate in the CAM visit and the Chinese New Year parade. Hoda volunteered to help set up a private tour of the museum; she'd get back to Trish to confirm.

II.

The following day, the group updated Ma and Charles Wu on the Dallas trip; it was assumed that Feng had made his own report to Ma.

That same day, Charles Wu reached Vandersloot Lear via their coded e-mail. The message stated: "Call me ASAP on secure telephone line."

One hour later, Wu's ringtone sounded four times; he pressed the tone button twice, as agreed. "Hello, Van. I understand your reluctance to get involved with Paul Wallach, but I think you should be aware of some new developments."

"Ok, but I don't like his trying to play *Secret Agent Man*. I gathered this project was really about lonely hearts and matchmaking; I still don't see the large-scale applicability to intelligence."

"Wallach apparently believes that the MSS might use scanning lenses to monitor the physical and psychological health of the American 'enemy'. This is supposedly based on Chinese face reading. He says, if we're slipping, our faces will look sicker and more stressed-out to their spying eyes."

"Charles, nothing against classical Chinese, but I think face reading is a fairy tale—the stuff of mediums and the occult. For one thing, it tries to combine mythology with hard science."

"Admittedly a tall order, Van, though I confess, I encouraged him by finding Five Element commonalities between *Mian Xiang* and *I Ching*, plus Chinese facial archetypes that correspond with Jungian ones."

"I know Jung admired the Chinese. To believe your premise, I'd have to believe that the Chinese returned the favor. I'm still not convinced. I have authorized surveillance on these Chinese technicians in L.A. and Dallas, as I told you, but that has to do with the subway murder, not face reading."

"I understand, Van, but what I thought you should know is this: these Chinese software technicians seem to be experts in cinematic face-recreation, and in humanoid robots. They've told Paul they believe synthetic faces can be used to propagandize and influence mass audiences …maybe even change history by replacing old documentaries with new, fake ones. I think it's plausible and possibly valuable."

"*That's* interesting."

"But I've saved the most interesting for last."

"Charles, I do love your sense of the dramatic."

Wu laughed. "I know you like to live on the edge, Van. It seems these Chinese technicians are not only willing to share information with U.S. Government operatives, but are curious to know whether Van is your real, or code name. Also, one of them, a security man named Danny, brags about being a hit man of sorts from Chinatown, New York. I have videos of two of them, and an audio of a third. Perhaps you'd want to see those?"

"Ok, I'll bite," said Van. "Or just nibble. None of these tidbits, alone, is conclusive, but add them up with my own satellite surveillance and there might be something there. Please forward by the usual mode; it's hack proof—we think."

"It should be, Van. As you probably know, Ma, the cinema tech, is affiliated with SCU's image re-creation lab. Feng-Tzu-Wo works for Branson Robotics in Dallas. The video of his driver, Danny, is self-explanatory. According to Wallach's team, Danny claims to be a martial artist. Also, Wallach passed along that he and his team are planning a trip to Chinatown during Chinese New Year on Sunday, February fifth. Maybe, in telling me all of this, he's still trying to draw you out."

"Possibly, Charles. There is an outside chance that these Chinese in L.A. or Dallas are connected to the subway murder. Their curiosity about me may be a clue. My contact at the Fifth Precinct—lieutenant Juen—wants to use a double of me to draw out Mary's assassin and/or possible cohorts. Whoever it was that hacked her files probably got my name. I'm considering Juen's offer. The double—also a cop—could act as bait. He could also provide security for Wallach's team, in case whoever wants me might harm Wallach or derail his project."

"Why would they want to do that?"

"If they are MSS agents, maybe they've already gotten all they need from Wallach and would just as soon see him and his project disappear—especially if it meant denying valuable technology to our side."

"I thought you said you didn't believe in this stuff."

"I'm not sure I do, but if I can believe that *they* believe in it, I might want to disrupt what they're doing until I can check it out with your help, Charles, and some from our own technicians. We're continuing our satellite surveillance on L.A. and Dallas,, but what I can do directly is limited without the help of my FBI liaison. He'll probably need to be involved."

Charles Wu now believed Van was beginning to take the face reading group's ideas more seriously, even though Van still ridiculed Paul Wallach's wanting to play spy. Wu remembered Van's stubborn streak from student days; that he tended to reject other's advice or conclusions until he proved something to his own satisfaction, or bent them to his way of doing things. Wu had to admit, that back in '99, Van had rejected his unit members' (and Wu's) advice to throw the Chinese agent Fong back to his handlers for termination. Van insisted that he could be turned to the Americans' advantage—a position that, fortunately for Van, was ultimately vindicated.

The possible propaganda value of digital re-creation had seemingly impressed Van. But, to be fair, Wu himself was not yet convinced that any spy services could implement Chinese-based face reading. (The Chinese themselves apparently hadn't produced anything like it.) He also wasn't sure that any of the current players could be linked to the subway murder or to possible attempts against Van. But he did know that Van wouldn't move decisively until he drew his own conclusions without being led or pressed. Wu had a plan now and Ma was the key.

III.

Two days later, Agent Vandersloot Lear met Professor Charles Wu for a light lunch in the Ivy Lounge of Columbia University's Faculty House. From a window table overlooking the monumental stone buildings comprising the East Campus, they reminisced about student days and inquired about families in Princeton and Taipei.

Van took a desultory sip of his white Merlot and pushed it away as if punctuating the end of small talk. "Charles, here's the latest on our people of interest in L.A. and Dallas. Satellite shows nothing suspicious about this Ma. Comings and goings are all apparently legitimate and business-related, and what lip reading we have confirms that. The two Chinese in Dallas speak together with their hands over their mouths. Nothing for sure there, although they may suspect surveillance."

Wu finished chewing a last mouthful of arugula, brown rice and beet salad. "Maybe they are experienced operatives. Anything else?"

"We're definitely setting up this double for me at Chinese New Year's. He doesn't look that much like me facially, but he's the same, lanky six-foot-six—a detective from the Midtown South Precinct that Juen found. He'll do the trench coat and fedora bit I'm known for in China-town and we'll put the word out that Van's around. Also, big crowds draw the bad guys. The double will shadow the Wallach team, and Fifth Precinct detectives will be right there, along with my FBI man."

"What if Wallach guesses that this cop is supposed to be you, and yet he knows the cop isn't you?" Wu's kindly expression became tinged with alarm.

"Tell you what Charles, maybe we should let Wallach in on this, at the outset. Tell him to play along. His team should be happy they're getting security, and Wallach should be happy we're paying all this attention to him. Call him. Find out when and where they're all meeting in Chinatown and tell him to expect company."

"I will. I see where you're going with this. If the Wallach team's ideas have merit and the Chinese are interested, you can still monitor events and keep your distance. I remain the go-between."

"That's it. Meanwhile, I'd be in touch with the FBI guy and the double on a secure line."

"I suppose I'll hear about it from both you and Paul Wallach," said Wu with a self-congratulatory smile.

"Yes, Charles, but if something big goes down and gets into the papers, it won't be me you read about."

***

Back in his campus office, Charles Wu was pleased that Van was getting increasingly involved without any arm-twisting. True, the subway murder was the main thing driving Van—to pursue leads in Chinatown and use himself (or his double) as bait. But how that affected the face-reading group, Ma and all his doings in L.A., remained to be seen.

IV.

The day after their 42nd Street Library meeting, Trish texted everybody that Hoda would be coming to Chinatown New Year's, and had arranged an insiders' visit to CAM, starting at 10 a.m., February fifth, thirty minutes before the doors opened to the general public.

Harold was happy to hear that, but for him, the hectic weeks spent researching faces and finding a Chinese technician had given way to anxious waiting and worrying. Could Ma complete the project in a reasonable time? Would shadowy figures like Van and the hit man impact events? Would things continue to go smoothly with the faces team? At least, he was not afraid to show his face in Chinatown. This long-delayed trip to CAM may or may not be useful for the face-reading project, but it represented another leg up that mountain to manhood that he still had to climb.

Two days later, while working on his face recognition article for Fortune-Estes, Harold made a disturbing discovery. Faces were being analyzed by U.S. government agencies using geometric lines that reminded him of the grids from Ma's Agora Dome demonstration and Dr. Quadrano's Esthetic Mask. This seemed to be a new program developed for face recognition based on biometrics and an analysis of the unique surface texture of skin. *My God—this sounds like Chinese Medicine facial diagnosis that we're working on with Ma. Are we behind the curve, and not ahead of it?*

His phone rang. It was his Uncle Paul. "Harold, I've got interesting news.

"So have I, Uncle Paul; we may have a problem."

"How do you mean?"

"The U.S. National Science and Technology Council—this is cabinet level—has a software program that analyzes skin texture for purposes of face recognition."

"So?"

"It sounds like very much like the Chinese Medicine analysis we're doing with Ma. They look at lines, pores, and consistency of skin."

"Not so fast, Harold. We've got at least two degrees of separation from them. One, we're doing virtual medical diagnosis and prognosis, versus their face recognition for security purposes. And two, we're doing shapes and sizes of features that mirror personality profiles. That second one is too hocus-pocus for those national science types."

"But I thought you really believed in this stuff, Uncle Paul."

"I believe in it because I have an almost religious faith in the Chinese to have gotten it right. So far, our theories are just that. Nothing's been proved. Unless your Chinese techies are really CIA or FBI agents, I wouldn't worry about our government coming up with this first—if Van's lack of interest is any indication. Except, something else has come up."

"Yeah, what's your interesting news?"

"Van wants in"

"What?"

"At least partially—and on his terms. Charles Wu is the intermediary and has forwarded all our research, the audio and videos, to Van. Charles didn't say Van now believes in our face reading work; rather, it's about the Dallas hit man who could be involved in the subway murder, and also about the Chinese techs' interest in Van and his code name.

Possibly this means that Van is currently operating against the Chinese...maybe even investigating the subway murder, along with the FBI and the police. So, I guess, based on the chance that the Chinese or local gangs might be threatening, we're getting some police protection for our Chinatown trip."

"Is Van going to show?"

"Like I said, on his terms. There's going to be a double for Van. A big, older cop that looks enough like him. According to Charles, Van was a well-known figure on Chinatown streets when the police and Feds cracked down on the gangs a few years ago. It looks like they're using him as bait, like we're doing, in a way."

"And we're caught in between."

"Well, they thought that if there was a chance bad guys were targeting us, we'd better have police protection."

"I guess that's a good idea with any large crowd. If something does happen, Uncle Paul, it's your chance to play the role with Van again, or at least his double," Harold sniggered.

"Not really. That's what the cops are for. Anyway, aren't you the Kung Fu Black Belt?"

"Strictly for sport, and besides I'm out of shape," said Harold. "In any martial arts exhibition, I'll just be watching," He thought, *So, Van seems to be hot on the trail of the subway murderer (like I fancied myself to be in Flushing). And ground zero could be the CAM museum. I might find myself confronting gangsters. Am I ready for this?*

V.

For the next two weeks, all members of the team stayed busy with regular work, having sent Ma all their research. Then, during the fourth week in January, Ma e-mailed a specially encoded message reporting major steps taken and the basic concepts involved: the scanning of facial shape and structure from thousands of publicity headshots and movie outtakes enabled his team of cinema archivists to match images to the known attributes of each actor compiled from various biographies.

To the categories of Power, Beauty, Intelligent and Happy faces, he added subtypes: under Power faces were Fierce, Strong, and Determined or Steadfast; Beautiful faces broke down into Innocent or Angelic, Glamorous or Handsome, and Alluring types; Intelligent faces to Competent, Cultured, or Sensitive; Happy included Joyful, Compassionate, Contented and Serene faces.

Such symbolic faces that reflect the general population, he explained, could be influencing factors in perception and subsequent personality development when observed by others and mirrored back to the individual, in this way creating "self-fulfilling prophecies."

Blends of these categories, producing average or composite faces, were constructed with matrix overlays. The sheer numbers read by the scanner yielded trends and tendencies that overcame individual inconsistencies or the possibility of error. Its high-resolution capabilities had also been enhanced by 3-D body scanning and ultrasonic technology, which recorded tissue texture and depth with exquisite precision—accurately corresponding to Chinese Medicine descriptions of physical condition and health status. Thus, the program innovatively read both facial shape and texture (symbolically and intrinsically) much like the human brain would do.

Using headshots of animals, he had incorporated matrices of their features that corresponded to and suggested human categories, for example: power or predatory animals to power humans, prey animals to more passive humans. (Useful because peoples' biases about "animal" features probably colored their perceptions.)

Facial shapes, of course, only suggested traits; necessary keys to reaction were the impressions and perceptions of the app's operator whose own face was being read. All of the various facial shapes could be integrated using an imaging process called "superposing"

Anyone using the app could submit their own face and a number of others. The program would rate compatibility based on one's live reaction to different expressions and facial types suggesting certain traits, but also factoring in different skin textures that reflected health or disease, such as stress and inflammation. The program's accuracy in reading live expression would be enhanced by correlating findings with those of police detectives experienced in spotting fear, stress, deceit and guilt in strangers or suspects.

Facial expressions could range from positive: friendly or amorous, joyful and peaceful to negative: angry, sad, fearful, scowling or sneering; any habitual expressions would leave indelible, telltale lines. Incongruous or repeated extreme expressions and atypical eye movements caught in the 5-second video could signal mental or personality disorders.

Ma had also factored in peoples' posture and voice type—recordable within twenty-five feet; deeper or resonant voices tended to command more respect.

The great advance over other programs was that working live it would enable the real-time reading of both expression and reaction, as well as how well faces mirror and interact with each other, thus truly incorporating personality into what would otherwise be a static appraisal of form or shape. Ma's final task would be writing the programs in code language, and electromagnetic imprinting.

(Facial recognition had been built only into the program's own database of faces but could be coupled into external data sources such as official ones if authorized by them.)

As to marketing, Ma thought these basic facial types (plus their blends into average faces) should be useful to people seeking mates, bosses seeking employees, doctors, or anyone surveying masses of people. He still needed a unifying concept to rate the different levels of compatibility, but expected to find one in time for the presentation.

As for input from Branson Robotics, Jennifer told the group she assumed Ma had access to whatever was needed or valuable from them. Paul was anxious to forward news of all this progress to Charles Wu for his opinion, and perhaps Van's.

Harold was experiencing some mild insomnia, worrying that Ma's genius was overshadowing his own "meager" contribution to the project. He had been astounded by the sheer volume and detail that Ma had entrusted to them. Did this mean that Ma was entirely trustworthy, after all? But then he realized the app was probably useless without Ma's programmer's codes and exact implementation. Also, fears about his romantic aspirations toward Trish kept surfacing.

He still saw himself as a self-doubting bumbler who could never gain the respect of a confident, tough-minded woman like Trish. He had taken more initiative early on in the face reading project. But he needed to clearly regain the role of leader that was naturally his with his advanced knowledge of science and marketing.

What was that unifying concept he had scribbled down? Based on the stress or confidence levels shown in the face and voice, can compatibility be assessed, say, between similar types? What about some conflict, for instance, between people who are basically honest versus those who are basically deceitful—or between courageous types versus timid types? Theoretically, you could even get high compatibility between two criminal types. There had to be room for natural confusion: a mix of positive and negative. Most people probably exhibited a mixture of traits and would not give clear-cut readings.

What's more, erroneous first impressions that powerfully affected perception were difficult, if not impossible, to overcome—necessitating multiple exposures or videos lasting several seconds! Hopefully Ma's sensors would be sensitive enough to pick it all up from complex skin tone readings and varying facial expressions within that time period.

Connection, Conflict, and Confusion—the alliteration of C's worked for marketing, but would all this lend itself to Ma's algorithms? Harold decided to e-mail his idea to Ma and get his reaction. Meanwhile, he had better tell the group about Van.

The next day, after e-mailing Ma, Harold called Trish with the news—electrifying to her—that Van's men would be escorting them around Chinatown. Trish had always seen Van's involvement as an unnecessary complication, but she could hardly say no.

Hoda then called to say that Dorothy Wong, her contact at CAM, had accepted police protection from a Lieutenant Juen, whom she knew, in case Mary Shun's murderer was still around.

VI.

Harold sensed he was navigating better through the stream of life. There were more encouraging signs: Ma had responded positively to his three C's concept for the face reading app saying he thought they helped tie things together nicely; then, the first week in February, he received kudos, a nice raise and the promise of a shared by-line when *Scientific Nation Magazine* opted to expand on his *Prosopagnosia and Autism* article. He had cleverly included a few hints about the "burgeoning field of scientific face reading". The marketing he had learned at Harris, Pearson—planting little seeds—became useful, after all, for promoting *Read My Face*, the group's new cell phone app. Harold had come up with the name; it had been approved by the group and duly registered in the patent office by Trish. They were all on the verge of an enterprise that could fundamentally transform their lives, especially his.

There were still some loose ends to clear up with Carlos. Harold texted him and arranged to visit that evening in Weehawken. After taking the ferry from 39th Street to Port Imperial, he hurriedly scaled the steep Palisade steps to Boulevard East, where Carlos's turreted townhouse offered a commanding view of the jeweled city across the river.

Still panting slightly, Harold braced himself as the door opened. "Carlos, I've got some things to get off my chest, before we embark on this grand adventure of ours."

"Funny—I had the same feeling." Carlos put his arm around Harold and led him through the entryway into the large, ultra-modern living room.

"You did? Tell me, have I been getting on your nerves?"

"No more than usual," said Carlos, with a knowing smile.

"I know...I'm always so serious." He stood stiffly facing Carlos. "But I do want to apologize to you for acting like a sore loser after the

Harris, Pierson episode, and then resenting your attention to Jennifer. I was afraid of your showing me up again in business and then with the ladies —not intentionally on your part, I realize—but it must have been obvious I was doing a slow burn—jealous as usual." Harold flopped down on one of Carlos's twin, plushy recliners.

"No apology necessary. In fact, I might owe you one." Carlos seated himself in the companion chair and leaned earnestly toward Harold. "I was aware of your feelings, but in a way, you were more honest about them than I was about mine."

"Really? In what way?"

"Harold, I know you thought my writing was creative and you helped promote me. You probably thought I was a smooth operator with women or something. And you always told me you didn't know who you were: the puppet on your parents' strings. Well, guess what? I am the smooth Mr. Cool who fools everybody. I may be a good actor, but you're the one I admire because you're sincere—maybe awkward at times, but sincere."

Harold laughed in disbelief. "How do you *mean*?"

"You may not know who you are, but you don't pretend to be someone you are not. The truth is, I'm really confused about who I am but I'm stuck in a masquerade—speaking of faces—and I'm afraid of what might be behind the mask. That voodoo doctor on the plane had my number. I'm just afraid that everybody may have expectations of me that I may not meet, and that could blow up this whole project. And I wouldn't want to ruin everything, especially for you. You and Trish really seem to be hitting it off."

"My god, what are you saying? You want out?" Harold looked stricken.

"I'm saying that, right now, while I am committed to the project, I'm not prepared to commit to Jen or to any other woman."

"Gosh, Carlos, I never thought that we had to wind up as a romantic foursome. You seemed to be taking everything with Jen in stride. I haven't seen any P.D.A.'s...or, for that matter, any tension between you either. I do admit it'd be icing on the cake for things to work out for Trish and me, but that's secondary to the success of the project. You needn't feel responsible for that."

"You're right. You see, Harold—you're the healthy one, and I'm the one confused and feeling pressure."

"Well!" Harold's jaw dropped. "You could knock me over with a feather. Don't get the wrong idea, Carlos, but I love you like a brother."

"I get the right idea bro' and I love you too. Don't forget it."

Both got up as if on signal, and stepping forward on the dark oak floor, clasped each other in a comradely embrace.

"Hey, why don't I brew a quick pot of Bustelo?" said Carlos, smiling broadly.

"Beats booze…but you'll have to scrape me off the ceiling."

They laughed like old times.

VII.

A few days later—February fifth—Harold awoke in the early dawn to the flickering of snowflakes illuminated by streetlights outside his bedroom window. *Oh damn, not snow!* He clicked on the T.V. weather for the forecast: cloudy with flurries; little or no accumulation expected...*shouldn't hold things up.*

Every member of the team was on their own to get to the CAM museum, but Jennifer had stayed over at Trish's so that they could travel together. During their taxi ride, they discussed what had been a non-subject between them for weeks: their "dating" of Harold and Carlos. Trish said, "Harold calls just to chat, he says, and he keeps it light and fun—no pressure, no problem. What about the Latin lover?"

"I think he lost my number," joked Jennifer. "But really, Carlos is an angel. He makes no moves and acts more like a brother to me, which is just as well because that is what seems to be developing. I think I've got a better shot at Harold." Jennifer intended her scoff of a laugh to mean she wasn't serious.

"You do? Since when?" Trish's eyes shot sparks.

"Ouch! Did somebody a hit a raw nerve? Look, Trish I've deferred to you on Harold from day one. But tell me true, are you really interested in him, or only because you thought I might be."

"Now you *have* hit a raw nerve", said Trish. "I guess I do have a soft spot for Harold; he's really been growing on me."

"I think he's a terrific guy, but unless you're serious, do me a favor: don't lead him on or play with him."

"I will promise you that."

"Good; let's leave it at that," said Jennifer. Finally, she had gotten in the last word.

Harold took the Q train and exited from the Canal Street Station where Mary Shun had been murdered—without trepidation, he noted coolly. It was 9:15 a.m.; the street was packed, mainly with East Asian people. Some were dressed in matching sweaters, jackets, caps or head-bands of various colors bearing the names of Chinese Benevolent and Youth Associations. A few young men carried batons that reminded Harold of martial arts fighting sticks; one youth with a warrior-like face explained that they were used for crowd control.

Harold encountered people costumed as rabbits, unicorns, lions and dragons. Band members blared horns, banged on drums and tinkled glockenspiels. "Safe" firecrackers shot red confetti upward that mingled with the white snowflakes spewing from an ashen sky. Some people waved multi-colored streamers; others played with stick-and string puppets. Pedestrians confined by snow banks could walk only two or three abreast. Imagining himself Jim Brown, the immortal NFL running back, Harold cradled his shoulder bag with both hands as if it were a football, and maneuvered his way through the dense crowd.

Two blocks east, then another two blocks north, he met up with Trish and the others waiting outside the large front windows of the CAM museum. All were wearing thick winter coats, but were hatless, except for Hoda who wore a headscarf. Even in flat walking shoes, Hoda was the tallest of the group.

Introducing her to Paul and Carlos, Trish and Jennifer noted the usual male reactions, smiled, and exchanged "Here we go again" looks. They complimented Hoda on her headscarf made of spun gold that they hadn't seen before. (Hidden underneath was an eye mask that she had received from Cairo only a few days ago.) The time was now 9:30 a.m.; the glass front door was being unlocked from the other side.

A small, pony-tailed Chinese woman stepped forward, raising her arms in greeting. "Hello, I'm Dorothy. Welcome, Hoda to you and your group."

Following introductions, she led them past displays and down a staircase to an office with a glass wall —through which they beheld an intimidating spectacle: uniformed police officers and tough-looking men in suits; one, very tall, and dressed in a trench coat with a fedora, towered above the others.

Once they were all inside the office, Dorothy nodded toward an officer with gold braid on his cap. "This is Lieutenant Juen. We've been getting acquainted."

Smiling, Lieutenant Juen shook hands all around for the introductions; the other men merely nodded. "Let me assure you," Juen said, "we have no reason to believe you or museum personnel are in any danger. We're always fully mobilized for New Years celebrations. Now, do any of you have any fears or concerns?"

A few seconds passed. "No, not really", said Paul Wallach. Juen's open-ended question had offered a chance to ask about threats to the faces group, but he wondered if the Lieutenant was really asking if *the group* knew anything.

"Good," continued Juen. "It is doubtful that Mary Shun's murderer has designs on you or your people. Dorothy has asked her staff to report any sign of trouble—even threatening looks from anyone. But we're always on the lookout for gangs or any other criminal activity, especially during holidays."

Trish was having trouble believing Juen's story that this "protection" was just routine. *I guess, it's to keep us all from getting apprehensive. Dorothy looks calm and so does Hoda, bless her. Harold looks slightly anxious, but that's normal for him.*

"We promise not to hang over your shoulder." The rumbling bass voice came from the tall plainclothes officer. He smiled. "We'll keep our distance. As the lieutenant said, we have to keep an eye on everybody. There'll be other officers, too, but it's just as well you don't know who they are. We'll be here if you need us."

"Act normally," said Lieutenant Juen. "Go about your business, and we'll go about ours. The place is all yours for about another twenty minutes, but let us know when you are ready to leave."

Ascending the stairs, Carlos whispered to Jennifer. "Where were these guys when we needed them—in Dallas?"

She stifled a giggle.

Harold was already engrossed in the displays. One chronicled an 1880s massacre of Chinese laborers in Wyoming "who had fled without resistance like antelope." Another showed a "Yellow Face" vaudeville act featuring garishly pigmented make-up, phony accents, and "The Heathen Chinee," which denigrated Chinese speech and behavior. Harold thought, *if I were Chinese, I'd have a major gripe. Hmm! I do anyway.*

Moments later, Paul showed Harold a display of the Exclusion Act of 1882 that singled out Chinese for ID cards, restrictive work rules, and summary expulsion. Included was the report of an American official, at the time, declaring that the act would 'absolutely destroy our growing commerce with China.' "That's ironic," said Paul, "in view of current events."

Harold grunted in agreement.

They noted examples of racist stereotyping where Chinese movie villains were contrasted with "good" Chinese. A large gallery of faces showed Chinese-Americans who had overcome discrimination to become aviators, scientists, politicians, and creative artists—even a local policewoman.

There were no restrictions on taking photos of any of the graphic displays or printed narratives that accompanied them. Harold shot pictures continuously. He said to Paul, "we can just skim the narratives now and read them in detail in the photos at our leisure." Within fifteen to twenty minutes, circling around, the group had surveyed almost the entire small museum.

At 10 a.m.; the front doors were opened, and a crowd that had gathered outside poured in.

Paul pulled Harold and Carlos aside. "I don't know whether we should stay close to the Van double for protection or avoid him because he's a lightning rod."

"I'd feel safer keeping him in my peripheral vision" said Harold.

"In a large room, he'd be hard to miss," offered Carlos. "But there are too many corners to see around here."

"What's this—men only?" cracked Trish, with Jennifer and Hoda close by. "The cops said not to leave without telling them. But where are they?"

"Let me find Dorothy," said Hoda. "Maybe she knows something."

"Let's not separate, at this point," said Jennifer.

"I'll call her," said Hoda. Several seconds went by. "No answer."

"Maybe," said Harold, "the cops are by the lobby windows, looking for gangsters, outside and inside."

The group followed each other around to the lobby but failed to see the officers. They headed toward a sign that said "Chinese Puzzles", which led to a large room that was crowded but navigable. They saw the tall plainclothes man and Lieutenant Juen along with two other officers they recognized—all in animated conversation.

"Hey, if they're all here, who's minding the store?" said Trish.

"I don't know police work," said Carlos, "but you'd think they'd spread out."

"We should let them see us," said Paul. "Let's get closer."

The tall plainclothes man was laughing about something the lieutenant had said when he saw Harold's group approach. He waved them over and addressed Paul, "Best not to stand right on top of us either, but now that you're here…"

"Why, is something happening?" asked Harold. Scanning the crowd, he observed several people looking in their direction--overlooking, among them, a pair of East Asian men who were comparing photographs: one taken from a security camera loop, the other from a 1999 Columbia College yearbook.

"Things are not always what they seem," said the tall plainclothesman. "Like the lieutenant is showing me an example with this…what is it called?"

"Tangram Puzzle" said Lieutenant Juen, smiling. "Illusions play tricks on the mind."

"What do you mean, things are not as they seem?" insisted Carlos.

"For instance," said the Lieutenant, "you might think, our standing here attracts attention to us. But we have men moving around, watching people's faces and their actions. And others are watching you. So, don't worry; it's doubtful that people would act badly here—it's too easy to trap them indoors."

"And yet you say," began Paul, "there are no credible threats against us, that you know of?"

"I will say," continued Lieutenant Juen, snuffling a soft laugh, "that the longer you hang with us, the greater likelihood you'll see action, if there is any."

"In other words, you could be bait as well as deterrent for that kind of action?" asked Paul.

"Some gangs like to challenge us in a game of cat and mouse," said Juen. "They think they can make us run like the Keystone Cops, but we know how to play the game too."

"Well, we're amateurs who depend on you pros for safety; so what's our safest route to the parade after this?

"Your safest route would be to head toward Mott Street, near the Fifth Precinct Police Station," said the lieutenant. "We'll be no more than half a block behind. Several parades form up around there; you'll see lots of celebration action, for sure." Juen nodded to someone across the room.

Paul beckoned the group, raising an upturned palm. "Has everybody seen everything here they need to see?"

"I believe so," said Harold. "Chinese facial images that correspond to roles; certainly evidence of anti-Chinese discrimination. Nothing on face reading itself, but we can forward our photos to Ma anyway."

Hoda went to Dorothy's office to say goodbye and returned a minute later. "I decided not to tell her police would be following us. I wouldn't want her to worry."

The group turned right out the door toward Canal Street; Paul waved them into another huddle in a closed store entranceway. "It's funny; we know this Van double is bait; the cops know we know. But somehow, everybody's pretending these are routine precautions against gang violence."

"You must admit, Paul," said Carlos, "they did clue us in on their street tactics, although that conversation in the puzzle room reminded me of Chinese double talk, just like in L.A. and Dallas."

Harold said, "I guess if you're a cop trying to give meddling civilians like us only minimum information, it's going to sound vague and ambiguous."

"Vague and ambiguous says it precisely," said Trish.

"What are we supposed to be meddling in?" asked Hoda.

"Well, Hoda," said Paul, "we've only given you minimum information. You know this Van double is supposed to be bait for gangsters who might have killed Mary Shun. What we haven't told you is that we might be bait too, if our face reading project is of interest to Chinese intelligence and therefore has national security implications."

"Really?" exclaimed Hoda, her already large, black eyes widening.

"Actually," said Harold, "We were originally trying to reach Van ourselves to ask if he thought the project had potential for espionage enough to interest our government or the Reds—not that such was our intention for it."

"So, we'd be bait for Chinese intelligence?" asked Hoda.

"Only if they heard about it" said Harold, "or thought Van was part of our project. And maybe if the gang murderer was tied to Chinese agents spying on us. That might mean... oh, never mind."

"What?" said Jennifer.

"Well," said Harold, "it's possible, but hard to believe...that the Chinese technicians...that Ma is a Chinese agent. But why would he target us after he's worked with us and given us the best of his thinking and technology?"

"By now, he's got all the information and the technology he needs," said Trish. "Like I said before—why does he still need us?"

"Right," said Paul. "So maybe after getting everything they can from us, we're dispensable if we're the key to Van and they get him—if that's their game. Listen, Hoda, maybe this is a little too hairy for you. Why don't we just find you a cab..."?

"Oh, no. I'm in—wouldn't miss this for the world."

"You know," said Harold, "I still find it hard to believe that about Ma. Wouldn't he have been vetted through U. of S.C.?"

"You'd like to think so," replied Paul. "Van claims, through Charles, to be acting as bait to trap Mary Shun's killer, and that he's not particularly interested in our project. But maybe he knows something about Ma and his buddy in Dallas?"

"And we're the bait too," said Jennifer.

"I think we should play it out," said Harold.

"If something is happening, like soon, we might have an answer right here in Chinatown, and you'll never have more police protection than you do right now." Harold wondered if he was reassuring them or himself...

Trish edged closer to Harold, gripping his shoulder.

"So, we're all still in this together—including Hoda?" asked Paul. "Ok then, let's go."

VIII.

Two blocks down from the CAM, the sidewalks and streets were jammed with pedestrians, as most vehicular traffic was blocked off. The faces group pushed their way through crowds along Canal Street and two blocks further to Mott Street. Linking arms at times to keep from being separated, they dodged bass drummers, dragon dancers, cymbalists and tambourine players. They looked back occasionally for the cops who were supposedly behind them; none were visible.

Real firecrackers thrown from apartment windows exploded on the nearby sidewalk. A woman screamed and jumped. Onlookers laughed. Teenagers, sounding toy horns and noisemakers, brushed by them, adding to the mayhem. Another firecracker went off—followed by an even louder bang; it was an engine backfiring up the street. They saw its smoky exhaust and a motorcycle rider in police uniform wending his way through the crowd.

The harsh wail of a siren announced the arrival of an NYPD patrol car behind the motorcycle. Its doors flew open; the tall officer from the museum, accompanied by a plainclothes man, leapt out and starting running after a group of youths in maroon jackets who started to scatter. Behind them ran a group of several other youths wearing golden colored jackets. Squads of blue-uniformed policemen gripping nightsticks closed in from both sides. All were running toward Harold's group, about fifty feet away.

Jennifer and Carlos, who had linked arms, were nearly knocked over by a human chain of costumed lion dancers charging out of the Oriental Rug Emporium. The dancers wore fanciful lion heads; young men sporting batons, maroon martial arts tunics and matching headbands flanked them on both sides.

All the participants came together in a blur of arms, legs, batons and police nightsticks.

Harold saw one of the baton carriers grappling with the tall officer; two of the lion dancers attempted to cover the officer with a net and pull him down. Another baton carrier jumped in front of Harold and swung the baton wildly. It comprised two segments connected by a chain—a nunchuck. Whipping it around with blinding speed, the assailant looked at Harold as if targeting him.

Harold knew such weapons were mainly used for training in martial arts; he remembered their showy display in Bruce Lee movies, but he had never faced one in personal combat. Harold hesitated only a split second to wonder "why me?" in what could have been a devastating lapse in concentration. Acting mainly by reflex, he raised his bag to intercept a glancing blow while lifting his knee high in a defensive stance. The nunchuc wielder read Harold's calm, confident demeanor and backed off. The other attackers began to retreat into a small cluster as an angry crowd advanced on them and blocked their escape. The melee appeared to be losing steam; a circle of plain-clothed and uniformed police stormed out of doorways and seized most of the attackers; other officers rushed toward where the faces group stood bunched together.

Another young man wearing a black tunic and headband sprang from behind Harold and wielded a baton above his head as if to strike him. Standing only a few feet away, Hoda whirled around and grasped the man's upper arm with one hand. Then, slipping over her eyes the blue-metallic mask of Horus hidden under her scarf, she affixed him with a stare so intense he seemed paralyzed and lost his grip on the baton, which tumbled to the street.

To Harold, the scene seemed surreal. Time and motion froze like a stuck frame in a horror fantasy movie. Then, events tumbled on, as onlookers cried, "Get him! He's one of them!" Blue-coated officers apprehended and handcuffed the tunic-wearer along with other dancers and baton-wielders. He was heard to mutter bitterly about his loss of face in being beaten by a woman. Other police vans arrived, sounding their sirens and flashing red and white lights. The attackers were quickly loaded into them through rear doors.

Once underway—despite the insistent shrieks of their sirens—the vans could only crawl down Mott Street while rousting clots of curious onlookers.

Still on edge and not sure the danger was completely past, the faces group stayed bunched together. The tall officer and the other policemen from the CAM were nowhere to be seen. Harold and Hoda stood nearly back-to-back as if standing guard—Hoda still wearing her mask—while Trish, Carlos, Jennifer and Paul stayed close beside them.

Some of the surrounding crowd seemed to back off as if in awe of the faces group, giving them several feet of space. Hoda took the opportunity to reposition the mask under her scarf. The group saw no threatening faces or moves toward them; standing motionless, hardly breathing, they seemed ready to burst with pent up emotion.

"Our heroes!" exclaimed Trish, simultaneously embracing Harold and Hoda, as Jennifer joined in. The hugs were returned, with smiles more of relief than exultation.

"So much for *watching* martial arts, Harold!" said Paul, his arm clasping Harold's shoulder. "And Hoda, where did you learn those moves?"

"Good show, both of you," said Carlos, embracing Harold and then Hoda.

"Just a defensive move," said Harold, shrugging. "I wasn't trying to hurt anyone." He wondered whether he could hurt someone if he really had to. He hadn't done much and certainly didn't deserve to be called hero. *What if Hoda hadn't intervened?*

"Lucky for them," said Trish. "And Hoda, what was that all about?"

"Beware the curse of Nefertiti," said Jennifer. "Make sure you stay on her good side."

"It certainly wasn't a curse," Hoda said with a reassuring smile. "More like a hypnotic induction. It works only with evil-doers." She smiled at the perplexed looks. "My uncle in Cairo sent me information that could be useful in your studies of faces. I'll explain later. Oh, and the arm bar was nothing—just a self-defense move I learned as a girl."

Before anyone could reply, a nearby crowd of East-Asian people began to chant loudly what sounded to Paul like a victory anthem. They hemmed in the faces group, and had completely refilled the street. Many were holding banners and pole signs advertising their community organizations in Chinese and English. A brass band and a parade with floats were forming down at the intersection of Bayard Street.

"We do need to get our bearings for the moment," said Paul, waving the group toward him.

"It may be déjà vu," said Trish, "but maybe it's time for our usual lunch break—Chinese, of course."

"If only to hide out," said Carlos, "from the Chinese—of course."

The others, not feeling relaxed enough to laugh, smiled and nodded their assent.

"It's a little early for lunch," said Harold, "but maybe that's in our favor."

IX.

Attracted by a day glow neon sign and an enticing whiff of Chinese food, the band of six plunged down a flight of stairs into a tiny restaurant festooned with black Chinese lanterns; they plopped into a red plastic booth as if exhausted from running. A glum-faced waitress shuffled over bringing menus and a tray of hot tea, crispy noodles and condiments.

Harold quickly polled the group and ordered a large tray of appetizer samplers.

"Let's try to make sense of what happened out there," said Paul, dipping a fried noodle into Chinese mustard. "They seemed to be going after the cop who was the bait. I guess they attacked Harold because he flashed a Kung Fu move—although I suppose any number of the wrong people could have seen us with the police at the museum."

"Maybe we'll find out when they question the culprits," said Harold, "…if they tell us about that. Meanwhile, we owe Hoda a full explanation as to what's going on here."

"After which," said Trish, "she owes us one about her magic powers."

"I promise," replied Hoda, removing her mask from under her scarf and sliding it under a menu. "But I want to assure you, it's not magic."

"Ok," said Harold, "see if you can follow this. Not counting you, Hoda, we have two face-reading consultants, both Chinese. One, we're not sure we trust; the other one works with an American agent who isn't sure he trusts us. Does that make sense?

"Of course not," said Trish with a sharp laugh.

"What do you mean," asked Hoda, "that the American agent doesn't trust us?"

"The American agent is named Van," said Harold. "With all due respect Uncle Paul, Van and you were classmates; he went into the CIA and you didn't. He may see you as a jealous would-be agent who might gum up his operation…" Harold's apologetic smile smacked of chagrin over challenging his beloved uncle.

"Maybe," said Paul, dryly. "So why is he encouraging us now?"

"I'll answer that in a second," said Harold. "The other thing he may not trust is that this Chinese face reading is computable and intelligence-worthy, which the Chinese, through Ma, may be leading us on about…"

"Leading us on for what purpose?" asked Carlos, edging closer.

"Why, to get Van, of course," answered Jennifer, matter-of-factly.

"I can see what Harold means about Van encouraging us," said Paul. "Maybe he thinks he can hit two birds with one stone: get Mary Shun's killers and deny the Chinese the face reading program, if it's valuable after all." Squeezing Harold's shoulder affectionately, Paul ignored any slight he may have felt; he was, in fact, proud of his nephew's boldness in confronting him, as well as his smarts in sizing up the situation.

"Who knows," said Jennifer "maybe the two birds Van wants to hit are from the same flock…both Red."

"A perfect example of circular logic," said Harold.

"Another Chinese puzzle," said Paul.

The others laughed.

"OK," said Carlos. "Where does that leave us?"

"Nowhere, which is great," said Harold. "We sit tight. There's nowhere else to go; nothing more to do. Remember, Trish—Ma quoted Confucius that you shouldn't try too hard. It's time to trust the universe, even if we're not sure we can trust Ma."

"True enough," said Trish. "At any rate, we've done everything we can do. If Ma *were* a spy, maybe it would take Van to really find out. And, Hoda," she said, smiling shrewdly and turning to the regal-looking Cairene, "now tell us how you came to practice the black arts."

"Nothing black about it," said Hoda, uncovering the shiny mask and running her fingers over it. "You may be surprised to know, your ideas on the mathematics of beauty happen to jibe with the numerology of Horus. I've done a bit of research myself. The hypnotic effect of symbols like the Eye of Horus lies in the geometry of their shapes— shapes that apparently resonate deep in the human psyche." Her right index finger traced the three parts of the design: the eyebrow above, the eye itself and the subtle curve of the appendages below, resembling the legs of the letter "R".

"Gosh, Hoda," said Jennifer, "You've stepped right out of Jung's book on symbols; how certain images can induce a trance-like state. That Haitian professor we met on the plane might say that voodoo can work that way too."

"Perhaps," replied Hoda. "Some voodoo is supposedly about evil intent, but Horus is only about protection, not aggression. And here's the key thing for the power to work: the user must have good intent and the recipient evil intent. There's nothing inherently scary or disabling about the falcon's eye—its effect depends on what you believe and intend. That baton attacker on the receiving end of my stare had evil intent. That's why his own power bent back and disabled him. Scientifically, I suppose you could call it rapid induction hypnosis. The ancients believed in it."

"Hmm," said Harold, "kind of like in martial arts where you use the opponent's power against him."

"If you like," Hoda replied. Her expression, usually dignified and aloof, seemed to thaw and become compassionate and soulful.

Paul thought that the dramatic contours of Hoda's face and her penetrating black eyes had entrancing power—enhanced by her stature and her voice. But she radiated the power of a benevolent goddess, not an evil sorceress.

Hoda continued, "It's also true that various segments of the Horus happen to add up to a factor of sixty-four..."

"Another coincidence," said Harold.

"...Yes," answered Hoda. "I'm aware of the coincidence of the 64 Horus segments to the 64 hexagrams of the *I Ching*."

"All of which leaves me in a hypnotic state of confusion," said Trish.

"I think we'd better stop there," said Hoda. "There's another scientific explanation too. But I promised my uncle I wouldn't divulge more unless...Well—he said I would know when it was time, and it can wait."

"It's Ok. I need time to digest all of that," said Harold, thinking, *this amazing woman may be sitting on an important scientific truth, and I'm dying to know it.*

"And I need time to digest all of this," said Carlos, reaching toward the plate of hot appetizers that had arrived.

The food was devoured in a few minutes, with little conversation.

"Time to leave and trust the universe," said Trish.

Carlos took a last sip of Chinese tea. "Does anybody really want to get back in that crowd?"

"I've soaked up enough local color," said Jennifer.

"Me too. I think we should meet somewhere safer, like my office," said Trish.

"I'd call a cab, if I thought one could get through," said Harold. Climbing the steps outside the restaurant, he spied an NYPD badge glinting in the mottled daylight and made eye contact with the officer. "Hey, here's a cop." Guiding Trish by the arm, Harold waved the group forward onto the sidewalk through the crowd.

The uniformed policeman nodded at Harold; another one joined him, blocking the sidewalk and forming a path for the group. A police van pulled directly in front of them. Doors opened and a smiling Lieutenant Juen, in the front seat, beckoned them inside. "Not to worry. We saw you the whole time. Now we'll see you home."

The group trundled into the second and rear seats of the eight-passenger vehicle. Two other officers rode along: one in uniform drove; the other, in plainclothes, sat in a rear seat. Carlos, seated behind the driver, while pretending to cough, switched on the audio recorder in his upper jacket pocket.

"Like you said, we certainly saw a lot of action," said Paul.

"You never know," answered the Lieutenant. "We have to be ready for anything, and we had enough eyes to go around, for you too." The van started up and proceeded slowly, south, on Mott Street.

"Not to sound ungrateful, Lieutenant," said Trish, "but what have we done to deserve valet service from the NYPD?"

The plainclothes officer replied, "You were in the middle of that disturbance back there. We wanted to assure your safety even though it was unlikely they were targeting you. By the way, I'm Agent Jacob Ritter, Federal Bureau of Investigation."

"Pleased to meet you," answered Paul, his smile bleak. "They may not have been after us at first, but my nephew was attacked after the main fracas when that tall officer impersonating Van was being assailed."

Agent Ritter twisted his squarish features into a grimace. "To be perfectly honest…"

Trish thought, *here comes the b.s.*

"…We're not yet sure of anything. Most likely your nephew was drawn into a collateral situation when they saw him step forward in a martial arts' pose."

"Are you saying I provoked them?" asked Harold, clenching his teeth.

"You certainly had the right to defend yourself," said Ritter, in a softer tone. "All I'm saying is, maybe they didn't see it that way. We've got to investigate further, question suspects and get this all sorted out."

"Listen folks," said Lieutenant Juen. "We understand you've got some kind of business project going on. But there's no evidence that bad people want to interfere with it. Let me ask, do any of you know anyone in Chinatown, other than the CAM staff?"

The group looked at each other, shrugged and shook their heads.

"Not really," answered Paul.

So that's it, thought Trish, they do want to pick our brains.

"Except," said Harold, "we do know some Chinese people who claim to have spent time here. That's Ma-Chang-Kuo and Danny the hit man we call him. But we assume you know that from the videos and audios we forwarded to Charles Wu."

The FBI man and the lieutenant exchanged non-committal glances. The FBI man said, "We'd rather focus on what you know. What else can you tell us about these Chinese people?"

"I don't know if you'd call it evidence," said Trish, "it's more like a woman's intuition."

"Go on," said Lieutenant Juen.

"Well, pardon me gentlemen, but I've learned to have a sixth sense when it comes to the opposite sex. To me, this Ma, charming as he is, seems a little too cute to be for real."

"How do you mean," asked Agent Ritter, eyes narrowing.

Trish replied, "I don't think he's as cool as he lets on. This whole 'don't try too hard, just trust the universe' routine seems a bit forced, like his smile, for instance."

"In L.A.," said Harold, "it's like we were having a smile contest, but he would always win."

"Not always," continued Trish. "He wore a sort of mask; nobody smiles that much. Except, it slipped at odd times, like when we were discussing surveillance or espionage, or the CIA…or Van."

"Do you think it's possible he's a spy?" asked Jennifer.

"Not enough evidence to jump to that conclusion," answered Agent Ritter.

"Anything else?" asked the Lieutenant.

"I remember when we first met him," said Harold. "The cowboy boots and R&B routine…shopping at Bloomingdales." Harold turned to Trish. "Do you remember what he said when I told him he'd make a heck of a spy? He said, 'Oh no, too obvious an attempt to blend in.'"

"Sounds like a pre-packaged excuse, in case he's accused of something," said Carlos.

"Like Harold said, Ma seemed to have the answers before the questions were asked," said Trish.

"Right," replied Harold. "Like, if he is a spy, he's playing with us."

"…Even if he's not," interjected Carlos, "he's still playing with us."

The others laughed briefly in agreement.

"Another Chinese person we know," said Jennifer, "would be Danny, the hit man from Dallas. If looks could kill, he wouldn't need a gun. He seemed to enjoy making scary faces and watching our reaction. Another disturbing thing was that the Chinese robot makers seemed anxious for government authorities to hear about their work with faces that could remake history."

"We're assuming," said Paul, "that you're fully briefed on our work with Ma, through Charles Wu and Van."

"Let's say," answered Agent Ritter, "that he lines of communication are open. Our interest in your work is only peripheral to our own."

"Which is what?" asked Paul.

"I can tell you only this: that we are looking into possible Chinese government involvement in the subway murder; that's confidential. The rest is speculation."

Lieutenant Juen smiled brightly. "We appreciate all your cooperation. But believe me, the less you know, the safer you'll be. We'll keep you posted as the need arises. Now, where can we drop you folks off?"

"How about my office, 810 Seventh Avenue, near 53rd," said Trish. "It's Sunday; the coast is clear." She turned to the group. "We can have a short debrief and decide our next move."

All agreed to the plan. The van circled around, turned west on Canal Street onto Broadway, and headed north.

X.

"Now, there is another reason for our picking you up here," said Agent Ritter.

*Ah so, the whole truth, and nothing but...*thought Trish.

Ritter reached into a jacket pocket and withdrew what looked like a disc-shaped metal locket, attached by an eyelet to a chain.

"What's that?" asked Paul.

"A sensing device. We have no information that you're targeted for anything, but, in case you *do* run into bad guys, this is a no-cost-to-you insurance policy with a potentially big payoff."

"How so?" asked Carlos.

"Once set, it transmits a continuous signal, showing your location. It adheres to your chest by its adhesive side, and as a safety, it hangs around your neck on this chain. These little colored buttons on the other side operate it. You can turn it off with the black button, but normally you would want to keep it on."

"Why?" asked Jennifer.

"Because a signal from it will bring us running on the double to wherever you are, which is the desired effect; but we don't want any false alarms," answered the FBI man, smiling. "The chip and sensor are calibrated to the wearer's normal heartbeat, brain waves, and blood chemistry picked up in his perspiration."

"In other words..." said Harold.

"...In other words, a stressor effect from a serious emergency will trigger elevated heart rate and the release of neuro-hormones. That would also set off the 'I'm in trouble' alarm."

"Impressive technology—but what if we're actually Ok?" asked Harold.

"It gives you a little warning, vibrating like your cell phone, that it's about to send the alarm. At that point, you can manually override it; pressing this button says, in effect, that you're Ok."

"Cool," said Carlos. "But yet you say we're not targeted, so why do we need to wear it?"

"Only if you find yourselves in a dangerous situation where we could possibly help," replied the Agent.

"You mean with Chinese gangs or enemy agents?" said Hoda, knitting her brows.

"You never know," said Agent Ritter.

Paul emitted a wan smile. "I think I understand, Agent Ritter. As you probably know, we are going out to Los Angeles to see Mr. Ma about our little project, which you probably know quite a bit about from Van."

"We don't need to know details, right now. But if you'd like to have a little protection, just in case, wearing this sensor would help."

"If we're in trouble in California," asked Harold, "how fast could you help us from New York City?"

"We have people out there who can act, if the need arises," said Agent Ritter. "This thing is entirely voluntary; you're under no obligation; but I will say this…"

Here it comes, thought Trish.

"…There's no downside, except for the small inconvenience of wearing it and remembering how it works. The upside is that we'll always be listening…I mean, be ready to respond."

Paul checked faces: they ranged from leery to hopeful. "It sounds like it could be beneficial, but can we discuss it and get back to you?" he asked.

"This is going to sound strange," replied Agent Ritter, "and yes, it is voluntary, but the offer must be withdrawn at the end of this van ride, for, let us say, security reasons."

"What?" snapped Trish.

"Expires like a discount offer on T.V.," laughed Carlos.

"We need to be assured," answered Agent Ritter, evenly, "since we've shared this very special technology with you, that you are entirely trustworthy and would keep it to yourselves."

"And if we agree?" asked Paul.

"Then all we ask is that you sign this little agreement." Ritter pulled a pocket-sized card from a coat pocket.

"May I?" asked Trish, taking the card; she read aloud: "Description of Functions …Confidentiality Agreement…This seems to say that we agree to not divulge operational details, or the purposes of this device."

"And if we don't agree?" asked Harold.

"You don't have to take the device, but…"

"But what?" asked Carlos.

"We'll still ask you to sign the agreement."

"And if we don't?" asked Jennifer.

"We can't make you, but…" replied Agent Ritter.

"…Let me guess," interrupted Paul, recalling his commander's line from the Army Reserve. "You can't make us, but you can make us wish we had."

Agent Ritter grunted a laugh, then turned to Paul with a 'cat that ate the canary' grin. "Something like that. No threats exactly, but we really must insist."

"I guess we're in this thing," said Paul, "whatever it is, whether we like it or not."

"Whatever it is," droned Trish.

"We'll pull over, to make this easier," said Lieutenant Juen. The driver pulled to the curb on 23rd Street and 6th Avenue.

Agent Ritter held out a ballpoint pen. "There are six lines for signatures, and five of you. You don't have to decide whether you will take the device until we drop you off."

His coat already open, Harold unfastened buttons on his plaid wool shirt and exposed the skin of his chest. "I'm the one who started all this," he said. "I'll be the first to sign and I'll wear the device; no discussion."

"I'm not fighting a martial artist for the right to bare my chest," said Trish.

"Us neither," said Jennifer, looking over at Hoda.

Everyone laughed, even the stolid policemen.

Harold wrote his signature on the card and passed it around; everyone signed.

Trish's legal brain whirled into action: "Don't we get a copy of that little agreement?"

"Uh, afraid you'll have to trust us on that," said Agent Ritter. "Pieces of paper could get lost or fall into the wrong hands."

"Like ours?" asked Trish, with a saucy smile.

"We basically trust you, but things can happen."

"I guess we do have to trust you," said Paul.

"It's best that you do." Agent Ritter affixed the adhesive-backed sensor to the middle of Harold's chest and pressed a black button. It took several seconds for base-line numbers to register on a digital screen next to a red indicator light. "Let's not forget the safety chain." He looped the thin metal chain over Harold's head onto his neck. "This little black button is the off/on switch, which you almost never use. The warning is set on vibrate, and this white one is the override 'I'm all right' button. Take the device off to shower or swim. The battery re-charges remotely. Otherwise, you're good to go."

"Obviously," said Paul, "you think we're trustworthy enough to send us off with this technology, and we're willing to let you track us to wherever. But, do you mind answering a few more questions?"

"Such as?" Agent Ritter's smile flattened out to a flat line, curved sharply upward at the corners.

"Well, now that Harold's wearing this wire…"

"…I wouldn't call it that—more like a homing device." Ritter's eyelids and lips briefly squeezed shut.

"…Homing device then," said Paul. "Do you need us to report to you about our activities or our plans, other than what is obvious from Harold's whereabouts?"

"No…not really…We don't want you to think we're breathing down your necks or interfering with your work."

"Can we call you directly if we have a question or a problem?" asked Paul.

"We prefer to initiate contact with you, but in case of a real problem, short of a life or death emergency, there is a way." Agent Ritter sucked in his lips, resignedly. "Press both the black and white buttons simultaneously. Just once.

The resulting message amounts to 'I'm all right, but must speak with you.' We'll be in touch pretty fast. By the way, I'll need everyone's cell phone numbers."

"Not that I'd refuse," said Paul, "but you could probably get them without our permission."

Agent Ritter's smile was bland. "We prefer to have your permission."

"Again, what about Hoda?' asked Jennifer. "Do we need to involve her this deeply?"

"We're not looking to get in the middle of your business transactions," said the agent, "but only to help you in case of trouble. Do you want her to be in the loop?"

"Again, think about your family, Hoda," said Trish.

"So far, I'm only a consultant here, but also a friend; so, I'd like to help in any way that would not intrude. Call me if you need me."

"Ok, thanks Hoda," said Paul. "But this device does seem to be a lot of responsibility on Harold. Are you all right with that Harold?"

"Yes, but I'd like to share the fun and keep my faces team posted in real time via cell phone."

"We're approaching 53rd and Seventh," said Lieutenant Juen. "Any other questions? No? Then thank you again for all your cooperation. You're on your own now—although not entirely." Smiling briskly, Juen pushed a button that opened the van door.

Nervous laughter, barely audible, arose from the group as they climbed out. None of them noticed Agent Ritter also exiting the van a moment later.

One minute passed. "Did you get all of that, Van?" asked Agent Ritter, on the secure line of his cell phone. He was calling from a black Ford Fusion that had been trailing behind, and was now parked in a restricted zone.

"Yes. Everything came through loud and clear. Two near slips though, Jake—on your part."

"You mean when I said 'we'll be listening to them', and then I recovered and corrected it with: 'we'll be ready to respond'. I don't know if they picked up on that."

"What made me think they picked up on it was when Paul Wallach said something like his nephew is now 'wearing a wire'. He might have been trying to trip you up and play agent there, and you said…"

"…Yeah—I said I wouldn't call it that, meaning a wire…"

"Right. You were careful not to outright deny that it's a wire. You said 'more like a homing device'. Good move; that way they can't claim they were duped into wearing a wire without their knowledge."

"Correct. Also, the Donlon woman didn't mention the fine print that called it an audio-engineered tracking device. That's our technicality, if it ever came down to a legal issue, which it won't. They probably don't have a recording of the verbatim conversation. But why don't you want them to know we can hear them?"

"Because it might cramp their style or keep them from talking to people of interest. Obviously, we're not always listening. We only activate it when we want it to, like when they're approaching trouble or in trouble, based on the sensor readings."

"Ok, Van. So, given what we found you on Danny Ching, what justifies the time we're spending on this group?"

"Well, thanks to your people, we have a complete ID on Ching-Li-Ho, a former Marine with a clean record, supposedly from Chinatown, New York. But according to Henry Juen, nobody ever heard of him. He could be one of those Chinese born here and sent back to China to be groomed by the MSS. We've confirmed he's a driver for the Branson robot outfit in Richardson, Texas. The NSA satellite camera shows that whenever he speaks outdoors with his Chinese boss, Feng, it's always in their van with hands in front of their mouths. Branson himself may be clean, but I swear these guys are operatives. I don't like their looks."

"As you know, Van, that may not be enough to convince a judge we need to plant a bug in their van. If only you could detect something suspicious, even from lip-reading… What do you have on the L.A. digital cinema guy?"

"Ma-Chang-Kuo comes up squeaky clean, although we do have a satellite camera on him too. You know, Jake, if this Danny is our man in the subway murder and if he's really an American, then it's your case and I stay background. If Ma or Feng are dirty and working for MSS, or if Danny's tied to them, we keep working together."

"Yeah, our two-man truce in the CIA-FBI war."

"It sure feels lonely. Meanwhile, I assume Henry is working on those Dragons he just busted on Mott Street; maybe something will emerge from that."

"Ok, Van. We have to assume they were trying to kidnap you. We must determine who's behind it. If I don't hear from Henry, myself, about possible Flying Dragon links to China, I'll call him."

"Do that, and keep me posted, Jake. I do think we need to tune in on Wallach's group—now. Can you activate their audio and patch me in?"

"Ok. I'm activating it now…"

XI.

In Trish and Jennifer's office, the group had been sitting around an oval glass conference table, drinking coffee.

"We may not need it," said Carlos, sipping the hot liquid, "but I have a recording of that last double-talk conversation."

"How do I befuddle thee, let me count the ways," hammed Trish.

"I did count the ways," replied Harold, putting his coffee down. "Like, did you notice, they wouldn't even admit this was a federal case, meaning FBI—let alone international, meaning CIA? And, they never once used Van's name, as if they won't commit that he's involved, or let on how interested he might be in what we're doing."

"Right," said Paul. "Only Charles Wu uses Van's name directly."

"And," replied Harold, "they continue to be vague and ambiguous about whether we're targeted or not."

"But," said Jennifer, "maybe they made us a target just by working with them."

"I'm new to this," said Hoda, "but I noticed how they always want to maximize the flow of information from you to them and minimize it from them to us."

"Probably normal police talk," said Trish. "But Hoda, we've got to define your role here and make sure you're shielded from harm. If bad guys are still out there, they're not likely to forget you and your little performance in Chinatown."

"For sure," said Jennifer. "Or some Chinese people here, who know Dorothy at CAM, could talk to her and compromise your role at the Met. Have you thought about that?"

"Don't worry. I already cleared this with Dorothy. I told her I might wear an Egyptian mask to New Year's. All she said was Chinese masks, Egyptian masks—what's the difference? As far as danger, I will never be afraid to protect my friends, and it looks like you all have more protection than ever."

Harold replied, "I believe I'm speaking for all of us in thanking you for your courage and support, Hoda. But I've been thinking about how we can use you even more, if you're willing."

"I'm listening," said Hoda.

"Wait a second…" Harold looked suddenly distracted. Quickly exposing the device on his chest—the shirt buttons had not been refastened— he immediately covered it with an empty plastic cup, to the consternation of the group. "…You say you're listening, Hoda…I wonder who else was listening?"

"Harold," Paul said, excitedly, "You must have noticed Agent Ritter's reaction to my wire question? Did anyone else?"

"Yeah," said Carlos, "Before that, I heard him say they'd be *listening.*"

"If this really is a wire," said Trish, "as a professional skeptic, I'm not surprised."

"So maybe," said Harold, "we'll find out. Like if they are listening and suddenly get blocked out, maybe they'll wonder why and call in."

"And if they don't?" asked Jennifer.

"Maybe covering the device affects your baselines or something and sets it off anyway," said Carlos.

"*Maybe,*" said Harold, "we should call them and confront this issue, so we don't set off false alarms. And maybe, we'll establish some trust at both ends."

"Isn't he masterful?" said Trish, affecting a swoon.

Paul answered his ringing cell phone. "Hello?" Smiling, he looked at the group and nodded his head. "Yes, Agent Ritter…No, we're all Ok. Did something interfere with the transmission? We thought so…"

Trish handed Paul a business card. "Have them call the landline and I'll put them on speaker phone."

"Agent Ritter," said Paul. "Can you call us at 212-636-7000, extension, 214?" It rang a few seconds later. "Yes, you're on speaker phone now…Go ahead."

"Dr. Wallach, did Mr. Savitt cover up the device?"

"Yes, I did Agent Ritter," called out Harold.

"Did you guess that it had a microphone?"

"Ah, the truth will out," sighed Trish.

"We all sort of guessed it," said Harold.

"Let me explain. It is used only selectively for that purpose. Again, we're not prying, only making it possible to respond more quickly. Your knowledge of the listening mode of the device might have compromised that."

"Trish Donlon here, Agent Ritter. Excuse me for asking, but, strictly speaking, don't you need a court order for a wire?"

"Yes, strictly speaking. But, believe me, we're not in an adversarial situation here. We needed to hear you folks right after our van ride; that's easily justified, based on what we heard a moment ago."

"What was that?" asked Trish.

"I believe Mr. Morales said he had a recording of that *double-talk conversation.*"

"And so?" rejoined Trish.

"So, if we're going to get on our legal high horses, it is a federal offence to record a conversation without permission, especially a confidential one concerning government business."

"*Oh,*" moaned Carlos.

"We're not about to play hardball with you, but…"

"…But, if you don't mind," said Paul, his voice rising, "I would like to get a few things straight, and with you too, *Van,* if you're listening, by any chance…"

A few seconds passed. "What is it, Dr. Wallach?" said Ritter, sounding more amicable.

"We may be meddling civilians, but you have trusted us quite a bit so far."

"That's true."

"You trusted us to participate in this little caper of yours and to wear this wire. At this point, I'm not trying to play James Bond, *Van,* but I am willing to participate in a fishing expedition, even if we are the bait. That's worth some answers."

"Let me ask you a question, Mr. Wallach," said Agent Ritter. "What if we told you that Mr. Ma or the people in Dallas might be Chinese agents, which by the way we really don't know—what would you want to do?"

"Good question," replied Paul. "What would we do?" He looked at the group.

The agent's tone sounded calm and patient. "Would you want to abandon your project, get out of whatever arrangement you had with Ma, and try to find someone else to do it?"

"I don't think we could legally do that, unless Ma proves to be a bad guy," answered Paul. "And even then, he could literally run away with the project. It looks like we're stuck with him, and…" he laughed, "unless we want to take all the risks ourselves, we're stuck with you too."

The lawman's tone seemed almost paternal. "I can promise you we'll be more help than trouble."

"Can you tell us if Van really is the bait?" asked Paul.

"I can tell you we're really going to find out."

Paul spoke, "Ok. I guess we're not bailing on the project or the protection. Can we address this wire thing, though?"

"All right. We're willing to do this your way. How about if it's your choice to activate it?"

Paul looked around. "Any objections?" There were none.

"None? Good. Here's how to activate and deactivate the wire. Simply press the black and white buttons simultaneously, but twice. That means activate; press them twice again—that's deactivate. Remember, pressing the white one once means you're Ok. Got it?"

Everyone nodded.

Harold uncovered the buttons and simultaneously pressed both twice. "Ok, we're deactivated."

"Ok. Good luck with everything. We won't be monitoring your every word; we were never were going to do that."

"Just every heartbeat," said Trish, under her breath.

"Like I said before, we'll be available if you need us."

"Goodbye," said Paul, with a gleeful smile, as the other phone clicked off. "I could be wrong, but it sounds like Van is going to L.A.—if not with us, then maybe right behind us."

"How do you figure?" said Carlos.

"Look at it this way: apparently, some bad guys are after Van and they didn't get him—actually his double—here. One way for Van to know if these bad guys are tied to people we're working with is to monitor us and then go to L.A., essentially offering himself as live bait."

"Yeah," said Harold, "maybe by saying we're really going to find out, the Feds were dropping a hint, intentionally or unintentionally, that Van is going to L.A."

"…In which case, we could drop a hint to Ma," said Paul, "that Van wants to come."

"Right," said Harold. "If Van is the big prize to keep Ma from going away with the software, we can help deliver him."

"So, Van does become our card to play now," said Trish.

"At any rate," said Jennifer, "we do have more reason to believe Van may be coming. And, the Chinese have acted like they'd welcome that."

"Like the spider welcomes the fly," said Trish.

"And we could be caught in the web," said Harold. "But, you know, I was thinking, Hoda—if for some reason our project with Ma is derailed by legal problems, we'd want you to be perfectly safe, and yet maybe you could still help us."

"By doing what?" asked Hoda.

"I think Hoda and Charles Wu are potentially our most important educational consultants," said Paul. "Hoda, with your permission, I'd like to call Charles tomorrow to set up a meeting between you two—see what we can come up with, for the future of this project. Maybe I could also pick Charles's brain about Van's intentions"

"Yes, that would be fine with me," replied Hoda.

"One more thing before we go," said Harold. "We still need to decide about dropping hints to Ma about Van."

"In other words, sweeten the bait?" asked Carlos.

"I've got an idea," said Harold. "Why don't we call Ma now. It's almost one-o'-clock; that would be ten, L.A. time—not too early. Why not tell Ma we've gotten interest from the Feds and see what his reaction is, and at the same time, while we've got the Feds' attention and maybe even Van's…"

"…Double click the two buttons on your device and cue the Feds to listen in," said Trish. "Great minds run together."

"Fiendishly clever, old chap," said Carlos.

"Wait…Let's think this through," said Paul.

"I think it makes sense," said Jennifer. "If Ma, all of a sudden, says the Feds shouldn't come, let's ask him why. Maybe it means he's a good guy after all, and was just humoring us about Van because we wanted Van's participation…"

"…And if he wants Van to come?" asked Hoda.

"…Maybe that's a clue as to his real intentions," said Jennifer.

"…And maybe not," said Paul. "Maybe he is still humoring us."

"…However, said Jennifer, "if the Feds are listening, they're experts at discerning that sort of thing, which they may tell us…"

"…Or not," said Paul.

"Ok," said Harold. "There may not be any certain answers, but I see no downside. The suspense is killing us, and we're just checking in to see how Ma's doing…"

"Trust the universe," said Trish.

Harold pressed the device buttons twice, waited about ten seconds and punched Ma's cell phone number…

"Hello, Harold. Good to hear from you. Everything all right?"

"Sure, Ma. But we were wondering how it's going, and yes, we do have news, sort of …"

"…Really? Hmm. Maybe I should put us on videophone. It's always nice to see your face, or is it faces?"

"Ok. Can we Trish? Yes…Trish and the other partners are here… She's hooking up the monitor now."

Trish quickly connected Harold's iPhone to the large-screen computer monitor. Carlos began to record with his video camera.

Harold continued, "Takes just a few seconds…We see you now. Do you see us? Good. We just got back from Chinese New Year, and you wouldn't believe what we just went through."

"Try me." Ma's usually splendid smile seemed a bit less so.

"Actually, it was more of a riot than a parade," said Harold.

"Chinese people sometimes get carried away at New Year festivities."

"Hi, Ma, it's Trish. Yes, somebody *was* almost literally carried away."

"How do you mean?"

"There was an attempted kidnapping of a very tall policeman right in front of us," said Harold, "by some of the dragon dancers. We had seen him, just minutes before, when we visited the CAM Chinese museum."

"As long as you folks are safe…" Ma's smile seemed genuinely warm.

"One thought occurred to us, Ma," said Harold. "My Uncle Paul's colleague, the federal agent named Van that we've spoken about?"

"Yes?" Ma winced.

"Van used to be a well-known figure on Chinatown streets, and maybe, because he's also very tall, the gangs thought they were taking him this time."

"But they didn't succeed, did they?" Ma looked uncharacteristically anxious.

"Apparently not," answered Harold. "We don't know for sure because we haven't seen or spoken to him ourselves." Harold was trying to read Ma's face to detect either genuine concern for Van, or disappointment that the kidnap attempt failed. He wasn't sure what he saw.

"By the way, Harold, to speed things up, I have farmed out pieces of the project."

"Why so, Ma?" asked Paul. "I'm Harold's uncle, Paul Wallach."

"Nice to meet you and your face, Dr. Wallach. Why so? Because I was able to break up parts of program writing and electromagnetic encoding to trusted associates. Even so, none of them knows enough to put it all together. Otherwise, it would have taken many more weeks. As it is, we are only a day or two away."

"We have to trust that aspect of it to you, Ma," said Paul. "In that respect, we have included in our circle another consultant—not a partner, but a good friend, Hoda Ramsis. She is a museum executive." Paul moved the monitor so that Hoda was visible. She and Ma exchanged greetings. Paul introduced Jennifer and Carlos to Ma as well. They saw each other as insets on the monitor screen.

Trish ventured, "…But you knew their faces from a video sent by Feng from Dallas?"

"Oh yes, I did recognize you both. All good faces." He laughed.

Trish thought Ma's response was instantaneous and sounded honest —proving nothing.

"We are still engaged in our regular jobs, Ma," said Harold. "If you could finish in time for us to come out on a weekend, that would be ideal."

"The program itself should be finished by tomorrow or next day. We have been working round the clock to prepare a special presentation that would even impress your friend Van if he should come." Ma's smile shone as goodbyes were exchanged.

Harold pressed the device buttons twice, turning off the wire.

"So, do we call the Feds and discuss this with them?" asked Jennifer.

"No, it's don't call us, we'll call you, remember?" said Carlos. "We don't even have their number."

"What's our take on this then?" asked Trish. "I can't read these jokers, including Ma."

"Neither can I," said Harold.

"Obviously," said Paul, "we have to wait and hear from the cops about what they think is the significance of this—if anything. Who knows if they were even listening? Hoda, give me your card and we'll set up this thing with Charles Wu."

Hoda handed Paul her card; the group, agreeing to stay in touch, soon went their separate ways.

XII.

"What do you make of that, Van?" said Agent Ritter.

"There was obvious verbal sparring between the group and Ma, and perhaps an element of distrust, which may be well founded. For sure, Ma didn't say anything about not wanting me to come. What he means by special reception, I may need to find out in person."

"So, are you going?" asked Ritter, "And will you need me and my men?"

"I'm not sure yet. But here's some Intel recently intercepted from an Agent White Lotus, in L.A., to MSS headquarters in Beijing: '...I monitor all work coming from our operatives in American cinema and T.V. Our initiative to bombard American media with attractive images of China progresses well...I can report on conversation between Los Angeles technician and American media group wanting information about Chinese face reading for use in fashion and communications.'"

"Who do you suppose that sounds like?" said Ritter.

"Who else but Ma-Chang-Kuo and our Wallach faces group? And one thing's for certain, unless White Lotus wears two hats..."

"What's that?

"Ma is not White Lotus. And in fact, he may not be dirty himself, maybe he's just being monitored by MSS, or..."

"...Or is being threatened to cooperate with MSS."

"All possible. As to how important they think face reading is...let me read the rest: '...Chinese face reading may have significance, particularly if the enemy thinks so. We will continue to report on developments.' It sounds like face reading to them is not a priority, unless it's important to us."

"Maybe Ma and the faces group made progress since then, and MSS may think it's more important now, if they're monitoring. And if not..."

"…And, if not, it's up to me to decide one thing," said Van.

"What's that?"

"If it's all about me."

"Isn't it usually?"

"Ha! Is my ego that big?"

"You are a big target in more ways than one."

"Sounds like cops' double talk, Jake." Van laughed. "To answer your question, though, I really don't know what my plans are. That's straight talk. Goodbye."

XIII.

Van's secure phone line on his Super Watch buzzed three times. He answered, "Hi, Henry."

"Hi, Van. We didn't get much from the Dragons on Mott Street."

"Not surprising."

"They're playing it tough. Dave Porter, another FBI man working with Jake, threatened them with jail or deportation, trying to get them to admit they were after a Fed, which was, of course, a bluff on our part."

"I know. Because the double for me is NYPD, and without proof of a conspiracy, it's only a local charge."

"Right. They seem to be local guys with local ID's but they didn't try to lawyer up or call families. There's one weak link though."

"What's that?"

"The rug emporium guy, Bao-Lin-Chu, Peter Bao. Very nervous, like he's got something to lose. He couldn't come up with a story fast enough to explain why the Dragons came out of his store."

"Is he clean?"

"No priors; got a green card. He came from Hong Kong in 2005. Agent Porter noticed a half-rolled rug in the store and remembered something from an old Charlie Chan movie where people were rolled up in a rug. Porter goes eyeball to eyeball with Bao and says: 'I know you're using this rug to smuggle people. We have tests to prove it.' Bao turns white, starts to shake; then he blubbers like a baby. We took him to Fifth Precinct for questioning."

"And?"

"He denies smuggling, but he did admit he does a lot of business with an L.A. importer who may do things with the rugs he's not aware of."

"Can the FBI guys in L.A. check that importer?"

"Porter and Jake Ritter are working that now and will probably let you know. Interstate Commerce makes it federal. I also have a good contact in Tommy Chin, LAPD, to keep the locals tuned-in."

"Good, Henry. I'm particularly interested if that importer is dirty and if he's one receiver of that Chinese chatter from the mainland."

"OK, Van. We'll keep working on the Dragons and Bao the rug guy to see if anyone flips."

"About the Wallach group, I noticed they tried to pry stuff about me out of you."

"I guess they were wondering if you suspected a West Coast connection to the subway assassin, or thought their Chinese partner might be dirty."

"Nothing there yet. And after hearing them call that partner through the wire Jake Ritter gave them, I still have nothing solid. You may not have heard that."

"No, I didn't hear it. But they certainly sounded suspicious of the Chinese partner, in the police van conversation."

"I realize that. Thanks for your help, Henry."

XIV.

Thirty minutes later, Van saw Lieutenant Juen's name flash again on his Super Watch, as it buzzed lightly.

"Yes, Henry."

"Van, we just broke one of the Dragon Dancers. He's got a long rap sheet. Doesn't admit direct involvement in the subway murder, but he did say some Flying Dragons went after Dr. Wallach's nephew in Chinatown because he challenged them out in Flushing—as if he knew something about the murder. I don't know what Wallach's nephew might know, but apparently the Dragons think he knows something and maybe they're involved. Otherwise, why would they go after him and his group?"

"Hmm—like uncle, like nephew. We've got wannabe agents coming out of the woodwork. All the more reason to monitor their activities, and I guess protect them too. I was hoping to avoid this, but anyway…talk to you soon."

XV.

Van called Charles Wu on their secure line. "Charles."

"Hello Van. I saw something about the attempted abduction of a police officer in Chinatown on T.V. news. I gather that was supposed to be you."

"Obviously, they didn't get him or me. We're assuming I was bait. Arrests were made. Even so, we caught only little fish so far and only local. There is a possible West Coast link—FBI is pursuing that. But Henry Juen just squeezed a Flying Dragon who admits a deliberate attack on Paul Wallach's group, specifically his nephew. Apparently, the nephew had gone out to Flushing Chinatown and confronted gang guys about their supposed involvement in the subway murder—I don't know details—and this is payback. The Dragons probably wouldn't bother unless they were involved, we figure. This leaves me pretty much committed to letting Wallach's group be players and at the same time, not letting them screw things up."

"I see that. It's ironic that Wallach's group could stumble onto your work and possibly disrupt it while only trying to get your attention about face reading. But ironically too, they could lead you right to the main actors and who knows, maybe the face reading is a link?"

"Who knows? I leave it to you, the Professor of Tao to explain such linkages."

They laughed.

"Meanwhile," Van continued, "I don't want them to get their hopes up that I'm joining their little party in L.A., if you get my meaning."

"I do understand. Good-bye, Van."

XVI.

Ma's second phone buzzed again. He recognized the Hokkien code used by his parents to text him: "We hope to implement plans with Ms. Ren and Mr. Ho from Hong Kong. We dare not contact them directly but trust that intermediaries will coordinate our comings and goings. But save yourself at all costs. Do not despair if we are caught, for our cause of freedom is righteous. Be careful as your messages may be monitored. Your devoted parents."

PART SIX

LONG BEACH STUDIOS PRESENTS…

I.

For his grand presentation, Ma called Harold to invite the group to L.A. for the weekend of February 25th. Everyone seemed enthusiastic, except for Carlos. He had been in a funk for some reason, not returning calls. Harold was puzzled, considering their recent reconciliation. But Carlos's prompt offering of his credit card for his share of the trip eased Harold's worries somewhat.

More good news from Vera Tang kept Trish and Jennifer in high spirits; their firm garnered a fee of a half a million dollars as the new Tang Asian styles were placed in high-end couture houses, with much more profit expected as new lines were added. Their own bonuses would be fifteen percent of Spence-Iturbi billings. Not only that, Esteban Iturbi was drooling over the possibility of Hollywood legend re-creations modeling both vintage and contemporary styles. Trish kept those expectations under control while she negotiated what she told him were tricky ownership rights to any re-creation program. Jennifer was meeting her other boss, Jim Spence, for lunch dates while feeding him juicy tidbits about re-creation stars in fashion and its varied possibilities. She had always had a crush on Jim—a real charmer with craggy, blondish good looks. But he was the boss, and they had always been careful to keep things strictly business-like.

Dr. Paul Wallach was contemplating a graceful exit from a successful thirty-five-year periodontics practice; surely the skilled hands that could perform delicate gum surgery could now be re-employed, together with his other creative faculties, to help Harold deliver his brainchild.

Only his ever-practical partner, Lorraine, seemed to dampen his optimism. What drives him, she had asked? Was it the thrill of adventure, or the need to be accepted by Van as a worthy player in international politics? And of course, she still had concerns for her husband's safety.

Paul didn't really have good answers to those questions, for Lorraine or himself. Anyway, current work was satisfying: implant surgeries with bone grafting; converting gummy smiles into beautiful ones. At home, he amused himself with pronunciation drills in an old Chinese conversation book. Grammar aside, he always did have a good Chinese accent—even Charles Wu thought so.

Paul briefed Charles and suggested he contact Hoda, as he had promised her he would. A few days later, Charles reported that Hoda had visited him at Columbia where they'd discussed such subjects as numerology and the wisdom of the ancients. The visit would have lasted longer than forty-five minutes, except that Charles, unexpectedly, had to type up his own notes again that day; it seems his shared secretary, Eileen Cheung, had taken yet another day off; this was something he must look into.

II.

A meeting of rivals was occurring in Beijing, between MSS Deputy Minister of Operations, Liang-You-Mien and the Science and Technology Deputy Minister Li-Jian-Shui who had conceived *Operation Spotlight*, the espionage and propaganda initiative against the American enemy. Mirroring the American intelligence services in this respect, Chinese Operations Officers like Liang prided themselves on "getting their hands dirty" and often ridiculed the analysts and other ivory tower types like Li. They accused them of having balloon heads from too much thinking and flat butts from too much sitting. Minister Liang's staff of six flanked him around one end of a bare, twenty-foot rectangular maple table in a windowless room reserved for confrontational meetings; chairs were made of plain wood without cushions, and the room was kept deliberately chilly in the February cold. Minister Li sat virtually alone at the other end, preferring to face his accuser with only a recording secretary—not trusting any personnel but his own.

Like his facial features, Liang's words were sharp, slashing through the air like daggers. "Your master plan seems too complicated. Too many paths create a maze that confounds our own forces. The New York rug operation you hatched to get the American agent Van was a complete disaster. Imbedding spy lenses requires too many operatives and really hasn't taken hold. Going forward, trusting Operatives Ren and Ho to travel with our best propaganda documentaries is risky and might give away our plans. Even if Ma's presentation draws Van to Los Angeles, we risk having to liquidate him and the face reading group there in case our plans—again your idea—come to naught. How do you explain yourself?"

Minister Li spoke slowly in resonant tones, "I am not impressed with your bluster. You sit here with your lackeys who mimic the ludicrous faces you make like masks in Chinese opera. Attempting to shift blame on my department for your operational errors is equally ludicrous. The Americans themselves may solve the spy lenses issue. They are in the process of putting scanning cameras on almost every street corner, and we can hack into their database. You, not I, run Ren and Ho, and you bear responsibility for their competence and trustworthiness...also true for Agent Green Dragon in Dallas who supervises the abduction of Van. As for Ma, you have been watching him for years and you must vouch for him. Don't blame the ideas department for failures in implementation. If your intelligence is correct, the Los Angeles meeting will be upon us in just a few days and we will see who will claim credit for success, or lay blame for misfortune and failure!"

III.

A few days later, the faces group met in a first class lounge a few hours before the Southwest Airlines 6 p.m. flight out of Newark bound for L.A. Carlos still seemed edgy, and knocked down a couple of scotches. Harold told the group they'd been booked into the Hilton at LAX. A limo would take them at noon tomorrow to a meeting at an undisclosed location.

Once the flight was underway and after a few minutes of relaxed chatting, sleep came easily; the five hours seemed to go by quickly. After disembarking at LAX and picking up their bags, they approached the exits and saw a limo driver's sign that read: "Faces Group."

Paul looked alarmed. "Should they be advertising our mission?"

"Maybe it's smarter, Unc'," said Harold, as the group drew nearer to the limo driver. "We know what it means; it's doubtful others would know. And if security cameras are sweeping, they couldn't tie us to a sign that didn't have our names on it…at least, that's my thinking."

"Thinking Chinese again, Harold," said Trish.

"…Or CIA," said Carlos. "Secret Agent Savi…" Carlos froze, looking in the direction of the limo driver. "It's…you!"

Danny, wearing a black limo driver's uniform and a ferocious smile, sprang forward. "My friends from the faces group," he announced with a flamboyant wave of his cap. Danny tried to embrace Carlos, who shrank back, offering a half-hearted handshake.

"Anyway," Danny laughed, "let's get acquainted and *re-acquainted.*" He turned to face Jennifer, then bowed and kissed her hand; she squeezed out a smile.

He let go, reached for her overnight bag and placed the sign under his arm.

Carlos hurriedly introduced everybody and apologized to Danny, saying he was shocked—er, no…he meant surprised—to see him in L.A.

Oh, Danny assured them, he understood Carlos's surprise and would deliver the same superior service they had received in Dallas. And he couldn't have been happier to meet Trish, Harold and Paul; their stupefied looks only seemed to amuse him more as he led everyone out the door and into a black, stretch limo with darkly tinted windows. Its passenger area consisted of a polygonal booth with leather seats surrounding a small table. Once on the road, from his driver's seat, Danny kept up a merry monologue; his passengers were still too stunned to reply.

Harold became aware that his heart was beating uncomfortably fast and decided to activate his sensing device. He depressed the black and white buttons twice—seeing the red indicator light go on—and then, a few seconds later, the white "I'm Ok" button once, as the FBI man had directed.

The Hilton was located directly outside the airport, so the ride was short. Danny wished them a "good night and sweet dreams", noting it was 11:30 p.m. New York time. His toothy smile barely slipped as he reminded them to be ready promptly at noon tomorrow. Danny's ominous presence seemed to pervade the atmosphere like a noxious cloud. In Dallas, Harold opined, he was working for Branson. So why was he now here in L.A.?

With a stab at black humor, Trish suggested they cab it back to the airport and take the next flight home. No one laughed.

After checking in and making their way to their interconnected suites, everyone, including Harold, downed room bar brandies that helped ease them into troubled sleep.

IV.

Next morning, strong coffee and a hearty brunch helped calm jitters from the night before. Harold told them his device had been on and transmitting since last night. Perhaps they were all jumping to conclusions. The authorities were probably listening and, after all, even Charles Wu and the Feds had nothing solid on Danny...Maybe he just talks tough to play with people. They had to trust Ma. He was too well known to really try and harm them. At any rate, the device could summon help if necessary. During check out, the clerk surprised them with the news that their bill had already been paid by a certain gentleman. What's more, he had arranged that their return airfare and their outbound fare had also been refunded.

"Very nice of Ma—who else could it be?" said Paul, turning toward the group. "But I thought we were supposed to be paying all our own expenses."

"Call me paranoid," said Harold, "but I would like to re-confirm those arrangements." He punched a few numbers on his cell phone and waited while recorded voices offered him a menu of choices.

Carrying their overnight bags, the group approached the hotel entranceway and prepared to sit on nearby armchairs. Just then, Danny charged through the main door. "Let's go, time's a wasting!" He waved for them to follow and turned to go back out. The group followed dutifully, and moments later stood waiting outside the limo doors as he put their bags in the trunk.

Harold finally reached a live Southwest Airlines clerk on his phone when Danny jerked open the limo door to deliver another shock: occupying the booth seat were a middle-aged man and woman, well dressed and East Asian-looking (probably Chinese, thought Harold). The couple turned to face them with impassive smiles, saying nothing.

"Part of the staff flown in special from Hong Kong," Danny said. "Pile in. I'll explain later." Bewildered, the group allowed them selves to be herded into the roundish booth, next to the expressionless couple.

Harold's cell phone went dead. "Hey Danny," he yelled as they began pulling away, "my cell phone cut out during an important call."

"Oh right, Harold. Sorry—Ma's orders. We don't allow cell phone transmission in the limos at certain times, like when going to undisclosed locations."

"You can jam cell phone transmission?" Harold said, wondering if his sensing device was transmitting.

"Why can't we know where we're going?" asked Paul in an annoyed tone.

"Sorry, Dr. Wallach. We need to have very tight security. This location is very secret for reasons you will understand later." Danny laughed.

Carlos exploded, "I've had enough of this secret bullshit, Danny; I want some answers. Where are we going?"

Harold reached over to his right, gripped Carlos's wrist tightly and whispered in his ear. "Let's stay cool for now, bro'."

"Mr. Morales," said Danny, sounding conciliatory, "I promise you in a short time you will understand and agree that these measures are necessary."

Carlos silently seethed. He would restrain himself for now; he had earlier turned on his phone with the Dragon Anywhere app that converts recorded voice into text; it would have to await clear lines of transmission to send and receive, but it could record.

All along, Paul had been watching the reactions of the Chinese couple. During the awkward moments between Danny and Carlos, the couple had exchanged glances, the woman saying something in Chinese to the man—he answering gruffly. She had glanced back at the group members with a mix of contempt and amusement. When the woman looked at him, Paul was careful to maintain an attitude of good-natured curiosity, and trusted that his face reflected that. He allowed his face to fully relax into a contented smile; the couple seemed to be fighting a desire to smile back, but grimaces won out.

Harold continued to hold Carlos's wrist, but loosened his grip as he felt the tension in Carlos's arm lessen. He gently squeezed the wrist as if to say 'You're Ok now' and then let go. Harold tried to see out the darkened window for clues as to where they were headed, but saw mainly murky outlines of cars and buildings. He finally spotted a sign—barely making out "405 South". So, they were on one of the main freeways, headed south. It was useless to argue or complain; making small talk seemed absurd. *Might as well relax and "enjoy" the ride,* he thought to himself, barely cracking an outward smile.

Trish had been watching the Chinese man opposite her, studying his dour expression, so she was startled to hear a male voice speaking Chinese that wasn't Danny. It also wasn't this Chinese man because his lips weren't moving.

"Qing wen, zhe shi ni di yi ci lai mei guo ma?" said Paul, in perfectly pronounced Mandarin.

…So thought Danny, who was also listening intently. Turning around, he looked expectantly at the couple, and then said something in Chinese that Paul didn't understand—at which point, the Chinese man growled, "Shi de!"

Danny laughed. "Very good accent Dr. Wallach. They understand you perfectly. I'd better translate for everyone. You asked, 'Is this your first trip to America?' and his answer was 'yes.'"

All eyes were now fastened on Paul, as he turned to face the Chinese man. "Ni weisheme lai?"

Danny translated, "Why do you come?"

Before the man could answer, the woman seized his arm and addressed Paul. "Xue xi yue du mei guo ren de lian, jin kan zhen ren."

Danny, his face partially visible in the rearview mirror, pressed out a tight smile—before translating: "…To learn to read American faces, close-up, and in person."

Paul hesitated, searching for the right words, "…Xi wang… wo men neng gou du dong duifang."

Danny roared with laughter. "Oh, very good Dr. Wallach! You said 'hopefully, we can read each other well.' A perfect answer…"

The Chinese man's face contorted in a spasm of rage; slamming the table, he spouted a flood of language that Paul couldn't follow.

The woman turned to the man and shouted, "An jing!"

Paul knew that meant, "Silence!" The enforced quiet lasted for several seconds.

Heads spun at the steely-faced woman's next words: "I think we have seen and heard enough to have an understanding between us."

Paul thought her English was perfect. A few more seconds passed.

Harold forced a mirthless smile. "Really? What kind of understanding comes from pretending not to know the other's language?"

Ballsy and right on the money, thought Trish, regarding Harold with a prideful glint in her eyes.

"In Chinese culture…" the woman enunciated slowly, "…it is permissible to test a stranger's intentions—sometimes pretending innocence." Her imperious expression reminded Harold of the Chinese Dowager Empress from an old movie.

"Innocence?" asked Trish, drawing out the word for emphasis.

Carlos's head shot forward like an enraged rooster. "Is there any end to the mind games you guys play?"

"Wait, Carlos," Harold said. "What *is* this understanding you talk about, Ms…?"

"…Ms. Ren," Danny interposed.

"…You were *saying*, Ms. Ren?" Harold persisted.

The Chinese woman's hardened eyes softened. "If we have an understanding about mind games, we should also have an understanding about…spy games."

Carlos exhaled through drawn lips.

"…As in you won't spy on us if we don't spy on you?" asked Paul, in grave tones.

No one spoke for several seconds; nothing moved except pairs of darting eyes. Everyone started to talk at once and then fell silent.

Harold put up his hand. "Speaking of us and you," he said slowly, "may I ask, who precisely *are* you?"

"We are," the woman continued, "myself and Mr. Ho, like a liaison between Hong Kong film interests and Ma's work at SCU."

"So, you are representing a foreign power?" asked Paul.

"No more than say, BMW discussing auto sales with their American counterparts over here."

Boy! There's a practiced answer if ever I heard one, thought Carlos.

"I gather you are Ma's supervisor, in a way," pressed Paul.

"More like the head of his alumni association from National Shanghai University. We have many cooperative ventures with American film and production companies and universities."

Alumni association—that's a good one, thought Trish.

"Well," said Paul, "we are conducting a private venture with Mr. Ma and, with all due respect, we have not been made aware of your participation at any point."

"Ma may not have explained it," the woman said, smiling, "but we have enjoyed good relationships exchanging information between our two great universities."

Exchanging information, or infiltrating? wondered Trish.

"So, when it comes to exchanging information," asked Harold, "exactly what *are* your concerns regarding spy games, as you put it?"

Ah, mind game parry and thrust! silently observed Trish.

"Excuse me," the Chinese woman replied, turning. She snapped off a few words in Chinese apparently aimed at Danny, who, with a sullen look, raised the barrier window behind him. "To be plain," she continued, "some of your group brought up the issue of the CIA.

I ask you directly, as I know the American preference for directness; was this a bait to lure possible Chinese spies, or do you actively seek the participation of an American spy agency?"

Uh oh, beware double questions again, thought Trish.

"Well…"

"I…"

Harold and Paul had both started to speak. Harold nodded respectfully toward his uncle.

Summoning a contrite smile, Paul began, "I take full responsibility for that CIA business. A schoolmate *of mine*," "because of his familiarity with intelligence matters, may have been able to confirm whether our face reading program had national security implications, or not."

"If you say so," the Chinese woman replied. "But let me propose a reverse situation. What if Ma had mentioned that he had a connection to the MSS—the Chinese Intelligence Services—would you have wanted to continue working with him?"

"That's a fair question," said Paul, remembering the Feds had asked it too.

"Here's another one," interjected Harold, looking directly at the woman. "*Are* you a member of the MSS?"

"I myself am not, but we are, shall I say, not unfriendly to the MSS, as I suppose you are not unfriendly to the CIA." Her smile was smug, almost insolent.

Trish couldn't resist: "Not if we know what's good for us. Oops, did I say that?"

"Fair enough," said Paul, ignoring Trish's joke. "But you folks, or at least Ma, have encouraged my former schoolmate to attend this presentation. We're not really sure he is CIA, or if he's coming, by the way—but you've practically invited him."

"I understand *Ma* invited his participation," the Chinese woman said. "But to again put the shoe on the other foot, can you imagine yourselves, under any circumstances, inviting a member of the MSS to your deliberations?"

A few more seconds of silence ensued. Then, loud laughter broke out that included the other Chinese man and Danny, visible in the rear view mirror.

Danny is probably linked through an intercom, Harold thought. *No surprise. The window raising was just a show. And the other Chinese man probably understands English. More double-talk and mind games...Who is in control of this wacked-out discussion? And where is it leading? Certainly, these people are in control of where they are driving us...*

Just then, the vehicle slowed and turned, indicating their exit down a ramp. Harold could just make out an airport control tower within the darkened field of view—a few hundred yards distant. "We're approaching an airport of some kind," he said.

Danny stopped at a gate, gained admittance, and drove slowly into a large fenced-in area visible through the driver's open window. The outline of a huge building loomed ahead.

"Where are we going? We have a right to know," demanded Paul.

"Ha, ha, ha. Don't worry. You will not be harmed." Ma's familiar voice seemed to float as if disembodied from somewhere in their midst. But, to Harold, it seemed more a taunt than reassurance.

Ma's voice continued, "My colleagues, I must intervene before you become too upset. I have reasons for being so mysterious. The easiest to explain is security. We are entering a little-used area at a small airport to help ensure utmost privacy; it provides special facilities for our purposes, as you shall see."

A two-inch disc in the limo ceiling was evidently the audio speaker. Examining it more closely, Carlos discerned a dark, glassy button at its center. "What's this, a camera lens? Are we being spied on?" he asked, sounding anxious.

"Not exactly," said Ma's voice. "It is integral to presenting the face reading app. If you had known you were being observed, you might have acted inappropriately. In fact, you acted wonderfully, helping to show how the app works. All was recorded on audio and video."

"We were guinea pigs in your experiment then," said Carlos, clearly irked.

"I know we agreed, jokingly, not to study each other," replied Ma, "but I promise you will have all the answers you need very shortly. Not just words; you will experience things that will tell the whole story."

Danny opened all the limo's windows, including the sunroof. The group saw that they were driving through a garage door type opening large enough to admit busses or trucks. Visible through the limo rear window was a small Air China Jet liner parked on a nearby runway. The garage door began to close, shutting out a last glimpse of icy-blue, February sky.

Carlos had been waiting for the opportunity. Unobserved, he pointed his phone through the roof opening toward the patch of sky and pressed *send*— with, he thought, a hope and a prayer.

The limo stopped several yards inside, revealing a cavernous, dimly lit interior space.

Ma's voice came on again. "Please excuse me now. I will be greeting you in person in just a few moments."

Everyone got out of the limousine. The faces group, somewhat dazed and apprehensive, peered about all directions, appraising the spectacular dimensions of the place. It was a curved-top airplane hangar the size of a football field that had been converted into a movie studio: banks of large lights were mounted at the nave and on the sloping sides of the roof structure. Cranes, trestles and catwalks ran across the under-side of the roof, at least one hundred feet above them. The superstructure lining the roof was crammed with cameras, smaller lights, sound and other electrical equipment, as well as pulleys, winches and cables, all neatly arranged, as if it had been operating for months or years, thought Harold.

Most imposing to him were three Jumbothon-sized monitors suspended from the roof. They formed a wide screen, perhaps two hundred feet wide and fifty to sixty feet high. Above them, an LCD display sign spelled out in bright crimson: *Long Beach Studios Presents.* Recorded processional-sounding music was playing at background levels from a full orchestra—including, Harold thought, exotic-sounding Asian instruments and an electronic synthesizer. A few feet below the monitors, situated on the floor, was a centrally positioned dome that reminded him of Ma's Agora dome, except that it was smaller and more open.

The unmistakable figure emerged from under the dome wearing his signature boots, jeans and bad tie. Ma started walking toward them, smiling and waving. Nearing a double row of theatre seats located a short distance from the screens, he gestured to his guests to seat themselves.

Two young men wearing white peaked caps and collared sport shirts emblazoned with *LB Studios* patches ushered them to seats in the first row—the faces group to the right of the staff. The seats were wide, plush recliners allowing upward viewing. Between seats were cup wells and retractable tables containing 3-D goggles and cups of coffee, tea, and apple juice along with fudge and granola-bars.

"No popcorn, but you can't have everything," Ma laughed while turning to an approaching figure. "Oh, here's another member of the staff some of you have met before…this is Feng."

Feng stepped next to Ma and nodded, issuing a brief, correct smile at no one in particular; the two men seated themselves on high-backed swivel chairs several yards in front of the theater seats, facing their audience.

Jennifer noticed that Feng was wearing a maroon sweatshirt like Danny had worn in Dallas—only without the hood. *Another mind game,* she thought, *or am I losing mine?*

The spectators sat upright in their seats, as the reclining mode used in cinematic presentations had not yet been activated. Some craned their necks to see the monitor screens towering over them. During the brief respite, a few helped themselves to drinks and snacks.

Ma spoke, "Feng will start because of his special expertise in our introductory presentation. It is titled *The Human Face in Promotion and Propaganda.* The video monitor on their left flashed the title above a close-up still of a serenely beautiful Asian female (thought Harold) who suddenly became "live", smiling and flashing dark, vivacious eyes.

Harold realized again something curious he had first noticed in the limo: Ma had lost all traces of an Asian accent or pigeon English that omitted articles like "the" and "a". He now sounded as fluent as a native-born American. *What was that about?*

Ma continued, "Part two will be *Former Faces in Cinema Give Way to the New.* The right-hand screen lit up with its title and a zoom-in of another finely wrought Asian face—this time male—befitting a leader. "This kind of presentation is not just a show. You will be immersed in a reality so vivid that you will feel much like actual participants." Ma paused, pointing at the screens. "Please note, we have saved the best for last, part three: *Read My Face,* a spymaster-tested app that rates your would-be mate or business associate. In this, you will certainly participate." The central monitor flashed its title over a circular montage of headshots.

Members of the faces group were amazed as they recognized themselves: Harold, Trish, Carlos, Jennifer, Paul—but also Lorraine Wallach and Charles Wu. Arranged around them were Ms. Ren and Mr. Ho, Ma, and also Feng and Danny. An oval shaped blank space occupied the center of the grouping; imprinted over the space was a black question mark.

Ma spoke again. "Some of these images you yourselves sent; some came from the limo. Mr. Wu supplied his own at my request." He laughed, seemingly amused by his guests' baffled looks.

Exchanging glances, Harold and Paul seemed to share the same thought: who had introduced Ma to Wu? Paul wrinkled his brow quizzically; Harold answered with a shrug.

The lights dimmed to near-total blackness; a message flashed on and off the central monitor: *Don your goggles, recline your seats, and enjoy the show.*

Ma and Feng adjusted their lapel microphones. Harold noticed Ma's smile was bright as ever but Feng's seem to fade; the overhead lights dimmed to half power.

Feng's words boomed out of the surround-sound system and throughout the huge enclosure without echo or distortion. "The following documentary marks the dawn of a new realism in revisiting history—one that permits truth to emerge."

The background music began with a march-like theme that sounded tinny and archaic to Harold. All three monitors showed a shifting array of faces—Western, African, Asian—taken from news film footage. The screens seemed to shimmer with uncommon brightness. The male voiceover narrator began speaking in stilted, portentous tones that Harold associated with film actors and wartime newsreels of the thirties and forties.

"*The Human Face in Promotion and Propaganda,*" said the narrator, "... describes a culture that is dated and dying. Why is that? Promotion and Propaganda are perfectly acceptable words in Western culture. That is the problem. It has become acceptable in the West to force so-called truths upon unsuspecting masses. But now the tide is turning toward an older and superior culture that trusts the observer to discern truth by simply observing the reality before him."

The music then transitioned from a Western sound to a blend of Western and Asian harmonies. All three monitor screens melded into an enormous wrap-around view of the Eurasian continent from one thousand miles up. A zoom-in began, accompanied by the voiceover, "Viewed from space, the magnitude of Eurasia is clearly evident. It occupies two-thirds of Earth's land mass and four-fifths of its population. As dawn breaks, the shadow of night slowly dissolves. At seven miles above you see details of dun-colored towns and green pasturelands separated by silvery rivers and dark, jagged mountain ranges. These are 3-dimensional satellite images of Central Asia...but the year is twelve forty-eight, A.D., nearly a millennium ago!"

Harold noted how the melodic line climbed majestically, sounding vaguely Wagnerian but with an Asian flavor. Drums, brass, Chinese-sounding strings and cymbals rose to a deafening crescendo; it barely masked a thunderous beating noise one hundred feet above on the roof of the hanger-studio: the landing of a U.S. Army UH-60 Sikorsky helicopter.

Its passenger had been briefed on how to enter the building through a roof hatch, which he accomplished easily. As he eased his large frame onto a steel platform below the re-fastened hatch cover, Van had to ask himself, *was this trip necessary?* Yes, he had seen the Air China liner parked outside. And yes, plugged into the wire worn by Wallach's nephew, he heard about Danny's "coincidental" arrival as a driver here in L.A. He also heard Ma's overdone secrecy like those ridiculous jamming attempts in the limo, and also the discussion about spying, the CIA and the MSS. Charles had called him at the last minute saying he couldn't guarantee Ma's loyalty, but that his presentation promised to be national security dynamite.

Maybe so; we'll see. Still, he had his doubts about whether this was worth bringing in the FBI, which awaited his signal from beyond the airport gates. Van's Canon 15/50 spy binocs had revealed a few possible hostiles outside the building…and now a few inside. His Taser M26 stun gun occupied the inside pocket of his trench coat. So here he was, traversing a catwalk suspended over an ear-blasting extravaganza. Everybody of interest was right below him. *Might as well enjoy the show. They even supplied 3-D goggles.*

On the screens, a bird's-eye view from about one thousand feet showed thousands of wicker-helmeted bowmen on horseback dashing across grasslands and clashing with battalions of sword-swinging infantrymen. Warrior-type faces exhibited a range of emotions: fierce determination, rage, exultation, grim resignation; their colorfully appointed mounts resembled the small but agile war ponies of the time.

The voiceover continued, "You are witnessing events from nearly eight-hundred years ago, re-created authentically from archeological and DNA evidence left by the warring peoples. This is the last great battle between invading Mongol Khans and the Han people of China. It depicts *not* the destruction of a noble, sophisticated culture, the Chinese, but their absorption of the militarily advanced and hardy invaders—unjustly called barbarians by the West. The result was an ultimate strengthening of that culture."

The scene faded, as the same narrator spoke: "Contrast that with another conquest of so-called barbarians, also carrying bows, but in relatively recent times…" The monitors showed a panorama of an American landscape of the 1870s, titled "Dakota Badlands". The camera zoomed in to within two hundred feet. "We now see another cavalry charge across grasslands led by dozens of blue-clad soldiers. They are sabering and shooting a small band of Indians huddled against a wide creek that had cut off their escape. Like time travelers on the scene, we experience the panic, anguish and hopelessness in the victims' faces. Contrast the hatred, contempt and bloodthirstiness in the expressions of those who butcher them. Unfortunately, in this sad case, there was no melding of cultures, only obliteration of one by the other—and both the worse for it."

Harold thought, *I know it's re-creation, but this is riveting…and convincing…a new level of documentary realism. Great effects.* He looked over to see group members recoil from the maelstrom of carnage as if bodies might tumble from the screens into their laps.

One hundred feet above, Van thought, *what a crock! America has atoned for all of that by absorbing the downtrodden like nobody else. How many people are running to China these days for freedom? And the Chinese are as racist as any whites. I'll admit, though, this is clever propaganda.*

The satellite camera shifted from the Dakotas "to neighboring Wyoming," the voiceover continued. "…where a hunting party of swaggering, former blue-shirts take dead aim with their Winchester repeaters on a band of Chinese coolies they had flushed out of tents by blowing bugles. See the uncomprehending fear of the pajama-clad Asians, pigtails swinging as they ran, not taking cover or defending themselves." The narrator concluded, "…these facts were documented by no less an authority than the New York Times of the 1880s—not that long ago."

Harold remembered: this was that Wyoming massacre they showed at CAM where the Chinese "ran without resistance, like antelope". Deep revulsion soured his stomach as he realized that Ma had incorporated the CAM display he had forwarded into this documentary. *You couldn't blame the Chinese for carrying grudges about such atrocities. But whose side was Ma on?*

"Ironically," intoned the voiceover, "the sound of bugles announces our next re-visiting of history. You are now zooming in on the Yalu River Basin separating China from North Korea. The year is 1950. You see faces of thousands of Chinese volunteer soldiers, made up of farmers and workers, streaming down hillsides, resolute and proud, blowing bugles and scattering the frightened enemy before them. The faces of defeated American and U.N. soldiers show befitting expressions of bewilderment and despair."

We did underestimate the Chinese in 1950, thought Paul. *This is a bit of revisionism, though, considering the way things turned out—in a stalemate. But let's face it, that war spawned "The Manchurian Candidate" and our recent fear of the Chinese.*

Paul's former Chinese language classmate reflecting from above had a somewhat different take: *Volunteers my ass! They were herded to the slaughter by their machine-gun toting commissars. But we did run, and oh, how they love to rub it in.*

The voiceover began again, as images of wheeling tanks and dog-fighting jets flitted across the screens. "As they say, the conquerors write the histories—along with all their justifications and biases. But true winners need not employ propaganda to combat truth—which will out in the long run…"

Martial music began as the left-hand screen showed Chinese military leaders, from ancient through modern in digital re-creation. The right-hand screen showed American counterparts from Revolutionary times to present. The center screen was divided into Chinese/English language captions on the left and English on the right.

The narrator continued: "The military sphere should draw any peoples' bravest, brightest and best…On the left, see the faces of Chinese warrior-sages that reveal the true mettle of a nation: sprung from the people, tanned and fit from hard work, clear, shining eyes reflecting the divine spirit of their ancestors, an unwavering determination to defend with valor and wisdom the motherland, and her incomparable five-thousand-year-old civilization.

On the right, see the soldiers of the would-be empire barely two-hundred-fifty years old and already in decline, dissolute sons of privilege who won their spurs butchering blacks, Mexican peasants and Native Americans...In two world wars, they are able to defeat virtuous and tenacious enemies only by overwhelming force of arms...until finally, they met the unconquerable Asian warrior who exposed them first in Korea and then Vietnam for what they really are: racist, debauched and cowardly."

Van laughed to himself, *I can't decide if Ma's trying more to impress his Beijing masters with this crap or to piss me off. He certainly succeeds on the second count. I'm still not sure whether he really wants me here and whether or not I'm supposed to arrest him.*

The music segued to a contemporary jazz beat. The screens showed throngs of shoppers streaming in and out of stores bearing signs advertising housewares.

A new narrator began, "Some say, the term 'truth in advertising' is an oxymoron..." After the mind-numbing intensity of the past several minutes, the faces group allowed themselves a brief interlude of faint laughter. "...If so," the voice continued, "it means advertising and promotion can only cloud or distort the truth, whether it be about people, or products..."

The monitor video showed quick-cuts of various consumer products, including T.V.'s, cars, computers, and clothes being manufactured, sold, and enjoyed by the end-users, all with "Made in China" labels.

"...Therefore, in the long run, the truth will out about products too—if people and governments permit free trade and free choice. Left to their own preferences, people invariably choose Chinese products..." Clips of angry politicians shaking their fists were superimposed over newspaper headlines of anti-China tariff bills passed by U.S. Congress.

I see where they are going with this, thought Paul. *But let's be honest, the Chinese don't really play fair: dumping, rigged exchange rates, pirating, espionage...*

The screens now showed clips of blackboard formulas, R&D laboratories, product-testing machines, and rats in cages. "...Some in the West praise so-called innovation, while disparaging so-called imitators. In fact, more improvements and new innovations come from perfecting products than from just ivory-tower brainstorming. Nevertheless, China, now becoming the world's leader in manufacturing, is poised to regain her once proud role as innovator as well…"

The screens showed a panoply of Chinese inventions: paper making, the compass, gunpowder, fireworks and rocketry, printing, metallurgy, the blast furnace, porcelain, the weaving loom, and recent advances in space engineering, neutrino particle physics, a non-invasive blood test for Down's Syndrome, and stem cell "educator" cells. Accompanying the images were rousing strains of recorded Classical Chinese music played by an orchestra featuring two-stringed fiddles, plucked lutes, wooden oboes and bronze bells.

The narrator continued, "The world increasingly turns to China, the font of ancient wisdom…a venerable civilization that has always valued the virtue of industriousness; something that is now declining in the West. China is the world's most populous country, now becoming the most prosperous, and the center of world affairs. After all, Jung-guo means Central Kingdom.

"Entrepreneurs and capital are increasingly attracted by China's highly educated work-force and favorable business climate, unfettered by hidebound regulation." Filling the screens were wide-angle shots of the futuristic Shanghai skyline, a thronged Tiananmen Square in Beijing, huge dam and hydroelectric sites on Yellow River, and the busy Hong Kong airport. The scenes were juxtaposed with close-ups of attractive Chinese faces in various working poses and garb.

Lights flashed on; Ma dropped off his perch and approached the group. "Ready for a short break? I see some of you squirming in your seats." He laughed. "Time for some feedback or questions."

"Yes, Ma," said Carlos, clearly agitated. "You appear to be shamelessly pushing propaganda like the paid agent of a foreign power. I thought you were an American cinema producer."

"Ah, thank you Carlos," Ma replied. "Immediately we get to the heart of the issue. The content and tone of this presentation so far, is definitely one-sided—and deliberately so. But my role as artist, for now, must be a neutral one."

"But how can you be neutral," asked Paul, sounding more sad than angry, "if you're promoting this propaganda?"

"Let me explain," Ma replied. "Two things. First, we see the power of what the American call "spin"— in this case, reinforced by life-like imagery. The information presented here is clearly slanted and selective, but there is enough indisputable fact to gain credibility from even you, an American audience, especially when it is presented with such realism. Also, there is another technology at work here, developed in China, which enhances the persuasive power of the presentations. Please trust me, I must withhold this from you until the end. Now the second point: obviously, this project has grown beyond the bounds of our own resources and even SCU, although I am indebted to them for refinements to the face-reading sensor borrowed from magnetic resonance imaging and spectrophotometry. That is why Ms. Ren and Mr. Ho are here, representing Chinese media interests looking into the potential of technology from both nations to benefit both sides in joint ventures." Ma smiled at the pair who smiled back, seemingly recovered from their previous fits of pique in the limo.

"But Ma," said Harold, "are you also selling our face reading technology to the highest bidder? We are your collaborators in this project. Aren't we to share in another colossal opportunity built on our program?"

"Ah, Harold. I'm happy to see your ambition is growing with your imagination. Feng, our staff, and myself would have accomplished the presentations you have seen so far even if you and I had never met. The face reading is separate and our faces group will retain full licensing rights. But now, far from being cut out, you are being let in on something rather fabulous; I would welcome your participation in this technology developed by the Chinese government. But bear with me a while longer."

Paul noticed furious whispering between Feng and Danny. He tried to ignore their distracting antics as he rose to address Ma. "Despite whatever assurances you may make to the contrary…these surprises… and the possibility of a foreign power having access to these projects …" Paul paused, turning first to Trish and then to Harold who started to whisper to him. All five of the group, now standing, engaged in a brief, sharp hubbub.

"Please friends, take your seats," said Ma in a conciliatory tone— which seemed to mollify the assemblage as they returned to their seats.

"Let me cut to the chase," continued Ma. "I am going to abbreviate part two, *Former Faces in Cinema Give Way to the New*, because you are already getting the idea, and so you can more quickly enjoy part three, the meat of what you really came for."

Still looking troubled, the group resumed their seats, readjusted their goggles and prepared to continue watching the presentation.

Accompanied by a flourish of big-band music from the nineteen-forties, the voiceover narrator began with the same intonation that had previously struck Harold as archaic and corny: *"Now introducing the Hollywood Cavalcade of Stars."* What followed was a beautifully integrated montage of vintage as well as contemporary stars.

Harold, however—while admiring the top-notch production value of this digital re-creation—noticed something peculiar about the facial images…

Something was bothering Van as well as he held his goggles at different angles to see better. The close ups, especially in 3-D, were indeed life-like: skin texture, pores, every tiny hair and blemish. The focus could not have been sharper and yet, the proportions, and the angles of the features…something was off.

Harold, the supposed film buff, had to figure this out. Why does everybody look the same, but somehow maddeningly different? Slight, subtle changes had made Bogy and Bacall look sinister, Katy Hepburn and Cary Grant looked deranged or idiotic. The newer stars suffered from the same kinds of distortion: George Clooney looked bloated and dull; Leonardo Di Caprio, piqued and sickly; Brad Pitt, swarthy and serpentine. All the "presidential" types used to portray leaders looked coarse and thuggish; and the younger actors' faces all seem to be stuck in an ugly duckling, adolescent stage. The changes were only barely noticeable, but had Ma miscalculated with his computer-generated grid lines? This was not a good audition for Trish and Jen as far as using Elizabeth Taylor or whoever for cosmetics or fashion. *Had anyone else picked up on this?*

Harold looked over at his partners; their faces began to tighten up as if pulled by drawstrings, as images appeared on the opposite screen. The contrasting faces of Asian actors were predictably perfect and idealized, resembling humanoid robots. But was this realistic and convincing? Everybody looked stereotypically noble or glamorous or wise or innocent, but also very phony. So, they aren't quite right either…Was this all deliberate? If so, what was Ma trying to prove?

The narrator continued, "As you can see, the faces of cinema reflect their cultures and are changing for the better. A civilization that looks decadent, shriveled and weak is giving way to one that is virtuous, vibrant and energetic. The fading culture that worships sexual immorality, greed, gluttony and sloth is being superseded by one that venerates traditional family values, hard work and healthy life-styles."

At first Van was steaming. Then he snorted a laugh, thinking, *this propaganda film is like badly made Chinese counterfeit money: hokey and amateurish. Is this the best they can do?* Still, he had to remember Hitler, Stalin and Mao always put over the Big Lie. The masses are asses, was the saying—undoubtedly true. Also annoying was this shimmering on the screens, a faint flickering, like a strobe light…

Harold raised his hand like a traffic cop. "Ma, excuse me but, like you said, we *have* gotten the idea. It's time for explanations that make sense, at least to me…"

"Fine, Harold." Ma swiveled in his chair to face Harold, smiled triumphantly and puffed out his chest. We've accomplished the exact desired result." At his hand gesture, the screens went blank, the sound cut, and lights came back on.

"This is way over the top, Ma," said Harold, his tone challenging. "The Hollywood types look like villains and the Asians like cartoon heroes. Maybe the Chinese—no offence—would buy it, but the Americans wouldn't nor would anyone else in the West."

"Precisely, Harold."

"What?" said Harold, removing his goggles and scratching his head.

Ma hopped down from his chair and stood facing Harold. "These historical narratives are precisely what masses of Chinese and others would believe: a straightforward hero or a villain. You in the West want everything nuanced these days; everybody is conflicted and confused under a mass of contradictions. You don't even believe in your own myths anymore." His laugh sounded sympathetic.

"So then," demanded Harold, looking befuddled, "What practical use or significance is any of this to us?"

"Don't focus on the content. That can be changed depending on the market or customer. The real message, according to your media sage, Marshall McLuhan, is the medium. In this case, digital re-creation and realistic history coming at you, enhanced by secret new technology, courtesy of, naturally, the Chinese."

Ah, thought a grimly smiling Van. *So that's their game: buy up American movie distribution rights and show the distorted versions worldwide—along with their own pantheon of perfect movie gods and fairy tale characters. Third World populations will eat it up like candy.*

"What's this secret, new technology again Ma?" asked Paul, now energized and waving his hands. "You're like a carnival barker, always hawking the extra added attraction."

"Yes, Dr. Wallach, but this is not an empty shell game. There'll be a real payoff for you folks and courtesy of the People's Republic of China, you're going to learn the secret of the trick! This is special communications technology I am now handing over to the West. Did everybody notice the shimmering quality of the monitor screens? It may have been annoying at first, but you get used to it. Thanks to these special goggles though, you have not had any lasting effects. They are not just for 3-D. If your colleague Van were here, Dr. Wallach, he would appreciate what I'm about to demonstrate…"

Feng began speaking under his breath furiously to Danny who looked sullen.

Ma glanced at them, showing a trace of a smile. He walked back several feet to the dome-like structure under the now blank monitor screens and manipulated some controls. All three screens began to show swirling black lines, similar to T.V. test patterns, which then blended, at high speed, into waves and circular pulses. Soon, all homogenized into a subdued, rapid strobe, followed by the shimmering effect seen earlier.

Ma switched the screens off and continued speaking, "You experienced something called flash induction, made up of intense subliminal flashing. It can directly program the subconscious mind, kind of like hypnosis. Through something called brain wave entrainment, it directly affects areas of the pre-frontal cortex involved with belief. I know how you value solid science; we believe flash induction can scientifically enhance belief in almost anything—especially doctored documentaries!"

Ma continued, "As you might imagine, repeated inductions are necessary to achieve lasting results. But let me ask the skeptics: isn't this technology important enough for governments to fight over?" Ma looked upward with hands outstretched as if imploring a deity.

Harold was confounded. *What was Ma's game?* The rest of the faces group also seemed confused—while the Chinese couple looked clearly elated. Ms. Ren was clasping Mr. Ho's left hand with her right. Harold saw that Feng and Danny were fidgeting in their seats, looking increasingly agitated and petulant.

Just then a huge shadow invaded the lit space in front of the viewing area. A catwalk swung down close to the startled and incredulous occupants of the first row.

"Don't be alarmed," said Ma, looking up, "I believe a special visitor may be joining us."

Van delighted in seeing the shocked faces below as he descended the last rungs of the catwalk and dropped the remaining several inches onto the floor. The sides of his trench coat had flapped out like wings, helping create the illusion—given his hawk-nosed appearance—of a giant raptor landing in their midst. Van observed that some people looked simply surprised, but others looked scared and guilty as hell.

"Van, I presume," said Ma, stepping forward with an outstretched hand.

Van enveloped Ma's much smaller hand briefly. "I just love surprises. Don't you? It's easier to see what people are about when you catch them unawares." Van's powerful gaze swung around like a laser beam.

No one moved or spoke.

Paul bolted forward and started shaking Van's hand as if pumping water. "Van! At last! We'd hoped you'd come. Things aren't quite right out here and maybe you can help sort them out." Harold, Carlos, Jennifer and Trish rose almost as one and surged forward to meet Van.

"Nothing against you or your people, Paul," said Van, disengaging from the handshake with some difficulty. "I would have rather *not* come, but my presence is often the best way to *make* things right…and flush out the bad guys." Van focused keenly on Ma, then Feng and Danny—who looked away.

"Van, you remind me," said Ma, "of a fictional detective named Charlie Chan. He put people on the spot and exposed the bad guys. I've got the perfect stage for your activities. Please—everyone take your seats. Van, please sit in the second row. We'll demonstrate how faces technology can tell good guys from bad."

Everyone, including Van, dutifully sat like students responding to a teacher's command. Feng and Danny continued to look blankly straight ahead.

Ma sat down again and poked at his Smartphone. The assembled group appeared live on the screen in a circular pattern. "Everyone here is on the spot, so to speak, including our mystery person, who turns out to be Van." Ma smiled pleasantly and nodded at Van. "Now the group is complete. The face-reading program can work on an individual level, in a group dynamic, or person-to-person. The sensors diagnose the emotional and physical health of the body by reading heat and moisture as well as textural and color changes coming from the facial skin. It also factors in the strength and timbre of voices along with body language. It detects cringing or evasive posture, signs of habitual positive or negative facial expressions and stress. By reading your stress levels and expression lines, it reveals degrees of confidence, courage and optimism; bad news if you sneer, scowl or pout a lot. Dr. Wallach—dentists will be happy to hear that healthy smiles are always good news." Ma chuckled. "And by the way, we discovered a direct correlation between happiness and good health, based on facts from the bios of the more than five-thousand actors we surveyed. So, you can't really fake looking happy, or healthy...they tend to run together." Ma shot another pointed look at Danny and Feng, whose snarly expressions seem to have returned. "Remember the Chinese proverb: 'When there is light in the soul, there will be beauty in the person.' Ha!"

Ma touched his cell phone screen. "This is how you look now—and how your camera phone would look showing the faces you'd scan and the voices you'd record if they were in range. How well you like the faces and bodies you scan is part of your reaction. To read yourself or any other individual, read the top gauge needle that swings between healthy and unhealthy; this is a composite measure of your stress and fitness levels.

To assess the compatibility of any two—or more—people, click on the viewing screens showing the scanned faces, and depress the shutter, as if taking a photo. Then refer to the three display gauges colored red, orange and yellow. They are labeled Connection, Confusion and Conflict: the three C's—brilliantly conceived, I might add, by Harold."

Harold looked pleased, as a few cheers broke out.

Ma continued, "The gauges also register low, medium and high. Next, press on any two or more faces, and depress the shutter. The faces will be read, giving an answer in any or all three of the categories. A reading of Confusion represents a mix of Connection and Conflict. However, we know that people can change and so can circumstance, especially as you act on your intentions. For advice on how to proceed in the future, press the button and see the message revealed, like a fortune cookie." Ma snickered. "Except, that *these* are derived verbatim from *I Ching* hexagrams. Select either of two modes: business or romance. First, we'll choose business."

Looking over at Van, Paul recognized the body language of a cynic: backwards slouch, twisted smile, fingertips splayed out.

Ma continued: "The program will accurately reveal your stress level and any tension in your face. If your motives are mixed, it will give mixed messages, so make your intentions clear and your motives pure— if you can!" Ma chuckled and pressed a button. Each of their headshots was enlarged by fifty percent. "We are all going to see how we look and interact; how we perceive our roles, and play them in real life."

Harold felt blood rush to his face again. He stole a look at Trish who was looking back with a thin, knowing smile.

Ma continued, "Working chronologically with the faces group— Harold, Trish, Carlos, Jennifer and Dr. Wallach—what do we see when we interface them? We see a medium-high level of Connection, and medium-low levels of Conflict...resulting in some confusion. I understand the intention was for business, but perhaps there are mixed motives, mutual suspicions or jealousies. Forgive my candor, but the most convincing test must be of ourselves. Anyone object, or disagree?"

Harold noted that no one spoke or gestured; Feng and Danny seemed to be glaring straight ahead.

Ma continued, "The sensor will read your demeanor and stress level based on skin emissions, expression and voice. With these five people, the readings will be a composite. Here's what the message says: 'Proceed with caution, make sure motives are pure, information is correct, and individual roles are understood clearly.' Exactly. It may sound vague or a cliché, just like *I Ching,* but it does give a green light, so to speak, as long as one is prudent."

Paul watched Van on the screen shift to an upright, alert posture, then begin to manipulate his large wristwatch and speak into it.

"Next, we add Mr. Wu to the mix. We see the needle rise to the same level of medium-high connection; again, not perfect. What is missing in this relationship? Perhaps lack of information, motives or roles that are again not clearly understood. The message says: 'New factor in enterprise creates possibilities for growth, but also for complications.' I admit, this answer is also pretty vague, but the overall direction remains forward, with no visible obstacles in the way."

Ma's cheerful expression, visible in close up on the screen, now took on a darker aspect. "Now I must submit myself to the process…"

A murmur arose from the spectators.

"…Your humble servant may be presented in a less than perfect light." The needles showed medium-high levels of Connection, but also medium levels of Confusion and Conflict. "You are wondering what is wrong with Ma?" As he poked at the device in his hand, Ma's wide smile seemed to shrink. "The message says: 'When taking middle course, be wary of possibilities for distrust.' Hahhh!" he said, as if conceding the sensor had read him well. "I have previously given some people grounds for suspicion, and now present myself as neutral between contending parties. Perhaps all suspect me and question my loyalty to their enter- prise, whatever it may be."

Harold saw everyone—even Van—seem to nod or smile somberly as if giving credence to Ma's "confession."

"But it's not all about me," Ma went on. "We add Ms. Ren and Mr. Ho, my *mentors* from Hong Kong…"

Ma's smile seems particularly warm, thought Harold.

"…Between them, we see high connection, low conflict—not sur- prising. Now, as we align their pictures with the group already studied…we see only medium Connection, and also medium Confusion and Conflict. The summary message says: 'One may not serve two masters without loss of freedom and loss of self.' Sounds like more ambivalence. Is there a lack of trust here also? Before answering, let's add in Van."

Van shifted forward in his seat, eyes narrowing.

"He shows low to medium Connection, Confusion *and* Conflict; not one to easily make commitment. The message says: 'When great effort has been expended to overcome doubt, it is easier to take action.' Really? Are we ready for action? Or do we still doubt? Finally let's look at Feng and Danny."

The two sat rigid at the sound of their names.

"Add them in and we see…Connection between the two of them is medium, but between them and the rest of the group it rests at…almost zero. Confusion is at a very low level and conflict, at a very high one. What does this mean?"

Feng huffed his disapproval; Danny's lower lip protruded defiantly.

Ma continued, "The message says: 'Enemies that pretend to be friends may be easier to read than friends who hold back truth.' Aha! Are you ready for the truth?" Ma pointed at Feng and Danny.

The two sprang up almost in unison and faced the group in a combative pose. Feng pulled a small, silver, automatic pistol from his pants pocket. "The truth is that you, Ma, are a traitor to the motherland." His hand shook slightly as he pointed the pistol at Ma and then waved it back and forth at the group. "But we are all taking a little trip to visit her. Danny, get the limo ready and I'll alert the pilot." Feng spoke into a cell phone, which he had plucked from his shirt pocket.

Danny started to run in the direction of the hanger entrance and then stopped as a deep voice rang out over Harold's right shoulder. "Hold it right there, little man. This airport's in lockdown and nobody's going anywhere." All eyes were on Van, as he rose and held his Taser gun pointed at Feng.

"Xu zhang sheng shi!" Feng shouted. Forgetting Van for the moment, he lurched toward Danny who hesitated, looking confused.

"You're wrong, it's no bluff," said Van, understanding Feng's words to Danny.

The loud crackle of the Taser resounded in Harold's right ear. With a mewing cry, Feng crumpled to the floor as the Taser strings snared his arm and body. With surprising speed for such a big man, Van vaulted over the front seats and rushed upon Feng, who lay sprawled and quivering—having dropped the pistol and the cell phone on the floor. Van quickly pocketed both in his trench coat and re-holstered his Taser. Leaning down on one knee, he spoke into his Super Watch, "Where's my backup?"

Ma walked over calmly, kneeled beside Feng and held his limp arms down. "Don't worry, I'll control him. You can trust me."

Danny started to sprint full out on the concrete floor and toward the parked limo halfway across the hangar floor. An instant later, Harold charged after him. Someone had turned on major lighting, which flooded the entire studio floor. A few uniformed staff gathered near the exit to watch the commotion headed their way, while others, further away, started to run in that direction.

Van bounded in long strides after the two men, followed closely by Carlos and Paul who were walking fast. Trailing them by several yards were Trish and Jennifer, trying to keep up.

Another witness to the scene—a well-dressed Asian man of advanced-middle age with a roundish face—was sitting in a modified golf cart at the rear of the studio. He watched as a trio of FBI-jacketed men converged on Ma and the prostrate Feng who was beginning to stir.

The FBI men propped Feng up to a sitting position, pulled his arms back and applied handcuffs. The Chinese couple approached and embraced Ma, babbling happily.

Still running, Danny slowed slightly as he neared the shut vehicle entrance and an adjacent door, which was barred by a security guard. Halting, he then shot off toward a mini-studio off to the right that was enclosed by a low fence. Harold was closing fast, only fifteen or twenty feet behind, when Danny jumped over the two-foot picket fence, apparently headed for a door left ajar that was emitting daylight.

Harold thought, *I was never a good hurdler, but I better be now.* He leapt over the fence with inches to spare, and in two big bounds caught Danny by the scruff of his jacket collar. Danny, in a quick motion, slipped out of the garment, spun around and assumed a martial arts posture—as did Harold. Danny made a threatening chopping gesture with his hands and kicked straight out toward Harold's head. Harold barely ducked the blow and began to circle his adversary. Danny took a running jump, followed by a backward spinning move and aimed another vicious kick at Harold's mid-section.

Harold moved in quickly to cut the radius and force of the blow, blocking it with an upward raised thigh. Focused on each other, the two were barely aware of the spectators surrounding them, like at a prizefight. Harold now stepped forward in a half-crouch, trailing a half-bent leg behind him, ready to spring. With only a brief hesitation, his trailing leg suddenly whipped high in a wide arc. The blow was so fast the only sure sign it had landed was an audible crack—as Danny's jaw whipped upwards and he crashed to the floor.

"I hope I didn't hurt him too badly," exclaimed Harold. He leaned over the prone Danny who, though breathing, was clearly unconscious.

"Way to go Harold!" yelled Carlos as he and the women gathered around.

Paul kneeled down and raised one of Danny's eyelids, looking for a pupillary response. He checked the airway, then felt the neck. "I don't think he's badly injured, Harold…Doesn't look like a concussion or a broken jaw, and his carotid pulse is strong and regular."

Several seconds later, Danny came around and started to get up, but two other FBI men held him back and handcuffed him. As they pulled him to his feet, Danny's eyes were downcast.

"Some mighty nifty moves there," said Van, still slightly out of breath. "Catching bad guys these days, I must admit, is more of a young man's game." He smiled. "I'm glad I could help, but it looks like everything's under control." Van looked toward the exit door through which several FBI men were escorting Feng, Danny and three other staff members who had apparently tried to escape; they also wore the distinctive maroon sweat suits—and handcuffs.

"So why did you finally decide to come, Van?" asked Paul, stepping toward him.

"I'll take some responsibility for that," said a familiar voice behind them.

Everyone looked over to see Charles Wu standing behind the gate barrier about fifteen feet away; next to him stood Ma, Ms. Ren and Mr. Ho.

Wu spoke, "Mr. Ma and I are previously acquainted, thanks to Skype." Wu smiled at Van who was looking at him open-mouthed. "Questions will be answered in due course; I'm sure Van has some of his own."

"Don't I though!" boomed Van, his look spearing Charles Wu.

"However, if I may, Mr. Wu," answered Ma, "the presentation for the faces group is not complete. We have not chosen the romance mode yet, if you are all willing."

"I'm ready for that," said Carlos with a strange smile, as the others turned to look at him. "Like the documentary said, the truth will out. So, let's have it all out."

"Good," said Ma. "But possible romance within the group is really none of my business, even for purposes of demonstration." Ma's smile was brief and gracious. "So, on your seats I have left mobiles for the faces group with the app already selected; you can run it yourselves. As I said before, the most convincing test for anyone is a self test." Ma beckoned for the others to follow as he headed toward an enclosed private office. Van, still shaking his head in disbelief, followed behind, accompanied by another man in an FBI jacket.

Carlos, Harold, Trish, Jennifer and Paul approached the theatre seats and prepared to sit together in the first row. Paul stopped. "I have no romantic interest aside from my wife, so maybe this is none of my business either."

"The perfect reason for staying, Uncle Paul," said Harold. "You and Aunt Lorraine are a tried and true love match. You would be a predictable control in this experiment."

"I agree," said Jennifer, smiling. "Dr. Wallach, you and your wife appear to be the perfect loving couple, and so this would be a kind of ultimate test for the app."

"Ok," said Paul, sitting down smiling. "I'm in. So if I'm the control, I'll go first." He lined up his headshot with Lorraine's and pushed the toggle. "Connection" registered very high; Confusion very low and Conflict, as medium. "Ha!" he said. "No surprise. I interpret the medium conflict reading to mean that we love and understand each other—

all too well. Lorraine thinks I'm playing a role that's not really me and I disagree, although I suspect she's right."

Paul enjoyed the hearty laughter from the group. He pushed the message button and read aloud: " 'Even if two hearts are one, minds may not be' ".

More laughter erupted.

"Ok, we're next," said Carlos, brightly, as if looking forward to the test. He lined up his headshot with Jennifer's and pushed the toggle… Connection was medium, Confusion low and Conflict low. The message flashed on the overhead: 'Your innermost nature is innocent and free from blame, unlike the outer person who plays a role. Move forward with integrity and don't form relationships out of convenience or formality.'

"Doesn't that just nail it?" said Carlos, a peaceful smile on his lips as he looked at Jennifer. "I was going through the motions with you, like with any female, just playing a role like Dr. Wallach described. The difference is, his role-playing was based on something real for him—an interest in international politics. The real Carlos—remember Harold, how I challenged you to discover your real self and what you really wanted in a woman? Well, that's ironic because—the *real* Carlos is a gay man. Not that I've ever really acted on it beyond my fantasies. That's *my* reality. There may be possibilities of romance for me, but before that happens, the real Carlos has to come out. Today, I took a step in that direction."

Wild applause and hurrahs broke out.

"I'll say you did, bro'," said Harold, turning to embrace Carlos standing at his side.

Jennifer looked over with a warm smile; she reached around Harold to grip Carlos's shoulder.

Harold spoke, "So Carlos knows who he is, and what he wants. As for me…" he shot an anxious glance at Trish, "let's get this over with."

"*Now* look who's all hot and bothered," said Carlos with his best rascally grin.

A burble of affectionate laughter arose from the group.

Harold fumbled with the mobile. "Damn thing! Which is the button to line up the images? Let's see, there's Jennifer. She's a possibility…sorry—bad joke."

Jennifer made her droll "silly boy!" face while Trish vamped a "highly insulted" expression.

Harold lined up images of himself and Trish, then read: "Connection, high… Confusion, low to medium…and Conflict, low…*Can you believe that?*"

Jennifer and Carlos yelled "Woo, woo!" and "Go for it, man!"

"Wait…" Harold said. "Let's hear what Trish has to say."

"Maybe I'm hedging until I see the message," she said.

"Ok, I get it," said Harold, sounding discouraged. "That's your out, in case the message is unfavorable,"

"Don't worry," she said. "I'm not afraid to overrule anything I disagree with."

"You could write that in stone," said Jennifer.

The others laughed.

"Ok, here's the message: 'Those who want the same things, may still need to make priorities.'"

"That's the lamest hedge I ever heard," said Trish.

"You don't think we want the same things?" pleaded Harold.

"Remember our talk on our first plane ride to L.A.?" Trish asked. "You said what really sells the client are those moments when you tell the truth and come across authentic."

"I do, Trish…And you said if you try to sell something you don't really believe in, they'll eventually cancel the project—something like that."

"Right—so the important thing is that *you* believe…not just in the project, but in *yourself*— Harold, you dumb Jewish hunk!" Trish planted an ardent kiss on Harold's lips; he responded in kind. They clinched for a good ten seconds—oblivious to cheering, backslapping and cries of *get a room!* and *hose them down!*

V.

Soon, the happy group joined the others in the opulent, wood-panelled lounge, where, fuelled by tap-beer and wine spritzers, all enjoyed what Harold later described as a "spirited interrogatory" of Charles Wu, regarding his "expanded" role as a CIA consultant.

There was lavish praise for the faces group who had soldiered through from concept to finished product, with Harold wearing the wire and even supplying martial arts heroics—but also gratitude as well for Van who had offered himself as bait in New York and enforcer in L.A.

But Van had never suspected that Charles Wu, who he now lambasted in good fun, was running Ma to help bait him out to L.A., thereby baiting Feng and Danny to go there. To be honest, Wu admitted, he hadn't really been sure of Ma's loyalties himself until the end, and he needed for Van and the FBI to take charge, just in case things went south.

Feng, Danny and others had hoped to scoop up Van, Ma, the Chinese couple and, if necessary, the faces group—plus all their technology —and fly back to the motherland in the Air China Jet. This was to have been facilitated by Agent White Tiger in L.A. who, thanks to Van's signal during the presentation, was intercepted by the Los Angeles FBI just inside the airport gate, along with his MSS cohorts and their jet pilot. The jet itself had been arranged by Ma, courtesy of S.C.U.

The Chinese couple, of course, turned out to be Ma's parents, who successfully defected by switching places with the real Ms. Ren and Mr. Ho. Ma, had overplayed and disguised their roles as MSS operatives in the limo in order to help provoke Van into intervening, but also to help deceive Danny.

Ma's parents had been fully briefed about Chinese designs on Van by Ms. Ren and Mr. Ho who were themselves successfully defecting in Hong Kong.

Ma evidently played the double agent role like a pro, telling Feng and Danny that he had inside information that Van would show, arranging for the Air China Jet, and keeping everybody guessing until late in the game; he didn't want to spook Feng and Danny and have them somehow escape.

Feng, suspected to be Agent Green Dragon, was successfully lured and arrested along with Danny in Long Beach instead of Dallas because previous, solid evidence of their guilt had been lacking. In fact, even with their self-incriminating behavior, nothing was conclusive until Agent White Tiger, who had been arrested in L.A., implicated Feng. That occurred only after MSS operatives in New York had flipped about the plan to kidnap Van. (Intercepted recordings of Agent Green Dragon would match Feng's voice, sealing the case against him.)

FBI Agent Ritter in New York reported the roundups of MSS Agent Blue Lotus in New York and gangsters from New York's Chinatown and Flushing, including a few purged from the House of Kung Fu, an otherwise respectable organization. Not eluding the dragnet were operatives Eileen Cheung and rug merchants in L.A. and New York. Saving their own skins, Ghost Shadows gangsters in New York squealed that Danny Ching was known to be Mary Chen's murderer, which subway witnesses would later confirm. Billy Shun, probably in China, would escape American justice, at least for the time being, although his status there would likely be as scapegoat for a failed mission, rather than hero. Nonetheless, the capture of Feng—an important operative—more than compensated for Billy's escape.

Finally, to tie up other loose ends, Branson and his robotics company were apparently clean, and would be properly briefed about Feng and related matters.

For his part, Harold still felt he needed to challenge Ma with a few more questions. "Listen, Ma...Needless to say, the wind-up was worth it. But you put us all through quite a Movieland performance: from the phony Chinese accent and the country and western routine to all the spy double-talk—not to mention, Confucius say this and say that...and winding up with, I'll admit, the greatest show on earth, here in Long Beach."

Ma's eyes twinkled as he laughed. "Thank you, Harold."

"You're welcome. I must say, I can understand any Chinese person resenting all the racism your people have faced, and even sympathize with a wish to retaliate. You seem to be a loyal American, and I'm grateful that all this technology is in the right hands, but where do you really stand on all this?"

Ma's smile seemed right-sized and natural. "You have a right to ask, Harold. First, let's talk about the racism. As despicable and inexcusable as American racism was, if the Chinese were the dominant culture, well … let's leave it there. Now, I was certainly playing a role … or multiple roles because there were many things out of my control and I needed to be ready for changing circumstances. Remember: 'anticipate and prepare yourself for good fortune.' Sound familiar?"

"Yeah," said Harold. "You were acting very *I Ching*: flexible and hard to pin down."

"Like Slippery Shrimp," said Trish. "No offense, Ma."

"None taken, Trish. I remember you enjoyed the shrimp — and I really do like Bar-B-Q and funny ties." Ma laughed. "But remember, the acting wasn't just for your eyes and ears. The MSS was monitoring me constantly and I needed for you all and for Van to think I might be a spy, and for him to intervene in case things got too sticky. But even after Mr. Wu got involved, I still needed to look useful to the MSS until I saw my parents safely here. They made it, by the way, thanks to Mr. Wu and his contacts at Air Asia."

"*Mr.* Wu was certainly a busy little beaver," rumbled Van, swigging a malt scotch. "You're lucky I turned up, and lucky the fidget midget didn't fudge things up. Even with this haul of bad guys and good technology, I'll have to explain away all these amateur agents." Van scoffed a laugh.

"*Beaver? Mister mad eagle!* " said Charles, with mock rage. "You're the one who's lucky Tim Peters didn't get called into this, Van. We might have lost everybody here and their important work. But you eventually came around after playing mighty hard to get on face reading. As it is, you should get full credit for all of this coming down on your watch—even if it was extra-curricular. So, I certainly expect you to help push this as the biggest advance in espionage and surveillance since satellites and…well, your *Helsinki Summer* and miniaturized electronic listening devices."

"OK, truce," said Van laughing. "No…you win. And thanks for the plug. I wrote that book in college."

Paul loved hearing Van and Wu needle each other like they were back at Columbia. "That book was an inspiration to me, Van," said Paul, smiling. "You could say, it prompted me, eventually…to go into periodontics."

Everybody laughed. The session wound down in about an hour after more good-natured ribbing and amiable chatter. Harold had to take a last, playful, parting shot. "So Ma, after all this high-priced programming, the best you can do is a string of fortune cookie sayings?"

"Ha, got me there, Harold. But don't forget. Machines can measure, but it takes humans to give context and interpretation. As long as we're so variable and imperfect, faces will never be an exact science…So, yes, subtle Chinese clues are the best you can do!"

Harold let "Confucius" have the last word. The faces group, plus Ma, Van and Wu agreed to stay in touch for all-important follow-ups.

The first, a coded e-mail from Wu and Van to Paul and Harold came the next day:

> Savor this victory; it was important. However, suffer no illusions that it was anything but a skirmish in what will be a protracted war against an implacable and determined enemy.
>
> Given their natural advantage in manpower, an enviable work ethic, and a regime that drives them relentlessly, the Chinese are operating with supreme confidence. They are building also on the sustaining vigor of their ancient traditions, their recent successes in commandeering capital markets and resources and their demonstrated prowess in the telecommunications, aerospace and military spheres.
>
> Perhaps most sobering: China's understandable self-assurance rests on their conviction that we, in the West, are in irremediable decline, and have already been softened up for the kill. Can we prove them wrong? Are we up for the challenge?

EPILOGUE

PIER VILLAGE, LONG BRANCH

Two weeks later, as sprigs of new spring grass poked through the sandy soil of the New Jersey shore, Dr. Paul Wallach took his wife Lorraine out to dinner at a favorite boardwalk restaurant to celebrate their forty-fifth wedding anniversary.

Eyeing the rolling surf through a large picture window, Wallach sounded serene as he reviewed the latest exploits of the faces group. "I got an early call from Harold as I was driving to the golf course, wishing us a happy anniversary. We talked about that incredible day at Long Beach Studios and he filled me in on the latest. I know I've told you quite a bit already, but we were reliving it today. The greatest moment was when Van hugged me like a long-lost brother...A hugger he never was. And complimenting me on my Chinese! That was rich. I loved his expression and told him so when he found out that Charles Wu was running Ma as a double agent. Plus, the Chinese have now lost two more important defectors in Ms. Ren and Mr. Ho. They alerted us to the plan of imbedding Skype lenses to spy on the U.S. and they brought over all the propaganda videos they co-produced with Ma. Their stand-ins, Ma's parents, could have won Academy Awards the way they baited us in the limo. But Ma assumed all along that Van would be listening and counted on his showing up to bait Feng and Danny and to make sure with his FBI guys that they wouldn't escape. Honestly though, up to the end, Van wasn't sure whether they might've had to arrest Ma too. Of course, another inducement was Ma buying our plane tickets and letting Van hear about that through Harold's wire, hopefully leading him to worry that we'd be literally Shanghaied. So, the bait was laid all around." Paul beamed.

"It sounds like Charles was the mastermind, but Ma made it all happen," said Lorraine, echoing Paul's enthusiasm.

"Exactly. Charles was like executive producer, but Ma became movie director, cinematographer, *and* actor. He let Feng and Danny think he had drawn Van into *their* trap, and then turned the tables on them by offering us all the flash induction technology, and then welcoming Van instead of helping to capture him. Their reaction was priceless."

"So, are you on Van's team now?"

"No." Paul laughed. "But, today I got an e-mail invitation for a Columbia alumni dinner forwarded from Charles. He and Van will be there and it's cause for another celebration: Van's unofficial retirement as an operations officer. I messaged Van back, through Charles, saying that we're both retiring from the wet stuff—meaning blood—as they say in police work. I told him my practice is up for sale and I'm exploring offers to consult and teach. I'm not expecting to work with him again, but that's all right."

"I know, dear, that you love to hobnob with these real operators. But I hope you got your fill of action. What's the latest with career changes for the others?"

"Harold tells me the government offer we got through Van for the basic program was seven figures. Ma showed them how to adapt his program into one for mass or individual surveillance. He says his publishing boss is interested in a new textbook Harold would write about scientific face reading. He wants me to help write a chapter on espionage for that. And with Charles leading the way, he's discussing with Columbia their offer to teach a seminar on face reading for their Media and Communications curriculum. He'd like me to guest lecture in that."

"Amazing. Your sister Sylvia and the whole Savitt family will be doing handsprings," said Lorraine.

"They already are. Harold said when he told them the news, Stuart apologized for wanting him to become *only* an ophthalmologist. They had a good laugh over that."

Lorraine leaned back in her chair while perusing the dessert menu. "What about Trish and Jennifer?"

"Well, in addition to sharing in the seven-figure windfall, they figure on striking it rich with an upcoming re-creation spin-off program for fashion. Both of them should share the patent for that with Ma. Trish told Harold that since Jennifer has given notice to Spence-Iturbi, she could devote more time to her relationship with Jim Spence, which apparently had been developing for some time. Jennifer is going ahead with her plans for a face reading institute primarily using the celebrity-matching spin-off of the program featuring character actors. Not only could people be encouraged to like their own faces, but improve their health and sense of self-worth, which shows up in the face. Jennifer wants to hire you as a consultant to possibly expand the idea into school counseling. She wants to include that Dr. Maupassant from Haiti and also Hoda, as consultants. Harold says she'll be calling you soon."

"Yes," Lorraine said, "After I retire in June, I'd help facilitate those things. Like you, I'm looking forward to better hours."

They both laughed.

"Hoda, of course," said Paul, "made a terrific name for herself with her input. Remember I told you about how flash induction affects belief in the brain, shaking things up a bit like electroshock? Well, it turns out that when powerful symbols like the Eye of Horus are projected into the brain—juiced up, you might say, by a powerful hypnotic stare—belief is affected.

The numerological constants for the Eye of Horus that she shared with Charles, and that he later passed along to Ma, happen to coincide with the frequencies in flash induction—which also induces hypnosis! Thank goodness we got that concept before the Chinese did. It is powerful stuff, and we are selling that to the government too. By the way, we're cutting Hoda in for a share. And Harold said Hoda believes the museum world might be interested in a spin-off from the main program that analyzes paintings and statues."

"You better close the deal with the Feds before they find an excuse to requisition it," said Lorraine. "…friends of Van and Charles or not."

"Of course, you're absolutely right, but think about it: belief, unless it comports with tangible reality, is only like blind faith. On the other hand, science, such as flash induction, can induce people to believe that fiction is reality, and perhaps lead them to do things they wouldn't ordinarily do —like in *The Manchurian Candidate!*"

"If you say so, Paul. I know you love to dabble in this stuff. For sure, Harold finally found faith and belief in himself, but it was based on the reality that his gifts to the world were real and had to be used on his own terms."

"Yes. He did finally believe in himself, and he made a believer out of Trish."

"Yes, I know quite a bit about that, Paul," said Lorraine with a crafty smile.

"What do you know that I don't?"

"Well, listen to this, mister know-it-all. Trish called me today while you were golfing. She said that Harold had popped the question. She said yes and they are making plans. I told her, speaking for both of us, that we're thrilled for them. But she also said she called to sort of apologize to you through me."

"Why?"

"For fighting you and Harold tooth and nail on the issue of convincing and using Van. That was until she realized that just filing a patent on the app could have exposed you all to government intrusion and maybe even a takeover. So, she said you were right; the team needed someone like Van to believe in it, and shepherd it safely through. So, just before they left for L.A., Trish said she took a chance and called Charles Wu and he said he would do his best to sell Van, which apparently, he did. But the best thing, she said, was that she and Jen and Carlos finally got everything sorted out between them."

Paul's dark brown eyes exuded compassion. "I'll say they did. You know, if Harold had a reality to fall back on, Carlos finally confronted a much harder reality to face about himself because of the world's intolerance. Facing things about himself led him to believe again in his own talent, and, according to Harold, it's paying off. A good friend in his men's writing group has facilitated a publishing offer for Carlos's short stories."

"Wonderful! He's so creative. We saw it in those faces games you all were dreaming up."

"Oh yes, I almost forgot," said Paul. "Carlos is negotiating with a major toy and game manufacturer on all our behalves. We'll get in on that merchandizing stuff too."

"*Estupendo*, as Carlos would say. So, what about you? What else are you planning on doing with all your spare time?"

"I don't know. I saw an ad for role-playing at an improv theatre in the city. I thought I might…" Laughing, Paul Wallach ducked the swizzle stick Lorraine playfully threw at him.

The End

About the Author

Philip Howard Wolfson, a native of New Jersey, attended Georgetown and Fairleigh Dickinson Universities before receiving his dental degree from the University of Medicine and Dentistry of New Jersey in 1974. As a dentist, he developed a keen interest in the art and science of facial esthetics.

Studies in international politics and Chinese language at Columbia University's School of General Studies led to his passing the Foreign Service Examination of the United States Information Agency, all of which helped develop his multicultural worldview; whereas his later stint as a medical advertising writer in New York City helped prepare him to communicate, as he does now, with that wider world through fact-based fiction.

About the Publisher

"A book should be a ball of light in your hands."
— Ezra Pound

This past year, **BLAST PRESS** expanded its publishing program in several new directions. We have our first anthology—which is distinct from a magazine—with representative New Jersey poets with our *Palisades, Parkways & Pinelands,* a generous almost 300 page collection of over 30 poets. Another direction is the illustrated collaboration between H. A. Maxson and Dorothy Wordsworth in a new kind of "found poetry" that is a beautiful mash-up of a living poet and his long-dead collaborator's nature notebooks. *The Changing Room* is another first for BLAST PRESS, a fully-illustrated long poem by Carrie Hudak that blends dream and reality as a child's story might, but with adult themes of death and a sophistication of tone unusual in an illustrated tale. *Surfing for Jesus* is a lively new work by Susanna Rich, exploring religious themes and impacts of growing up in a church tradition in late-twentieth-century America. Joe Weil and Emily Vogel's "responsorials," are an ongoing dialog with poem answering poem in their unusual and emotionally intimate *West of Home.* Last year, **BLAST PRESS** released the widely published author Emanuel di Pasquale's *Knowing the Moment,* a delicate paean to his life on the Jersey Shore. And **BLAST PRESS** continues its primary tradition of supporting uncollected poets with a first-time poetry book by Mathew V. Spano, *Hellgrammite.* I would like to extend a special thank you to our authors and editors, and to our enthusiastic readers, for all you do to enliven the world of poetry.

With best regards,

Gregg Glory
(Gregg G. Brown)
Publisher

Also Available

Anthologies
Palisades, Parkways & Pinelands
Jersey Shore Poets

Susanna Fry
30 Poems

James Dalton
Instead

Magdalena Alagna
The Cranky Bodhisattva

Rusty Cuffs
[Thad Rutkowski]
Sex-Fiend Monologues III

Sarah Avery
Persephone in Washington

George Holler
Erotic Logic

Jacko Monahan
One-Legged Poetry

Daniel J. Weeks
X Poems
Les Symbolistes
Self-Symphonies
Virginia

Carrie Pedersen Hudak
Yoga Notes
The Arms of Venus
Queens Arms
The Queen of Cakes
The Changing Room
Bee Loud Glade

Sharon Baller
Venus Has Gone Insane Again

Joe Weil
West of Home

Emily Vogel
West of Home

H. A. Maxson
Grasmere
Call It Sleep
A Commonplace Book

Emanuel Di Pasquale
Knowing the Moment
Poems in Sicily and America

Mathew V. Spano
Hellgrammite

Linda Johnston Muhlhausen
Elephant Mountain

Warren Cooper
What Happened at Dinner, and After

Gabor Barabas
Collected Poems

Lord Dermond
[Daniel B. Dermond]
13 Stories High
Ghosts and Princes Revised
Hourless Grail
Inner Dominion
Lords Miscellany
The Mortal Words
Sacred Blades
The Unaging Muse

John Dunfy
Spinning Wheels

Joie Ferentino
BELM

Chuck Moon
God-Speck Exhibitions

Brandi Mantha Grannett
Floaters

Mary Jane Tenerelli
'Til Death Do Us Part

Gregg Glory
[Gregg G. Brown]
Adoring Thorns

The Alarmist
American Bacchanalia
American Descants
American Songbook
Antirime
Ascent
Assembling the Earth
Autobiographies
A/voi/d/ances
Benedict Arnold
Black Champagne
Brain Cell
Burning Byzantium
The Cabana at the Equator
Constellations in December
Chaos and Stars
Contemporaries
Dear Planet Jesus
The Death of Satan
A Deepening Sea
The Departed Friend
Deus Abscondis
Digital Boy
Disappearing Acts
Divine Revolt
Dr. Kilmer's Ocean-Weed Heart Remedy
Down By Swansea
Eating the Cliffside
Evil Interludes
The Falcon Waiting
Ghosts and Princes Revised
The Giant in the Cradle
Greetings from Mt. Olympus
Hell, Darling
The Hummingbird's Apprentice
Hurry Up, Hurricane!
Hymns
The Impossible Mesa
Interregnum Scribbles
It's the Sex Pistols!!!!
Jan and Marsha
The Life of Riley
The Maybe Plagues
Mercury Astronauts
A Million Shakespeares
Naked Eloquence

Nobody Poems
Night, Night
Of Flares, Of Flowers
On Being a Human Bean
The Pilot Light
Platinum Lips [CD]
Prometheus Bound
The Queen of Cakes
A Raven's Weight
Red Bank
Repetitions on the Rappahannock
Rose Lasso
Saving Cinderella
Shreads of Verity
Seven Heavens
The Singing Well
Sipping Beer in the Shadow of God
The Sleepy Partridge
The Soft Assault
Soul-Splitter
Spotty the Spot-tacular Cat
Supposing Roses
Supreme Day
The Sword Inside
The Timid Leaper
Torturous Splendours of the Dream
Ultra
Unimagined Things
Venus and Vesuvius
Vindictive Advice
A Volcano Island
Wild Onions
XXX Sonnets
Youth Youth Youth

Date Due →

Books returned after due date are subject to a fine.

Fairleigh Dickinson University Library
Teaneck, New Jersey

T001-15M
11-8-02

CPSIA information can be obtained
at www.ICGtesting.com
Printed in the USA
BVHW031816100419

545182BV00001B/17/P